THE THIRD LIFE OF OPHELIA

AN OPHELIA LEGACY NOVEL

SPENCER STONER

INDIGO

Livonia, Michigan

Published by Indigo
an imprint of BHC Press

Library of Congress Control Number:
2016954824

ISBN-13: 978-1-946006-15-8
ISBN-10: 1-946006-15-7

Visit the author at:
www.authorspencerstoner.com &
www.bhcpress.com

Also available in eBook

ALSO BY SPENCER STONER

THE OPHELIA LEGACY

BOOK 1
OPHELIA & LYAN ARE DEAD MEAT

MULTI-AUTHOR COLLECTIONS

IN CREEPS THE NIGHT
CONTAINS THE STORY "ON THE WAY HOME"

To my family,
especially Mom and Malia
who read and reread this until it was right,
and Pete from DFQ
who helped me find closure.

SO ENDS THE FIRST

OPHELIA'S JADE GREEN eyes opened a crack, the first sign that she was still alive. They opened wider to see gray and white swirling patterns, albeit blurry. The young woman was laying face down on a slab of marble in the middle of a cold room.

She tried shaking the cobwebs in her head loose but quickly learned that was a mistake. A wave of nausea washed over Ophelia and a dry heave welled up inside her. The sound of gagging was muffled as the young woman realized a roll of leather was shoved between her lips. It was fastened around her head in a way that reminded her of a horse's bridle.

Whatever it was, it sealed her mouth off from being able to speak beyond incoherent mumbles. She could bite down on the gag and push against it with her tongue but it wouldn't budge at all.

As the rest of her senses started working again, Ophelia realized that her wrists were bound together under the polished marble, so that she was practically hugging the slab. Her legs were also tied down against the top of the stone. Chilling air washed over her skin, raising goose bumps, and telling the young woman that she wasn't wearing any clothing. She did feel some kind of material draped over her rump and hips. Even in a situation like this there was such a thing as small favors.

What was going on here? The last thing Ophelia remembered was being in her family's farm house and extinguishing the fire in the living room before turning in for the night. This obviously wasn't her home.

The room was dark. Blackness surrounded her so completely that Ophelia couldn't tell how big or small the room truly was. The only light that came into the room was from a frameless window to the young woman's left. The window appeared to be floating in mid-air rather than embedded into a wall. The sky outside was cloudless and blue. Golden desert sand flowed along the slope of a tall dune, making little crescent shapes along the surface as the wind weaved its path.

In all the fairy tales Ophelia read that involved kidnapped princesses or other damsels in distress, they all took place almost exclusively on dark and stormy nights. What was happening to her seemed impossible on a bright, sunny day like it looked outside.

Sand dunes? Ophelia lived on flat plains where she and her parents farmed wheat. At least this year it was wheat and the crop was just teasing at being ready to harvest. There wasn't a desert within hundreds of miles of her family's farm. Where in the world could she be?

The sound of movement behind her, no more than a couple of steps of shuffling feet, made Ophelia's entire body stiffen. The new arrival must have noticed and hurried to the side of the table.

"Awake now?" a male voice said, nearly squeaking with excitement, "And ahead of schedule, too. Promising, very promising indeed."

Whoever it was seemed to be talking more to himself than Ophelia. Her entire body jumped when she felt a hand press down on the small of her back.

"Ooh, nerve reactions are very well timed," that was the only indication the stranger gave that Ophelia had moved at all, "Subject is well within the ideal age range of late teens to early twenties. Appears to have attained full maturity and lacks any signs of degeneration that aging brings."

She felt his hand start to glide up her back along her spine. Ophelia couldn't suppress a shiver as she tried to control her breathing. Panicking wouldn't help now.

"Fine core musculature due to actual use instead of preening and sculpting," the hand slipped between her shoulder blades and into the young woman's chin length chocolate colored hair, "Protein extractions along the cranial sphere indicate no history of serious illnesses nor defective genetic conditions. Unfortunately, our benefactor doesn't want the protein extractions removed even though it would likely improve efficiency of my process. Still, it is expected to perform within expected tolerances."

What process? Tolerances? What was he planning to do to her?

The stranger gave a soft tug at one of the two thin braids that Ophelia wore on either side of her face. For some reason, it brought back the memory of the brush fire last year. Her braids had just reached her shoulders and her mother had said that she would likely be able to tie her hair back with them by next summer.

But as she was helping fight the fire, the flames found her hair and burned one of the girl's braids down to her chin before her father doused her with a bucket of water. So Ophelia cut not only her other braid but the rest of her hair to the same length.

The stranger let the weaved length of hair go and when Ophelia finally saw the man's hand, she let out a scream the leather could barely muffle. It looked human, until you reached his fingertips. His nails were obsidian black claws the shape of the waning crescent moon with little tufts of brown fur just at the base.

The stranger let out a quiet grunt, "Subject seems to have mild xenophobic tendencies. Will need to check if another rune will need to be imprinted upon the canvas."

The more the man spoke, the more Ophelia struggled with her bonds. She grunted with effort, her saliva soaking into the leather in her mouth. She could feel whatever tied her wrists together stretching enough so that the bonds wouldn't bite into her skin but they also wouldn't give enough slack to free herself.

The man, not seeming to notice or care about the woman's efforts, stepped into her field of vision. Even with as little as Ophelia could move her head, she could see that he was rail thin, quite possibly the thinnest man she had ever seen. That was with him wearing a loose fitting cloak made of tweed.

Her neck muscles screamed in protest as she tried to look at the man's face. It was draped in shadow, although Ophelia did see that he had white hair and wore a tall, black top hat. Then her neck cramped and the girl dropped her head back to the surface of the marble table.

The stranger walked out of view again. The sound of his shuffling feet didn't seem like they were getting further away but the noise suddenly stopped as if it was interrupted. As best as she could tell, Ophelia was again alone in the room.

She had never felt so helpless before. Whatever was going to happen to her, the young woman had no way to stop it. Ophelia wondered if her parents would be able to find her or if they had even started looking. The doubt that washed over her made tears begin to well up in her eyes.

The only sound in the room now was Ophelia's muffled sobs and sniffling. Even though it wasn't accomplishing anything, she kept tugging at the bonds around her wrists, hoping against hope that something would snap loose and at least give her a chance to escape or fight back or something!

After who knows how long, the shuffling feet returned. Her cheeks still slick with tears, panic finally won out and Ophelia redoubled her efforts to free her wrists.

Ophelia felt her chest tighten and she started slamming her hands against the bottom of the table. One way or another she had to get free, even if it meant breaking all her fingers to make her hands squeeze through the bonds.

"Ah, still tempestuous, eh?" the man made a clicking sound with his tongue, "Now, now, dearie. I admire your energy but we can't have you hurting yourself before the procedure, can we?"

Ophelia felt a fingertip, complete with one of those black claws lightly scratching along the back of her neck. After finding the place it was looking for, the stranger pressed down and the girl felt her arms suddenly go limp.

In spite of the fact that she was tied down and couldn't really move anyway, Ophelia realized that her entire body had followed suit. She couldn't even wiggle her toes or raise her shoulders any-more. Ophelia wanted to ask him what he'd done but it, of course, only came out as a series of grunts and slurps against the gag.

"I disabled the entirety of your nervous system from your C-four vertebrae and below," he answered the question as if Oph-elia had spoken clearly, "Now I must commence the final inspection of the canvas for any imperfections. So if you please..."

Even paralyzed, her entire body jumped when he touched the souls of her feet. Again, the stranger let out a noise that sounded surprised but still pleased at her instinctive action. His claws slipped between her toes, she could even feel him scratch between the nails and skin.

As his hands slowly, methodically made their way up her legs, Ophelia felt his warm breath on her skin. She wanted to yell for him to stop but, even if she'd been able to speak, she knew he wouldn't. Ophelia closed her green eyes tight and prayed for this to be over quickly.

"For working on a farm, the subject shows remarkably little scarring," the stranger muttered, his hand slipping between Oph-elia's knees and the smooth surface of the table.

As his hands made their way up Ophelia's thighs, her eyes closed tighter. When she felt the material that had been covering her backside, the only modicum of modesty she had left, slide off, Ophelia did the only thing she could do. She cried. Sobbing that would have rocked her body only made quiet groans against the leather in her mouth, her own body's lack of reaction seeming to mock the girl's emotions.

The stranger's fingers and hands probed along every part of her body. He made comments every step of the way but Ophelia couldn't listen anymore. She struggled to shut him out. She shut everything out, hoping all of it would go away.

She felt his hands cradle either side of her face. He pulled her head up until it was as close to vertical as the bound woman could get.

"Open your eyes," he commanded simply.

Ophelia didn't. She wouldn't. But the stranger's hands held her firm. His fingers were splayed out, her ears sandwiched between two of his digits. She could feel his breath, the warm air from his lungs wafting against her cheeks in a slow steady rhythm.

The man's grip was like a vice. It didn't exactly hurt, but Ophelia could feel the pressure pressing into the sides of her head and could tell that he hadn't even put any effort in… yet. The idea that he could literally crush her head made Ophelia feel that much more hopeless.

He was as still as a statue. The man wasn't going anywhere until Ophelia did as she was told and he didn't bother to ask again. Her eyelids slowly rose.

The stranger looked like an old man. His skin was pressed so tightly against his bones that it looked as if he had missed a decade's worth of meals. The black top hat had a red band around the base and rested perfectly level on top of his head.

The man didn't have any eyebrows and circular panes of glass rested in front of his eyes. They were held together by thin, stiff gold wire across the bridge of his thin, long nose and then stretched back to behind his long lobed ears. Behind them, though, the stranger's irises glowed softly, an inhuman shade of red.

His mouth was little more than a straight line until he saw Ophelia do as he commanded. Then it stretched into a smile that was far too wide for his face. His white teeth and moist crimson gums were fully exposed to the cool air and the girl's vision.

The stranger leaned in closer, his face only inches from hers. His attention shifted from one eye to the other before her head slipped out of his hands, like holding her didn't even occur to him once he had what he wanted. Ophelia's chin impacted against the marble with a dull thud, her teeth sinking into the leather gag.

"The perfect canvas," he declared to no one.

Straining to look higher, Ophelia saw the stranger reach into his tweed cloak with his left hand. The motion seemed... off somehow to the right handed woman who couldn't even tie a knot with her off hand. She wondered, with everything else happening, why that suddenly took her attention.

But a fresh wave of panic rushed through the girl when his hand emerged again. He held a glass vial that was almost as long as the stranger's hat was tall. It was a wonder he could hold it in one hand. Inside was a purple fluid that bubbled and shimmered in the light that shot from the floating window.

The part that Ophelia's eyes locked on, though, was the bunch of needles that protruded from the bottom of the vial. They were all the same length, easily as long as Ophelia's longest finger, but they were different thicknesses. Some were so thin that she could barely see them, but some were too wide to be called needles with any honesty.

She was the perfect canvas? What was he going to do with that thing?

He stepped out of her vision again. Ophelia felt the cloth that had been covering her rump slip back over her. It would have been a comfort if she hadn't seen the vial and needles the man held in his hand. She tried to find a way to speak around the leather in her mouth but her voice only came out in quiet grunts.

"Shh, shh, shh, dearie. Some moments are too special to ruin with words," the stranger said as his hand once again glided along the small of her back, "Besides, the gag is there for a reason."

The needles dug into her flesh. Ophelia let out a yelp of pain but, moments later, an acidic burn under skin turned it into a wrenching scream.

The needles pulled out and plunged back in. Then again. And again. The stranger started slowly but the stabs came quicker each time as they made their way up her back.

The pain only got worse the longer it went on and Ophelia was screaming so continuously that the leather in her mouth soaked through and saliva dribbled down her chin into a puddle on the marble. The stranger kept pushing in and out of her with no sign of stopping. In fact, he only seemed to get more energized as he continued. Ophelia finally, thankfully, lost consciousness...

ONE
THE DEMONSTRATION

OPHELIA'S EYES FLUTTERED open, the pale irises expanding as her pupils contracted at the exposure to light. A sensation of warmth washed over her back while cool marble pressed against the front of her body.

She heard the shuffling feet of someone enter the room. After a few moments, the man in the tweed cloak, Doctor Efreeti, stepped into view. How she knew his name was a mystery to her. Ophelia couldn't recall them ever being introduced to each other.

Rolling onto her side, she watched as he closed the distance between the door and table. The woman smiled as his clawed fingertips reached down to run through her short hair. Then Ophelia lifted herself to a sitting position on the stone table.

"And how are we feeling?" the man's mouth spread into a wide grin that showed every tooth and a good portion of his red gums as he sat on the table beside her.

The woman looked down at her hands, flexing and stretching her fingers several times before turning her head to face the man. She knew she'd been laying there all night but why? Ophelia's mind quickly shifted to what was to come and a smile rivaling the thin man's spread across her face.

"Ready," she answered.

"Very good, dearie," Efreeti tossed a cloth bundle onto her lap, "Put these on. They are what all neophytes wear when they arrive here."

The woman hadn't realized that she was naked until that moment, "A neophyte?" her fingers lazily tugged the rope wrapped around the bundle loose as she spoke.

"Do not take it as an insult," the thin man sat beside Ophelia and bumped his shoulder against hers, "All it means is that you are new to the Al Razheem. Once you prove yourself, you will be their elite, second only to the General himself."

"The General?" she couldn't explain why but a warm feeling washed through the woman's chest at just the mention of him, "You think he will like me?"

Efreeti nodded, lifting himself back to his feet, "He will come to depend on you, dearie. Now get ready. We go to the Oasis within the hour."

AN HOUR LATER...

"So this is, what, lap eleven or twelve?" the bearded man asked.

"The thirteenth, actually," the thin man answered.

Outside the immense sandstone walls of the keep that the occupants called "The Oasis" was nothing but sand as far as the eye could see. Inside, though, was a grove of trees surrounded by a circular trail. It was a miraculous feat in this climate, a force of will to create a forest in such a desolate place even with the edifice of the tall walls to protect the plants from the scorching sun, stinging winds and deadly sandstorms.

And that will belonged to the bearded man, the General of the Al Razheem. It had taken years to fulfill this vision and, as the deep lines on his stern face could attest, they had taken a toll. While he had a long and full beard, it only served to show how little hair remained on top of his skull. The black hair had gray creeping through it in thin streaks now and what grew along the sides of his head was tied into two massive braids that rested on his shoulders.

The General's white uniform had lengths of weaved gold looped through the epaulets on his shoulders and under his thick arms. More of the precious metal was embroidered into the cuffs of his sleeves forming words in a language that, on this continent, only he understood. To those under him, they knew only that it denoted his rank as their ruler. On the buckle of his belt, the only piece of metal he wore that wasn't gold, his family crest was etched with each symbol representing a different god that his lineage had paid homage to over the passing generations.

He stood on a balcony that overlooked his literal oasis, watching a young woman run along the trail again and again and again without any sign of tiring. Beside the General stood the being who called himself Doctor Efreeti.

Thick round pieces of glass obscured his eyes while a tall black top hat kept the sun off his face. The long tweed cloak he wore would have brought sweat raining down the face of a normal man in this arid heat but Efreeti looked more than comfortable. In fact, the inhumanly wide smile on his face showed that he was enjoying his time in the keep.

The General stroked at the three braids that lined around his chin. "Is there a point to this? So far all I've seen is a woman who can jog well."

"You wound me, sir," the grin never left Doctor Efreeti's face, "It was you who demanded demonstrations of your newest acquisitions, my dear General. The first trait I've shown is her endurance. Not flashy, admittedly, but it is of import none the less."

The thin man's beastly hands rose and pointed down toward the woman running below. His clawed fingers bounced in time with the rhythm of the woman's pace.

"I have also made her unquestioningly loyal. An important trait among assassins, don't you agree?" Doctor Efreeti smirked.

The General let out a soft grunt, "But to whom?"

"You wound me again, sir!" the thin man lifted his hand to his chest as if injured but unable to hide the giggle in his voice, "Have you not noticed the lovely design within her runes that precisely matches your own crest?" he pointed at the crest on the bearded man's belt.

He didn't have to look down at his own waist to know what was there, "I had. I was trying not to take it personally."

He was lying, until that moment anyway. The General had been too enthralled by many of the woman's other attributes to give the glowing tattoo on her back more than a passing look.

The piece of cloth that passed for a shirt only covered a portion of her chest with only a couple of strings stretched between her shoulder blades holding the fabric in place. He should have realized that Efreeti had dressed her as such to leave his view of the tattoo that stretched from the top of her back down below her waist unobstructed, as well as entice him to accept his newest creation.

On her right arm was a small buckler. It wasn't much more than an oval of wood that barely covered her forearm. The metal wrapped edge stretched out just past her hand, an unusual design that the bearded man wasn't confident was battle efficient. He would wait and see if he was wrong or not.

She was also wearing a pair of shorts that couldn't have been at all shorter. No doubt to show off the musculature of his organization's newest recruit and he had taken in that view well.

On her right hip was a curved scimitar that bounced with every step. The red sash hanging from the other side of her belt denoted her rank as an Al Razheem neophyte, a courtesy the General had agreed to give Efreeti when he brought Ophelia into the Oasis for demonstration.

"Oh, indeed sir, you should take it personally," Doctor Efreeti leaned in closer to the other man, who resisted the urge to step away, "You should take it as the compliment it was intended. You of all people know the power of symbols. That symbol, designed to precisely match your family crest, shows that she gives her allegiance to no one but you, who has taken it as his own."

Still unconvinced, the General decided he would test this loyalty himself later, "She is an attractive specimen, I'll give you that. But a well endowed woman doesn't make a perfect assassin." He said, tugging at the braids on his chin.

Doctor Efreeti sighed, "Her name is Ophelia, General. I take great pride in my work and wish it to be addressed with a proper title."

"Wasn't that her name when you procured her for this? What else did you let her keep from her past?" the bearded man leaned against the balcony's railing, his eyes fixed on the woman below, "What happens when she gets homesick, Efreeti?"

"Impossible," the thin man answered, "This place is home to her now. I removed all her memories of her life before coming here. Whatever family, tribe or clan name that came with Ophelia has been thoroughly expunged. I needed the space to create her new abilities and make her your finest murderer."

The General frowned at the murderer jab but let it go, "Tell me about these abilities then. So far I haven't seen anything worth paying for."

Doctor Efreeti removed his hat as he leaned on the railing beside the bearded man. The front half of his head was completely bald. The hair on the back was totally white and long enough to reach his narrow shoulders.

"I do believe I've moved from wounded to emotionally maimed! Fortunately, my dear General, that would be the next phase of the demonstration and it would be far more effective to show rather than tell. Indeed it would," he laughed as if he'd told a joke.

As if some silent cue had been given, a clump of trees that Ophelia was steadily approaching started to shudder, although there was no way she would have been able to notice from her position at ground level. Still, the woman slid to a stop much quicker than the General would have thought possible when a massive beast leaped out from between the tightly spaced trunks. It landed right where Ophelia would have been if she'd continued running.

The creature easily towered over the woman. The beast's biceps were bigger around than Ophelia's entire body. Two tails whipped back and forth behind its rump as the creature clawed at the ground, not yet realizing the prey wasn't there.

When it saw that it had indeed come up empty, the monster lifted itself onto its two hind legs. Ophelia could have easily walked between them and barely have to duck her head to get through.

"What is that thing?" the General's arrow shaped eyebrows pressed together as he glared at the tweed wrapped man, "And how did it get into my forest?"

"It is a crinotaur, my good General. It's an older, more malicious cousin to the minotaur. It doesn't bother with silliness like labyrinths. It simply goes straight for the kill, " Efreeti answered, seeming to not notice the other man's anger, "I brought it from home."

The beast was covered in dark violet fur. Two massive horns curved from either side of its head that looked like an immense wolf. Its heavily muscled body looked almost human, a ripple running from one bulge to the next as it turned to face what was to be its next meal.

Mucus flew from its black nose as the crinotaur let out a heavy snort, the ooze slowly sliding down the metal ring that looped through the creature's nostrils. It reared back and let out a massive roar at the woman, who had yet to even draw the sword sheathed on her round hip.

"Are you crazy?" the General seethed but couldn't bring himself to look away from the spectacle.

"Indeed not. I prefer to believe that it is creativity with a splash of initiative. And perhaps some chocolate sauce? I do so enjoy chocolate sauce," the thin man looked positively giddy as he watched the woman and crinotaur below.

The monster could easily chomp down on her entire body and barely have her limbs poking out of the sides of its maw. With this intent, the beast closed the distance to Ophelia as it roared, the force of the air coming from its mouth causing the braids on either side of the woman's face to whip around.

Once the crinotaur was within her reach Ophelia's buckler reared back, balled her hand into a fist, and then launched for the crinotaur's jaw. One of the beast's sharp teeth, easily the size of the woman's hand, snapped loose from its mouth at the impact of the shield's metal edge. The monster stumbled into the closest tree, ripping the trunk from the ground by the roots from as the beast fell over.

"I'll plant you a new one," Efreeti grinned when the General turned to express his rage at what had just happened to his precious plant, "A better one. One that can grow various blade weapons, if you like."

Shaking its head, the crinotaur wrapped its massive arms around the laid out tree. Its feet dug into the soil as the creature hefted the trunk up with little effort. Turning toward Ophelia, it swung the trunk like a hammer down for the woman as she pulled her sword from its sheath. The blade wasn't even half way out before the wood splintered against the leveled soil of the trail.

"Perhaps I should buy the monster from you, Efreeti," disappointment was obvious on the face of the General, "The girl didn't even have enough sense to dodge."

"Oh?" the thin man's smile was almost literally ear to ear, "Perhaps you should look over there."

He pointed behind the crinotaur. In a flash of purple mist, the woman was suddenly standing at the monster's back with her sword drawn. With a flick of her wrist, the blade lopped one of the crinotaur's tails off. It flew into the trees and disappeared.

The General tried to hide his astonishment behind a passive mask but some of the emotion still made it through, "What just happened?" he asked.

"I call it *blinking*, good General," Doctor Efreeti chuckled, "Unlike teleportation spells that require preparation through physical ingredients and/or incantations, one only need be attacked and they are immediately blinked out of harm's way. Rather ingenious, don't you think?"

With a howl of pain the crinotaur spun around to face Ophelia, leaving a trail of blood dribbling from its rump and over the gravel trail. The beast launched itself at the woman, its black claws extending as far as they could reach.

Another flash of purple mist shaped like the woman and Ophelia was suddenly standing beside the creature. Lunging forward, she drove her boot into the creature's side.

"And what is the range of this 'blinking'?" the demonstration had the bearded man's full attention now.

"Out of the range of immediate harm," Doctor Efreeti answered, "Otherwise, your assassin would be out of range for a counterattack of their own."

One of the beast's ribs broke with a muffled, sickening crunch. As the crinotaur fell onto its side, one of its arms swept toward the woman, trying to snatch her into its massive paw.

With acrobatic grace, Ophelia back flipped out of the creature's reach. When she returned to her feet, the woman brought the sword down on the beast's hand and severed two digits away from its palm.

"Why didn't she blink out of the way of that attack?" the General asked.

"She wasn't in any real danger," Efreeti practically beamed with pride, "The runes can sense that. Besides, what kind of sport would the demonstration have if there was no back and forth between the participants?"

The master of the Al Razheem nodded silently, his eyes staying locked on Ophelia and the beast lifting itself back to its feet. Blood welled down the crinotaur's arm as its injured hand reached up to cradle its aching side.

The monster huffed for breath as it and Ophelia circled around each other. It looked for an opening while the woman took one step in front of the other in a way just short of a strut.

Doctor Efreeti pushed the two circles of glass higher up along the bridge of his narrow nose, "Ahh, here it comes, my General. The grand finale! Don't blink! Your eyes, I mean. Ophelia will almost certainly blink, if I were to presuppose."

The crinotaur lunged forward, dropping the full weight of its body behind the claw of its undamaged arm, intent on crushing every bone in the woman's body. Ophelia didn't even try to get out of the way. She simply lifted her arms from her sides as if she was welcoming the attack before blinking away.

And she suddenly found herself standing atop the beast's head, one foot on a curved horn while the other balanced precariously on the end of its snout. Before the crinotaur could react, a smiling Ophelia reached down with her right arm, the one with the buckler, and wrapped a hand around the ring in the creature's nose.

Giving it a solid wrench, the monster reared back and screamed in pain. Ophelia's foot rose from the beast's horn and stomped down on the front of the crinotaur's lower jaw. Spreading her long legs, the woman pushed the beast's mouth open even wider, using her handhold on the metal ring to steady herself.

The curved scimitar thrust into the roof of the creature's maw, burying itself into the moist crimson flesh. With a grunt of effort, the woman pushed forward until, finally, the blade emerged from the crown of the crinotaur's skull.

One last whimpering moan escaped the animal's mouth as it tumbled to the ground for the final time. Ophelia leaped away from the rolling beast, effortlessly landing on her feet in front of the creature.

Looking up toward the balcony, the smile on her face was easy to see. She gave both men a playful curtsy as they turned to face each other.

"Well, my good General," Efreeti slipped his tall top hat back onto his head and gave it a little slap to elicit a soft pop, "what do you think?"

"I'll take her," the other man answered, his voice the definition of awe.

The General idly waved a hand at the thin man, as if to dismiss him, and turned his attention back to the woman below. She stood at attention, the curved blade already back in its sheath. Her pale gray eyes were locked on the bearded man, waiting for him to say something, anything to her.

"Welcome to the Al Razheem, Ophelia," he declared, "Go back through the gate and you will be provided with new accommodations."

"Thank you, Master," the woman gave the General another curtsy before starting for the barred gate that waited immediately below the balcony.

The ruler of the Al Razheem noticed that Ophelia didn't even turn a glance toward Efreeti. He felt the corner of his mouth tug with pleasure at the idea that she could truly be as loyal as the thin man had promised.

The gate opened with a quiet squeak. As Ophelia stepped through into the much cooler tunnel, she noticed another woman leaning against the wall.

Her hair was red, almost the exact shade of blood. The ends curved in around her chin. A crimson and black corset was wrapped around her shirtless torso, making her pale skin stand out.

On her left arm was an unusual metal sleeve that looked to be made of chain mail but the pattern gave more of an impression of snakeskin. The sleeve got steadily wider until it passed her wrist, where the weaved metal sank into a bronze loop that could easily fit someone's head. It also had four bladed hooks protruding from the bottom.

The other woman's skintight black pants fed almost immediately into equally black thigh high boots. The heels of the boots were so narrow that it was a wonder they didn't stab and sink into the ground below. The sapphire sash on her hip denoted her higher rank in the clan of assassins.

Lines formed at the corners of the woman's emerald green eyes as they narrowed, staring at Ophelia as the newcomer closed the welded bar door behind her. The assassin's heavily painted lips were tugged down into a tight frown even though her words appeared complimentary.

"Very well done," she said to the neophyte, "An excellent show. I especially liked the bowing at the end. Very classy."

"You're the peon sent to show me to my room?" Ophelia smirked, resting her hands on her rounded hips.

A quiet hiss slipped from between the red haired woman's lips, "Absolutely not! I'm Kitanah, the Great General's personal assassin," the assassin's chest puffed out proudly, making the lacing of the corset strain.

"Oh?" the brunette woman felt a smirk wash across her face, "Is that why he was looking for a new recruit? Are you getting a little long in the tooth?"

Ophelia turned to continue down the tunnel and the metal sleeve suddenly shot in front of her, stretched across the newcomer's path and embedded itself into the wall opposite of the red haired woman.

As Kitanah stepped over to the other woman, the sleeve shortened in length to stay taut while the other end remained attached the far wall, "Watch yourself, girl. You may have just come shiny from the showroom but you haven't proven your worth yet!"

"I have no need to watch myself, old lady. The Great General was doing plenty of that for me," Ophelia's pale eyes scanned up and down the body of the woman with red hair before letting out a mocking chuckle.

Ophelia stepped under the still stretched chainmail and continued into the darkness of the tunnel ahead. Kitanah wrenched the metal sleeve from the wall, shaking out crumbs of stone and dust from inside as she glared after the other woman.

TWO

JUST A COUPLE OF QUESTIONS

"SHE HAS TWO braids on either side of her face," the hooded man ran his fingertips along his partially shaded cheeks to emphasize his description.

He was easily one of the biggest, muscular men in the mostly full tavern. The hooded man was also one of the few not seated, although that was starting to change the longer he talked. The stranger had stepped inside only moments ago and strode straight to the bar to speak to the barmaid behind the polished wooden barrier.

His simple charcoal colored cloak showed signs of wear from long travel, at least around the edges. The cloak was still in good enough shape to obscure his body. The hood hid his face well in the flickering lantern light save for the tuft of blonde hair, with the thinnest streaks of gray, on the end of the man's chin.

"I'm sorry. I have no idea what you are talking about," the woman behind the bar chewed on her lower lip as she focused far more attention than was necessary on wiping down the mug in her hands with a soft rag.

The hooded man leaned forward onto the bar, his baritone voice barely above a whisper, "Please. She's family. I need to bring her back home."

The woman's hazel eyes flicked back over his shoulder, "I wish I could help, mister. It's just, um, uh,"

The barmaid wasn't built for deception. It was obvious that he had struck a nerve in the woman and that she did, in fact, know something about Ophelia. But while the hooded man had made the barmaid nervous, the three men creeping up behind him had a completely different reaction to his questions.

Their answers involved drawing a rapier, a scimitar and a pair of daggers as they closed the distance with the hooded man. The stranger's hands balled up into heavy fists that pushed against the flat surface of the bar to help him straighten back up to his impressive height that dwarfed even the tallest of his would be attackers.

"I just want you to know that I don't blame you for this," he gave the woman behind the bar a kind smile, "But I'm going to want some answers after this is over," And he turned to face the armed men.

The closest of the three men, only coming up to the hooded man's chest and holding the rapier, stabbed at the larger man. He must have been counting on the stranger being larger meaning that he would also be slower.

The rapier wielding man was wrong. A simple side step from the stranger brought the attacker within the robed man's reach and the smaller fighter fell away with a jaw that hung loose behind the skin of his face.

The man with the broken jaw must have been the unlucky one that drew the short straw to test the hooded man's skill because the other two kept their distance. These weren't merely ruffians looking for an excuse to brawl. They were organized.

Neither of the men standing before the massive stranger wore a uniform in the strictest sense but each wore a sash around his waist. The man laying on the floor wore red while the other two wore violet sashed. All three sashes had swirling script that ran the length of the material.

"That was unwise, friend," the one holding the scimitar announced, "This is an Al Razheem tavern."

Everyone else in the bar rose to their feet around their tables. There were indeed many sashes dotting the crowd behind the two men speaking to the hooded stranger.

The big man frowned. He hadn't wanted this and he tried to tell his opponents just that. A heavy brass lantern flew out from the middle of the crowd and struck the side of the stranger's head, pulling his hood away and revealing his face.

The now revealed man's elbows slammed back down onto the long bar. His hair was cropped close to his head, the same mix of gold and silver as the tuft on his broad chin. Thin lines formed between his eyebrows as he blinked, trying to clear his suddenly blurred vision. The muscular man touched the side of his head where the lantern struck. There wasn't any bleeding but it was a clear message of how unwelcome he was.

"Very well, Alvin," he muttered to himself, "At least you learned we're on the right track."

The two remaining men had their weapons drawn and took the opportunity to charge. Lucky for Alvin, the lantern had stayed in one piece as it fell onto his boot (it smashed his little toe when it landed but he could live with that). With a flick of his leg, Alvin sent the brass and glass light flipping into the air and into the face of the man wielding daggers in each hand.

The second hard impact was too much for the lantern and it shattered, spraying embers and licks of flame all around Alvin's target as the man landed flat on his back. The other attacker's scimitar missed Alvin's torso but sliced through the material of his cloak as Alvin stepped out of the weapon's path.

The large man wrapped one of his massive hands around the second assassin's wrist and squeezed. Alvin's other hand followed suit on his opponent's throat. The scimitar fell and impaled itself into the well-trod wooden floor.

All fell to silence in the building. Then the second assassin dropped to the floor unconscious and everyone in the tavern who had been a spectator suddenly joined the fray. After that was only chaos.

OUTSIDE

The sun had been well obscured by the leaves of the trees surrounding the woman, keeping her from being able to tell precisely how much time had passed. She endeavored to keep herself busy mending a thick cotton shirt that obviously mean from someone far larger than her to wear. It was only partially effective.

The rip in the seam between the sleeve and the torso of the garment had been stitched and restitched several times in just the last hour and she was starting to run out of thread. Her leg had moved from toe tapping to outright twitching the more she tried to focus on the manual, menial task in front of her.

The vest she wore was made of hardened strips of leather, tied together in a way that left gaps revealing the shoulderless lavender silk blouse underneath. Its long sleeves were rolled up to stay out of the way of the sewing. The long charcoal gray skirt the woman wore billowed away from her legs, keeping the cloth from tangling with her limbs.

The woman's long brunette hair was tied back with the two equally long braids that grew from the hair line at her temples on either side of her face. Streaks of white hair were mixed within, gleaming in the fading light. The leather choker around her neck had a simple iron medallion hanging from it with a list of names etched down the face, each name getting written steadily smaller and smaller as they scrolled down the metal.

She just couldn't stay still anymore. Jumping up to her feet, the woman threw the thoroughly mended shirt onto the two backpacks that sat side by side. She picked up the sheathed dagger that rested on the log she'd been using as a seat.

She slipped the dagger between two of the pouches in the belt and turned to start into the forest, only to run into the broad chest of the very man she was so very eager to find. The woman's thick eyebrows alternately rose and sank together as conflicting emotions and thoughts crashed together, trying to decide which would get precedence over the others.

The large man's cloak was the same color and, coincidentally, made from the same material as the woman's skirt. It also had a long tear down the side that revealed the man's heavily muscled bare arm that should have been covered with a long sleeve of white cotton. The sleeve was nowhere to be seen.

There, thankfully, didn't appear to be any wounds on the man beyond a couple of scratches. The woman turned her jade green eyes up at the much taller man to see that his face covered with dark soot.

Without a word, the woman gently pushed the man aside and looked back in the direction from which he had come. A pillar of smoke rose into the sky from a couple of hills away and she let out a heavy sigh before turning toward the man again.

"I thought we agreed to keep the scorched earth to a minimum until we find her," she gave the man her sternest look, the one that had become perfected being used on not only the man but also their child over the years.

"This one wasn't my fault!" the man pulled his hood back and ran his thick fingers through his spiky, silver peppered hair, "I was just asking the barmaid a couple of questions and half the tavern decided to jump me!"

"So you just had to burn the building down?" She folded her arms across her chest.

He shook his head, "One idiot decided to try and use a lantern as a weapon."

Alvin unfastened his cloak and slipped it off his broad shoulders. He wore a hardened leather vest much like the woman's, with a white cotton shirt underneath that was now missing a sleeve.

Over his black pants, Alvin wore leather chaps that showed the wear and tear of years of work on a farm. His black boots were covered in ash.

"But it wasn't for nothing, Perse," Alvin said as he stepped up to the woman, wrapping his hands around her bare shoulders, "I got a lead. The men that attacked me were Al Razheem and the barmaid said she saw a girl matching Ophelia's description!"

Perse's face lit up at the news. But an eyebrow cocked as another part of the man's sentence registered.

"Barmaid? How is it that in a room full of men you always find the one woman and talk to her?"

"She was more open to conversation than the men holding swords?" Alvin grinned in a way that came off equal parts silly and charming as he slipped his hands around the woman's hips, "But, baby, you know I've only eyes for you."

He softly pressed his lips to hers and felt them already stretched into a smirk of their own. Perse wrapped her arms behind the back of her husband's neck, having to lift herself onto the tips of her toes to do so, and once their lips pulled apart, the woman rested her head against the man's chest.

"I want her back, Alvin," She felt a lump suddenly start to form in her throat, "I want our daughter back."

"I know. I do, too," he wrapped his arms around Perse and effortlessly lifted her from the ground, "We'll get her back and then the Al Razheem will be sorry they even looked at our little girl."

Still holding each other, Alvin and Perse slowly sank down to sit on the dusty ground. The married couple didn't let each other go for a long while. It wasn't until the sky had reached an almost black shade of cobalt that Perse finally pulled away from her husband and rose to her feet.

"We won't be able to do anything until morning, anyway," she said, slipping a hand into one of the pouches around her waist, "I should patch up your cloak and you should find some wood to keep this going through the night."

She pulled out a small leather bladder that fit perfectly into her palm and uncorked the top. Between two fingers in her other hand was a small vial that found itself open with a practiced twirl of her fingers.

Two drops of the liquid from the vial found their way into the bladder. The vial was sealed, then the bladder was given a quick shake. The leather started to expand. Perse tossed the bladder onto a small pile of kindling she'd made near the spot she'd been using for sewing. The kindling flared up into a cozy looking campfire.

Alvin lifted himself to his feet and gave his wife a playful bow, "Baby, your wish is my command."

Perse let out a quiet laugh as she gathered the torn cloak and settled onto the log to start working. The smile lasted until her husband was out of the clearing and among the trees to search for more kindling. Then tears of worry threatened to make her needlework crooked.

THREE
HER FIRST ASSIGNMENT

"TEN... NINE..."

Ophelia leaned against the cold stone wall, her boot idly tapping against the floor. The intersection of hallways was deserted, save for her at one corner, yet she didn't make a move to go in any of the four directions available.

"Seven."

She pulled the curved sword on her hip from its sheath, the metal of the brass handle cool against her left palm. And her foot kept tapping.

"Four."

Ophelia wiped her short braids behind her ears as she lifted her scimitar to shoulder level. Holding the blade horizontally, she pressed the dull back edge against her right shoulder, readying the blade.

"Two and one."

The woman whipped the weapon into the intersection. The blade met some momentary resistance but, after the sound of a dull thud, Ophelia followed the weapon out of the hallway.

The headless body of the man who had been walking down the hall dropped to its knees. The chain mail the man wore protected much of his body but stopped at the base of his neck. Ophelia aimed for the couple inches of space between the armor and the heavy metal helmet. It still held the head as it rolled several paces behind his body.

The body tumbled down to lay flat on the floor but Ophelia was well on her way in the direction from which the guard had come. The sword in her hand was covered in red ichor, causing her to hold it well away from her body until she passed one of the many tapestries lining the walls.

Wiping the blade back and forth across the cloth, she finally got the blade clean enough to slip the weapon back into its sheath without fear of getting messy herself. Still, Ophelia felt the need to wipe her hands against the little amount of material that was her shorts, as if she needed to clean her hands as well.

She continued on. Her destination wasn't a long walk from there. The Squire's audience chamber was just down the hall.

When Ophelia reached the hickory double doors, she pulled one open a crack, just enough to be able to peek inside. She let out a soft groan and threw the door open to step inside the room to meet its lone occupant.

Kitanah stretched herself across the Squire's massive chair. It would have been referred to as a throne if it had still belonged to the king that occupied this castle decades ago. As it was, the chair was made of polished wood with velvet armrests, backrest and, of course, the heavily cushioned seat itself.

The red haired assassin had made herself comfortable. One long leg was draped over an armrest. Her bare right arm rested on the opposite one while her metal sleeve enveloped arm rested on her flat abdomen. The chair was large enough that Kitanah looked very comfortable, without a hint of feeling cramped.

Ophelia frowned as she looked around the room. The *throne* sat along the middle of the back wall, allowing plenty of room for a group to meet in front of the former seat of power. There were two more doors, besides the door the younger assassin had entered from, across from each other in the side walls.

The sapphire colored carpet ran in T-shaped pattern. The line of the top led to each side door. The thick fabric absorbed the sound of Ophelia's steps as she walked deeper into the room.

The place was deserted, save for Kitanah. In fact, it didn't look like anyone else had been in the audience chamber in quite some time.

"Where's the Squire?" Ophelia asked.

Kitanah shrugged, "Not here."

"I can see that," the younger assassin rolled her eyes, "Our intelligence said that he would be meeting with his Captain of the Guard now. He's supposed to be here!"

The other woman scowled, "You think I don't know that? Obviously, he changed his schedule," Kitanah took a long, slow look around the room, "I don't think he knows about us though."

Ophelia scanned around the room herself, trying to figure out what Kitanah could have possibly been looking for, "What makes you say that?"

"Something you don't have. Instinct," the other woman grinned, her white teeth standing out between her ruby lips, "If he knew we were coming, why didn't he have any soldiers waiting to ambush us?"

Ophelia frowned, realizing Kitanah did have a point, "You are the old hand at this. What do you think we should do then?"

The higher ranked assassin bristled at the word *old*, "Find the Squire, of course. If I were a betting woman, I'd wager he's back in his living quarters."

"Why there?" Ophelia asked.

Kitanah slipped her leg off the arm of the chair and straightened up in the seat. "All the man does is read about historical military conquests. Where else is he going to do that? The kitchen?"

"They do have a library here," the younger assassin answered.

"Tell you what," the other woman lifted herself onto her black leather boots, "If I'm right and I kill the Squire, you have to give me your share of this job's payment. It's only fair since I'd have done all the work."

Ophelia felt a tinge of excitement in her chest, "And if I kill him?"

"I'll give you the same stakes," she answered.

"You take that door, I take this one?" the younger woman nodded from the side entrance to her right then to the one on her left.

"Fine," the spiked heels of Kitanah's boots dug into the carpet, leaving little pock marks with each step toward the agreed upon door, "Don't get yourself killed. I want to have a chance to rub this in your face."

With that the older assassin was out of the room. Ophelia let out a quiet sigh as she started for her own exit. There was a set of stairs leading up almost immediately on the other side of the door.

Ophelia made her way down the network of hallways on the second floor. She couldn't help but notice that she hadn't needed to hide or dash across any intersections to avoid being seen. This part of the castle seemed quite empty.

On the way to the audience chamber, there had been the usual assortment of maids, guards and other denizens of the castle wandering through the halls. Ophelia had been able to avoid all but one on her way.

That was because of the guards patrols were efficient and systematic, not leaving any hallway unattended for too long. Assuming Kitanah didn't leave any evidence of her own passage, Ophelia figured that she had less than an hour before the body she left was discovered. Then this part of the castle wouldn't be so empty.

The assassin didn't bother opening every door as she walked past. Most of them were too close together to hold a library behind them. The doors appeared to lead to quarters for residents of the castle and visiting guests.

This castle only had two floors. Ophelia hadn't been able to explore all of the first, concentrating on getting to where she thought the target was going to be waiting, but she hadn't seen any library. Judging by how many small rooms she had gone past, Ophelia was starting to think that she should have taken the door she pointed out to Kitanah.

As Ophelia approached yet another corner, she heard a couple of voices drifting from the adjacent hallway. Crouching, she sneaked along the wall and poked her head into the other hallway just enough to catch a peek of what was there.

"You think it's really them, Vermilion?"

Two men stood beside each other. The first was massive in muscle but also in gut. His bushy brown beard obviously hadn't been combed through in a long while. The ham bones he called fists were wrapped around the hilts of two swords that looked too small for him. But that could have been why he carried two of them.

The second man was nowhere near as large as his compatriot but he was hardly a pipsqueak. While he was clean shaven, his long straight hair reached down almost to his waist. He wore a long sword across his back in a fancy looking polished leather scabbard.

Both men were dressed so similarly it had to be some kind of uniform. They had black vests wrapped around white shirts that had frills along their collars and the cuffs of their long sleeves. Instead of pants, they wore kilts with intricate patterns of yellow, green and blue lines crisscrossing and overlapping against each other. Ophelia actually thought it was an attractive look for them.

The two men stood between the two doors closest to the corner. The door closest to Ophelia had a massive, intricate lock built into the wood. It also had a keyhole that was oddly shaped, not meant for any kind of traditional key to open.

The two men were obviously guards but not the same heavily armored, showy type that lined the halls below. The assassin had to assume they were more skilled than those who relied on heavy metal wrapped around their bodies for protection.

If they were indeed the more skilled fighters in this place and there was such an unusual lock on one of the doors they were protecting, that meant the men had to be guarding something important such as, say, the owner of the castle. That could be the

Squire's living quarters and the men were very likely the Squire's personal guard.

"It's possible, Tunicle," the long haired man nodded at the bigger one, "The Al Razheem aren't the most forgiving of folks. If that message is to be believed, they've sent one of their assassins after him. We have to be ready."

So the Squire did know they were coming somehow. Ophelia slowly, quietly pulled her curved scimitar from its sheath. She had been thinking of trying to flirt her way in, perhaps pass herself off as the latest plaything for their master to gain entry. With the guards on alert, however, there was no way they would let a new face past them without a fight.

So a fight it was to be then. Straightening up against the wall, Ophelia took a deep steadying breath. She was suddenly thankful for the sensation of warmth from the runes tattooed on her back that offset the cold feeling of the stone.

Stepping around the corner, Ophelia pointed her sword toward the men, making her intentions known. The big man, Tunicle, stepped away from the doors to fill up the majority of the hallway ahead of Ophelia. Both his blades were in his hands in an instant.

The other one, Vermilion, took a moment longer to draw the long sword from his back. Both men stood ready for the coming violence but neither stood between Ophelia and the door with the strange lock. Either the guards had confidence in the mechanism's strength or the room wasn't as important as the woman supposed.

Ophelia thrust her blade at the larger man first. He crossed both his swords over each other and slammed them down onto the back of Ophelia's weapon.

The curve of the assassin's sword only helped Tunicle get the leverage to drive the blade of her sword to the stone floor, bending Ophelia over and pulling her off balance. Stumbling forward, she presented the perfect target to Vermilion, like an executioner waiting to behead a criminal.

The long sword blade dropped for the woman's neck but both men only succeeded in severing the neck of the violet silhouette left behind when Ophelia blinked. She reappeared behind the long haired Vermilion, who found her sword thrust into his back. The blade pushing out through his chest, Vermilion's white shirt quickly changed its color to crimson.

"No!" the big man turned to face the gruesome sight.

Ophelia jabbed a knee into Vermilion's back to push him off of her curved blade. The blade wouldn't budge.

Vermilion held the curved end of the blade tightly, blood pouring from his hands. He chuckled back at the assassin without turning to face her.

"Take... her... Tunicle," he wheezed as a stream of blood spilled from his mouth.

Ophelia tugged again on the scimitar, trying to free it, when Tunicle's blades started down for her like steel fangs. Letting the handle of her sword go, Ophelia shoved Vermilion at the other guard, letting the man take her sword with him.

The now dead guard's body slammed into Tunicle, knocking him back into the wall and away from Ophelia. The woman's eyes opened wide in shock as the tip of Vermilion's blades slipped between her eyelashes before falling from the big man's grip.

She didn't disappear and reappear. She didn't blink. Ophelia wasn't in another part of the hallway. She didn't blink!

Vermilion slumped to the ground in front of Tunicle. The big man dropped his thin straight blades to catch his falling compatriot, aiding him to the floor.

A long, superficial cut stretched down the front of the still standing guard's abdomen from the tip of the woman's scimitar still protruding from the slain man. The injury wasn't anything that kept him from stepping over Vermilion's body and away from the wall toward Ophelia.

Grief washed over the face of the heavy man as Vermilion's eyes lifted toward the assassin. Neither of them were armed now.

"You teleported," he growled, "Just like the message warned. I didn't believe it was possible."

Tunicle's knuckles cracked as his bulky hands rolled up into fists. Ophelia ducked under the first swing and had to jump out of the way of the second.

A scream of turmoil and rage erupted from the Tunicle as he swung for her again and again. Ophelia was barely able to stay ahead of the big man. Tunicle's fists slammed into the walls on either side of the woman. Tunicle didn't seem to feel any pain as the stone, and surely his bones, crumbled from the force. He just kept swinging.

Finally, one of the guard's punches connected. Stars filled Ophelia's vision as she fell to the floor. One side of her face already felt as if it had been hit by the stone floor before her other cheek connected with the cold, hard surface.

Ophelia didn't blink. He hit her and she didn't blink.

Ophelia felt her last meal lurch up her throat when Tunicle's gargantuan foot found its way to her stomach. Her arms wrapped around his vomit covered leg before he could rear back for another kick.

But rear back he did. Tunicle whipped his massive leg back with such strength that Ophelia was flung away from him. Rolling along the floor, her head finally hit the smooth wood surface of the door with the strange lock.

She didn't blink. Why wasn't it working?

Ophelia scrambled up to her knees, scratching at the surface of the polished door before finding the handle. Tunicle's knee slammed into her back, the runes sending an acidic shock through her body at the unexpected strike.

Why wouldn't she blink? Blinking was supposed to protect her...

"Get up," the heavy man ordered, "Turn and face me."

Shaking, Ophelia forced herself to her feet. It took her far longer to accomplish than she thought it should.

Turning, she had to put her full weight against the door to keep from falling over. One of Tunicle's enormous mitts wrapped around Ophelia's throat, pulling her face up to look straight at him.

"The only reason you get an honorable, face to face death is because Vermilion would have wanted it," and his fist flew for the woman's face.

Ophelia closed her eyes, readying herself for the coming pain. When it didn't come, her pale eyes slowly opened. All she saw was polished wood.

The door in front of her suddenly shuddered as if struck by a sledgehammer on the other side. Landing flat on her backside, Ophelia's eyes were locked on the door and the strange lock embedded in it.

She was in that room that Tunicle and Vermilion were protecting. Ophelia had blinked through the wood and the big man's punch slammed into the door instead of her.

"Oh my, how did you accomplish such a feat, my dear?" a voice popped up from behind the woman, "I do trust you didn't permanently injure anything."

Ophelia tried to scramble to her feet and shuffle around to see who was talking at the same time. She was on her hands and knees when she was finally able to see was what behind her.

There was nothing else in the room but a sword in a scabbard, resting on a pedestal with the handle pointing toward the ceiling. The scabbard had jewels encrusted all along its surface, with gold filigree all along the edges and the opening where the wide hilt protruded.

The sword rested on a pedestal that was decorated in the same manner. Jewels were embedded in the sides of the pedestal while gold was wrapped around the corners and edges.

The rest of the room was completely bare. Just the stone walls. There weren't even any torches.

That was when Ophelia realized that the sword itself was the lone source of the light in the room. The room was so small that it didn't take much to light it but Ophelia still couldn't see who it was who spoke to her.

"Who's there?" she said, her buckler mounted arm resting against the wall.

"Oh, my apologies, dear. My name is Havarti," the voice came again.

"Where are you?" with a heavy grunt of effort, Ophelia finally lifted herself to her feet, "What kind of name is Havarti? Isn't that some kind of cheese?"

"I'm a bastard sword, a hand and a half sword, and still I get comments about cheese!" Havarti shrieked, "I bet a claymore never has to deal with this kind of disrespect!"

"She's in the shrine!" Tunicle's muffled voice came through the wood, "Squire Trelaine has the key!"

"Didn't mean any disrespect," Ophelia groaned as she finally pushed away from the wall and thankfully didn't collapse under her own weight, "I didn't realize swords spoke. I thought you were someone hiding in here."

"And where, pray tell, would someone hide?" Havarti asked.

There was a red jewel at the base of the sword's handle. The way the light hit the jewel (or somehow came out of it?) changed with every word that the sword said, like the facets themselves shifted with the sound.

The wood that served as the room's door shuddered as something heavy was slammed against it. It held firm in the frame but it wasn't going to last long.

Ophelia's eyes snapped back toward the door, "What's funny is that was what I was just about to ask you."

"Ask me what?" the sword sounded confused.

"If there was a place to hide," Ophelia felt her insides jump when the door bent in again.

"A place to hide what?"

"Me," the woman stepped toward the weapon, "They're going to kill me when they get in here."

"That is most regrettable, dear," the bastard sword said, "but how am I to know that your death by their hand isn't justified?"

Ophelia's teeth ground together, "I guess wanting to kill your Squire would be justification for you."

"My Squire?" Havarti harrumphed, "That ninnyhammer has been holding me in this room for years."

She cocked a thick eyebrow at the sword, "Ninnyhammer?"

"What descriptor do you feel would be more appropriate, my dear?" the bastard sword asked, "Milquetoast? Pedantic? Gormless? Clodpole? Sch-"

The door cracked with the next slam. It still didn't give but it was no longer sitting flush in the frame. One or two more hits and it would crumble completely, allowing everyone outside entry.

"I get it. You don't like him," Ophelia stepped up to the end of the pedestal, resting her hands on the gold edging, "If I die here, you stay here. Nothing changes."

"Despite the redundancy of your phrasing, you are correct," Havarti let out a soft sigh, "I suppose your plan would be to use me as your weapon in your dramatic last stand?"

"Part of me stopped working for... some reason," Ophelia jumped again when the door shuddered with another crack, "but I can still fight and I can win. But I'll stand a better chance if I could do it on my terms. If you want to help, I'll take you with me when I leave the castle. If not, yeah, I'll be making my stand here."

The top half of the door was ready to topple to the floor. It was only being held together by several splinters at most. Tunicle was seconds away from entering.

The sword literally vacillated back and forth on its pedestal. The jewel that shifted whenever the weapon spoke did so with the sound of a quiet grunt. It had come to a decision.

"Take a hold of my handle then step to your right as far as you can," Havarti said immediately followed by, "Antre."

Ophelia did as she was instructed. Her boot met the wall and, instead of being stopped by the stone, continued moving past. Her body immediately followed just as the remains of the door littered the entire width of the floor of the room Ophelia had just vacated.

"I suggest you pull me in after you, dear, unless you want them to see where you are currently ensconced," unlike before, Havarti's voice was directly in the woman's head.

Immediately the sword was pressed against tightly against Ophelia's side in the gap, although not quite as tightly as the walls were against her back and chest. She wanted to ask how he'd spoken directly into her mind but Tunicle came into view at the passageway's entrance.

The big man almost completely filled up what space there was in the shrine. Tunicle barely had enough room to rest his hands on his hips as he frowned at the now empty pedestal.

The guard's narrow eyes scanned along the room until they turned in the direction of the gap in the wall where Ophelia stood. She could have sworn he was looking right at her but Tunicle kept turning until he was again facing the shrine's shattered entrance.

"She took the Squire's prize!" he announced as he stomped for the door, "She must have teleported out but she can't be far! The message said it had limited range."

Havarti's voice, again in her mind, spoke up, "It would appear you have a traitor within whatever group you are allied."

"What are you talking about?" the woman quietly hissed.

"You asked how they could have known you were coming," Havarti answered. "Especially with this being your first assignment."

How did the bastard sword know that? "Are you reading my mind?" she whispered, her tone making her discomfort obvious.

"You are my wielder now," the weapon said as if it was obvious, "We have a telepathic link so I am aware of important information and we may converse without fear of being overheard by most standard means of detection."

"But I still have to talk to y-"

Havarti interrupted, "No, you don't, my dear. You can simply think back to me, as well. And I would recommend doing so as long as Tunicle and whoever is with him may still be close enough to hear."

"Speaking of which," Ophelia chuckled as she thought those words, catching a hint of irony to the statement, "I thought he looked me dead in the eyes when he came in. How didn't he see me?"

"That is because of an enchantment on this passageway that conceals the entry from all but the Squire," the sword explained, "Trelaine uses it to leave his room and leer at me in the night without alerting his guards. He seems to enjoy our, as he calls it, *alone time.*"

"He does seem to think highly of you. Why?" she shook her head as she realized something else, "Forget that for now. You said this passage leads to his room?"

"Indeed," Havarti answered, "I would hazard to guess that it would be the perfect place to, say, assassinate him?"

"Glad to see you're enthusiastic about the idea."

Ophelia nodded and started shuffling sideways down the thin spacing between the bricks. After only a few steps, all the while scraping against the wall, the white fabric that covered her chest was now much closer to the black end of the spectrum.

"How can the Squire fit through here? I barely do!" the woman said, feeling the rough brick scraping against the tattoo on her back, making tingling waves shoot through her body.

Havarti took a moment before he finally spoke, "Let's just say that he isn't as *ample* as you in the chest area, my dear."

"Ha ha," Ophelia physically said through gritted teeth.

Thankfully the secret passageway wasn't long so, even at the slow pace she was forced to go, it didn't take long for the woman to reach the far side. When her right shoulder met up with solid stone, she turned her attention back to the sword.

"Antre," Havarti said aloud.

The mortared stones silently pulled apart. Another part of the enchantment, Ophelia supposed. After all, what use would a secret passageway be if everyone could hear it opening and closing whenever it was used?

Ophelia pulled her body free of the narrow tunnel, taking a moment to roll her shoulders and enjoy the new found feeling of freedom. Looking around, the woman found that she was indeed in the bedroom.

In front of her was his bed. It was so heavily cushioned that, once the comforters and blankets were added, the bed came up to the bottom of Ophelia's rib cage. How did the Squire get into it? Jump?

The one lit torch in the room was barely enough to illuminate the whole room. A small window that had crisscrossed bars in the opposite wall let in soft moonlight helped. The angle the light was coming from told the assassin that the night still had some time to go before morning came to take its turn.

Other than the bed, the only other furniture in the room was a writing table. There were stacks of papers laid across the surface, only one of them held blank sheets to write on. The rest had various scribblings spread over their respective surfaces. The table didn't have any drawers for storage. Squire Trelaine apparently wasn't a fan of things he couldn't see being in his immediate vicinity.

The only thing on the wall to Ophelia's left was a portrait of, according to the small plaque mounted in the thick frame of polished wood, the Squire himself.

"You're sure this is his room?" Ophelia felt her thick eyebrows press together. "Why would someone want their own picture in their room?"

"I'm positive, my dear," Havarti's voice popped into her head, "He is a man of certain, shall we say, eccentricities?"

Ophelia stepped around the bed to get a closer look at the portrait, "Meaning?"

The man in the painting was thin, not quite Doctor Efreeti thin, but close. On his head of long, curly ginger hair was a puffy hat that looked half full of air. Like most of the rest of his clothing, it looked like it was made of fine silks, the cravat around his neck, the yellow sash around his narrow hips, all the way down to the ribbons that tied down the front of his leather boots to hold the footwear firmly on his feet.

The only thing he wore, save for his boots, that wasn't silk was a kilt. It looked very much like the ones Vermilion and Tunicle were wearing out in the hallway, although silver chains held a black pouch on the front of the garment. The flap that held the pouch closed had a series of feathers radiating from the button that fastened it together.

Ophelia let out a soft grunt, "I would have thought that you'd be in this portrait with how much he seems to treasure you," she said to Havarti.

He let out a grunt of his own, "This was painted before my arrival. I can tell because time has had quite an effect on him from his depiction here to when I see him in that closet he calls my shrine."

"Why did he make a shrine for you anyway?" the woman asked but before the weapon could answer, the lock holding the door in the wall now opposite her started to let out the telltale noises of a key being pushed and turned into it.

Her pale eyes darted over to the bed. There was no space under it to hide, although if there was going to be a search for an intruder that would be the first place any guard would look. The writing desk provided no cover from view. The Squire really did not like things around him he couldn't see.

That, of course, only applied to people who didn't know about the secret passageway. Ophelia quickly dashed back into it, whispering the code word just as the door started to creak open.

In first came the massive heap of muscle and gut, Tunicle. Holding a thin sword in each bruised hand, his narrow eyes scanned the entire room before nodding back into the other room.

"I'm sorry we weren't able tell you about the intruder entering the shrine earlier, my liege," the big man said as he stepped further inside.

"Indeed," a new voice came from the other room.

A man who looked much like the painting stepped into the bed chamber. He was tall and thin but the mop of curly ginger hair from the portrait had been replaced with a limp, thin draping of hair where the gray had taken dominance from what streaks of red remained.

His face also looked much more gaunt. The entire way he carried himself reminded Ophelia of Doctor Efreeti and a shiver ran through her body. For the life of her she couldn't figure out why but she was sure it had to do with the target suddenly being in front of her.

"Where is this secret passage, sire?" Tunicle kept his weapons up as if he was expecting a fight at any moment.

Ophelia's grip around Havarti tightened. While the opening or closing of the secret passage may be silent, her trying to squeeze through it surely wasn't. And while Tunicle himself couldn't possibly fit to chase after her, he didn't really have to do so. All he would have to do is position guards on either end to skewer her when she came into reach or even wait for her to starve to death in the tight confines.

The much smaller man pointed almost exactly where the woman was standing and spoke the code word. Quietly as she could, Ophelia pulled the bastard sword out of his decorated scabbard as Tunicle closed the distance.

"And it is open now?" the big man asked, still unable to see through the enchantment.

Squire Trelaine nodded in the affirmative.

Havarti was free of his scabbard but Ophelia had to stretch to get the long blade out. She didn't have time to get the sword into a position to attack or even defend before Tunicle's two blades stabbed into the narrow space.

And Ophelia suddenly found herself staring at the big man's back. She had blinked!

"Tunicle!" the Squire's voice came out as a shrill squeak, "Behind you!"

Her left hand still up in the air, holding Havarti's handle with his blade hanging down just like in the passage way, Ophelia flexed her wrist to pull the sword up into a horizontal position.

The big man turned to see the woman holding the bastard sword over her head with the blade stretching out to her side, pointing toward the Squire. Even as he started to pull his blades free from the now invisible secret passage, Ophelia lifted herself to one foot, all the way to the tip of her boot covered toes, and spun around in a pirouette that would have been the envy of a professional dancer.

Her second foot dropped back down to the floor, followed shortly by Tunicle's head, which was suddenly sporting a beard that barely passed the end of his chin. Both the woman and disembodied guard's skull faced the Squire, who started to visibly shake.

Havarti let out a shuddering gasp in Ophelia's mind, "What did you call that? Blinking? It was quite invigorating!" the sword vibrated in her hand.

The blood that had been clinging to the steel of his blade shook off in small droplets, each falling away from the woman and onto the floor. Once the bastard sword was still again, with his polished steel glistening in the torchlight of the room, Havarti physically spoke up.

"But it is dirty work being your sword."

A pained look crossed the Squire's face, "Her sword?"

Ophelia was finally able to get a good look at her target. Havarti was right. There wasn't much of the man in the painting left. His hair was indeed thinner but so was his face. Squire Trelaine's cheeks were sunken and the dark circles under his eyes made the whites truly stand out.

The Squire was dressed for bed. He would have likely been in here when Ophelia initially arrived if not for the altercation in the hallway.

He wore a long cream colored night robe made of what looked like the same silk he wore apparently at any given point of the day. Three buttons ran down the front of his robe to hold it closed against his gaunt frame.

The sleeves billowed around his wrists, obscuring the involuntary shaking of his right hand. Only his right hand. The way he acted, either he didn't notice it or it was something he actively tried to ignore.

"What is the meaning of this, Havarti?" his lower lip projected out in a deep pout, "Have I not been a good steward to you?"

"Good steward?" Ophelia felt as if Havarti was pulling her to step in the other man's direction, "I can't remember the last time I saw sunlight! I've been in a room that, if I had feet, I could have paced in five steps! In circumference!"

"I explained to you that it is too dangerous for you to be outside of the walls..." Trelaine started to speak.

"Yes, yes, yes. Your precious research," the sword interrupted, "I was never consulted on being a part of it. Nor was I given any choice! Can we slay him now, please?"

The last question was directed at Ophelia. The woman looked from the sword and back to the thin Squire. Shrugging, she started toward the man.

"But why her?" the man inched backwards toward the still open door, "I can understand being displeased or even hating me. But wanting me dead?"

Havarti suddenly leaped out of Ophelia's hands and shot through the air like a spear. The man jumped, letting out the least manly yelp that the woman was sure a male could let out when the sword just missed his shoulder.

The sword embedded into the wood of the bedroom door and slammed it shut, wobbling back and forth from the impact. Trelaine lost his footing and tumbled to the floor, looking gobsmacked.

"Ophelia, engage the lock! He has a small army in that foyer!" Havarti yelled, "Quickly!"

The assassin did as she was told, dashing for the entrance and dropping the latch that served as the door's lock in place. It was designed specifically to not be able to be manipulated by any soul outside of the bedroom.

"You heard him," Trelaine slowly pulled himself away from the woman, crawling face up on his hands and heels, "There's a small army out there. Even if you kill me, you won't be able to get out alive."

Ophelia tugged the weapon free of the wood and turned to look at the man, "They don't know about the secret passage. If you had told them about it there would be men in here by now to come to your rescue."

The Squire grumbled under his breath, reluctantly nodding in agreement, "Do you even know why they want you to kill me?"

Ophelia felt herself smirk, "Would it make a difference if I did?"

This was the next stage of trying to save himself for which the General had prepared her. The first was him trying to lure her into the superior number of troops. That failed when she locked the door.

"You're the new one, aren't you?" his voice trembled ever so slightly as he spoke, "Efreeti's newest girl?"

She hadn't expected that. Her pale eyes narrowed as they focused solely on the man. How did he know that name?

Trelaine's back straightened and he sat up a little taller when he saw Ophelia's reaction, "It's easy enough to figure out. He figured out the procedure to create you. I was the one the Al Razheem called upon to make the physical materials to actually perform it."

Ophelia's shoulders actually relaxed as he explained. She had feared that whatever traitor had informed the Squire's people of her arrival had somehow betrayed her masters to them, as well.

She gave the man a sweet smile as she stepped closer to him, "So that means you're part in this affair is over, right?" the assassin pressed the sharp tip of Havarti against Trelaine's silk covered, bony chest.

"But, but," his eyes were opened so wide they looked as if they would tumble out of the holes in his face, "I know how they did it! I can reverse it, make you like you were before!"

"Like I was before?" Ophelia didn't bother to hide the confusion on her face as she pushed the cold steel of her sword into Trelaine's heart, "Why would I want to be anything but what I am now?"

She pulled Havarti free of the man's chest and immediately wiped his blood from the blade on the silk robe of the now still man. The locked door suddenly shuddered as something heavy being slammed against it on the other side.

"Aside from a little more reliable blinking, that is," Ophelia added as she turned for the secret passageway.

A soft knock on the bedroom door came as Ophelia was stepping over Tunicle's body, now half on the floor and half slumped against the wall. The assassin looked down at Havarti in her left hand, not only wondering why they had stopped trying to break the door down after only one attempt but also why they would knock on the door after the fact.

"Are you in there, Ophelia?" the muffled voice of Kitanah came through the wood, "Is the target dead?"

"Who is that?" the sword asked.

Ophelia gave Havarti a quick explanation as she stepped back over Tunicle's body. The weapon let out a soft grunt when she reached the part about the wager but didn't say anything after that.

The assassin leaned in close to the surface of the door, "The target's been eliminated. All clear out there?"

"Yup," Kitanah answered, "It looks like you succeeded in pissing a whole lot of people off by the look of things."

Firming up her grip on Havarti's handle, Ophelia's free hand started for the latch that held the door locked. It wasn't that she didn't trust the other woman, it was just that... she didn't trust the other woman.

The latch flipped up. Ophelia slowly pulled the door open and peered outside, ready to strike anything that approached.

Kitanah was the only one standing in the room, right in front of the door. She looked the same as when she and Ophelia parted ways a short time earlier, except now she carried a heavy looking pack over her shoulder.

Also, the metal sleeve she wore on her left arm had flecks of red up and down its surface. Crimson streaks were all along the hooked ring at the cuff. It had seen some action. Very recently.

And that was when the smell hit the new assassin. It was a sickening mix of copper, offal and urine? Ophelia was pretty sure it was urine.

All around the red haired assassin, dead bodies that were missing one, two or more limbs, many their heads lined the floor and the base of the walls. It was more like there were puddles of stone because there was so much blood covering the floor. And the space between the dry patches would make it hard to get through the room without soiling one's boots.

"Nobody even noticed when I came in," Kitanah smirked, pushing the door wide open and stepping into the bedroom, "They were all looking here, trying to figure out how to save their precious Squire from you."

Ophelia slipped Havarti back into his scabbard, "He wasn't much of a challenge."

The other woman stepped over to their now dead target, kicking at his ribs as if to check whether he was faking or not. When he didn't react, she let out a soft chuckle and looked back at Ophelia.

"Still, it looks like someone gave you a run for your money," Kitanah's green eyes traveled up and down Ophelia's body.

Her face and torso were starting to show the bruises from Tunicle's attacks. It wasn't until Kitanah mentioned that she looked injured that any real feeling of pain started to wash through her. Then it started to come back in a very heavy handed way.

"Nothing I couldn't handle," Ophelia replied and started to undo the belt wrapped around her hips.

"What about your precious blinking?" the other woman idly made her way around the room, the Squire's painting suddenly catching her eye, "I thought it made you untouchable."

"It's only for when I'm in real danger," Ophelia said as she pulled the curved leather sheath from her belt, "A couple of punches are nothing to worry about."

"If that's what a couple of punches can do to you..." Kitanah trailed off with a quiet whistle, though her eyes never left the painting.

Ophelia looped her belt around Havarti's scabbard and fastened it back snugly around her hips. With her new sword in place Ophelia stepped toward the red haired woman, wondering what had so intently grabbed her attention in the Squire's portrait.

"They definitely caught him during his prime in this, didn't they?" Kitanah motioned to the stern looking face of the Squire.

Before Ophelia had a chance to answer, the other woman slashed the hooks on her metal sleeve through the canvas. On top of that, Ophelia thought she heard Trelaine's corpse grunt at the same time.

Kitanah brought the hooks down the surface of the painting in the opposite direction. This time, Ophelia turned to look at the Squire's body and saw it shudder, then lay even more limp than before if it were possible.

The neophyte assassin knelt down beside Trelaine's corpse, holding her hand under his nose to feel if air was still moving in and out. She felt nothing. Resting her hand on his throat, his body had already started to get cold. He was most definitely dead. Then why did he react to the painting's destruction?

"Something wrong over there, kid?" Kitanah arched a thin eyebrow at the other woman.

"No," Ophelia answered, "Nothing at all."

Lifting herself to her feet, Ophelia made sure to crush the Squire's windpipe under her palm. She just wanted to make sure. With no reaction from the body, she started over for the secret passageway.

"We can leave this way to avoid your mess," she said.

Kitanah's eyes narrowed at the other woman for a moment before a smirk crossed her face, "I guess this means I win the bet."

Ophelia's head emerged from the illusion of bricks that hid the passageway's entrance, "And just how do you figure that?"

"Look around," the other assassin did just that before focusing again on Ophelia's head poking out of the wall, "We're in the Squire's living chambers."

"Where I killed him," her gray eyes bore into the other woman, "Not you. So I won."

"I told you he was going to be in here!" Kitanah growled, "Did you even find your precious library?"

"No," Ophelia confessed but didn't look at all troubled as she did so, "The important part was who actually killed him. And that wasn't you so…" and the new assassin again disappeared into the hidden passage, leaving Kitanah alone with a deep scowl on her face.

Four

THE REMAINS OF THE DAY

AT THE KNOCK on his office door, the scroll the General was reading disappeared into a drawer in his desk. The motion was so fast the two women entering the room didn't even realize he'd been holding anything.

First inside was Kitanah with the bulky knapsack over her shoulder. It must have been heavy as well because the red haired woman was leaning to the side as she walked.

"*BeHey TeraHyb,*" Kitanah said in the native tongue of the General and gave the man a shallow curtsy as she cleared the doorway.

Frowning, the man nodded back with his elbows resting on the heavy stone desk in front of him. It was made from the same tanned sandstone as the walls of his castle, giving the illusion that it was perhaps carved or even grown out of the floor without the closest of inspections.

After the red haired woman came Ophelia. The General had heard his newest assassin had taken some lumps on this mission but he honestly couldn't tell where.

Her mostly bare torso swayed from side to side as she walked. Then the woman gave the man a deep bow and it took him a moment to look up from the low cut of the gray cloth that served as what she called a shirt.

"It's an honor to see you again, Master," Ophelia said as she straightened up.

Having such an eye for detail did have its advantages. Like in the midst of assessing her legs for any signs of injury the man noticed a different weapon hanging on her hip than the one with which she left.

"New sword, Ophelia?" he asked simply.

"Yes, General," She nodded, wrapping a hand around the long handle, "I procured it from Squire Trelaine's castle. It dealt the killing blow to the target."

"Killed with his own sword then?" the man grinned to himself, "Is that the legendary Havarti?"

Ophelia didn't bother to hide her surprise, "You know this sword, Master?"

He nodded, rising to his feet, "It was because of that bastard sword that we enlisted the Squire's assistance in the first place. I'm glad to see that it didn't stay in the hands of his people after the fact."

The younger woman looked down at the sword than back at the General, "He didn't like it there. He wanted to leave, to see more of the world."

The man tugged at the braids on his chin for a moment before speaking, "And how better to do so than in your hands, Ophelia?"

Again, the young woman was surprised, "You'll let me keep him?"

"Him?" Kitanah slipped the heavy bag off her shoulder, "You talk as if the sword's alive."

The red haired woman put the bag down with ease, considering how long she'd been carrying it. She wasn't surprised to see the Ophelia glaring at her when she looked back up but the General having the same look on his face hit Kitanah almost like a physical blow.

She had suspected that something was unusual about the sword but Ophelia didn't say anything about it, or much else, to Kitanah the entire trip back to the Oasis. The younger woman garnered all her attention onto the bastard sword but never heard either speak to the other as if they were living beings conversing. As such, the experienced assassin figured to get under Ophelia's skin with her remark. She hadn't counted on, however, upsetting the General as well.

"You know better, Kitanah," the bearded man rested his hands on his hips as he stared the woman down, "Now remain silent until I am finished with our newest recruit."

Kitanah bowed obediently, not even having to look up to see the dopey grin surely stretched across Ophelia's face. It must have pleased her greatly to see the higher ranking member of the Al Razheem getting berated for her benefit. It would have done so for her.

The General turned all his attention to Ophelia, who told him of the events leading to Trelaine's death. She spoke like an excited child back from some kind of field trip. Although, Kitanah silently noted, that the time where they met up in the audience chamber to when they found each other back in the Squire's living quarters was more vague than the rest of her tale.

Kitanah would have corrected the story, except the bruising that the younger assassin's bruises and other injuries faded much faster than they should have. Even if the older woman had spoken up, it was her word against Ophelia's.

The General rested a hand on the young woman's smooth shoulder as she finished speaking, "Very good, child. You are a credit to our family out here in the desert."

"Master, there is something that is troubling to me, though," Ophelia's cheeks flushed soft pink at the man's touch, "One of the guards I killed mentioned a message warning him and the rest of the Squire's people of an assassin that can teleport. This was my first assignment for you, so how could anyone outside of the Al Razheem know about my ability?"

Kitanah felt her entire body stiffen as the other woman spoke. The General's eyes closed narrower and narrower, shifting in her direction as Ophelia finished.

"Indeed," he said, then his demeanor shifted to that of an accommodating parent, "Go get yourself cleaned up and settled into your new room. You've earned a rest."

The younger woman wrapped both her hands around one of his. Bowing down, her soft lips pressed to the gold ring on his finger.

Slowly, Ophelia straightened up and gave him a wide, flirtatious smile, "Thank you, Master," and she was out of the room seconds later.

The General straightened to his full height, bringing him half a head taller than the not at all short Kitanah, and motioned for the woman to approach him. She did so, leaving the knapsack on the floor.

"Did you get all of them?" his face looked as if it was chiseled from rock as he spoke.

"Yes, Sire," she nodded, adding a little bounce to her entire body, "All twenty of the soul orbs."

"Making twenty-one with the one already in my possession" the man nodded, "Efreeti can go into full production now."

The red haired woman frowned, "Can you truly trust him, Sire? I mean, he isn't Al Razheem, or even human, for that matter."

"Don't judge him too harshly, Kitanah. After all, it's thanks to him that you have..." the General reached out and tapped his fingers along the long metal sleeve encompassing her arm.

"But I was and am Al Razheem," she said, "To take someone you've never met and claim to make them unquestioningly loyal? I don't see how that is possible, no matter what kind of tools that man claims to have. And, if he could, why make a person loyal to someone else?"

"And there it is," the General folded his arms over his broad chest, "It isn't Efreeti as much as it is Ophelia's loyalty you question. Tell me, are you jealous of our new recruit?"

"Jealous?" Kitanah physically reared back as anger washed over her, "Of a farm girl whose only special talents come from a vial?"

The man arched a pointed eyebrow at the woman, "Why do you call her a farm girl?"

The woman's teeth ground together for a moment before she answered, "She had to come from somewhere, Sire. To me she has that bovine glaze in her eyes you see in cows before they either mate or are slaughtered."

The General grunted. He made his way back to the chair behind his desk, although only his hands rested on the heavily cushioned back. He didn't sit down.

"Tell me why you warned Trelaine's men that she was coming for him."

Kitanah's eyebrows furrowed, "I needed to make sure they were protecting him rather than the vault. She is the lower ranked, I used her as bait to lure them away from your true goal."

"The more important goal," the General corrected, "I did want Trelaine dead."

The woman nodded back, "I'm the senior, I sent her off to find the Squire as I did your bidding with the orbs. Once I attained them, I rescued Ophelia from the corner she dug herself into and brought her home safely."

The man's fingers dug into the cushion so hard Kitanah could hear the fabric ripping, "And it was necessary to tell them of her ability to blink?"

"I..." her mouth went dry, "I did what I felt was necessary to goad them into action."

"Or to give them an edge to eliminate a competitor," the General hissed, "Would she have been in that *corner* if you hadn't given away that strategic edge?"

"Sire, I..." her breath started to shudder, "I only want what is best for the Al Razheem."

"I decide what is best for the Al Razheem. Not you!" he bellowed back, "If I find out you ever try to sabotage one of my investments again, I will have you disarmed and fed to the hell hounds! Do you understand?"

The General was not using hyperbole when he said he'd *disarm* her. Kitanah had witnessed another assassin that had betrayed the clan literally have his arms severed from his body before he was tossed into a pen full of wargs.

Without his arms, the assassin had no hope to defend himself as the monstrous canine beasts started eating him alive. Hell hounds were even worse. They don't just eat their prey, that was just the last thing they did to the unlucky victim and by that point it was almost a mercy. But only because there was only so much meat on the body so the end of the suffering was in sight.

"Yes, Sire, I understand," Kitanah's cheek twitched, an ember of rage in the back of her mind only growing as she stepped over to the bag she'd brought into the office.

"Leave it," the General ordered as Kitanah started to reach for the handles.

Again, she nodded to the man, stepping away from the pack. She stood in place, not knowing what to do next. The bearded General stepped over to the bag and picked it up himself before again facing Kitanah.

"I've doubts about Ophelia's loyalty as well," the General's face softened as he looked back at his assassin, "Efreeti said I was free to test her fealty and I do intend to do so.

"Until I'm satisfied, you are to treat her as a member of the family. If you witness anything that causes you suspicion, tell me but do not act on your own. Ophelia's fate is mine to decide," with that he motioned to Kitanah that she was dismissed.

She left as ordered. Kitanah made her way down the hallway, her stomach churning from one emotion to another and she wasn't able to get it to settle on any one feeling. She was so caught up in trying to process what had happened that she almost walked into the unearthly thin Efreeti.

"My dear Kitanah, I dare to suppose that you're a bit distracted," he said as he tipped his tall hat in her direction.

"I'm fine," she responded, starting to step around the man in the tweed cloak.

Even though he didn't move, Efreeti's presence alone seemed enough to keep Kitanah from getting by him, "The only words in the mortal tongue that are guaranteed to be lies. What is troubling you, child? Perhaps Doctor Efreeti can help make it better?"

Kitanah shook her head so vehemently her hair whipped across her eyes, "I have no need. Not from anyone in general, or you in particular."

The thin man's lips pulled together into a tight purse, "Ah, then I am to presume that I am part of your troubles and, by extension, my Ophelia as well?"

"Your Ophelia?" her green eyes dug into the being.

"Ah, pardon me, a slip of the tongue," his usual, discomforting smile returned to his face, "While I did create Ophelia, she is no longer mine. She belongs to your beloved General, body and soul."

"You say that," Kitanah rested a hand on her hip.

Efreeti adjusted the circular lenses mounted on the bridge of his bony nose, "And you do not believe it. I hypothesize that you feel I gain nothing by making a totally loyal soldier for someone else so I must have some ulterior motive."

It was as if he were reading her mind. Kitanah didn't let him know that, though, and kept her face an expressionless mask. What he said next, though, surprised the assassin.

"And, of course, you are correct," he chuckled, "While I made her unquestioningly devoted to the General, I did not make her so to the Al Razheem."

"But," Kitanah stopped herself from attacking the man while he spoke, "the General is the Al Razheem."

"Is he now? Then I conjecture there is nothing to worry about," Efreeti arched an eyebrow, or at least the part of his face where an eyebrow would have been, "If you'll excuse me, I have to attend to your fearless leader and procure the parts for our next project."

And with that Dr. Efreeti stepped aside, pressing himself against the stone wall to give Kitanah plenty of room to pass. As she did so, Efreeti again bowed his hat toward her.

She knew he was referring to the soul orbs. As far as the General was concerned, Doctor Efreeti had every right to them. Once the thin man started toward the office, Kitanah turned to watch him.

Even the way he walked seemed sanctimonious and condescending. How could a man like that have garnered such unmitigated trust in a man who created an organization that traded in suspicion and deception? Perhaps that was his secret. Efreeti was trusted simply because he acted so untrustworthy.

And Ophelia... how could one be loyal to the leader of the Al Razheem but not to the organization itself? Particularly when the General is the embodiment for which everything the Al Razheem stands.

If there was a loophole in that logic, Kitanah was sure that Efreeti would be the one to find it. She had to know more about Ophelia. She'd sent agents to investigate where the Doctor had come from with the woman in tow. That was truly how she knew that Ophelia grew up on a farm.

With the General just now forbidding her from actively looking into Ophelia, he would surely punish Kitanah for her inquiries, even if they were made before he'd ordered her not to make them. The only solution was to not tell him, in the name of protecting the Al Razheem.

Now, with that same goal in mind, it seemed time to check in with her people and see if they had uncovered any information about the farm girl from the west and any potential threat she posed to Kitanah's clan, her family.

EFREETI'S WORD

OPHELIA TREAD OVER the familiar steps of the hall that led to her first memory. Stepping up to the heavy wood door, she didn't even have to raise her hand to knock before Doctor Efreeti's muffled voice gave her permission to enter.

She did so. Stepping into the familiar darkness, Ophelia had expected a sense of comfort to wash over her, but it didn't. Looking around, there was the single rectangle of light showing snow covered peaks rather than the shifting golden dunes outside that she remembered.

The marble table she awoke upon was no longer in the room. Without it for a sense of scale, the blackness of the room seemed both vast and claustrophobic all at the same time.

The man Ophelia had been looking for stepped out of the shadows with the same grin on his face that made him look like, well, comforting was the wrong word but more... normal to the young woman.

"Of what service can I be for you, child?" Doctor Efreeti bobbed his tall hat in her direction.

She knew what she wanted to say but Ophelia hadn't thought of the actual words to say to her... father? Creator? What exactly was Efreeti in relation to her?

"I'm back from my first assignment," the assassin started with a simple report.

The thin man nodded, "Despite the impression the glasses I wear give, dearie, my eyes do in fact work."

"Is that what those things are called? Glasses?" Ophelia pointed from her own eyes to his.

Efreeti let out a quiet sigh, "Yes. Now, Ophelia, my time is precious so please do not squander any more of it with inane prattle," he pulled the pair of glasses off and tucked them into some unseen pocket inside his tweed cloak.

Ophelia's teeth tapped together behind her closed mouth. Her hands rested on her hips for a moment before she folded her arms across her chest. After a couple of seconds, though, her hands slid back down to her round hips.

She didn't actually speak until her left hand unconsciously wrapped around the hilt of her new sword. "I had a fight with two guards. I killed one after I blinked around their initial attacks."

Efreeti's smiled broadened.

"But the second nearly beat me to death with his bare hands before I blinked again," the confusion and uneasiness she felt in that fight washed through the woman again as she spoke, "Is something wrong with me?"

Efreeti's mouth flattened.

The thin man stepped up to Ophelia with a stern look on his face. "Wrong with you, dearie? I can assure you that there is nothing wrong with my work. And you are my finest work."

"But," the woman felt a shiver run through her body, making her tattooed runes itch. "why was that guard able to keep hitting me again and again and again?"

"No *buts*, girl. You are perfection. Perfection, though, doesn't mean you don't experience pain," Efreeti said, folding his arms across his narrow chest, "That would be boring, especially since some pain can be quite pleasurable."

"So what use are the runes on my back then?" Ophelia frowned at the man.

Like a wave washing over a beach, anger splashed over the thin man's face to be instantly replaced by sadness, then finally settling on what she could only describe as... concern, "The runes keep you from receiving a killing blow, Ophelia. Your death cannot happen on any timetable set by mortal hands."

"You mean they will only keep me from dying?" the woman asked.

"It is a means to keep things interesting, girl," he answered, "Your death would make you wholly not so. However, if comfort is what you are seeking from me, I will tell you that each time you blink will accelerate your healing processes."

Doctor Efreeti pulled his glasses free from his cloak and put them back on as he scanned up and down the young woman's body. Ophelia looked down at herself, almost expecting to see something she hadn't noticed before simply because Efreeti was checking her over at the same time. She didn't.

The thin man wrapped his hands behind his tweed covered back. "Just like how the bruises from this beating that guard gave you are already faded well to the point of nonexistent." The corner of his mouth twitched up.

"Alright," Ophelia nodded slowly, her pale eyes moving from her own body and back to the thin man.

"Now you should go, child," Efreeti turned away from the assassin, "It would not do to have any of your Al Razheem colleagues begin to think that we are somehow conspiring against your beloved master."

Ophelia stiffened at the mention of the General. She hadn't thought of the impression her coming to see Doctor Efreeti would give anyone who had seen her enter his laboratory. She immediately turned and started for the door.

The unearthly thin man chuckled as the door closed behind the tattooed assassin, "Perfection, Efreeti, perfection," he muttered to himself.

FIVE

CLOSE CALL

THE OASIS

"You're telling me that two farmers got the drop on two assassins?" Kitanah scowled.

The heavily bandaged man nodded. All the woman could see of his face were his eyes and his chin, his bald head was completely enveloped in strips of cotton. The wrapping continued down his neck, torso and arms. His legs were surely wrapped as well, although he was covered by a blanket from his waist down to protect his modesty as he sat in one of the many beds lining the long wall of the healing ward.

The bandages themselves were treated in some kind of concoction that smelled of aloe and gave the bandages a subtle yellowish hue. The injured man looked as if he'd been mummified.

Kitanah bit down on her lower lip hard enough that the metallic flavor of blood teased at the edge of her tongue, "Tell me how they were able to fool you, Withermore. You were one of my most skilled agents."

His left hand kept twitching. The man grunted in a mix of frustration and pain as he flexed his wrapped fingers, trying to make himself still. But no matter what he did, it just kept moving.

Finally giving up, he sighed and started speaking, "It was after the Waning Moon tavern burned down..."

TWO WEEKS AGO IN THE WILDERNESS

The campfire in the middle of the small clearing wasn't burning as brightly as it was at sunset but it still had hours of wood to burn through when Withermore peeled away from one of the nearby trees, looking more like a shadow than a man.

After Withermore let out a soft call that perfectly mimicked a laden swallow, another figure stepped out from between the bark wrapped trees. Both men slowly, silently, made their way to the two mounds under a thick blanket beside the flames.

Daggers emerged from their belts as the two men closed the distance. Their intentions were clear and the targets open and exposed.

Withermore stood over the thicker mound while the other knelt by the smaller right beside, closer to the warmth of the flames. Nodding to each other, the assassins stabbed through the blankets simultaneously, right about where their targets' hearts and kidneys would be.

If the couple had actually been there, that is. When the men pulled their blades out of the blanket they found the metal coated with lantern oil instead of blood. The mounds quickly shrank as the liquid spilled out, soaking the thick material of the wool blanket and the ground around the assassins.

That was when they saw the first sparks. From the same tree Withermore had hidden behind, on the branch that hung over the two figures and combustible oil, Perse slapped a heavy piece of metal against a craggy shard of flint.

Her positioning looked awkward, with her laying on top of the branch, her skirt pulled taut as her legs wrapped around the bough to keep from falling. Perse rained sparks down on Withermore and his partner. It only took three strikes before the blanket erupted and only moments after that for the fire to spread to the clothes of the assassins.

Both men started screaming and shrieking almost immediately, jumping to their feet in a panic. It took a few seconds for the actual pain to register and send the screaming to a whole new level.

In that time, the earth under the campfire itself swelled until the mound towered over the two panicked assassins. The dirt tumbled down, burying the embers of the campfire under cold soil to reveal Alvin standing before the two burning men. He spat out the leather bladder that had been resting between his lips so that he could breathe under the earth and charged at the men.

"Didn't anyone ever tell you to stop!" extending both of his massive arms he clotheslined the men into the dirt, "Drop!" he gave each man a swift, solid kick to the ribs.

Withermore involuntarily hiccuped as both rolled away from the muscular man that was supposed to be their target. The dirt smothered the flames that were burning away at both him and his partner but the smell of sizzling flesh still hung in the air.

"And roll when you're on fire?" Alvin finished, turning toward the branch his wife rested upon.

"See what happens when you blow up people's livelihoods?" Perse said to her husband as he raised his hands to catch her as she let herself drop from the tree.

"Oh no, don't put this one on me!" he smirked back, not letting her feet reach the soil just yet, "These guys were in the bar, sure, but I think they were going to try this whether or not it was still standing."

Alvin kept his wife in his arms for a long moment before Withermore groaned. Reluctantly, Alvin let her down onto her feet and they both stood over the attempted murderers.

"You think these two are Al Razheem?" Perse's eyes narrowed down at them, her jaw setting hard.

"They were part of the group that started the fight," the massive farmer nodded, "They must have gotten out before the fire got too out of hand."

The woman knelt down beside Withermore, the closer of the two burned men. She rested both her hands on one knee, her fingertips idly sliding back and forth across the material of her long skirt.

"Is he right? Are you part of the Al Razheem?" She asked simply.

The bald man turned to look in Perse's direction. What little was left of his ear smoldered on the side of his head and it took him a couple of quick, struggling breaths to get any words out.

"How did you... why did...?" he rasped.

"Answer the questions given to you!" Alvin growled, his voice rumbling like a dragon's, "Or I will give you a blanket to keep away the night's chill."

He motioned over to the still burning blanket that still had two small mounds that had served as decoys representing himself and Perse. It didn't show any signs of going out soon and the heat could be felt radiating even from where they now conversed on the far side of the clearing.

The bald assassin's eyes opened wide and his head twitched in a way that was similar to a nod, "Yes, yes we are Al Razheem," his entire body started to shiver but not from the cold.

"Your people stole my daughter," the woman's voice had an edge like a blade to it, "Where have they taken Ophelia?"

"O-Ophelia? I- I don't know..." one thing about having burns over more than half of your body- when they are fresh it makes you lousy at lying.

Perse dropped her hand onto the man's now bare shoulder. The fabric of the shirt that had been there was long since burned away, along with several layers of skin only to be replaced with throbbing blisters. If his condition hadn't been so, the woman's gesture would have almost been considered comforting. As it was, though, the assassin only screamed in pain.

"Where is my daughter?" she screeched.

"Akshar!" the bald man hollered through his torment as Perse only pressed harder and harder down against his scorched skin, "Akshar! The Desert of Akshar!"

Only then did she lift her hand away. Slipping a cloth from her belt, she wiped the blister discharge and blackened skin that came off along with her palm away as she nodded down at the man.

"And where in the Desert of Akshar can we find her?" Alvin asked as he stepped up beside Perse, closer to the assassin.

"No, no please," tears spilled from the bald man's eyes as he gasped for breath.

"Then tell us what we want to know," the farmer's heavy leather boot suddenly hovered over the shoulder his wife had just released, "And not only will we stop hurting you, we'll even patch you up."

THE OASIS

"You told them our location?" Kitanah seethed as she interrupted Withermore's tale, "And you had the gall to return rather than honorably killing yourself?"

"I, I had no choice but to tell them, Mistress," the bald bandaged man stared down at his hands, the blisters on his fingers weeping, "I had to survive long enough to come warn you that they were coming."

The woman practically leaped to her feet, "They wouldn't be coming here at all if you hadn't told them where we were! Where was your spotter during all this?"

"It all happened so fast, Mistress," Withermore sounded as pathetic as he was sure Kitanah thought he was, "After the farmers treated my burns, they forced me to leave their camp. Vendilay found me just after I reentered the tree line. We came here post haste."

"And what of your partner?" Kitanah hissed, "What happened to Joseph?"

Withermore gulped, the bandages around his neck suddenly feeling uncomfortably tight, "His burns were too severe, Mistress. He never left that camp."

The woman let out a roar that echoed throughout the open expanse of the healing ward. Before the bandaged man knew what was happening, Kitanah's long metal sleeve slammed into his torso and pushed him flat down into his bed.

The weight on his chest only increased as the woman closed the distance between them. When she was finally standing beside his bed, she bent down so that her face was only inches from his. Blood started dribbling down his sides from where the hooks from the woman's sleeve sliced into his scorched skin.

"Remember when I said that you were one of my most skilled agents?" she whispered into his ear, "I was lying. Joseph was better. He was the one I trusted. You were only alive as long as there was a chance he'd survived."

Withermore felt his entire body tense as the metal ring that served as the cuff to Kitanah's metal sleeve started to turn on top of him, slowly at first. Bandages ripped and cold metal pressed against his skin. Then his flesh followed the example of the bandages after only a few rotations of the sleeve.

The bald man couldn't get a breath to scream. His brown eyes watered as he stared up into the woman's hard green ones.

The smile on her face told the man all he needed to know as he felt his life fade away. Kitanah wasn't doing this out of any sense of honor, or even for Joseph (though there had been rumors that they were secretly bedding each other since she'd achieved her higher rank). None of those reasons were why she smiled. Kitanah simply enjoyed watching others in pain.

Once Withermore's eyes turned dull and lifeless, the woman straightened up beside the bed. Wiping her sleeve clean on the bed's sheets, she motioned for one of the nurses.

"Take this sack of roasted meat to the kennel. They deserve a late snack," she ordered.

Kitanah didn't even wait for the nurse to respond before turning and leaving. It didn't take long for a part of Withermore's tale to start gnawing at the woman. One little detail that didn't quite make sense.

It took almost three turns in the hallways on the way back to her quarters before she realized what it was: How did a simple pair of farmers know of the Al Razheem?

The woman snatched a passing messenger by the arm.

"Tell Vendilay to come to my room," Kitanah ordered, "Now."

The man, barely more than a youth, protested, "But, Mistress, I'm already to deliver a post to Maester Shem—"

"I said now!"

The venom in her tone made the messenger jump to action. He launched off in the opposite direction and was around the corner and out of the woman's sight before she could take a breath to say anything else.

THE WILDERNESS

It was well into the morning but there was still a cool crispness to the air that was betrayed by the steam puffing from the man's mouth. The forest was left behind at daybreak and was well out of sight now. The grassy clearing stretched out before Perse and her husband almost uninterrupted except for the slight dips and rises in the ground that could laughingly be called hills and valleys.

The couple came upon a flat boulder that was almost the perfect height for a table and Alvin took the opportunity to drop his pack onto the rock and pull their map free from one of the many pockets. The unfolding parchment just kept spreading out wider and wider along the flat surface until it filled up all but the very edges of the granite.

"We should be somewhere around... here," Alvin dropped his thick finger on the east side of the Cantlebury Forest.

Perse rested her head on the man's shoulder, which was much easier when he was hunched over to look down at the parchment. Her pale green eyes ran over the point of the map he indicated and she frowned. If Alvin was right, they were so far northwest of this "Oasis" in the Akshar Desert that it would take them weeks to reach it.

"We'll have to go south to Paimae to get extra water bladders and maybe even some horses or something to get to where they're holding Ophelia," the farmer's finger traced over the map along the route he had in mind.

"I'm worried, Alvin," Perse said, wrapping both her arms around the one of his she rested her chin on, "It's taken us so long just to get here. What if Ophelia is already–"

"Don't," her husband interrupted, "If they wanted her dead, they wouldn't have dragged her across an entire continent."

"What else could a group of assassins want with her?" the woman's grip around his bicep tightened.

She felt her husband's entire body tense. Perse knew that he somehow felt responsible for their daughter being kidnapped but he never explained why and she hadn't pushed the issue. But after being attacked by the very group they were hunting down...

"Honey, maybe it's time you told me how you knew who the Al Razheem were," she said in as soft a voice as she could.

Alvin was still, leaning against the flat boulder like a statue for the longest time. Perse wasn't even sure he was breathing until he slowly nodded.

"Before I met you," the words came slowly at first, "I was a very different man. No, not a man, a boy. A stupid kid angry at the world and pretty much everything in it.

"You know I was an orphan. All I knew about my parents was that they abandoned me with some order of monks. Those monks were aligned with a group of mercenaries that did everything from taking bounties to guarding caravans."

Perse nodded, not having heard anything he hadn't told her before. Still, the look on his face, the effort it was taking him to speak, she waited for him to continue.

"When I was strong enough, I joined the group," the color drained from Alvin's face as he continued, "The new recruits always guarded caravans until they proved their worth in a fight. The idiot I was kept hoping someone would try to attack any of the caravans

I was assigned to so I could get recognition for my skill and then the high paying jobs. That was where the glory was.

"The last caravan I guarded was attacked. I thought I had my shot at the big time when I saw them coming. They actually introduced themselves as assassins from the Al Razheem before charging at us. They said that our group had sold the shipment we were guarding out from under them to another buyer and gave us peons a chance to run."

"But you didn't," Perse said.

Alvin nodded, shame covering his face like a mask, "It was my chance to prove myself. So they attacked and we defended. One of the wagons was set on fire and I started to hear screaming coming from inside. Female screaming."

Perse's hands slid from down his arm to wrap around his hand.

"I was so bloodthirsty I didn't even think about the fire until the assassins ran off," one tear slipped from his eyes to drop onto the smooth surface of the map, "After we put out the fire, we found a dozen women inside the wagon. Three of them died from smoke inhalation but the rest were okay.

"The dead were tossed out like rotten meat and the survivors were put into different wagons. That was when I learned that the caravan was shipping slaves. After all the caravans I went along with, it never occurred to me to ask what the cargo was. I slipped away that night and decided to start over someplace completely new. I didn't try to free the women or anything. I just left."

"And you think these same people took Ophelia to sell as a slave?" Perse asked.

She thought she knew everything about her husband. After thirty one years of marriage, the woman knew her husband was strong but to carry this weight for so long must have been an immense burden.

"I didn't at first," Alvin took a deep breath and let it out, looking like a steam dragon thanks to the cool air, "But when we got those horses, remember the ones that ran off on us? I also looked up an old contact from those days, Carden Boggs. He's the one who told me the caravan routes were still active and that Ophelia had been on one."

"You knew and you didn't tell me?" Perse suddenly felt her blood thump harder in her ears.

Her husband shook his head, "Not exactly. Boggs said that she was in a separate wagon from the rest of the shipment. And then it went off in a different direction once the caravan reached Middlemount."

"Near the bar you burned down," she frowned up at Alvin.

"She isn't part of the caravans I used to guard. I would have told you, I swear," the muscular man wrapped his free hand around his wife's in case she tried to pull away, "Boggs didn't know why and I just can't figure out what they could possibly want Ophelia for!"

His wife didn't pull away as Alvin feared, "You said they want her alive. As long as she's alive, we can get her back. And we will get her back," she declared.

Alvin pulled his wife into a tight embrace, resting his head on the crown of hers, "We will. I swear it."

"We can't do that standing around here," Perse said after they stood together for a good long time.

Alvin nodded and pulled the map from the surface of the boulder. It was going to take a while, weeks even, but both knew they weren't going back home until they were three again.

SIX

A STAR IS BORN

THE MAIN GATES of the Oasis pulled away from each other, their heft only matched by the ferocity of the winds screaming just outside the walls. The squared off tree trunks, lashed together with bands of metal as tall as a man, were attached to an intricate series of chains that made such a monumental effort as opening the immense doors a job that required only four men alternately spinning two wheels on either side of the entrance. Without them, it would have taken a small army of at least fifty, maybe even a hundred men to push it open.

Once there was a gap wide enough, a figure wrapped in a heavy cloak slipped inside the fortress. Almost immediately the men on the wheels opening the doors reversed their motion with the doors themselves following suit.

Even with as short of time as the gates were parted, sand buried the woman's boot wrapped feet. Kicking through the grains of loose earth, Ophelia pulled the amber colored cloak from around her shoulders and tossed it to an approaching assassin.

The red sash on his leather belt showed that he was the same rank as Ophelia. He actually stood several inches shorter than her, though the width of his shoulders stole away any impression of being more diminutive than her.

He threw the cloak to the ground with a quiet scoff, "The General wishes to hear your report."

"That's exactly where I'm going," Ophelia answered.

The woman's hand rested on Havarti's hilt as her hips swayed with every step. The stretch to her lips betrayed a pride that the straightness of her spine only reinforced.

As the returning assassin made her way through the halls, a familiar red haired figure suddenly blocked her path. Kitanah leaned against the wall, much like she had in her first encounter with Ophelia. This time, though, the metal sleeve was pressed between the wall and the small of her back.

Her right hand rested on her pale, bare abdomen with her fingers tapping away to the rhythm of some unheard tune. When she noticed Ophelia's approach, she pushed herself away from the wall and in between the younger woman and the door to the General's office.

"Was your mission a success, Neophyte?" Kitanah asked.

Ophelia's knuckles cracked around her sword's pummel, "I don't answer to you, witch."

The other woman had a look on her face that made the lower ranked woman think she had just tripped some kind of a trap. Ophelia's pale eyes flicked from one side of the passageway to the other. When she wasn't skewered by blades or spikes that had been designed to hide and then spring from the walls, she looked back at Kitanah quizzically.

That was when the voice of the General came from inside his office, "But you do, Ophelia. As long as she outranks you, you will answer her inquiries. Once she is satisfied by your answers then Kitanah will give you clearance to see me."

"Now now, my dear," Havarti's soft voice echoed in Ophelia's head, "Don't let the bespawler know that she upset you."

Ophelia wasn't sure if it was because of or in spite of that advice (to be honest, she had no idea what a bespawler was) that the woman chewed back the growl that was percolating at the back of her throat. The fabric that stretched across her chest strained as she took a deep breath before speaking.

"Alright, Mistress," Ophelia forced the words past her lips, "Yes, my mission was a success. The Vicomte that was threatening our people up north is dead."

Kitanah's green eyes narrowed and folded her arms across her chest, "And your proof?"

The younger assassin pulled a small leather pouch that hung at the small of her back off her belt and held it up at to the other woman's eye level, "Ring finger complete with signet."

She started to order Ophelia to "Show it to m–"

"And that is where your authority ends, Kitanah," the leader of the Al Razheem's voice again floated out into the hall, "Send Ophelia in, please."

SEVERAL WEEKS LATER...

"Of what is this man guilty again?" even though it was in Ophelia's mind, Havarti's voice was barely above a whisper as they slowly made their way between jutting rock formations.

The Gornack Plains, which served as the southern border of the Akshar Desert, were riddled with boulders ranging in size from that of a fist to a small house. The ground under the woman's feet was transitioning from arid sand to grassland but only with wisps of the plant at this point.

The sun was approaching the horizon but the shadows that the boulders cast seemed to go off in almost any direction, as if to mock from where the slowly fading light came. The shadows hid the assassin as she slinked from one formation to the next.

Voices echoed between the chocolate colored rocks, making it hard to pinpoint what direction they were coming from but she was close now. Ophelia moved very, very cautiously. The rock the woman hid behind was big enough that she didn't even have to crouch which, with her new attire, was a definite plus.

The cloth that had served as her shirt when she first joined the clan of assassins was replaced with a black leather vest that covered the top half of her torso but left the runes tattooed on her back completely unobstructed.

Around Ophelia's waist was a violet sash with gold swirls and waves that spelled out "Al Razheem" in the General's native tongue. And below that was a tight black leather skirt that was only slightly longer than the shorts she had worn before. Not exactly the standard uniform for an assassin but it was a gift from her Master so she could not refuse it.

Shaking her head, Ophelia glanced down at the bronze hilt of her bastard sword. "Doesn't matter. The General wants him and his friends dead so we're going to do that for him." She was not only used to speaking telepathically with Havarti but, in all honesty, had grown to enjoy having his almost constant presence with her.

Adjusting the new steel buckler strapped to her right arm, Ophelia hoped to catch the reflections of whatever was on the other side of the boulder where she found herself. There were four men gathered around a broken boulder that was shaped like an almost perfect basin that they were using as a fire pit.

The flames licked over the edges of the stone, bathing the immediate area in orange light. The man closest to Ophelia had his back to her but when the one sitting across the way looked up she snatched the buckler back to keep from being spotted.

It was enough. The one who almost saw her was the primary target. He fit the description perfectly: Wavy blond hair, chain mail armor, red leather vest and a necklace with a basilisk talon holding a shield hanging from it.

Between Ophelia and the target was the man with his back to her. He was the closest man but also the biggest. His silhouette alone almost cut off Ophelia's view in her buckler's reflection. Two other men, unseen by Ophelia but easily heard, meant that the campfire was effectively surrounded and left no undetectable path to the primary target.

The intelligence given to her said that they were all dressed very similarly to the primary target, only without the necklace. That suggested they were all part of some organization, although one with which the assassin was unfamiliar.

Ophelia slowly pulled Havarti from his scabbard. It may have been because of the air cooling in the waning day but she could have sworn that the sword felt cold in her hand.

"I'm afraid I have to express my doubts about this," the bastard sword said.

She didn't let Havarti express his misgivings about killing the Vicomte. Afterward, the sword let her know every reservation that he had during the entire trip back from the nobleman's estate. The Vicomte mentioned that the Al Razheem had been blackmailing him to do their will. That he had only taken her fellow assassins hostage to try and leverage control of his life back.

Much to the sword's chagrin, Ophelia never learned the details. She ran the man through, took his finger and freed her captive brothers in arms before he had even gotten cold. But still, Havarti felt the need to talk about it again and again on the way back to the Oasis.

Wanting to avoid another occurrence of that the woman rolled her eyes and let him speak now, "Fine. Okay. Express away."

"Why didn't the General tell us what this man did to warrant targeting? He told us why we went after the Vicomte, even if it wasn't the whole story," the sword spoke quickly, knowing the peace they were now experiencing was... fluid.

"It doesn't matter," Ophelia answered without her mouth moving, "I'm a member of the Al Razheem and my Master gave me a task to accomplish. The rest isn't important."

"Isn't important?" Havarti whispered back, "Assassins are supposed to have some code of honor by which they live, are they not? At the very least to swear fealty to their clan and to oppose its enemies?"

The woman shrugged, "What's your point?" her pale gray eyes snapped in the direction the camping men were talking when she heard one lift himself to his feet.

"Would he not have told us if these men were enemies of the Al Razheem?"

Ophelia stepped back, away from the corner of the boulder, as one of the men started walking in her direction. Both her hands wrapped around Havarti's handle, readying to strike.

"Tell you what, when we get back home, I'll ask the General what they did to get them a death sentence. Until then..."

The primary target stepped around the boulder, looking down at his trousers as he fiddled with his belt, struggling to unfasten it. When he looked up, all he saw was the glint of a long, sharp piece of metal before he stopped seeing altogether.

THE OASIS

The heavy doors spread apart, a rush of heat from the still, stagnant morning air washing inside the thick walls. Ophelia stepped into the courtyard, pulling the amber cloak off her shoulders.

The same man who tossed her robes to the floor in disdain before now obediently bowed as the garment fell into his hands. When he looked back up, he had to stifle a look of surprise when he saw how Ophelia looked.

Streaks of dried blood ran up and down the length of her body all the way from her forehead down to the tops of her boots at mid calf. One of her eyes looked even more starkly pale surrounded by the crimson ichor. It almost looked as if she'd covered herself on purpose as some kind of camouflage.

"All you alright, milady?" the assassin holding her cloak asked, his voice trembling slightly.

Ophelia looked down at herself for a moment, then back at the man, "Oh. Yes, I'm fine. It's not my blood."

Nodding to give the man permission to leave, Ophelia marched deeper into the keep. Again, Kitanah was waiting for her beside the General's office.

"Your mission?" the woman ran her bare hand up and down the snake skin like metal surface of her sleeve.

Ophelia's eyes narrowed at the older woman. It felt like another trap but, this time, it felt as if it was Kitanah who was afraid of getting snapped up in it.

It wasn't anything specific. Perhaps the fact that she wasn't standing quite so tall as she usually did. She had a defiant look on her face, much like just about every time she spoke to the younger assassin, but... was she fidgeting?

Ophelia's eyes moved from the woman's hand caressing the sleeve up to Kitanah's face itself, "What mission?"

"Don't play dumb with me," Kitanah stepped away from the wall but didn't get any closer to the other woman, "The reason you left the Oasis."

"She's keeping her distance," Havarti's voice popped into Ophelia's head, "And I cannot be sure but I believe I just saw a shadow scamper behind us to hide behind one of the pillars."

Perhaps Ophelia was the one in the trap after all. Instead of just trying to make her look bad, like last time, the other assassin may just try take her life. But the set up felt awkward.

Kitanah still outranked her but Ophelia was no longer a Neophyte. The General had also mentioned that no one else would know of her task and that she was to speak to no one but him about it. That meant that Kitanah not only found out about it but also had to be acting outside of her authority. A bold action, considering their proximity to the man who they both served.

"I just felt like taking a walk," Ophelia's hand slid from her hip to the hilt of her sword.

"Overnight?" Kitanah slowly walked around the other woman, like a hunter stalking its prey, "And coming back covered in blood?"

"It's a dangerous world we live in," Ophelia shrugged.

"She's moving to keep you from noticing the archer at the far end of the hall ahead," Havarti reported.

"Yes it is," the older assassin agreed, "Especially for some of our brothers out in the Gornack Plains. You wouldn't know anything about that, would you?"

Kitanah was surprised when Ophelia stepped toward her. Her green eyes doing their best impression of tea saucers told the younger woman that. The archer didn't have a clear shot now.

Brothers in the Gornack Plains? Ophelia hadn't seen anyone but the group she was ordered to eliminate out there. Did the General send her after them after a first group of assassins was assigned and failed? Regardless, her Master told her not to speak of her mission with anyone and, as much as Ophelia loathed to admit it, Kitanah was someone, particularly within the Al Razheem.

"I wasn't in the Gornack Plains," the brunette woman lied.

The other assassin obviously didn't believe her. She again tried to step away from Ophelia but found the wall in her way. Kitanah's green eyes flicked back in the direction of the first shadow that Havarti spotted.

"He's not moved," the bastard sword noticed the gesture as well, "Don't take your eyes off of her!"

Ophelia's left hand slipped along the top edge of the violet silk that served as her skirt's belt but was actually much longer. She readied herself to strike Kitanah down before the other assassin could try to do the same. The ring that served as the cuff for Kitanah's sleeve started to rotate like a carousel just starting up. She must have had the same thought.

"And what is going on here?" the unexpected voice of the General came down the hall.

The bearded man, dressed immaculately as he always was in his white uniform, stepped out into the hallway from his office. Immediately, the archer and shadows disappeared in directions that took them as far away from the scene as fast as possible, leaving only the three of them.

Ophelia felt herself suddenly stretch taller to stand over Kitanah, the leather of her vest creaking as it stretched to contain her puffed out chest. All was silent as the two women stared at each other. One wore a growing frown while the other had a smile that only got wider.

Finally, Ophelia brought an end to the quiet, "Nothing, Master. Kitanah was just giving me some pointers on how we sisters in the Al Razheem have to look out for each other."

Every line that had only been hinting at intruding on the red haired woman's smooth, pale skin suddenly came into full view as she scowled. Her face was a mask of rage and confusion as she struggled to understand why Ophelia, who obviously knew what she had just tried to do, didn't sell her out to the General.

"Sisters. I've always enjoyed how my people think of the clan as family," the bearded man stepped up beside Ophelia, "It makes me feel a joy that can only be described as pride."

His head turned in Kitanah's direction. The look on his face told her that he knew Ophelia was covering for her true actions. That was when she understood. The General had let what happened here go as far as he did as a test of Kitanah's motives. A test she had failed.

"Come, my child, we need to clean you up," the General wrapped his hands around Ophelia's with such tenderness that the other woman felt her own spirit drain from her body.

There was another test here that Kitanah hadn't even realized. That of Ophelia's loyalty and she had passed with flying colors. The older woman felt as if her feet had lost the will to hold her up and she was about to collapse into the wall.

Pulling Ophelia along, the General focused his attention on the path ahead while Ophelia kept her attention square on Kitanah. Her pale gray eyes stayed locked on the other woman until they turned the corner into the hall that led to the steam baths that were so luxurious that only the highest ranking of assassins were allowed access.

ANOTHER WEEK...

Kitanah downed another shot glass of the burning, cinnamon colored liquid. It was far from her first but it was her last because, when she slammed the glass back to the end table that sat beside her, it shattered and sprayed glass all over the floor around her.

She didn't even notice her hand was bleeding until she saw the first drops of red land on the arm of her heavily cushioned chair. Even then, all she did was turn her palm enough to watch the blood well out of the short gashes.

The fireplace set in the wall of her sleeping quarters blazed heat. There were no windows in the walls of the fortress called the Oasis so the fire was also the only source of illumination. She let the torches stay unlit, finding comfort in the dim light.

Kitanah's green eyes, feeling like wet sand as they moved, scanned the walls of her room. Trophies from her long history of successful missions lined the walls, though most were obscured in shadow because of the limited reach of the fire's light.

Lifting herself to her feet, the assassin felt her stomach protest the motion. Standing as still as she could, though there was a definite wobble to the room, Kitanah waited to see if the burning that was pushing up the inside of her chest would settle back down to the comforting warmth she'd just attained or if her body would expel the liquid courage she'd been steadily swallowing.

After her stomach stopped complaining, the woman turned for the door. Curling her injured hand into a fist, the woman's fingers slid next to each other as blood seeped between the digits. It wasn't a long walk to the sleeping quarters of the patriarch of the Al Razheem, the General.

He would listen to her. He had to. The General didn't want to be disturbed but she knew that he gave that order when he either wanted time to reflect on the potential threats and opportunities for the clan on the horizon or if he wanted some private time with Kitanah. And she wasn't with him so...

He had to know about the danger Ophelia posed to the Al Razheem. Even with Efreeti's assurance that Ophelia was loyal to the General, that didn't mean she was to the clan, Kitanah's family.

But the General did order Kitanah to not look into Ophelia's past. What she learned from her informant came from before she was able to relay the order but would the General see it that way?

The woman stood before his door for a long, long moment. Finally, though, she brought her hand up and knocked on the door.

Kitanah could hear the General's voice, although not his specific words from the other side. When the door opened, she was surprised to see the older man wearing nothing but his loose fitting pants. They were wrinkled as if they had been laying in a heap before he put them on. He never looked like this except when…

His broad, hairy chest rose and fell at a quicker pace than usual, like he'd been doing something physically strenuous, and the assassin felt the hairs on the back of her neck stiffen and her fist tighten.

"What is it, Kitanah?" the man's voice sounded gruff.

The woman felt her tongue, which she'd been soaking for hours, suddenly go dry. "Sire, I've been trying to put off talking to you about some concerns but I feel I can't anymore." Speaking formally made it a little easier.

The General's brow furrowed, pressing his arrow shaped eyebrows together, "What are these concerns?" the hand that wasn't holding the door open made its way up to the braids in his beard and started to idly tug.

"I know you told me not to look into Ophelia's background, Sire," she continued, "However, more and more of our brethren have been dying lately and she is the only one of us I have not been able to learn the whereabouts of at the times of their deaths."

The General frowned, "Whose deaths have you found suspicious?" even only half clothed, the man radiated authority.

"Trey and Garth in the Gornack Plains were the first," Kitanah said, "Then Inigo in the desert on the road to Paimae."

The man let out a quiet grunt, "And were they found alone?" Kitanah had a feeling that he already knew the answer.

"No," the assassin answered anyway, "Each of them were found with men I have yet to identify."

"There won't be any need for that," the General waved the hand that had been stroking his beard dismissively, "I told you that there was information you were not privy to, my dear."

Kitanah felt beads of sweat form and cling to her smooth skin, "Yes, Sire, but their deaths…"

"Are none of your concern," the man snapped.

"Who is that, Master?" A familiar voice came from inside the room.

"Your trainer," the General scowled at the red haired woman as he answered.

"Oh, Kitanah?"

Ophelia, awkwardly wrapped in a twisted bed sheet and wearing nothing else, stepped up behind the muscular man and rested her head on one of his broad shoulders, "I thought you left orders for us not to be disturbed."

While the words were directed at the man, Ophelia's gray eyes never turned away from the other woman. Her arms slipped away from holding the sheet aloft to wrap around the General's solid torso.

"I did," he said, leaning his head back against the younger woman's, "Apparently she didn't get word."

"She knows now, right?" Ophelia's lips brushed against the nape of the General's neck as she spoke, "So she should go away…"

The solidly built man shivered as her warm breath washed over his bare skin. To give him further incentive, one of Ophelia's hands that had been resting around his waist slowly slid down into the front of his pants.

Air rushed out of the General's mouth almost faster than the words he spoke, "Do not disturb us again, Kitanah!" and the door closed so fast that the wind from the motion almost blew the woman off her feet.

It took a long moment for the assassin's mind to process what had just happened. Even as the shock loitered through her, Kitanah could hear Ophelia giggling as she and the leader of the Al Razheem made their way back undoubtedly to the General's bed.

Kitanah had always thought of the Al Razheem and the General as one and the same. Inseparable in motive and united in method. But what she just saw wasn't her leader, it was a mere man seduced by the most common of temptations. To blind him from the threat that Ophelia herself posed to their clan.

The two supposed farmers that were following Ophelia to the Oasis must be playing a key role in whatever machinations were being brought to fruition. The upstart assassin was to gain a foothold into the Al Razheem and turn the General's eye away from this new threat. A danger from within to hide the threat from outside the walls.

But Kitanah couldn't prove that they were affiliated to Ophelia without betraying that she knew of the girl's origins. There had to be some way to prove their connection independently...

The assassin tugged at her metal sleeve as she started back for her living quarters. Men and women saluted as she walked by but Kitanah ignored everyone as her mind churned and ground every possibility down to find one that could stand and solve her problem.

Ophelia was being used as bait to lure the General's attention away from a very real danger. Perhaps she could use the upstart in the same manner Ophelia was meant: a distraction.

SEVEN

A TRAP LAID BARE

OPHELIA PULLED THE rumpled sheet up from the floor beside the bed. Wrapping it around her naked body, she slid back up beside the General and wrapped one arm around his bare, thick torso.

Resting her head on the General's broad chest, she could hear his heart beat as it slowed to find its steady rhythm after the physical effort they had just gone through. His heavily muscled arm wrapped around the girl's shoulders, which she enjoyed but it didn't serve to comfort her after what had just happened.

She looked away from him, it was hard to look pleased after the way he just treated her. Having sex the way he "liked it" made Ophelia feel less than human but he wanted to do it so she obeyed. Ophelia always obeyed the General.

It occurred to her that, thinking back over the past weeks, she had never said "no" to him. Not once. Was that what love was? Doing anything you were told without question?

She shook her head to herself, coming to a decision. The next time he asked to make love the way he "liked it", Ophelia would refuse. Kindly, of course, after all he was her Master but he would understand if she explained why she had no desire to do it that way again.

When a flicker of a smile returned to Ophelia's face, the girl looked up at the man. His eyelids drooped heavily as if he was drowsy. The General liked silence after they laid together so she thought better about speaking and turned away again.

In the long quiet that followed between them, Ophelia could hear his teeth start to grind behind his closed mouth. He was thinking and it was about something that troubled the older man. That was the only time he ground his teeth.

But the woman didn't ask. He would tell her when, or most likely if, the mood struck. Until then she ran her fingers through his thick chest hair and tried to put the last hour behind her.

"Ophelia," the General's voice was rough and he cleared his throat, "I have another errand for you to run."

The woman looked back up at the older man, "Of course."

He arched an eyebrow, "I have not told you what it is yet."

"I know," she rested her arms on his firm chest and lifted herself to look him the face, "But it's what you want so I'll do it for you."

His lips spread into a wide smile behind his dark mustache and beard, "I need you to go to Paimae. There is a couple of people looking into my affairs there that need to be dealt with."

"When am I going?" Ophelia leaned forward, pressing her lips to his.

"After I give you the details, I would have you leave tonight," he answered when the woman finally pulled away.

"Tonight?" she smirked back, again kissing him as her hands caressed down his body.

This time the General returned the kiss deeply, "Perhaps it can wait until morning. If we do that thing I like again," he chuckled as he pulled the sheet covering the girl's body away and exposing her to the cool air of his bedroom.

Despite the decision she made and everything her body told her to do, Ophelia felt herself smile and nod at her Master, "Of course. Anything for you."

He told her to do it so she had to do it. For him. Even if she screamed and wailed within her own mind the entire time.

THE TOWN OF PAIMAE

"Her name is Perse," the man in the red vest reported.

He stepped up to the table next to the wall opposite the bar. Behind it was the newly identified brunette woman with silver streaks in her hair, already with a fresh drink in hand for another customer.

The other man sitting at the table nodded. He wore a long red coat made of the same leather as one who just returned. They both also wore thongs around their necks with pendants shaped like basilisk talons holding little shields.

He lounged back in his chair, idly spinning his empty glass around. His brown hair stuck up without any real assistance and his nose has obviously seen the business end of a fist more than once but it seemed to fit the rest of his body: rugged and used for fun and violence, sometimes simultaneously.

The man still standing, Connelly, hadn't seen as much action yet. To try and counteract the visage of youth, he had a bushy beard that still had some bald patches. His hair was cut so short it was barely above stubble, so the indirect light from the early afternoon sun still glinted off the smooth skin of his scalp.

"She's been focusing all her attention on our little troll for a while now, hasn't she?" the still sitting man said, motioning to the barmaid.

"Yup," the (not that much) younger man answered as he took his seat at the round table, "Think a woman like that can really be that lonely, Travus?"

The man in the long coat shook his head, "Notice how her eyes keep flicking back toward the entrance? She's stalling, trying to keep Marque here for some reason."

"Sounds like trouble for us," Connelly just had to say the obvious and the look on his superior's face told him that he had succeeded.

"Maybe," Travus scanned the less than half full bar, trying to get an idea of what could be in store, "We'll just keep watching. Take what comes when it does."

The (not that much) younger man nodded in agreement, "There are worse jobs." He muttered as he slouched back into his own chair.

Perse leaned forward further than she really had to when she refilled the shot glass of Marque, the one sitting on the other side of the long bar. The young man only stopped staring down the front of the woman's shirt when she finished pouring the hickory colored liquid and straightened up.

Marque was dressed like many in town did, with a simple white button up shirt and brown pants that wrapped around the top of his worn leather boots, but with one important difference. Around his waist was a red sash with the flowing script that displayed that he was a member of the Al Razheem.

"There you go," Perse smiled at the man who could barely be considered fully grown, "Want another?"

Marque's brow furrowed as he looked from the full glass and back up to the woman, "Another, ma'am? I haven't even had a chance to drink this one yet."

The woman smirked and rested her elbows on the polished wood of the bar, "I wasn't talking about your drink. I was talking about the view down the front of my blouse."

When she leaned down again, it was as if her chest were a magnet and his eyes were metal. His attention turned directly where she wanted it to go. When Perse called him on it, the assassin forced himself to look down at his drink and then close his eyes. As he lifted the drink to his lips, he kept his eyes that way until the entire contents of the glass spilled down his throat.

She gave the young assassin a kind sounding laugh, "It's okay, sweetie. If I minded I wouldn't have invited you for another look, would I?"

"I think she's actually trying to seduce him," Connelly hissed.

Travus didn't even look back at him, keeping most of his attention on Perse, "I swear, have you ever had any dealings with actual women?"

The (not that much) younger man scowled at his superior. Just as Travus thought: he hadn't. That only made him wonder why someone so inexperienced would volunteer for an assignment like...

The doors to the tavern opened and in came a man so large he had to duck to avoid hitting his head. His blonde hair had flecks of gray that caught the light from the lanterns that illuminated that half of the building, furthest from the windows filtering in the sinking sun's rays. He was heavily muscled, wearing a white shirt with a stiff black vest and heavily worn leather chaps over his black pants.

The man had a large leather bladder full of some kind of liquid over his broad shoulder. It wasn't water, the way the leather sack was tied shut would have made it too cumbersome to sip from, and the question of just what the contents could be worried Travus. Then he noticed the violet sash around the waist of the gigantic man and that brought a new level of creasing to the man in the long coat's brow. But it wasn't until the newcomer started over to the bar that Travus let out a quiet curse.

"What? What's wrong?" the other man asked as he looked from the newcomer and back to the table.

"He's a higher ranking Al Razheem," Travus said softly, without moving his lips.

The look on Connelly's face told his superior that he understood, at least in concept, that what Travus said wasn't good. But there was still enough confusion that the man in the long coat motioned for the other to lean in closer so they would surely not be overheard.

"Did you see the big guy's face?" Travus asked but continued before he could even get an answer, "He saw Marque staring at the barmaid's chest and now he looks ready to mow our little troll into mutton!"

Connelly turned back to look at the large assassin as he marched over to the two at the other end of the long, polished slab of wood. After watching for a few steps, he found himself thankful the massive man wasn't approaching them and turned back to his superior.

"What are we going to do?" he asked, "We can't let Marque get killed before we've gotten what we need."

Travus' mind raced. The very reason Marque, and by extension both men in red, were even in this tavern at this time of day was for the scant amount of people inside. That made the only option all the more difficult...

"We're going to have to start a fight," the (not that much) older man frowned at his partner, who looked dumbfounded, "I know there's nobody here so you'll have to hit me and I'll just have to sell it!"

As they spoke, the mountain of a man closed the distance between himself and Marque. His massive fist curled up as the assassin in the red sash came within arm's reach. Travus motioned for Connelly to attack.

The large blonde man's hand sailed past Marque's shoulder and smacked the polished wood of the bar like a gavel, "A honey-bark ale, please," his baritone voice came out in a much mellower tone than either man at the table expected.

That made Travus rethink his tact. He raised his hand to order the (not that much) younger man to stop but it was too late. Connelly's fist clapped against the (not that much) older man's cheek, making Travus' head snap back as if he was looking over his shoulder. Again, Travus waved the other man off.

Perse, her cheeks turning the same shade as a rose petal, nodded and turned away to retrieve the gigantic man's order. Taking a mug from the shelf, she started over to the barrels that contained the requested drink.

"Have you received your orders, Neophyte?" the massive man asked as he rested his elbows on the bar.

Marque couldn't help betraying his surprise that he was being addressed. He turned to look at the new arrival and his brown eyes only got wider.

"N-no, sir. I couldn't get the barmaid to leave me alone long enough to loose them from the compartment," Marque's voice left his mouth at just above a whisper.

"And yet I got her to leave just by ordering a beer," he scowled back at the lower ranking assassin.

Connelly didn't notice Travus' signal to stop and threw his other fist at the man in the red coat. Travus had to stop him before anyone noticed that they had started to try and make a scene.

He turned his body so that his partner's fist smashed against the hilt of the sword that protruded from a pocket between Travus' shoulders, concealing the rest of the blade inside his coat. Before the (not that much) younger man could yelp in pain, the other snatched Connelly's drink from the table and stuffed the edge of the glass into his mouth. Half the contents went down Connelly's throat, the rest down his beard.

Both men dropped back into their chairs, getting odd looks from a couple of people at the closest tables but, thankfully, seeming to go unnoticed by the only people that mattered: the three at the bar.

"So what are you waiting for now?" the mountain of a man's words were directed at Marque even though his eyes lingered on the barmaid as she bent down to retrieve alcohol from a barrel.

Obviously anxious, Marque's hands slipped under the bar. Working some unseen mechanism, a muffled click came from under the polished wood and a piece of parchment fell into the assassin's hands.

"Good. Now give it to me, Neophyte," the massive man ordered, holding his hand out toward the young man even as he continued to face the woman.

"But, sir, it's my assignment," Marque began to protest.

"That a woman was keeping you from just by lingering around you," a hint of menace found its way into the higher ranking assassin's voice.

"Still, why would that make me...?" Marque wrapped both hands around the parchment and pressed it to his chest.

The gigantic man sighed, "Are excuses and questions the only things that can escape that stink trench you call your mouth?" he turned his full attention to the Neophyte in the red sash.

Again, he held his hand out toward Marque, whose entire body was shaking. After what appeared to be an rattling internal debate, the parchment found it's way into the grip of the much larger man.

Travus let out another quiet, but much more energetic, curse. Their target had just changed and neither man knew him. Not like they had gotten to know the little troll, as Travus liked to call him. Marque was not too bright and predictable. Now things were going to get complicated.

"I'll have to report this when I get back to the Oasis, sir," the crestfallen Marque said, although there wasn't much conviction behind his words.

"Fine," the mountain of a man tucked the parchment inside his vest as Perse returned with a mug filled to the brim with foam, "Head back at nightfall and tell them that I'm doing your job for you."

With that, the massive man took a deep drag from his pewter mug. When he placed it back on the bar, he let out a contented sigh and seemed to forget that Marque was still there.

With a deep frown on his face, the smaller assassin didn't stay there much longer. He smiled at Perse as he rose from the stool but she seemed as oblivious to Marque's presence now as the assassin who just dismissed him.

"They planned this," Travus declared to his partner as the tavern's door closed behind their former target, "She was stalling the troll so that this fake Al Razheem could come and steal his orders."

"How do you know he's fake?" Connelly looked at the massive man quizzically.

"You heard him order the troll to leave at night fall," the other man in red leather answered, "Any Al Razheem knows that you can only enter the Oasis while the sun is up. It's sealed up so tight at night that even the rats can't get in or out."

"I don't know. That sash looks pretty real to me," the other man ran his fingers through his patchy beard, "It's not like you can just buy one at the corner market."

"I have no doubt it is," the (not that much) older man answered, "I think he took it from the previous owner just so he could get his hands on those orders."

"How would he even know those orders were there?" Connelly didn't try to hide the skepticism in his voice.

"That's where his partner comes in," Travus pointed at the woman with silver streaked hair.

"Perse?" Connelly was starting to forget to control the volume of his voice, "What would a barmaid know about the Al Razheem and their message drops?"

A solid kick to the (not that much) younger man's shin reminded him to keep quiet, "She's worked here for weeks now. Plenty of time to watch a few drops and learn how they work." Travus replied, "But they couldn't figure out how to open the lock box so they set this up to intercept this set of orders."

"To what end?" Connelly grumbled, trying to rub the ache out of his leg.

For that, the (not that much) older man didn't have an answer. But he wanted one. To get it, he would need some time but there were two barriers to him having it.

The massive man didn't make any motion to the parchment tucked in his vest and Travus expected that the giant wouldn't until he was alone in whatever hideout he had for himself. Travus also knew that Perse got off work at sundown and that wasn't too long from now.

"Go after the troll," the (not that much) older man ordered, "I'm betting he knows the big guy's a fake, too, and I don't want the assassins getting word of this until I've had a chance to talk to these folks myself. Take him into custody before he can talk to anyone."

Connelly didn't share the other man's sense of urgency but he rose from the table and left to do as he was told anyway. Travus stayed at the table, watching the mountain of a man as he sipped at his beer and spoke to Perse at a volume he couldn't quite hear. The man in red didn't even notice when the tavern's door closed behind Connelly.

ELSEWHERE IN TOWN...

The door opened without so much as a creak. On the front of the slab of wood was a plaque that read:

LIGHT BRINGERS
PAIMAE OUTPOST
#6384

Ophelia felt as if she should have the hood of her amber cloak up over her head, considering what was about to happen. But that would have tipped the Light Bringers off that there was something amiss about her and she needed them off their guard.

She slipped the door back into the doorjamb where it came to rest with a quiet click. Looking back over her shoulder, Ophelia found herself in a room that was much smaller than the size of the two story building. Across from the entrance was a window that was as high as the woman's collar bone, behind which was a man in a scarlet cape that hadn't looked up from the piece of parchment in his hands yet.

That meant he wouldn't notice what she was about to do. With a quiet grunt, Ophelia pushed all her weight onto the handle of the door until it snapped off. Now nobody could get out this way.

There was only one other door that allowed access into the building from outside and the assassin had already been warned off from trying to use it due to enchantments that prevented all but the Light Bringers themselves from getting in. Still, that didn't stop her from barricading it beforehand so no one, especially the Light Bringers themselves, could get out.

With the handle still in her right hand, Ophelia turned and stepped to the middle of the room. The only way to get into the rest of the building from here was through a door to Ophelia's left that didn't have a handle on this side and didn't look at all inviting. While it was made of wood, strips of steel were wrapped around it horizontally and vertically with spikes as long as the assassin's forearms protruding from each point where the lines of metal intersected.

Surely it was meant to deter whatever criminal the group captured from struggling against the Light Bringer as they were escorted in, lest they find themselves impaled. Another Light Bringer, already inside, would open the door only once the suspect was submissive to their orders and no longer a danger to anyone inside. Ophelia had to change that.

"Ophelia, dearest, please reconsider this," Havarti's voice rattled through her mind, "We know these people are guiltless. They needn't die and you needn't be the one to kill them!"

The muscles in the woman's jaws bulged while her teeth ground together. The sword had been saying the same thing to her in one variation or another the entire way across the desert. Each and every time, Ophelia's response was the same:

"The General ordered me to do it, so I have to do it. For him."

That didn't stop her stomach from twisting into a jumble of knots as she stepped up to the man behind the desk. Behind him was a wall that gave him just enough room to push his chair back to stand and also hide the rest of the building's layout from the assassin.

Ophelia's amber cloak hid Havarti from view and, if he had his way, he would stay there. She found herself tugging at the hem of her short leather skirt as she came to a stop.

Ophelia had to clear her throat several times before she could get words out, "Is Inara Browder here?"

The man at the desk finally looked up. The symbol of the Light Bringers, a sword with streams of golden light emanating from it, was embroidered on his chest, but it was on a simple tunic rather than the plate armor that the ones out in the field usually wore. He was nothing more than a mere office worker.

"What is your relation to Inara Browder?" he asked back, his hand slipping down to rest on the dagger in his belt.

"She's a friend. I was told she was here. Could I see her please?" the lie tumbled out of Ophelia's mouth with the aid of repeated rehearsals even though she knew that the charade wouldn't work.

The Light Bringer nodded his head, but not to her. It was a cue for a heavily armored Light Bringer, covered from head to toe in steel, to step into the entry room with Ophelia. His sword was already drawn.

The door was pulled closed behind him immediately. She'd expected this, in fact, it was confirmation that she was on the right track to her objective. It should have pleased her but, instead, she had to stifle the urge to throw up.

"Surrender immediately," the man behind the desk said, "You are under arrest as a member of the Al Razheem league of assassins."

"Then we have a problem," Ophelia tried to put a defiant smile on her face but it defied her as well, "I didn't come all this way to surrender."

The handle wrenched from the main entrance flew from her hand and struck the man behind the desk between the eyes. As he fell to the ground to writhe in his newly given pain, Ophelia wrenched the protesting Havarti from his scabbard and charged at the armored Light Bringer.

As their swords clashed, Ophelia's pale eyes met the jade green ones through the slit in the helmet wrapped around his head. The look he gave her, there was anger to be sure, surely also surprise at the suddenness of her attack, but there was something else. Something that made Ophelia's step falter, if only slightly.

But it was enough for the armored man to shove her away and rear back for a strike of his own. The room was cramped, with barely enough room for both combatants to even hold their swords unsheathed. She wouldn't be able to parry, Ophelia couldn't get out of the way of an off balance, lumbering suit of armor that took up so much space.

For anyone else, that would only leave one other option: to block. Of course, Ophelia also had the option to let the sword past her defenses and count on her blinking to save her. But, at best, that would only get Ophelia behind her attacker and still unable to get deeper into the building.

She decided against it and did what was expected of any decent sword fighter in a situation like this and blocked the heavy handed slash. The force of the strike drove her into the wood slab that served as the main entrance. Ophelia was now thankful she'd removed the handle so it didn't dig into her back at the impact.

The assassin retaliated with a slash of her own and the armored man reacted the same way she had moments before and blocked. If not for the suit of armor, the assassin and the Light Bringer would have been about the same height. Of course, he still would have weighed more because of the muscle he surely had to move around in so much steel but the armor also gave him more mass to counter the force of Ophelia's strike.

The attack only made the Light Bringer take one step to steady himself and he was already able to attack again. The sword came at the assassin and she raised Havarti to block again, but this time she positioned her feet to purposely be off balance.

Again the blades collided and, again, Ophelia stumbled back, straight for the spike covered door. Just as the first sharpened point of metal would have skewered through the back of her rib cage, the woman disappeared in a flash of violet light...

...and found herself suddenly standing beside the man behind the desk. His eyes were still watering and blood streamed from his nose as he laid, curled fetal, on the floor. Ophelia lifted Havarti, turning his blade to point down toward the ground.

It took the armored fighter a moment to figure out what happened and where the assassin had gone but when he saw what she was about to do... "Don't! He's defenseless, no threat to you!"

Normally she would agree with him, more likely than not. Havarti definitely agreed, yelling the same thing so loudly it echoed in Ophelia's mind over and over again.

Still, the bastard sword fell, running through the prone Light Bringer's heart and stopping it instantly, "The General told me to do it. I... I have to do it. For him," was the only thing she could say in response to either of the voices.

A quick glance around revealed that the wall that hid the rest of the building from view was completely open at either end, no other doors to get through. It only took Ophelia a couple of steps to get out of the reach of the sword of the armored Light Bringer.

"She's inside!" he screamed, "Open the door!"

The assassin stepped around the corner that led to the flat side of the spiked door and beheaded the man standing there before he could reach the handle. Then she leaned in close to the door wrapped in steel strips.

"If you want to continue living, stay in there and don't get in my way again!" Ophelia bellowed but then what came out of her mouth next surprised Havarti and even her, "Please!"

Shaking her head, the assassin didn't wait for the armored man's answer. She turned and marched deeper into the building.

All the Light Bringers inside were armed with daggers and swords but none of them wore any armor. Only one, a woman Light Bringer, was able to get lucky and stab Ophelia from behind but the assassin blinked, ending up behind her and thrusting Havarti through the woman's chest.

Anyone who stood in Ophelia's way fell in a bloody heap. As she reached the stairway that led to the upper floor, only one more Light Bringer stood in her path.

He barely came up to her shoulders. His blonde hair was freshly cut and his uniform tunic still had taut creases that betrayed that fact that it was new and, judging by how shaky and awkwardly held the dagger was in his hand, he had not even had any combat training yet. Still he stood on the bottom step, keeping her from progressing.

"Please, Ophelia. There is no one that can stop you now. You can let him go," Havarti pleaded in her head but his next words came out so that the terrified Light Bringer could hear, "Young man, drop your weapon. Surrender and I promise that you will live."

The blonde man looked from the massive blade that was Ophelia's bastard sword and back to the thin blade of his dagger that was barely longer than his fingers. He tossed the weapon away and raised his hands over his head.

"I surrender," his breath shuddered as he stepped from the stairway and out of Ophelia's path, on the side opposite the bastard sword's wide blade.

The assassin nodded, marching for the newly unblocked stairs. As she passed the Light Bringer, her buckler suddenly shot up and the steel edge crushed the young man's throat.

As he collapsed with a confused, pleading look on his face, Havarti wailed, "Why? He surrendered, he was letting you get your way! I gave him my word!"

Ophelia froze, her foot hovering above the first step. Her mouth moved as if to start to answer but nothing came out. The hesitation only lasted a moment, though, and the assassin started back up the stairs again.

As she reached the landing for the second floor, words finally made it past her lips, "The General told me to... do it. I have to do it. For him," was her only answer.

EIGHT

TAKEN

ALVIN TAPPED HIS foot against the wooden floor so quickly it almost sounded like a wood pecker going ballistic on a pine trunk. His meaty hands wrenched at the sealed end of the heavy leather bladder that rested between his legs as he sat on the bed.

He practically jumped to his feet when he heard the door to the room finally open. Perse slipped in quickly, barely giving her skirt enough time to follow before the door closed.

"Some Light Bringers came to arrest Marque and he ran off," she reported to her husband, looking ready to burst into tears, "He's not going to head for the Oasis now, Alvin. He's not... going to lead us..."

The massive farmer wrapped his thick arms around his wife as she started to quietly sob. Her body shook against his but all he could do was hold her. Alvin had no comforting words. He was crushed by the news just like his wife. Their only way to find their daughter fled into the wind.

It was no secret that the Light Bringers were working to take control of Paimae away from the Al Razheem but, up until now, they had only arrested one of their assassins in the act of trying to fulfill his contract. Why did they have to get more aggressive now?

Alvin felt anger start to burn in his chest, making his breath quicken. Perse noticed and looked up at him questioningly. The grief in her eyes smothered the rage building inside him, replacing it with worry for his beloved.

"We'll find another way," he leaned down and softly whispered into the woman's ear, "They're not all powerful. We will find another way to get to the Oasis and Ophelia."

"I know," she whispered back, although the tone of her voice didn't fit the reassuring words.

Blinking hard, Perse spotted the leather bladder still sitting beside the bed, "You were able to get more drake gland oil!"

Alvin nodded as his wife pulled herself away to go and inspect the latest purchase, "It wasn't easy to get. We've bought out most of the vendors in the whole valley and the ones that we've been to before were starting to wonder what we need so much oil for."

Kneeling beside the liquid filled leather, Perse loosened the string holding the nozzle closed. She gave the oil a quick sniff. Cringing, she pulled the string taut so the opening was again tightly shut.

"They should be paying us to take such old oil off their hands," the woman waved her hand in front of her nose as she lifted herself back up to her feet, "Can you get the door for me, please?"

Perse motioned to the closet beside the door leading out to the hall then hoisted the hefty bladder over her shoulder. Alvin wrapped his hand around the closet handle when a series of knocks suddenly racked across the room's entrance.

Both farmers froze. When the knocks came again, Alvin motioned for Perse to come to the closet. Snatching the bladder from her shoulder, he tossed it inside and closed the door without even checking to see if it landed safely.

He poked his thumb at the entryway and, as quietly as he could, sneaked out of eye shot of the door. Perse frantically straightened out her streaked hair and rubbed at her eyes and cheeks to try and remove any hint of her emotional outburst.

The woman opened the door with a smile that was well practiced thanks to the bar, "Yes? How can I help you?" she said.

"I wasn't expecting to see you here," the unfamiliar man's voice floated into the room.

The confusion on Perse's face was genuine, "Excuse me?"

"I was expecting to see a really big guy. Big muscles, a not too bright look on his face," the voice trailed off.

Alvin scowled through the wall in the direction of the voice. Still, he didn't make a move toward or away from the door.

"You must have the wrong room then," Perse offered and then started to push the door closed.

The stranger's boot met the bottom of the wooden slab before it could move more than a couple of inches, "I really doubt it. It's more likely that he realized that he's too ugly to not be noticed by us normal people when he goes out. That's a more realistic guess, don't you think?"

The woman couldn't help but look offended for her husband. The look the man must have had on his face only served to make her angrier.

A grunt came from the stranger, "I suppose you could be right, though. I guess that means you should invite me in."

"And why in the name of holy Juna would I do something like that?" the idea looked as welcome to Perse as the smell of the drake gland oil before.

The tone of the stranger's voice lowered, giving an air of malice to his words, "Listen, I may be no giant like the man I'm looking for but I'm plenty big enough to knock you out of the way. Maybe even teach you how to properly treat a man–"

That was it. Alvin stepped into view of the man at the door. His fists were clenched tight ready to crush the man if, or more likely when, the need arose. Likely only seconds from now.

"Let him in, honey," Alvin glared at the stranger as he spoke, "I'd hate to have an audience when I make his nose retreat completely into his head."

Perse had a silent conversation with herself on whether or not doing so was a good idea. She didn't seem to like it but she did as Alvin requested anyway, pantomiming a standard welcoming motion as she stepped off to the side with the door in hand.

As soon as the man in the red coat was across the threshold, the woman had the door closed. The farmer's words about his nose suddenly reoccurred to the man and that made his step hesitate. He wasn't sure if it was from anxiety or being insulted.

Perse recognized him from the bar in which she had been working the last few weeks. He was quiet, mostly. He was around the same age as the farmers, maybe a few years younger.

He wasn't as tall as Alvin, his eye level only coming up to about the farmer's fuzzy chin, but he towered over the woman. Nor was he as heavily muscled as the farmer, few men were, but he was no stick figure in his long red coat.

His nose seemed... flatter than normal (likely the source for her husband's crack) but, for some reason it didn't seem to make him look disfigured or deformed. Perse may have even gone with the word "distinguished" if she'd been asked to describe him before his arrival here in their room.

"First, my apologies for even alluding to threatening your wife," the man held his hands out wide, trying to appear nonthreatening, "I'm married myself and would have hated hearing someone say such things to her but I'm short on time and I needed you to react."

Neither seemed too receptive to his excuse, but at least neither moved to attack him. The stranger stepped deeper into the room, keeping both the man and woman in his sight with his back to the closet door.

"Who said we were married?" Alvin moved so that the stranger's view of Perse was obscured by his massive frame.

"You didn't see her reaction when I was insulting you," he answered, "Until then, I knew Perse here was a part of your plan,

I just didn't realize she was so... integral. But it was you spooking Marque Clay that made me decide I had to talk to you," he pointed to the other man.

"Who in all of Honua's jolly greenness is Marque Clay?" Alvin felt his breath starting to quicken again.

"The assassin whose orders you stole," the man in red shrugged, "He was our likeliest suspect."

"Likeliest suspect? You had better start making sense or I'm going to ask you to leave. Out that window. Head first," Alvin pointed at the framework of glass panes.

The stranger nodded, his eyes tracking from the window back to the massive farmer, "I'm with the Light Bringers. My name is Travus Browder."

Both Alvin and Perse narrowed their eyes at the man, "You're no Light Bringer," Alvin said for both of them.

"I didn't say that. I said I'm with them. I'm actually a member of the Night Shield," Travus said back.

He got blank stares back in response. The man in the long red coat rested his hands on his hips while he figured out the best way to proceed. When he started talking again, he wasn't sure if he'd found it but started anyway.

"The Light Bringers are the ones who arrest criminals or augment armies fighting forces accused of or attempting to commit war crimes," he started, "The main responsibility of the Night Shield is to defend the accused in their tribunals."

"Am I accused of some crime that I need defending from?" Alvin folded his arms across this broad chest.

Travus shook his head, "The other, less known responsibility of the Night Shield, is investigative and undercover work so that the Light Bringers know who to arrest," the man in red looked a little bitter to have to explain all this.

"So you're investigating Alvin then?" Perse said, figuring that her husband wasn't going to keep his anger in check much longer.

"Only because he took Marque's orders that detailed who his next target is," Travus answered, "When I went back to the Light

Bringer outpost. They told me that they had received a threat that an Al Razheem assassin was planning an attack on our headquarters using explosives. That made me think of you (He motioned back to Perse.) stalling Marque Clay until he (He motioned back to Alvin.) arrived. Add the reports of everything your husband's been buying..."

The woman's jade green eyes narrowed, "Everything he's been buying?"

"Nothing in suspicious amounts but there was scrubbing powder from the laundry lady on Castle Street, dried hops from the mill and, most interestingly, oil from drake salivary glands from over a dozen different shops. You know what you can make with those specific items?" the Night Shield listed before turning to face the massive farmer.

"Beer," Alvin answered, "The hops are an ingredient for that. The drake oil is to keep a nice steady temperature for the fire in the brewing process and the scrubbing powder is to clean up afterward," he shrugged, keeping his arms folded across his chest, "The type I brew has a crisp bite that balances perfectly with sweet honey undertones."

Travus nodded, "That sounds very tasty. If you didn't have this much."

With a step back the man in red grabbed the handle to the closet and pulled it open. The bladder that had been tossed in haphazardly tumbled out, a thin dribble of the stinking indigo oil oozing out of the mostly closed nozzle.

"Oh, and you haven't bought a shaft of wheat, barley or yeast," Travus looked very pleased with himself, "So a makeshift bomb is something else that can be made from those things. Is that what you're making?"

"We're not planning to attack any Light Bringers," Alvin looked down at the purple sash still around his waist, "I'm not even really a member of the Al Razheem."

Travus nodded, "I already figured that one out while you were talking to Marque."

"If you knew he wasn't an assassin already, why are you investigating Alvin?" Perse asked.

"If I thought he was a member of the Al Razheem, I wouldn't have come here to talk," The man in the long coat said back, "You're lucky it was me watching and not someone else. I'm one of very few in the Night Shield who has an... intimate knowledge of how the clan works."

That caught the farmer's attention, "What knowledge? You know where the Oasis is?" he asked.

The Night Shield realized he'd said something that threatened to take control of the situation away from him, "What I know isn't the issue, *Alvin*. It's whether or not I've stopped you from being a real threat to my people or someone else and I'm still not completely convinced you aren't."

Perse stomped up to Travus, speaking up before Alvin could with a very, very firm tone, "One: We were never planning to attack the Light Bringers. We're searching for our daughter. She was taken to the Oasis by the Al Razheem. Two: Just because you opened a closet doesn't mean you will stop us from getting her back."

The man in red picked up the bladder and, after securing the nozzle again, placed it back with the rest in the closet, "I'm affiliated with the Light Bringers, remember? We can't just let random people cart around a wagon's worth of explosives, no matter what the reason."

Perse rolled her green eyes as she stepped over to her husband, "You would really try and take everything we've gathered to fight the Al Razheem, who you are effectively at war with? Whose side are you on?"

"It's not a question of sides," Travus's attention shifted from the leather bladders in the closet and back to the married couple, "It's a question about public safety. You don't know where the Oasis is, anyway. Do you really think you can find it before this all became too unstable to use safely?"

"That was what the dried hops were for," Alvin answered, wrapping a thick arm around his wife's shoulders (if only to keep her from attacking the Night Shield herself), "They're acting as a stabilizing agent for the drake gland oil until we can find the assassins' hideout. Which was supposed to be tonight."

Travus, very gently, closed the closet door, "Oh yeah, you're little scheme with Marque Clay. It wasn't going to work. If I knew you weren't true Al Razheem, he did, too."

"How?" Perse simply asked.

"All Al Razheem know that you can't enter the Oasis at night," he turned away from the closet, clapping his hands together, "For one thing, visibility is terrible because of the sands stirred up by rocs taking off and landing, which leads to the second thing. Because of the visibility issues, it's considered to be too much of a security risk to let anyone in after sundown."

"So the next assassin we intercept we just tell to head for the Oasis the next morning," Alvin shrugged, still holding his wife.

"The only reason you'd get a second shot at that is because I had Marque arrested," Travus took his turn to fold his arms across his chest, "I can't let you endanger my op like that again. I'm sorry but all your explosives have to go."

Alvin felt his wife start to lunge at the other man but held her back, only to slowly, methodically step up to the Night Shield himself. As his fists clenched, the farmer's knuckles cracked so loudly that it could have been mistaken for snapping planks of wood.

"A very audacious order for a man here by himself," the massive farmer said, slowly closing the distance between himself and Travus, "What's to stop me from beating you down and taking our supplies elsewhere? We'll be able to find a way to the Al Razheem's stronghold. And our daughter."

"You don't think I was stupid enough to come here alone, do you?" the Night Shield stepped back but resisted the urge to reach for the sword handle behind his shoulder.

Perse stepped over to the window and looked over the street, "If you're not alone, why weren't we swarmed by knights in red capes from the start?"

"I told you. I didn't know what your plan was," Travus had his attention squarely on the mountain of a man that was making the room shrink around him, "I wanted to give you a chance to tell your side of the story, a chance to find out if you were really a threat before I brought in the cavalry."

"Well, we're still no threat to your Light Bringers, only the people who took our child," Perse pressed a finger against one of the small panes of glass that made up the window, "Why don't you join your compatriots who seem to have decided that without even seeing us."

Both the Night Shield and Alvin looked back at Perse with confusion all over their faces, "That doesn't make any sense. I didn't send an all clear signal or anything," Travus stepped around the farmer and, after not having any part of his anatomy battered or crushed, continued on to the window beside the woman.

"Then you *are* alone now," Perse stating the obvious made Travus that much more uneasy.

"Something's wrong," the man in red narrowed his eyes at the sight of the Light Bringers rushing down the road.

Every last one of them turned left at the next corner. That was the direction where the outpost rested... and all the color drained from his face. Travus immediately turned for the entrance and dashed out of the room.

"What do you suppose that was all about?" Alvin asked.

Perse shrugged as she walked over to the bed. She picked up the folded parchment, forgotten during the confrontation with the member of the Night Shield.

"He seemed interested in getting this," she said as she unfolded the orders they had taken from the assassin, Marque Clay.

"I... I don't believe it," Perse whispered, as she looked up at her husband, "How is it possible that they could be after him, too?"

"Who?" Alvin took the parchment from his wife and read it himself, "Karma is a fickle harlot."

THE LIGHT BRINGER OUTPOST

Ophelia slowly sank to her knees. The Light Bringer in her grip struggled for his life but the man's neck still snapped as his head was finally wrenched around.

All along the hallway laid dead, unarmored knights. Their red capes concealed and, at least partially, soaked up the blood that poured from their wounds. Ophelia's cloak laid forgotten at the top of the stairs, just out of reach of the nearest corpse.

Just beside the woman, another Light Bringer was impaled against the wall by her bastard sword. Havarti visibly shook as he protested.

"It's almost over," was Ophelia speaking to the sword or to herself?

Lifting herself back up to her feet, another of the dwindling number of Light Bringer office workers charged at her. His sword slashed for her throat and Ophelia blinked, but she was surprised to find herself in the exact same place. The only thing that had changed was the blade had passed through what was unoccupied space for that split moment.

The assassin hoisted Havarti from the rib cage of his last kill and the dying knight let out one last groan of pain as he fell to the floor. Ophelia thrust the bastard sword forward, impaling the neck of her next would be assailant.

The look on his face was very familiar to the woman by now. His eyes stretched as wide open as they could, the irises shaking with some hope or regret that the man knew was moments from becoming nothing. No tears fell from this one's eyes so Ophelia guessed it wasn't a regret that occurred to him.

He slid from Havarti's wide blade down to the floor. Suddenly, the woman slapped her hand over her mouth. All was still and quiet for the briefest of moments before everything in Ophelia's stomach lurched out of her mouth and onto the floor.

Her entire body shook, Ophelia's pale blue eyes turning away from the only door she'd not been through yet. The room that housed the holding cells. It was the only place left for her quarry to hide.

"Please, Ophelia," Havarti's voice was desperate, "No more. You've forced yourself to come this far and I've had no choice but to aid you in this massacre. Neither of us can abide this any longer. Please, do not make me slay another defenseless victim. Please don't make yourself."

The woman stared back at the bastard sword, her face sweat drenched and gray, "The General told me to find Inara Browder and I must do it. For him."

"I understand that," Havarti replied, "But he did not say I had to be the instrument to accomplish that end, did he?"

Ophelia blinked, "No, no he didn't. I'm sorry," she slid the bastard sword back into the scabbard on her hip.

"I am thankful you are finally listening to reason," Havarti said, "Wait? What are you doing?"

The assassin's shaking hand reached out for the door handle but the metal didn't budge, "The General told me to find Inara Browder," she said as she stepped back from the locked threshold.

"I thought we just–" any words that Havarti had after that were drowned out by the sound of shattering wood as Ophelia kicked down the only obstacle keeping her out of the holding cells.

Two voices shrieked at the sight of the door reeling uncontrolled on its hinges and slamming into the wall. Ophelia forced herself to step into the room.

The assassin could see them clearly because each cell was simply interconnected bars. There were no solid walls between the cells so that criminals that were usually inside didn't have even an illusion of privacy. All there was inside was a straw mattress on the floor and a bucket in the opposite corner.

A woman that only came up to about Ophelia's shoulders stood in the furthest cell with her arms wrapped around a little girl that barely came up to the bottom of her chest. She couldn't have been any older than twelve years old at most.

The two looked so alike that it was obvious that they were mother and daughter. Both had short cut mahogany colored hair and the same brown eyes that were locked on the assassin as she made her way closer and closer to the bars.

There wasn't much room for the assassin to walk. The barred cells took up most of the space, Ophelia could barely extend one arm as she walked along them. Just enough room to get prisoners in and out.

"You are Inara Browder?" Ophelia asked as she wrapped her hands around the bars that made up the door to the cell her target awaited in. She hoped that the other woman couldn't tell it was so Ophelia could keep herself upright.

"Please," the woman slowly pushed her daughter behind her back so that Ophelia could barely see her, "Please don't hurt my daughter."

"You are Inara Browder?" Ophelia repeated and wrenched the bars.

They didn't budge. The door to the cell was locked.

Looking around, Ophelia saw the row of studs on the wall that would usually hold the separate keys to each cell but they were all bare and below that the equally empty stool where the guard assigned would sit and watch over his charges. Surely this was a last ditch effort to protect Inara and the little girl by the Light Bringers.

Ophelia chewed on her lower lip as she turned her attention back inside the cell, "The General ordered me to kill you, Inara. I have to. For him."

It looked as if it pained the assassin to say that. Even still her hands drifted over the heavy lock, studying to see if there was another means to pry it open.

"But he asked me to do something else first," Ophelia had to clear her throat three times before she could continue, "He wanted me to tell you what will become of your little girl after you die."

The way Ophelia spoke to Inara was as if she was going through a list of chores that were to be done during the day. The was no passion, no emotion at all to her voice. Havarti felt as if the woman had, emotionally at least, turned herself off. It was the only way Ophelia was able to continue.

Every sentence drew more horror from the other woman's face. She even wrapped her child's head in her arms to try and shield her from the future the assassin was laying out for her.

"You're a monster," Inara whispered, tears streaming down her chin to land on the crown of her daughter's head, "But they took the key and hid it well away from here. There's no way you can reach us. Not even with that hand and a half sword of yours."

As if to demonstrate just that fact, the mother and child of the Browder family shifted to stand next to the back set of bars that rested against the outer wall of the wooden building itself. They were indeed out of Ophelia's reach, even with Havarti.

Regardless, the assassin found her hand reflexively reaching for the handle of her bastard sword but stopped herself, remembering what he'd said before, "The General told me to do it, so I have to do it. For him," the assassin looked around the room again to try and find a solution to her predicament.

There wasn't enough room for her to try and smash the door in. She didn't even have enough room to extend her leg fully in the space between the wall and the cells.

Havarti's blade was too thick to wedge into the space between the door frame and the bars and no other way of prying the barred door open came to her. Inara would have laughed at the look on other woman's face if she didn't know what was coming if the assassin succeeded in reaching herself and her daughter.

Ophelia spun where she stood, slamming both her fists into the blackened steel bars. "The General told me to do it. But I have to it. For him." She muttered to herself like a rehearsed chant, looking as if she was in physical pain.

Inara knew then that the assassin wasn't going to leave without accomplishing her goal. She also realized that, with Ophelia being there at all, it was likely that everyone else in the building was dead so she had nothing but time to find another way.

That was when the woman in the cell noticed the intricately tattooed runes on Ophelia's back. The runes were glowing a soft violet, all the swirling symbols and runes forming a rough diamond shape that went from the base of her spine and peaked up between her shoulder blades.

It reminded the mother of the targets her husband had used to teach her how to use knives to defend herself. The worn parchment had a simpler design, of course, but the bright red diamond in the middle of the target drew the eye much like the purple glow of the tattoo.

"The General told me to do it, so I have to do it. For him," Ophelia mumbled again, the hand without the buckler rising to rub either side of the bridge of her straight, aristocratic nose.

Inara bent down to pull one of those very blades her husband taught her to use from her boot, taking care not to draw the attention of the woman trying to figure a way in to kill her and take her child, Tilly.

The woman hushed her daughter before starting toward the assassin. She moved slowly to keep Ophelia from noticing her.

Inara crept toward the other woman. She barely allowed herself to breathe as she closed the distance. Tilly let out a stifled whimper as her mother finally came within reach of the assassin.

"Mrs. Browder!" a voice came from the hallway.

Inara froze at the sound of her name. A steady thumping became louder and louder. Both she and Ophelia turned to look toward the door.

The armored Light Bringer Ophelia fought on the first floor burst into the room. His sword was drawn as he turned to face all three women.

When he saw Inara with little more than a wrist flick from the assassin's back, the man raised his free hand, "Don't Mrs. Browder! She has some kind of enchantment that can teleport her in there with you if you stab her!"

Ophelia turned and snatched the other woman's wrist in her left hand. With a wrench, Inara's dagger fell into the assassin's other waiting hand, the blade lightly scraping against the edge of the buckler before her finger's closed around the handle.

"No!" the armored man charged and swung down with his sword like a man chopping firewood.

Ophelia had to let the mother go to avoid having her own hand chopped off at the elbow. She wasn't sure if blinking would have kept that from happening since it wasn't a lethal blow, at least not instantly.

The sword embedded itself in the floor. It was obvious the moment it made contact that it wouldn't be coming out easily. That didn't matter much to the armored Light Bringer. With so much metal wrapped around his body, there was no way Ophelia could get around him.

The man reared back to smack the assassin with a gauntlet covered fist. Ophelia turned away and covered the three steps toward the corner, giving her as much space as she could get.

The assassin jumped, lifting a boot onto the wall and pushing away. With a twist of her body, Ophelia slid over the rounded pauldron on the Light Bringer's shoulder. She stopped her momentum by wrapping her arms around his neck, so it looked as if she was a little girl getting a piggy back ride from her big, metal encased brother.

"I don't suppose you have the key to their cell on you, do you?" the assassin slipped the blade of her stolen dagger into the space between the Light Bringer's helmet and the breast plate, pressing it against the soft flesh of his throat.

"No," he growled back.

"We'll have to do it the hard way then," Ophelia snarled back.

Throwing her weight to the side, the man's helmet slammed into the bars of the Browders's cell with a heavy clang. She twisted him around so that he was facing the mother and daughter, who huddled against the back wall again.

Wrenching back on his neck, the Light Bringer was forced to step back or slice his own throat. Ophelia kicked her legs up until she felt her boots press firmly against the wall opposite the cell.

Pushing forward, the assassin slammed the armored man against the barred door. She pulled back again and the sound of faintly echoing gagging came from inside the helmet as he again stumbled backward.

Ophelia threw her boots back up against the wall and forced the Light Bringer forward again. The metal suit and the barred door slammed together again with a deafening clang. Blood started trickling out from under the helmet.

The Al Razheem assassin did it over and over again until the bars started to bend from the repeated force of the hits. Finally, the door gave and the armored man fell into the cell in a heap. Crimson liquid quickly pooled under the helmet as the assassin stepped over his body.

Inara hugged her daughter tight against her chest, her eyes locked on the blood soaked dagger in Ophelia's hand as she came closer and closer...

NINE

AFTERMATH

THE LIGHT BRINGERS outpost was made of wood, like most every building in town, but it was a two story rectangle with a flat rooftop rather than the angled ones with which most of the homes were built. It did have, like many of the homes in Paimae, a white picket fence surrounding a thin tract of land immediately around the structure.

And behind that fence, separated by about five paces on each side, were seven of the nine armored Light Bringers that had accompanied Travus to his meeting with the farmers Alvin and Perse. They all stood at attention, shooing away curious civilians but mostly looking intimidating.

He had planned to ride back in the wagon with the explosives they were to confiscate from Alvin and his wife. When the Light Bringers rushed back here, it left Travus on foot so he was the last to arrive. As he neared his compatriots, he could tell that something was indeed wrong. Very wrong.

No one tried to stop him as he stepped past the white fence and the Night Shield did notice that none of them looked directly at him. Like a hobgoblin scratching at a wall blocking the way to its prize, every dark thought started coming to the surface of Travus's mind.

The door into the outpost had been rammed open and laid in two loose halves hastily tossed aside on the lawn. As he stepped into the building, the familiar figure of his partner and his bushy, patchy beard came into view.

When the (not that much) younger man saw his fellow member of the Night Shield, Connelly quickly stepped between Travus and the spiked door that led deeper inside. He was sweating even though it was approaching the end of the day when things were quickly starting to cool down.

"You don't have to be here, Travus," Connelly said, "I can come and find you later so you can make…"

The older Night Shield's eyes narrowed at the other man, "Make what? Where is Inara?"

His partner started to say, "Travus, you don't want-"

"Don't pretend to know what I want!" Travus snapped back, "Where is my wife?!"

The other Night Shield swallowed hard, "Upstairs. But, please, you don't w-, I mean, you can't-"

While Connelly stumbled over whatever words he was trying to find, Travus stepped around him and through the spiked door. It had been rammed so hard that the spikes were bent flush with the warped wood and wedged tight so it was unable to close again.

Travus almost tripped over the first body that rested just on the other side, a wide puddle of blood already starting to congeal under the lifeless frame. The corpse's head rested beside his right hip, his expression stuck in a state of permanent surprise.

"Adam?" Travus hadn't expected this.

He stepped over the body of one of the youngest members of the Night Shield and continued on. Bodies littered the entire floor. Sister Beckett died clutching at her chest, trying to stop the geyser of blood that was gushing out. Dogberry's head was nowhere near his body. Travus was only able to recognize that it was him because of his lanky build. He was easily the tallest of all the Light Bringers' office staff.

Even young Joey Buchanan, who only just arrived from training last week, laid dead at the base of the stairs to the next floor. And that was only the people the Night Shield encountered taking the direct route to the stairs. Judging by the steeping silence all around him, Travus guessed that he was the only living thing on this floor.

His legs moved as if they were buried in sand as he forced himself up the stairs. Drying blood rested over most of the steps, having run down like a macabre waterfall. There were three sets of boot prints in the red, presumably the remainder of the party of Light Bringers that had been with him... wait, that would only account for two.

Travus forced himself not to cringe at the noise his feet made when they pulled away from the sticky surface of the wood steps. When he reached the hall that ultimately led to the holding cells, he heard voices coming from that room.

But that wasn't where he checked first. The second door on the north side of the hall. It was wide open and what sparse furniture there was in the room was tossed around as if the living space was hastily searched.

His family, alive or dead, wasn't in there.

He didn't turn to look into any of the other rooms as he walked toward the voices. No good could come of it. In the event of an attack, there was only one place left that his family would have been taken to ensure their safety.

Another armored Light Bringer laid dead beside the door to the holding cells. Judging from the blood trail that led back into that very same room, he had apparently been dragged out. He would have been the last line of defense for his family.

When Travus appeared in the doorway, the muted conversation of the two Light Bringers stopped. Both armor clad men looked at the Night Shield, unable to think of any words to say to him.

In the cell nearest to the door was a very pale looking Marque Clay. He stared, very intently, at his own feet as he sat on the bed of straw.

The middle cell was empty. The blood trail from the dead armored man outside led to the furthest cell...

Travus couldn't remember what happened next. The next thing he knew, the two armored Light Bringers were holding him by his arms while he was kneeling over his wife. He hadn't even realized he'd been screaming until just then.

Inara was laid out on the straw bed flat on her back. Her hands rested on top of each other over her chest. Under them rested the dagger with which he had taught his wife self defense. The blade was clean but Travus suspected that it was the weapon used to end her life.

Her eyes were closed, creating the illusion that Inara was only napping. The only things betraying the fact that she wasn't just sleeping was the gray pallor of her skin the red ribbons of blood that soaked into her dress on either side of her torso.

He forced himself to detach, to be calm, at least for the moment. The armored men let him go, ready to pounce on him again if he was going to leap to another rage. He wasn't.

"Did you position her like this?" Travus asked the Light Bringers while still looking down at his wife.

"She was already like that when we came in," the one on the left said.

Travus' brow furrowed. That would mean that the assassin did this. Whoever it was showed no quarter to anyone else in the building, leaving all their bodies where they fell without their heads and laying in puddles of their own bodily fluids.

Inara wouldn't have died without putting up a fight first. So the killer put her onto the bed after the fact. Did it mean that he or she felt remorse? Unlikely, judging from the carnage downstairs. That meant it was probably some kind of message to him from the General?

The hobgoblin started scratching again. This time, instead of bringing up dark thoughts, it reminded him of something that was missing. Someone.

"Where is my daughter?" his rekindling anger crept into Travus' voice.

There was no answer for a long moment. Not until the Night Shield turned to glare back at the other two men.

"She wasn't here when we arrived, sir," the one on the right answered this time.

"Was her body found downstairs?" against every desire in his heart, Travus stood up to move away from his wife and pulled his long red leather coat tighter around his shoulders.

"All the bodies have been accounted for," the one on the right answered again, "There were no children."

The Night Shield felt as if he'd been kicked in the stomach and had to grab for the bars to remain standing at that news. If Inara was here, she would have never left Tilly. The Al Razheem took his little girl.

"It was the Blinking Horror," Marque Clay chimed in from the far cage, "I heard she was coming into town."

Travus marched over to the troll's cell, "Who is this Blinking Horror?" he'd never heard of such a thing within the clan of assassins.

The neophyte shook his head, "No one my rank knows for sure. You should ask the one who took my orders. He would know."

Alvin's face flashed in the Night Shield's mind. The farmer was only masquerading as an Al Razheem so he would be less than useful. But Clay would likely know that...

"He wasn't really one of you," Travus informed him of what he figured the troll already knew, "Him asking you to go to the Oasis at night told you that much."

To the Night Shield's surprise, Marque seemed shocked at the news. In all the time he watched the little troll, he never seemed to be that good of a liar but Travus had to make sure.

"We're taught not to question the orders of our superiors, no matter how crazy they sound," the assassin replied, shaking his head and resuming to stare at his boots, "Usually, if the order is strange, it's some kind of test."

It made sense. Information control was one of the oldest ways a secret organization worked to maintain control of its members. The main weakness to such a plan of action, though, was that lower ranks were easier to manipulate. That was what Travus himself did before.

"Tell me what you know about this Blinking Horror then," the man in red rested his arms on the bars of the door, "Prove to me that you're not trying to make something up to save your own skinny hindquarters, Marque."

Again, the troll shook his head, "I told you, we don't know anything at my rank-"

Travus kicked the door, the impact making the entire cell shudder. One of the armored men started toward the Night Shield but the other held him back with a touch on the shoulder.

"You're telling me there isn't one rumor, one hushed little story about something you've given such a flowery title to?" Travus made a clicking sound with his cheek, "Pull the other one, Neophyte."

The man in red pulled his arms away from the door and turned toward the hall. Just as he was getting ready to take his first step, the assassin spoke up. If you can call just the louder side of mumbling speaking up, that is.

"Word is she joined the clan a few months back. Some kind of magical monster given as a gift to the General from someone outside the Al Razheem," some of prisoner's words weren't enunciated well, but Travus could get the gist, "Supposedly, she only answers to the General, does anything and everything that he asks of her."

The Night Shield's eyes narrowed at the other man, "If it's some kind of monster, how do you know it's a she?"

"That's the word," Marque shrugged back, "I've heard that Kitanah isn't getting as much play time with the General these days because of her, too."

The first hint of amusement came to the assassin's voice with that statement. That made the hobgoblin's cynical nature scratch back up.

"If you don't know who this Blinking Horror is, how could you possibly know who the General's First is?" he spread the disbelief thick on his question.

"I told you. The Blinking Horror only answers to the General. But Kitanah is my Mistress within the Al Razheem," the assassin looked at Travus as if he'd let loose a loud fart in the church of the Wind Goddess, "She's the one who ordered me into Paimae in the first place. Told me my other assignment would be rerouted to that bar."

"What other assignment?" the Night Shield leaned back on the prisoner's door, "If the orders the fake assassin took from you were your second assignment, what was the first?"

Only then did Marque look up again, his jaw set tight as he looked at the Night Shield, "When they find out I lost my orders to an outsider, they'll kill me. Maybe even send the... the Horror after me. I want transport out of Paimae. I don't want *anyone* to be able to find me so no records of me ever leaving here, not when, not what coach, nothing. Agreed?"

An odd request, especially considering that Marque surely knew that the Light Bringer's resources, particularly manpower, had been decimated by the very "Horror" he was so worried about. Investigation and dealing with defendants were the Night Shield's area of responsibility, though, and considering that the Chief Prosecutor was laying dead downstairs, Travus didn't have anyone else to consult without sending a post. That message would have to include the details of the proposed agreement, which Clay outright stated would violate it.

"Okay," Travus nodded.

The armored Light Bringers looked at each other uneasily. They knew that the Night Shield had just breached protocol but they also knew that the circumstances surrounding them were not normal.

"I'll have my partner, the man who brought you in," Travus waited until he saw a glint of recognition in the Neophyte assassin's face, "take you south, out of the Al Razheem's reach. These two will go with you as your personal guard until you're locked up in whatever Light Bringer facility they see fit. Not even I will know. Good enough?"

Marque looked like he had to work way too hard to think. Both the Light Bringers watching the exchange quietly bickered among themselves. It was a sneer in the face of protocol but it was done under Travus Browder's authority as the highest ranking (living) officer of the outpost.

Finally, the little troll nodded. He must be truly afraid of whatever this Horror is to not try to gain his freedom in the negotiation. Staying a prisoner would automatically give him protection. Even if it wasn't the surest against the Blinking Horror, it was the best Marque could get.

"I was sent to tell you about a planned attack on your headquarters," He winced as he realized what he said could be considered incriminating and immediately started to back pedal, "It was supposed to be a feint, though! A trick to keep you busy while the Horror fulfilled whatever her assignment was going to be."

Only after he actually heard the words in his own ears did Marque realize his explanation didn't really help him, "I mean, the attackers I told you about were going to use a bunch of drake gland explosives to blow up your building. A story like that was going to clear... out your headquarters... and keep... you busy searching," the neophyte's face sank into his hands.

It was a clever story and tactic. It had just enough truth to it that, if Marque Clay hadn't been arrested to refute it himself, Alvin and Perse would have been the ones the Light Bringers would have focused all their attention on.

It also eliminated another enemy of the Al Razheem, by claiming them as friends. The farmers would be disarmed and the Light Bringers distracted, leaving the outpost open to attack by this Blinking Horror.

Travus motioned to one of the guards, who stepped up to him. He whispered something to the Light Bringer and the armored man marched out of the room.

"It's alright, Marque. I'll honor our deal," the Night Shield, returning his attention to the assassin, said and the Neophyte's face brightened, "If you explain something else to me."

And his face sank again, "What else can I know?"

Travus had to stop himself from chuckling at Marque inadvertently self deprecating statement, "You call this thing the Blinking Horror. You've made the 'horror' part pretty clear but what's the deal with the 'blinking'?"

As the Night Shield and the Neophyte assassin continued to talk, the armored Light Bringer that had left earlier returned with Connelly in tow. It took some time before Travus acknowledged their arrival, he was so focused on gaining what information he could from the little troll.

When the (not that much) younger man finally interrupted, the (not that much) older Night Shield was about finished with Marque Clay anyway. Travus turned to face his partner and saw a not at all pleased face looking back at him.

"What's this I hear about you sending me south?" Connelly asked Travus.

The man in the long red coat motioned to the caged assassin, "He needs protection. Specifically from the one that did this," he used the hand gesture for silently ordering to set up a perimeter to indicate the entirety of the building, "And that means taking him away from here, and taking him somewhere outside of the Al Razheem's area of influence."

"So why don't you take him then?" Connelly protested, "You could use the air."

Travus shook his head, "I'm the highest ranking officer now. I have to stay and I need someone I can trust to secret the troll away from here without anyone outside this room knowing."

Connelly reluctantly nodded, "Okay. We'll leave tonight. What are you going to do?"

"Request reinforcements to get this outpost back up and running," Travus didn't let the guilt he was feeling at lying to his partner's face creep into his voice, "Then try to get back to business as usual."

Again Connelly nodded, oblivious to what Travus truly had planned next, "What about that fake Al Razheem and his explosives?"

The (not that much) older Night Shield really had to sell this part, "Assuming they haven't already run off, I'll take what men we have left at first light and disarm them."

IN ALVIN AND PERSE'S ROOM...

"Is there any way we can speed up the process? You know whatever made them leave won't keep them away forever," Alvin pulled the drawn curtains aside just far enough to peek outside.

The street was empty in the middle of the night. It was so late that even the drunks had made their ways back home to wherever they went to sleep off their stupors. But for how much longer?

"Sorry sweetie. The hops can only soak up the oil so fast and if I put in too much at once it will all spill out," Perse bit her lower lip as she dropped another set of handfuls of the dried plant blooms down the nozzle of the leather bladder.

The massive farmer let out a sharp curse, "Why did the Light Bringers have to come now? We were this close to getting Ophelia back!"

She put in as many hops as she dared into the nozzle, the excess oil getting uncomfortably close to the brim of the treated leather, "Maybe it was some kind of divine intervention to make us actually look at those orders. We would have never known he was involved otherwise."

Alvin grunted. It was true but that didn't mean he had to like it. The married couple was now considered an enemy to public safety and that meant that the Light Bringers would be coming after them as hard as they did the Al Razheem. They didn't care why

Alvin and Perse were preparing such weapons, or that the family and the knights had an enemy in common.

The Light Bringers only saw them as criminals now. To that end, that meant that they needed help now. Until they looked at that parchment, they didn't realize that they even had a hint of assistance possible.

There was a knock on the door. Perse stifled a gasp while Alvin felt his stomach tighten. There was no way a large group of Light Bringers got this close unseen. Whoever it was knew how to avoid being detected.

The woman pulled another leather pouch out of a cloth bag that rested on the floor next to her where she sat. Wrapping it around the nozzle, she pulled the drawstrings tight and looked up at her husband. Taking a deep breath, he nodded that the smell of the oil wasn't on the air anymore and the large farmer started toward the door.

Alvin opened the door enough to just look out in the hall while the rest of his body stayed behind the door to keep anyone from being able to shove the door open and force their way inside. The man's entire body betrayed surprise at who he saw.

"Alvin, may I come in?" Perse could hear the voice of the member of the Night Shield, Travus, drift into the room.

She actually had to lean in the direction of her husband to be able to understand what was being said from the hall. Unless she was mistaken, Perse thought she heard a sadness in the tone of their visitor's voice. No, that was far too simple. He definitely sounded regretful but the Night Shield was also trying to not be heard beyond the range of Alvin's ears.

"Where are your Light Bringers?" The farmer answered back in the same hushed tone, though he wasn't sure why.

"I'm alone," Travus said. "We need to talk."

"You made your stance very clear when you were here before, Night Shield," Alvin said back.

"Things have changed, Alvin" There was a long pause, followed by a heavy sigh from Travus, "I need your help."

Her husband looked back over his shoulder at Perse. They were both curious but, more so, suspicious at the other man's sudden change of heart. She shook her head and Alvin nodded back.

"Go back to your Light Bringers," Alvin started to close the door.

Travus lunged forward, cringing at the pain as his bicep was pinched between the edge of the door and the frame, "Please! The Al Razheem took my daughter, too!" the words quickly rasped out, struggling to stay at the volume of the whisper.

Perse felt her entire body tense. Did they dare believe him? The timing was convenient but they did see all the Light Bringers that had come with him rush off.

"Let him in, Alvin," she said as she lifted herself to her feet, "But be ready with the window option you gave him before."

The massive farmer nodded, sternly staring down the other man as he let Travus into the room. The Night Shield tugged on the collar of his long coat, trying to steady himself as he entered the admittedly uneasy situation.

Alvin closed the door and turned to face the man in red, "Talk fast," he ordered.

And Travus wasted no time, "The Al Razheem attacked the Light Bringers' headquarters. My wife and daughter were staying there in protective custody. Now my wife is dead and my child is being held by them."

Perse felt an ache in her chest but they had to be sure it was true first, "How did the Light Bringers get news of the attack?"

Travus wanted to yell at them, to scold them for wasting time, but if he were in their position, he would likely be doing the same, "The Chief Prosecutor has an enchantment that unleashes an alarm when he's wounded or killed. That enchantment, we call it a *panic button*, was tripped. That was why all the Light Bringers ran off."

"But not you," Alvin's hands were no longer clenched into crush ready fists.

The other man nodded, "As a member of the Night Shield, we don't usually have the receptor to that enchantment, particularly if we're assigned work in the field."

The farmer's hands threatened to close again, "But you're working in the city."

The other man frowned, "Not until recently. My family and I lived in the south before... all of this."

Perse spoke up, "All of this?"

Travus sighed, forcing himself to stay still, "Years ago, I went undercover within the Al Razheem. A few months ago the teams of Night Shield that I helped join to replace me in the organization started showing up dead. The Light Bringers brought my family into Paimae for protection."

Alvin resisted the urge to mock him. The Night Shield would likely get angry and, at least in the farmer's mind, prove that he was speaking truthfully. But if he was being honest, that could make him reconsider whatever help he had come for from the farmers.

It was Perse who asked the stinging question, "Did you not consider your family at all when you decided to infiltrate a group of assassins? That they could become targets if you were discovered?"

"It was years ago!" genuine pain washed over his entire body as Travus protested, "I hadn't even met my wife then. I got out of the assignment before I was even married. For all the Al Razheem knew, I was dead!"

"Then you have a betrayer betraying you among your knights, Night Shield," Alvin cringed at the awkward alliteration that just spilled from his mouth.

It didn't occur to Travus to even be amused, "The thought had occurred to me. That's why I came here now. I told everyone we'd come to confiscate your explosives tomorrow at first light."

"And what did you expect from us for giving us this warning, Browder?" Perse asked.

"You need someone to guide you to the Oasis," Travus pressed both his thumbs into his chest, "Not only can I do that, I even know the layout inside the fortress. I'm the best chance we have of getting both our girls back."

Both husband and wife stared back at the man in red silently. They mentally chewed over his words, the possibility of truth, the likeliness of deception, even whether or not he used proper grammar (although that only occurred to one of them).

Perse crossed her arms over her chest, "Why us, though? Why not just take a team of Light Bringers on a rescue mission for your daughter? Why team up with a pair of farmers you thought were dangerous to the public a couple of hours ago?"

"Beyond not knowing who is betraying me and mine to the Al Razheem?" Travus didn't like the feeling of being at the mercy of anyone, especially now, but he continued and hoped, "The Light Bringers would treat the Al Razheem taking my daughter as a hostage situation and they have a strict policy of not negotiating with kidnappers and terrorists."

Neither farmer looked surprised at the revelation. Admittedly, that surprised the Night Shield. Still, he continued.

"I don't have the time to tip toe around, trying to find Light Bringers who may be willing to help me and, besides," Travus shrugged at the married couple, "we would have just as good of a chance of survival."

"Meaning you believe it's a suicide mission," Alvin sighed and dropped to sit on the bed, making it release a loud squeak.

Reluctantly, the other man nodded, "Still, it's the best chance we have of getting my daughter, our daughters back."

"What if I told you we had a way of improving our odds?" Perse pulled the folded parchment out from under her husband on the bed.

Holding it out to the member of the Night Shield, she motioned for him to read the missive. He did so but Travus couldn't see what miraculous thing they thought the stolen orders contained and he told them so.

"Look at the target," Alvin motioned to the parchment, "He just happens to be an old friend of Perse and me. And we have a sneaking suspicion that he'd be very open to help us out when he learns he's on the Al Razheem target board."

"You must be kidding," Travus looked back and forth from the orders to the wife and husband several times, "You know this guy?"

Both farmers nodded back. The hobgoblin in the back of the Night Shield's mind was as stunned into silence as he was.

"Then, uh, I guess we should get going," he was finally able to say, "Did you need help loading up the drake oil?"

Alvin shook his head as he stood back up, "Already loaded. We have a cart in the stable ready to make a run for it."

Travus was impressed. Alvin looked strong but to haul that many bladders that were as heavy as drake gland oil became when it was treated with a stabilizing agent, let's just say that the Night Shield would maybe, if he still had energy after these last few hours, would have been lucky to have half the bags of leather out by now.

There was a sudden pop and all three jumped. Perse let out an uneasy chuckle and stepped over to the forgotten bladder and the much smaller leather pouch that had just launched from the nozzle and landed on the wood floor.

"Alvin will grab this," the woman sealed the bladder shut, "Then we'll all go the cart and head north."

TEN

THE FERDINAND

"YOU WERE THE one who brewed the Honeybark ale for the tavern?" Travus was finding both farmers full of surprises.

Perse sat on a bench at the front of the cart, driving the horses along the road as the late morning sun beat down on all the travelers. The entire back half of the bed was covered with a thick tarp, obscuring the leather bladders filled with explosive oil.

In the front half, Travus sat with his legs crossed and his long coat folded in his lap. Beside him, leaning in the corner, was the sword that usually hid within the red leather. Alvin laid down at the bottom of the cart, taking up most of the remaining space all by himself. He had a broad arm over the top half of his face to shield his closed eyes from the light, having just finished a turn driving the horses himself for the last eight hours.

Alvin nodded back at the other man, "We had a lot of drake oil to buy. In addition to food we couldn't do all that on Perse's barmaid pay, now could we?"

Travus shrugged, "How do you even know how to brew ale, anyway? I thought you were a farmer back west."

"I was and will be again once we have our daughter back," the larger man responded, "Brewing was just a hobby. I made a couple of barrels and would have a mug with dinner and, sometimes," one of his hazel eyes popped open to peek back up at his wife before he continued and his voice lowered to a whisper, "I would let Ophelia sneak sips when she was little. She liked the honey undertones in the flavor, even without me actually putting in any honey."

Travus smiled at the first piece of truly personal information Alvin had volunteered, "How old is Ophelia now?"

"Old enough that she can drink Alvin's ale and all I can do is look disapproving," Perse said without even turning back to face the men.

"She's an adult?" the Night Shield's eyebrows pressed together, "Why are you so worried about her, then? Can't she take care of herself?"

"Barely an adult," ire seeped into the woman's words, "Would you not be here to help your daughter if she was of marrying age?"

Travus had to admit she had a point. Even if Tilly was old and gray, instead of a prepubescent child, he would still go after her. But that did beg another question:

"Why didn't you go to the Light Bringers back where you lived to ask for help?"

Alvin could just feel his wife tense up so he sat up in the bed of the cart and answered for her, "We did. They said that we should wait for a ransom demand and then they would do something. After we learned Ophelia was being taken to the east, they said it was out of their jurisdiction. So we came out here for her."

They continued on in silence for a while. The cart rolled past clumps of trees, maneuvered around stray rocks in the road, and the horses whinnied and whined when they started to tire.

Coming up to a small pond, the three people dismounted and unhitched the horses. Once the animals made their way to the water, Alvin spoke up again.

"Travus, how exactly did you find us?" the farmer asked the other man as he walked around the vehicle to check that the knots in the ropes holding down the leather wrapped explosives were still secure, "I was so careful not to buy too much drake oil from one place. And I needed the hops to brew my ale anyway, so that shouldn't have raised any alarms. What drew your attention to us?"

"I went to every drake gland oil seller in the area with your description. But without the tip we received we would never have given you a second look," Travus said as he stretched his legs... and suddenly felt a familiar scratching at the back of his mind.

His brown eyes scanned over the horizon as he idly scratched at the left side of his chest. Nothing appeared out of the ordinary but that could have been the problem right there.

"How much longer to this Ferdinand's place?" he started back toward the cart.

"We should get there right before sundown," Perse wrapped her hands around either horse's bridles as they finished drinking and led them in the same direction, "Why?"

"I knew I said I'd take a turn driving but I just realized I don't know this area too well," Travus didn't answer the woman's question, "If I take the reins, I'm pretty sure we wouldn't get there until well after moon rise."

Both farmers frowned at him as he lifted himself back up into the bed of the cart. Looking at each other, Alvin shrugged, Perse rolled her eyes. The husband sighed, the wife nodded. It was decided.

Alvin, after hitching the horses back to the wagon, lifted himself onto the bench that served as the driver's seat. With a quiet whip of the reins, the group was underway again.

As they rolled along, the clusters of trees started to become more frequent. In fact, the road they were on cut through several in the span of less than an hour.

When the shade from the trees draped over the cart, Travus always seemed to perk up in the back of the wagon. Neither Perse nor he had spoken much on this leg of the trip and, even when he sat up straighter, he still didn't address the woman.

"We're almost there," Alvin announced, "It should be just on the other side of these trees."

Ahead of the group was a wide line of trees that couldn't be described as a clump or bunch. They were lined up more like they made up the border of a different territory and, in a manner of speaking, they did. Those trees marked the edge of the land that the Ferdinand had claimed as his own and built a grand house upon.

Again, Travus straightened up in the back of the cart. This time he actually lifted himself so that he was sitting on the side of the vehicle.

Once they were inside the trees, the other side wasn't immediately visible. The temperature quickly dropped with most of the sinking sun being blocked out by all the green rustling above their heads.

Travus looked up into the overlapping foliage but then immediately looked down at his feet, idly scratching at his chest, "You guys go on to the Ferdinand's place without me. I'll catch up."

Before Perse could ask a question, protest or anything, the Night Shield tumbled out of the cart and rushed into the trees at the side of the road. Both farmers immediately lost sight of him.

Again, the couple looked at each other. Perse bit her lower lip as if to say, "bringing him was a bad idea." Alvin wordlessly grunted, "What choice did we have, really?" in response. The woman reached up to rub her chin, silently asking him, "What if he was just leading us on and is going to get the Light Bringers to come and arrest us?" He shrugged back, "If he was just waiting to get us out of the city, he could have done that this morning."

"But he knows where we are going. What if he tries to stop us or beat us to Ferdinand?" the worry in her jade green eyes said.

"Beat us? On foot?" Alvin scoffed, "Besides, we're committed now. The Ferdinand is our best chance to be able to get Ophelia back. Travus wants his daughter back, too, but he doesn't have any history with Ferdinand to get him to help."

Perse nodded and slipped up onto the bench beside her husband. Resting her head on his thickly muscled shoulder, they silently watched the trees pass as they neared their destination.

Calling what just happened a conversation would be inaccurate as much as both parents having the same worries at the same time but each coming up with the same arguments to calm each other simultaneously. It took over a decade of marriage for that to start happening without a word.

They left the coverage of the trees, the sinking sun providing them the last effort at warmth for the day. Most of the terrain was clear at this point, no more trees, but the house they heard about still wasn't visible.

That finally appeared as the sun reached the distant rolling hills to the west. It was as if the orb had to frame the house, making it appear as important and regal as the Ferdinand no doubt thought himself.

It looked like a wide two story fortress, rather than a house, made of massive logs laid and shaved flat. The corners of the structure were made with the logs standing vertically and still rounded with little rooms at the top used for look outs.

As they neared, though, there was already a bustle of activity. The lookout spaces had silhouettes of men moving around inside and others marched along the edge of the rooftop, aiming bows with nocked arrows at the couple as they dismounted their cart beside the main entrance. Unusually high security for a home.

The main entrance was made of two immense, heavily polished oak doors. Metal bands held the slabs of wood planks together seamlessly. A knocker rested on each door, life sized carvings of the heads of griffins, one the shape of a lion with the black ring of iron in its maw and the other an equally grand falcon's head, the same size as the lion, where the feathers faded into fur at the base. It also had a black iron ring in its beak.

Husband and wife stepped up to the doors, making sure not to make any sudden movements that could be considered threatening. Then Alvin lifted the ring in the mouth of the lion head without much effort and with an echoing thud, the knocker announced their presence to the inside of the house.

After two more reverberate knocks, the door opened to reveal an old man with a thin layer of white hair all around his head but without any on top. He came up to Alvin's shoulder, an impressive height for most, and didn't appear in any way infirm.

He opened the door enough that he fully revealed himself to the newly arrived travelers but not so wide that they could step in around him, "Have you an appointment to confabulate with the honorable Ferdinand de la Granger?"

"Confabulate?" Alvin looked over at his wife.

Perse didn't look back. A bevy of memories came flooding back to her that made what was happening now almost an afterthought. The woman felt herself start to shake, remembering why she and Alvin parted ways with the Ferdinand so long ago, but she struggled to keep her husband from noticing her uneasiness.

"No, we don't have an appointment," Alvin spoke up when it was apparent Perse wasn't going to do so, "We are old friends of the Ferdinand, from the time when he lived out west in Mirabar, and we come with important information for him about his safety."

The door man's nose curled up as if he'd just encountered a foul stench, "The Ferdinand is a man of tremendous import. He receives innumerable threats upon his life and none of them have come to fruition yet," he motioned to the guards lining the roof. "Whatever makes your assertion so credulous then?"

Alvin pulled the folded parchment that held the orders that were meant for the assassin, Marque Clay. He unfolded the document so that the door man could read it, but didn't hand the parchment over.

The aged man had to squint to read the writing, "That is calligraphy of the loveliest order, sir, but as far as I am aware you could have magnificent hand writing and created that yourself."

The farmer had to stop himself from growling back. The next action that came to mind was grabbing the old man by his neck, using him as a human shield for the archers, and then finding the Ferdinand inside the building himself.

Perse, though, spoke up before the large farmer's plan could launch, "Do you really think bumpkins like us could create such an intricate tale for you and the Ferdinand?" she asked and continued without waiting for an answer, "Regardless, we are no friends of the Al Razheem and do not wish to see the Ferdinand fall victim to one of their plots."

The door man stood in silent thought. His eyes scanned up and down both farmers slowly, like he was trying to find some excuse to turn them away but another part weighed the consequences of doing so with the possibility that they were telling him the truth hanging in the air.

"Very well," he stepped back and pulled the door open wide enough to allow the couple entry, "Though it is inconceivable to me that the Ferdinand could be embroiled in such a nefarious plot that would make him quarry to such a scandalous organization, I will leave it to his excellency to decide on the cogency of your asseveration."

As soon as both farmers stepped into the foyer of the immense house, the old man pushed the door closed. Candelabras filled with little wax pillars that lined the walls were already lit in anticipation of the coming dark of night.

Two curved stairways lined either side of the foyer, leading up to a set of double doors that were gilded with gold leaf carved into the shapes of deer and antlers, both elements in the coat of arms of the Ferdinand's family.

Two armored guards rested at either side of those double doors with their swords drawn. There were surely more in the manor proper where those doors led.

The door man, though, led the couple to a port way that rested under where both stairs met on the first floor. It had no doors and, as Alvin and Perse neared, they could see that it was a simple sitting room lined with shelves of books.

There were no candelabras in here so the corners of the room were draped in darkness. But it also didn't connect to any other room inside so there was little need for guards.

In the wall across from the entrance was the fire place, the flame already rolling inside was the only source of illumination. In the middle of the room, resting on a rug that had designs heavy with angular patterns scattered between arching curves was a round polished table with four equally shined chairs surrounding it.

Motioning to the table, the old man turned back for the entrance he just guided the couple through, "Please feel free to footle here. I will inform his excellency of your presence."

With that he stepped out of the room, leaving the farmers alone. As soon as he was out of sight of the entryway, Alvin started rubbing at his temples.

"Just listening to that man talk was giving me a headache," he grumbled, "Where did Malcolm dig up that guy?"

Perse couldn't help chuckling but the uneasiness in the pit of her stomach quickly brought it to a halt, "It was just his way of feeling important, I guess. I just hope that Malcolm doesn't make us wait..."

Before she could finish her sentence, a man wearing a thick fur robe entered the room. He was breathing heavily, as if he'd just sprinted some distance, but was trying to hide it as he walked slowly with a practiced regal posture. His black hair was tied back in a long ponytail that draped back over the brown and gray striped fur and his face was mostly bare, save for the stubble that formed throughout a day after shaving in the morning.

It was the Ferdinand, Malcolm de la Granger . Both Alvin and Perse recognized him immediately. He stepped up to the table and the door man, who made sure to stick close but stay behind "his excellency", pulled the chair closest to the fire out to allow his master to sit.

And sit he did. The Ferdinand flipped his heavy furs open, revealing obviously expensive clothing made of red silks and black satin with thin golden chains running from one pocket to the next.

He crossed his legs tightly as he leaned back and motioned to the other chairs at the table.

"Please sit," the old man voiced for him.

The farmers did as they were asked. Alvin leaned forward, resting his forearms on the edge of the round table while Perse sat stiffly in her chair, her pale green eyes looking anywhere but at their host.

The Ferdinand smiled politely but his demeanor didn't give any sign that he recognized either of the farmers, "So I hear that I am a target of assassination by this group called the…"

He looked up at the old man who said, "Al Razheem, sir."

"Ah, yes, that was it," the nobleman nodded, "He also said that you had a copy of the orders?"

Alvin nodded back, placing the parchment on the polished wood surface, "I took these from a member of the assassin's guild right after he pulled them from a secret compartment they use to deliver orders at a tavern in Paimae."

The other man reached out for the paper, the light from the fire glinting off the rings and bracelets wrapped around his fingers and wrist, "A secret compartment, you say?" he unfolded the document.

Though his expression didn't change, Alvin was fairly sure that the other man's complexion went a couple shades paler as he read. He tossed the parchment back onto the table, where it slid off to rest on the rug next to the large farmer's feet.

"I trust you have more evidence than an anonymous note and your word it came from an assassin?" the tone in his voice said that he didn't believe them.

"I thought you were never going to ask," the voice of Travus came from one of the dark corners, "Do you know how boring it is to wait for a dramatic moment to reveal yourself? It is a lot like waiting for an opportune time to strike a killing blow."

As he spoke the Night Shield stepped out of the shadows and he wasn't alone. Beside him was a woman in a black tunic and pants with a violet sash proclaiming her to be a member of the Al Razheem clan of assassins.

Her arms were forced awkwardly behind her, the blade of the Night Shield's sword pressed across her back and resting just below where her biceps met her shoulders. If she moved too suddenly, the woman's arms would be sliced down to the bone, making her limbs useless and also very likely that she would bleed to death in short order.

"I'd like you to meet Vendilay," Travus motioned to the woman beside him, "A member of the Al Razheem that has been following these two for some time. The fact that she is a trained assassin is the reason she was able to get in here without being detected by all those armed soldiers, sir, and the fact that I'm affiliated with the Light Bringers is the only reason you know she's here at all. Would you like to hear more?"

THE OASIS

The General stood before the main entrance to his fortress, awaiting the arrival of his new prize. Beside him stood the unnaturally thin Doctor Efreeti. That painfully wide grin just wouldn't leave his face. To the other side of the General was Kitanah, who had not stopped pouting since her master had sent Ophelia on this highly personal task.

The broad, tall doors of the Oasis were pulled open, allowing Ophelia into the fortress. Blood had soaked in along the hem of her amber colored cloak and she had her hood down. That made it so sand had buried itself in her dark shoulder length hair, making it look like a powdered wig.

Beside the General's preferred assassin was a much shorter figure. This must have been young Tilly. She wore a simple dress that was baggy on her thin frame, as if it had been originally made for someone a might bigger than the girl.

Her short hair was caked in dust as well and, unlike Ophelia, once they were inside the fortress walls she shook her head to try and rid herself of some of the desert's dust. The cloud that suddenly engulfed her head made her sneeze... then yelp in panic.

That was because of the blade that was being held between her arms, that were forced awkwardly behind her, and her back. At the sudden motion of her sneeze, her biceps should have been severed but Ophelia was quick enough to slip the longsword blade down along her spine far enough to keep the girl from slicing herself.

Once Tilly was done, though, the blade was again pressed against her bare arms. The General noticed that Ophelia's usual blade, Havarti, still rested on her hip and that the sword she was using to hold the girl was a longsword that had belonged to a Light Bringer. A likely deceased one judging from the fact that the tip of the blade had somehow been snapped off.

Both women stopped immediately in front of the trio waiting for them just as the doors fought against the desert winds to close behind them. Once the gusts ceased and the courtyard was again still and quiet, the assassins that manned the chains that controlled the doors quickly marched out of the courtyard. Such action was obviously prearranged when news of Ophelia's arrival became imminent.

Once it was only the five of them, the General spoke with a kind smile for her, "I am pleased to see that your assignment went well, child."

Ophelia nodded, "All for you, Master."

The General smiled and then turned his attention to Doctor Efreeti, who stepped forward as if by silent cue. He stepped up to the little girl, towering over her as the space between them shrank. He got so close that Ophelia had to push the flat of the long sword blade into Tilly's back when she tried to step back.

He pushed the round lenses on his nose higher onto the bridge of his skinny nose as he let out quiet clicking noises with his tongue. To Ophelia, it sounded like he was trying to do the impression of water dripping from the clepsydrae, the mechanism in the training room that kept track of the time of day.

When his clawed hand emerged from under his cloak, Tilly again tried to step away but was again stopped by the steel blade at her back. Efreeti ran his fingers through the girl's short dark hair. What he was evaluating, Ophelia couldn't guess.

"Open your mouth, girl," the thin man ordered.

He wasn't surprised when she refused. It didn't stop him, though. The curved claws of Efreeti's forefingers slipped between Tilly's lips and pulled them apart to reveal her teeth. He seemed pleased by what he saw and even more so as his fingers pushed in and felt around between her cheeks and gums.

"Excellent!" he declared, "No obvious signs of decay, showing a strong genetic disposition."

When Efreeti pulled his fingers free of her mouth, Tilly reared back to spit. When the sharp tips of the thin man's claws came to rest on her throat, she changed her target from his face to the sand at Ophelia's feet.

Efreeti's hands ran over the girl's chest as he continued his examination. His palms rested where her breasts had just started to grow and he turned back to face the General.

"She is quite young," Doctor Efreeti observed, "You are sure you don't wish her to... ripen more before I make her yours?"

The patron of the Al Razheem shook his head, "The sooner you can perform the procedure, the better."

Efreeti turned his attention back to the little girl as he bent down to kneel in front of Tilly. His hands continued downward, running all over her torso. The only thing keeping from trying to wriggle away from his touch was the sword at her back.

When his hand slipped between her legs, though, her brown eyes opened wide and a shocked squeak escaped her mouth. Efreeti frowned as he looked first up into the little girl's face, silently telling her that her reaction was inappropriate, then looking back at the General.

"This one has not had her first matronly cycle yet," he said as he straightened back up. "She is an acceptable specimen but I cannot use her until she's at least matured to that point."

The General looked disappointed, "Have you any idea how long until she has this... cycle?"

Efreeti looked up, as if reading numbers off the back of his opened eyelids, "Within a fortnight. I doubt any longer than that. Until then she is useless to me."

He turned and started for the hall that led deeper into the fort and his laboratory. The General rested a hand on the thin man's shoulder and leaned in close, his voice so quiet Ophelia couldn't hear his words. Havarti could and relayed them to the woman.

"Would using her for my recreation in the meantime cause her to somehow become an invalid subject for the procedure?" he motioned to the little girl as he whispered.

Efreeti let out a soft sigh, not bothering to lower his voice when he responded, "If you can guarantee me that your sexual exploits would cause no bruising to her dermis... her skin, " he added in case the General was unfamiliar with the word, "or any other damage to her body in the mean time, she is all yours."

The General seemed embarrassed for a short moment at Efreeti's loud answer to his somewhat private question but his usual air of authority quickly returned to his countenance. Tilly, on the other hand let out a horrified shriek at the idea and started to drop to her knees, not caring that her arms would get cut off or that she would likely die.

Ophelia quickly pulled the sword away from the girl and tossed it away, she was told that the General's prize was to return unscathed. The woman's head tilted to the side for a moment, the voice of the bastard sword on her hip in her ear. She lifted the little girl back to her feet by the nape of her collar and turned to the General.

"Perhaps it would be better to tie the girl down until her fealty is fully yours to take, Master," Ophelia's gray eyes narrowed at the little girl, "She is likely as much a danger to herself now more than ever."

The General's tongue ran over his lips as an avalanche of thoughts ran through him. His skin flushed as he looked from the small Tilly to the far more developed Ophelia.

"That is why you are my Second, Ophelia," he smiled, "Kitanah, take the girl and lock her down so she cannot harm herself until Efreeti calls for her."

Kitanah started to protest but stopped herself before the first word could fully form. Instead, she forced herself to bow and took the grip on Tilly's dress from the other assassin.

The General turned his attention to Ophelia, as she pulled the cloak from her shoulders. Tossing it to the sand covered floor, the rest of her firm body didn't have as much exposure to the desert winds as her hair. The braids on either side of her face lightly bounced against her chin as she ran her fingers through the shoulder length strands to loose some of the sand away.

The blue sash around her waist, complete with gold embroidery, swayed with her hips. It took a strong act of will for the man to pull his eyes away.

"While she's doing that, Ophelia, clean yourself up and then I want both of you to come to my chambers," he ordered.

"Anything for you, Master," Ophelia bowed.

"*What*?" Kitanah roughly pulled the child around as she turned to face her patron.

"You heard me," the General smirked wickedly at the red haired woman, "I won't have disharmony in my house any longer. I intend to teach you the true benefits of cooperation, supernal one."

Though she had been ordered to do something she was sure to despise, Kitanah reflexively smiled at hearing her old pet name from the General. She hadn't been called that since... since Ophelia had arrived.

THE FERDINAND'S MANOR

The Ferdinand had more anger in his eyes than shock as the Night Shield and the farmers finished their story, "This is... disheartening."

Vendilay, the Al Razheem assassin captured by Travus, sat at the table between the two farmers while the Night Shield stood behind her with his sword still in hand. The assassin glared at the Ferdinand de la Granger, her eyes seeming to shift color between black and blue with the flickering of the fire light, because she couldn't turn and direct it at the Night Shield without risking getting cut down by his sword.

"Have you had any dealings with the Al Razheem, Mister..." Travus trailed off when he realized he wasn't familiar with the noble titles like Ferdinand in this region.

"Ferdinand or excellency will suffice, *Mister* Browder," the nobleman made sure there was just enough disdain in his voice, "And why do you ask questions to which you already know the answer?"

The Night Shield didn't even bother to resist the urge as his lips pulled into a smirk. The Ferdinand was right, of course. Travus saw the mercenaries that had been hired as security. No one had that much muscle if they didn't feel threatened. He also knew that the Al Razheem only killed without gold changing hands when the target was those who somehow worked for or with the organization and either betrayed them or were no longer useful. And Marque didn't receive a single coin with his orders.

"What your true question is then," the noble continued, "is what exactly did I do to warrant elimination by my now former business associates?"

He drained the wine from his flute before setting the glass back on the table. Wine sat in front of everyone at the round piece of polished wood. The glasses in front of Perse and Alvin remained untouched. The assassin, apparently waiting for the Ferdinand to drink to prove the beverage was not poisoned, reached out and took finally took a sip from hers, leaving her flute just about half full.

The silence that filled the room made the air feel thicker, like it would take heavy effort to speak and each person was still deciding whether to expend such energy. Vendilay was the one to break the unspoken stalemate.

"He was commissioned by our General to work with Squire Trelaine to develop some kind of super assassin," she said.

Travus arched an eyebrow, "You're saying that Squire Trelaine's death was an Al Razheem hit?"

Ferdinand's eyes locked onto Vendilay with that. Her intention was clear: to make herself as useful to her captors as possible and gain Light Bringer protection from her guild mates. With her life forfeit after being captured anyway, at least to the Al Razheem, it was her only real chance at survival.

The nobleman, though, had information that she did not. If there were to be a race for protective sheltering, surely the Ferdinand de la Granger had the edge.

"Super assassin is overly simplistic," he spoke to Travus but kept staring at the assassin, using his words as if he was raising a bet in some kind of card game, "The goal is to make a man unkillable."

"How do you mean *unkillable*?" the man in red asked.

"I mean precisely that." the noble answered, "To create a means that neither violence nor time can destroy the chosen among us."

"By chosen, the General meant himself and those in the Al Razheem he trusts," Vendilay added, raising her own stakes.

The Ferdinand started to argue but stopped himself. The fact that he was marked for death provided credence to the woman's words.

That was when Alvin unexpectedly spoke up, "You were a man of honor, Malcolm. Why would you involve yourself with a group like them?" he motioned to the assassin.

The nobleman felt an anger he had almost forgotten about reignite in his chest as he looked at the walking, talking mountain of flesh. Still, he kept his control and forced himself to look at Travus.

"Immortality. Realistically within reach," he said with as much dramatic flair as he could, "There were three of us commissioned, actually. Trelaine was to develop the apparatus to contain a human soul. I was to figure the means of selection."

It took his conscious mind a moment to notice but, when it did, the nobleman found his eyes had drifted over to Perse, who had not looked up from her boots the entire time they had been in the reading room. He quickly looked back at the Night Shield, hoping his... distraction had not been noticed.

"Why would you need a selection process if you were only going to use this process on members of the Al Razheem?" Travus apparently didn't see Malcolm's eyes wander.

"The General wanted to control who could even possibly undertake the procedure. Even among his people," the Ferdinand explained as the old man returned with a platter of sliced fruit and set it down in front his master, "We needed specific criteria that could make it so that anyone he and I would deem worth turning immortal could also be controlled and not betray either of us."

"The General," Vendilay corrected, "That he deemed worthy and be controlled by the General."

Again, the Ferdinand was forced to agree with the assassin. He slouched in his seat, looking like a petulant toddler who had just been chastised.

Travus stepped up to the table between Vendilay and the nobleman, "What's this apparatus that Trelaine was supposed to develop?"

Again, Alvin spoke up, "Do we really care about that right now?" he turned to the Ferdinand, "Malcolm, the Al Razheem kidnapped our daughter. We need your help to get her back."

The Ferdinand couldn't stop himself from laughing at the farmer's plea. When even Perse looked up, along with everyone else, at him with confusion on their faces he cleared his throat.

"I already know that Ophelia was taken, Alvin," he sneered at the gigantic man, "I was the one who told the Al Razheem to take her."

The only thing that stopped the farmer from wrapping his hands around the noble's throat was the tip of the longsword that he suddenly found poking at his broad chest. Travus nodded back down at Alvin's chair, silently telling him to sit back down.

"Why?" Perse spoke for the first time since they had all assembled.

The mother looked on the verge of tears as she finally looked up at the Ferdinand. Her hands were wrapped around her midsection. It was as if she was afraid she would physically fall apart if she didn't hold herself together.

Malcolm sighed, "You know why, don't you, Perse?" it wasn't a question.

She literally stopped breathing mid inhale. Panic filled her eyes as they darted back and forth between the Ferdinand and Alvin.

The nobleman turned his attention to the larger farmer, "Do you remember the night you proposed to her, Alvin?"

"Please," the farmer's wife closed her eyes tight, as if doing so would stop what was about to happen, "Please don't."

"After you parted ways, she came to me," the Ferdinand continued anyway, "She was frantic, railing on and on again about how she suddenly felt leashed. That she'd given her freedom away for nothing. Nothing, Alvin."

Travus firmed his grip on the sword handle in case the heavily muscled man decided to try something foolish again. He didn't. In fact, the only reaction the man had to what was being said was confusion. It was all over his face like a mask.

"Do you know what I did, Alvin?" Malcolm leaned forward, resting his elbows on the table, "I tried to talk her into breaking off your betrothal."

Alvin turned to look at his wife, "You never told me that."

"Well, it didn't work, did it?" the nobleman said, "Looking back, I should have told her every word you said to me. Remember? Prior to your proposal, you came to me, got slobbering drunk and confessed the whole thing. You had told me about your mercenary days and the women killed in that caravan. Frankly, it disgusted me and I tried to get Perse to change her mind about marrying you. But I gave you my word and didn't tell her the details. How different things would have been then if I hadn't followed that moronic code of honor then."

"Maybe not, Malcolm," Alvin's face was twisted with the effort of balancing his confusion and the desire to beat the other man into a bloody pulp, "After Ophelia was taken, when I figured out it was the Al Razheem that took her, I told Perse everything. She's still with me."

His massive hand reached out and wrapped around both of his wife's. Tears were freely rolling down her face now and she couldn't bring herself to look back at her husband.

"Did she reciprocate in kind?" the Ferdinand asked.

Alvin tried to ask his wife what the other man meant but she still wouldn't look at him. She kept her eyes shut and shook her head back and forth, silently begging for what was about to happen to not.

"She may have gone back to you, *farmer*," Malcolm's eyes dug into Alvin as he spoke. "But that night, she was so unsure of herself, of everything, that she begged me for comfort, Alvin. Then I took her to my chambers and I bedded her. I took her in every way I could imagine, Alvin."

Now Alvin had forgotten how to breathe. His face was as pale as the moon that crowned in the night sky.

Perse expected his hand to pull away from hers. It didn't. It would, though, once the shock passed, she was sure.

The muscular farmer's jaw hung open. It reminded Perse of the time when the horse that pulled the plow reared back and kicked Alvin, shattering his ribs. The woman thought she was going to lose him that day but he survived.

"How old is Ophelia now?" Malcolm smiled.

The farmer's eye twitched.

The noble continued, "Are you sure you are truly her father, Alvin? After having had Perse in my bed for so long, so many times, could you really be?"

The massive man swallowed so hard that everyone in the room heard it, "But never again right? Never after we wed? After we made our vows to each other," the husband asked her.

"Never again. Ever," Perse sniffled.

"That was why you left," The words worked past his lips with momentous effort as he looked back at the nobleman, "You were afraid that Perse would tell me what happened and I would confront you. You crossed an entire continent to avoid me."

"Don't flatter yourself, you hippopotamic land mass," Malcolm sneered, but a shiver ran through him that he wasn't able to conceal.

"You don't know what happened after you moved away," Alvin squeezed his wife's hands in his, "She made me wait almost a year before actually having the wedding. I always wondered why but now it makes sense."

"She wanted to make sure her guilt was well hidden," the Ferdinand answered.

Alvin looked over at his wife, his free hand gently lifting her chin to face him, "No. That wasn't it. I know my wife, Malcolm. We finish each other's sentences. We don't even have to talk much to communicate these days."

The realization that her husband wasn't going to abandon her made Perse sit straighter. She nodded at the man she loved, took a long deep breath to steady herself and focused her attention on the Ferdinand de la Granger .

"I wanted to make sure that I wasn't pregnant or," she looked the other man up and down, "diseased in some way. I made a mistake and I wasn't going to make the man I love pay for it with me."

"And yet you still never confessed your *mistake* to him," Malcolm leaned back in his seat again, "That is the very reason I chose Ophelia as the test subject."

Alvin felt his anger boil up again but this time it was his wife that stopped him from attacking the nobleman. Travus leaned toward the Ferdinand and started his own line of questioning again.

"What exactly is this procedure you developed?" the man in red asked.

"You know what death is, yes?" the nobleman realized that it was to his benefit that he work to show his worth to the Night Shield again after such an unflattering revelation, "It is when the body is damaged to the point that it can no longer contain its soul.

"Trelaine developed an alternate container to hold a mortal's soul, hereby sealing it away from the ravages of time. Just like when apples are sealed in a barrel and rested in cold water are preserved, so too can the soul.

"The major difference, though, is that the soul is part of the whole. If you take a portion of a soul and seal it away, it cannot leave this mortal plain. If the soul isn't connected to the body, it cannot age and if the soul cannot age, neither can the body."

Vendilay reached out and took a piece of fruit of the tray on the table. She didn't say anything. As she physically chewed on the morsel, her mind worked to piece together all the information she was hearing with the many rumors that had been shuffling around the Oasis over the passing months.

"Immortality," Travus nodded, not sure he was believing everything being said, "What was this about selection, though? And what does it have to do with their daughter?"

"I had to figure a method that would only allow souls of Al Razheem and their compatriots access to the soul orbs," the Ferdinand got a blank look back from the Night Shield. "The containers, we call them soul orbs. We didn't want just anyone to make use of our work and threaten efforts.

"You are familiar with the cliché that secrets weigh a soul down? I labored under the theory that it was more truth than hyperbole, that a soul burdened with secrets was actually heavier than one that was free of such an encumbrance."

"What does that have to do with Ophelia?" Travus motioned to the farmers, "They were the ones who had the secrets."

"That was where the beauty of my hypothesis rested," the Ferdinand looked very pleased with himself, "It is based off the adage that the sins of the father will be visited on the son or, in this case, daughter. I surmised if you knew the heaviest burden connected to a soul, you could use it to force the energy into the orb.

"I had kept tabs on Alvin and Perse over the years. I knew them well enough to know that they were too cowardly to confess their most egregious failings to each other. I did not, however, want to have to deal with either of them for eternity if the procedure was a success," he pointed at Alvin and Perse, "Then I realized that family is connected not only physically but spiritually as well. My spies reported no burden for Ophelia to carry, at least none that outweighed the ones of those connected most closely to the girl. She was the perfect test subject."

"And when Ophelia wanted to go back home? If she couldn't be killed how could you stop her?" Travus looked at the nobleman like he was a mess on the bottom of his boot.

"I merely found a way to stop the aging process. Countering violence and controlling the subject, that came down to the third man commissioned by the General," the Ferdinand de la Granger sighed, "It wasn't my problem to solve."

"You bastard," Perse muttered at the man, "Ophelia is my little girl."

"Not anymore," Malcolm shook his head at the woman, "Assuming she's still alive, that is."

Perse lunged for the man so quickly even her still enraged husband wasn't fast enough to stop her. Her fingernails ripped into the nobleman's face like claws as her other hand snatched one of the assorted pouches from her belt.

"She'll outlive you. I promise you that, you monster!" she ripped the cord holding the pouch closed off with her teeth.

Travus pushed the woman off of Malcolm, the contents of the pouch dumping all over the rug beside the noble rather than into his mouth. Alvin rushed over, wrapping his arms around his wife before she could attack the man again while the Night Shield simply pointed his sword at the Ferdinand's chest.

"Get up," he ordered.

"What did you think was going to happen when you came here, Perse?" the Ferdinand coughed as he struggled clear the rasp from his throat, "You would come to your rejected lover for help and he wouldn't let your misdeeds become known to his supplant?"

As the door man rushed back into the room with armored guards in tow, the Night Shield's sword moved to the noble's throat, silencing him. At the same time, it also served to stay the hand of the hired soldiers. One of the mercenaries drew his bow back but didn't let the arrow fly. Not yet.

"Order them away, Granger," Travus dropped any pretense of respect for the man's rank as a noble.

The Ferdinand remained silent, laying flat on the rug until he felt the cold steel bite into his skin, "Get back. The harpy is under control now. You're services will not be necessary for the moment."

The old man frowned as he scanned over the scene. Finally he nodded at the mercenaries and they turned to leave.

The Ferdinand rose and retook his seat without assistance. Keeping his weapon pointed at the nobleman, Travus turned his attention to Alvin and Perse.

"What was that you tried to use?" he asked about the crimson powder that laid on the floor in a pile.

Still restrained by her husband, whose thick arms were wrapped around her from behind, the woman again looked down at her boots, "Red quicklime," she said, "It is a powerful acid when combined with liquids like saliva and blood."

The noble's hand reflexively ran over his lips and the scratches on his jaw as he imagined the effects of what could have happened. He turned his attention back to the member of the Night Shield.

"I want her arrested," he hissed, "I want her in chains and away from me before I give you any more information! Do you understand me?"

Travus looked from the woman, with rage and grief running through her entire body, over to the sanctimonious man sitting before him, "Yes, I understand you. You won't give me any more reason to protect you from those who wish to do you harm. So maybe I should turn you over to Perse. After all she is a good standing citizen and not part of any league of assassins intent on killing you."

The almost forgotten Vendilay started to laugh at the expression that started to form on the Ferdinand's face when she suddenly started to cough. Her eyes opened wide as she realized that she was suddenly unable to breathe.

"Finally," the nobleman whispered.

The long sword whipped back to the Ferdinand's neck so quickly he fell back onto the carpet. He struggled to get his own breath back as the Night Shield stood over him.

"What did you do?" Travus demanded.

"Binary poison," Malcolm croaked, "Only works when the wine and fruit are mixed."

The assassin doubled over on the table, her hands sinking into the soft fruits as if somehow gaining leverage would make her able to force air into her chest. Her face was already transitioning from cherry-red to asphyxiated purple.

"You forget that I was your first teacher in chemistry," the Ferdinand sneered at Perse.

The farmer wracked her brain for what possible compounds the man could have used. Unfortunately, she didn't have a countering agent for any that came to mind. But there was something she realized.

"Let me go," she turned to look back at her husband, "I think I can save her!"

Alvin did so without hesitation and Perse immediately dove for the nobleman.

"Keep him still!" Perse ordered as she plunged her hand into one pocket of the Ferdinand's vest and then the next, "He would have the antidote handy just in case he somehow triggered the effects of the poison on himself."

Travus again rested his blade on the despicable noble's neck to keep him complacent. The noble growled with impotent rage but didn't react any other way.

As Perse moved from one pocket to the next, Vendilay struggled for life. She pushed one of her fingers down her throat in hopes of forcing the airway open, only to vomit all over the tabletop. The acidic contents of her stomach parted around the metal tray to become two foul waterfalls spilling over the far edge of the formerly pristine piece of furniture.

It did give the assassin one last gasping breath before the edges of her vision started turning black. She stumbled around the table, shoving Perse away from the Ferdinand so that she could tackle him back to the floor and kneel on top of him.

Vomit and saliva dripped from the woman's lips as she pushed a handful of the fruit from the platter into the man's face. Instinct made him pull his face away from the poisoned food but he had forgotten about the pile of red powder. The juice covering his face and the powder met and the Ferdinand de la Granger screamed as his face started to melt away.

Travus' sword sliced into the woman, too late to stop her. Her body had given any grip on life it had left by then.

"Blast it! I just found the vial!" the farmer woman's face tightened in a mix of anger and sadness as she held out the liquid filled glass.

The mercenaries again rushed into the room but this time they were met by Alvin who slammed them to the floor with his massive fists before they even realized what had happened. Perse intercepted the old man, the vial in her hand replaced by the small dagger from her belt and pressing against his chest.

The Ferdinand's screams didn't last long. He joined the assassin in death but no one, not even the old man, looked overly grieved by his passing.

Travus stepped over the corpse of the former noble and ex-assassin and stepped over to the old man. Noticing his lack of emotion at his master's passing, the Night Shield had an idea.

"Did the Ferdinand have any children or siblings?" he asked.

Alvin answered for him, "No family since his parents passed twenty-five years ago. He was sterile so he couldn't have children of his own."

Both Travus and Perse looked over at her husband quizzically.

"He never married and after being seen with so many women, no bastards ever popped up," the large farmer shrugged, "I started to think he was working to be seen with women to keep up appearances but was really attracted to men so I talked to his parents. They're the ones who told me he was sterile rather than being charmed by, um, guys like me. Apparently, they never told him about our conversation."

"Or you me," worry was still etched over Perse's face but she chanced giving her husband a playful, unsure smile, "Still, I'm glad. I would have hated the competition."

Alvin's reaction was slow in coming. At first, his pale eyebrows pressed together as if he were going to be angry. But then his lower lip twitched as if he were going to weep. Finally, though, he let out a long sigh and, pulling her and the dagger away from its target, wrapped a heavily muscled arm around his wife.

The Night Shield felt his shoulders loosen up once Alvin didn't push the issue brought up by the Ferdinand's revelation. He was even more relieved when the old man didn't move to try and escape or fight once Perse was pulled away.

"Then I guess his property reverts to the state," Travus sheathed his sword as he stepped up to address the Ferdinand's former door man, "As a representative of the Light Bringers, what would you say if I offered you and the other mercenaries all the riches of that pouf's estate in exchange for one very dangerous job?"

ELEVEN

INCURSION

THE DESERT OF AKSHAR

Violet and mauve swirls curled around each other in the ink filled blackness of the night sky. Stars still managed to poke their little white kernels of light through the curtains of color that broke up all that encompassing dark. And even though only a sliver of the moon was visible, it still showed that light, no matter how small, could still find its way down.

At least that was what Perse wanted to believe as she laid in the sand and stared up into the cosmic show above her. But her stomach twisted and squeezed, not letting her forget what was going to happen very, very soon.

She found herself thankful for the warmth radiating from her husband's bicep under her head and neck. Perse found herself shuffling in closer to her husband's side as he, outwardly at least, didn't seem to share the shivering nerves she had.

When Perse rested her hand on his chest, only then did she realize that his heart was beating like a fowl being chased down by a pack of wargs. That only made her cuddle tighter against him and his heart slowly returned to a rhythm that was still fast but, judging from his arm wrapping around her shoulders, more from the pleasure of her company than the dread from what was to come. Perse smiled, her heart matching his, when she realized she still had such an effect on the man she loved.

"You wouldn't think torchlight would drown out as much of the night sky as it did," Alvin said, breaking the long silence that had stood since everyone else left.

"You do forget all those nebulae and colors up there when you're in the city," Perse agreed.

Then all was silence again. It didn't get much more still than the middle of the desert in the middle of the night. Any indigenous animal life was where whatever sparse vegetation was and that was nowhere near where the married couple lay.

The only exception to the stillness was the muffled hoof beats of two dozen horses just over the next dune. But they were trained to wait patiently for their riders, staying in one place so they did not disturb the peace of this moment.

Neither husband nor wife spoke again, nor even looked at each other, but they were together now. And now was when it would matter most.

The old man from the Ferdinand's estate made his way through the shifting sand toward Alvin and Perse. On the journey into Akshar, they had learned his name was Quisling. He was the leader of the company of mercenaries hired to guard his now dead benefactor, the Ferdinand.

Now he was under the employ of Travus Browder and, technically, the Light Bringers. He and twenty men volunteered to join Travus, Alvin, and Perse's quest to rescue their daughters. His arrival meant that the preparations must be complete.

"I do abhor interrupting… whatever you are doing here," his voice was quiet, as if he was afraid it would carry and give away their position to the assassins they were readying to attack, "But the formulation of the design you concocted has been consummated."

As Alvin lifted himself, along with his wife, up to a sitting position he let out a pained, quiet grunt. Perse smirked, recognizing it as the sound me made when he was annoyed and didn't want to show it. Like when the old man used such unnecessarily long words that he suspected weren't being used completely right.

"We were just enjoying the calm before the storm," Perse said.

Quisling nodded then motioned back over his shoulder. In the distance was the looming silhouette of the Oasis, the fortress that Travus said served as the home base for the Al Razheem assassins. It was about a half hour walk away from where they stood now and the aged mercenary didn't waste any time starting back in that direction.

Alvin drained the last of the cup of almost forgotten honeybark ale at his side opposite his wife before hopping up and aiding Perse to her feet. That only took a few moments but still they had to rush after Quisling.

Alvin wished they could light a torch to be able to see ground under them more clearly. In the darkness, the sand seemed to move with a mind of its own and an intent to twist or break the ankle of the unwary. With the moon a mere crescent in the sky they couldn't be spotted easily by any sentries patrolling the outer walls of the fortress but even a small torch's light would be a beacon to the assassins, revealing they were not alone in the desert.

Even as they closed the distance to what Travus described as the back wall of the Oasis, they couldn't make out any real details in the wall. It was as if it was a solid slab of stone.

The winds that whipped around the structure had worn away any easy to spot sign of mortar and there were no windows. In fact, the stone was the same color as the sand all around the farmers. That, combined with mirages causing the desert heat to make the horizon look like floating water and distorting any sense of distance or scale, made it doubtful that anyone who didn't already know where the fortress was would be able to find it.

At the base of the wall was the wagon that had carried all the leather satchels of drake gland oil. It was flipped over and resting at an angle against the wall, the night wind spinning the wooden wheels around.

Around the capsized vehicle were twenty armored men and Travus in his long red coat. He was the only one to step away from the wagon and toward Alvin, Perse and Quisling as they approached.

"We're ready for you to light the fireworks," he whispered.

Perse nodded at the Night Shield and started digging through the myriad of pouches on her belt. The old man rested a hand on Travus's shoulder.

"Just so we are clear," he whispered, though with a hint of demanding, "my men will not follow you or them throughout the entire fort. They will stop at strategic points to guard our escape through here."

Quisling pointed at the wall and the wagon. The younger man nodded back.

"That's what we agreed," he said, "Then each of them get their choice of one of the Ferdinand's estates or a share of plunder from his accounts throughout the continent."

"If you die, this deal had not better die with you!" Quisling growled, his white hair glinting in the faint moonlight.

Alvin couldn't help but notice that when it came time to discuss business, the old man's vocabulary became much clearer. He would have laughed, if he didn't know what was about to happen.

"I already sent word back to Paimae," Browder assured him, pulling his long coat closed around his chest, "You do your job and you'll get your reward."

Quisling looked back at the farmers, "Just remember that our agreement doesn't include getting your daughter out. If you don't find her, we leave without her. If you die, don't expect us to continue the search. We leave with our skins intact for our money!"

"We got it," Perse scowled at the old man as she twisted a metal nozzle onto the end of a leather bladder that quickly expanded to become big enough that she had to cradle on her other arm, "You'll find it a hard race to beat us with my daughter back to the horses."

Quisling huffed as the shorter woman stepped around him and toward the wagon. She inspected the bags resting under the vehicle in the sand and against the wall. Running her free hand along the side of the wagon, her face contorted as she did some last minute calculations.

She nodded to herself then looked up at the surrounding mercenaries, "This will direct most of the force of the blast at the wall but we should all still back off at least fifty paces. And where are those four bags I asked you to set aside?"

Alvin stepped over to the pile of four bladders, pulling two short lengths of rope from his pants pocket and tying the massive bladders together into two pairs. Then he slipped his broad shoulders under the ropes and lifted all four all at once.

The farmer was a big man but even still the leather bags full of oil stretched from the top of his chest down to the middle of his thighs. They were also heavy with a typical man only being able to handle one on his own. He was able to carry them, to be sure, but he wasn't going to be able to get anywhere in a hurry.

He was the last of the group including Travus, Quisling and the mercenaries to hurry away those fifty paces that Perse had prescribed. Perse herself was still beside the wagon, standing between both axles and holding the bladder with whatever mixture she had just concocted by the base of the nozzle while tucking the leather itself between her arm and side.

She squeezed, loosing a stream of liquid onto the wall just above the wood lip of the wagon. After spraying the entire length of the vehicle twice, she turned and hurried for where her husband and the others waited.

She was just short of the group when the liquid dripped down the wall far enough to reach the bags. After what sounded like a bell ringing for a servant's attention, the entire base of the fortress wall was engulfed in flames. Perse flew into the arms of Travus, who quickly pulled her back to her feet.

For as big of a fireball as the explosion was, there was very little smoke and when what there was cleared out, a whole four people could easily walk side by side through the wall where the wagon had been. No one said anything but the mercenaries immediately started rushing for the opening.

Quisling ordered two men to stand guard at either side of the newly formed entrance then he continued inside. Perse and Travus were right behind him, along with the rest of the mercenaries. Alvin brought up the rear, though the load didn't seem to be straining him yet.

Neither the farmers, nor the mercenaries, expected the sight they saw as they stepped inside the thick walls. It was a literal oasis inside the building that shared the name. Immediately ahead was a grove of trees and underfoot was green grass save for the trail that went around the grove.

"Don't go into the trees," Travus instructed as he pointed his now unsheathed sword at the trail in the grass, "Go around and you'll find a gate that leads into the fortress proper."

A couple of men questioned why they shouldn't cut through the grove but they did as they were instructed anyway. The gate that Travus mentioned came into view, complete with a wide balcony looming over it.

"You were cognizant of this location's existence," Quisling said to the Night Shield in a matter-of-fact manner, "Therefore you knew there would be no protection awaiting us."

Browder ignored the man and instead pointed at the now near and very closed gate, "What do you think, Perse? One or two bladders?" he asked the woman.

Perse stepped up to the latticed metal, wrapping her hands around the bars and giving them a quick shake. They didn't budge.

"Two, I think," she answered. "It's like they knew we were coming and fortified this spot."

Travus shook his head, "The General is very picky about who he lets in here. This place is his baby."

"Then maybe we should take it from him like he took ours," Alvin said as he laid down two of the leather bags where his wife indicated.

Once one shoulder was free of its load, the farmer looked back at the grove, then at the two remaining bladders he held. It was obvious what he had planned.

"Maybe on the way back, big guy," Travus wrapped a hand around Alvin's arm to get his attention, "This is our only way out, after all."

Alvin reluctantly agreed and each mercenary, as well he and Travus, gave the gateway a wide berth. Leaning against the wall, they waited for Perse to spray whatever it was that ignited the oil through the leather bladders.

"It came from the oasis!" echoing voices suddenly came from the hall the group was working to enter, "How could they get through the wall like that?"

Perse, hugging the wall, stepped as near as she dared. Trying to get the bag closer while keeping her body as far away as possible, she held the nozzle tipped bag in her hands outstretched awkwardly. She squeezed the half empty bladder. The liquid fell short of the closest bag.

"Quick! Somebody get the key! We can take them out before the General even has to hear about this!" one voice said.

The farmers looked at each other hopefully. Maybe they wouldn't have to use the drake oil explosives after all. Alvin thought his wife was already dangerously close and she would have to get even more so to reach a range to spray the igniting solution.

"Idiots!" a shrill female voice suddenly came down from the hallway, "Buffoons! You will leave those gates shut! You know you cannot open them without express permission from our General! Let them stay... trapped... in... Get out! Get out of there!"

The change in the woman's tone was obvious. She had noticed the leather bladders and knew they were out of place. She probably figured they were to be a repeat performance of what happened to the outer wall.

Perse stepped up and again squeezed the leather bladder. The first bag erupted instantly, followed immediately by the second when the flames from the first hit.

The farmer was knocked flat on her back and into the grass. Screams came from the hall as the men inside that survived the initial blast burned and joined their already dead colleagues moments later.

Again, Quisling ordered two men to guard either side of the smoldering hole as the rest of the mercenaries rushed into the hall. Travus, lingered around the contorted remnants of the gates outer bars as Alvin rushed to his wife.

"Baby? Baby, are you okay?" he wrapped both of his massive hands around either side of her face, his tremendous thumbs stroking her forehead so gently the carbon that colored her face black was barely disturbed.

Her eyelids fluttered for a moment but then her jade green eyes focused on Alvin hunched over her. Perse smiled up at her husband as she lifted herself to her elbows.

"Let's get our baby back," she declared.

DEEP INSIDE THE OASIS

The only sound in the wide open training room was the dripping of the clepsydrae, the funnel that dripped water from a small fountain into a bucket that rested along the wall to her left. It kept track of the time of day and told of the ungodsly early hour that usually found the woman sound asleep in her silk sheets.

Kitanah sat in the corner with her armored sleeve on her knees and her bare arm resting on top of the cold metal. She wiped at the tears that welled in the corners of her emerald green eyes.

She didn't know what to do. The General's lesson was... distasteful to say the least. The fact that it had happened several times now and with Ophelia of all people!

Doctor Efreeti's words from when he described Ophelia kept going through her mind, "While I made her unquestioningly devoted to the General, I did not make her so to the Al Razheem."

His voice repeated again and again. Kitanah had always considered the Al Razheem and the General synonymous. Now she wasn't so sure.

He'd never asked Kitanah to degrade herself like that before. Something about that girl's influence was, was... what? Corrupting the General? Surely, he could see past a long pair of legs and skimpy clothing? The General wasn't some typical man.

Was he? He started the Al Razheem! He personally recruited Kitanah into the family. He taught her every precept that defined her life! How could he reject the very ideas that made him and his family so great?

Every problem, every concern the assassin had landed at the feet of Ophelia. Kitanah felt herself bristle just having the other woman's name occur to her. But she had failed to show the General the danger the mewling calf was to the organization.

The ground vibrated and the water dripping from the clepsydrae stuttered, interrupting the steady flow of passing seconds, as well as Kitanah's increasingly poisonous thoughts. What had happened? The red haired woman forced herself up to her feet.

A moment later, a messenger rushed into the room. He already looked frazzled but when he stepped into the wide open room, the barely grown man froze mid step.

"What is it?" Kitanah hissed.

"M-Mistress," he couldn't make himself look at her, "there was an explosion in the General's oasis. We're under attack!"

The woman felt herself tense up. A knowing smirk fought to take its place upon her ruby red lips but she forced it down. It had to be the farmers. They had somehow found the keep.

But to blow a hole in a wall into the only part of the Oasis not under constant patrol... that denoted inside information. And that informant had to be Ophelia. Whatever plot she was a part of was happening now. That meant that now was Kitanah's chance to expose her duplicity and have Ophelia removed from her life once and for all!

"I will go down to the oasis and take control of the situation," she announced as she marched to exit through the same door which the messenger had entered, "Be a dear and dispose of that for me, will you?"

The woman motioned to the very spot the messenger had been staring since his arrival before stepping out into the hall. The corpse of a heavily muscled, red sash wearing member of the Al Razheem rested in a puddle of blood and *other* fluids on the stone floor.

Kitanah barked orders at passing assassins as she marched through the halls. None of them had ever even considered the possibility of coming under attack in their own sanctuary and the General's Second (soon to again be his First) needed them to focus their efforts.

She turned into the hallway that not only led into the oasis in the middle of the desert that Kitanah's beloved General created but was also the first place that she had met and instantly hated Ophelia. Reginald, one of the long list of assassins over which Kitanah commanded, rattled the gate with his free hand.

"Quick! Somebody get the key!" he hollered back down the hall, "We can take them out before the General even has to hear about this!"

Behind him were eight more assassins that Kitanah recognized as being in her command, all of them armed with curved scimitars. They started back down the hall to fulfill Reginald's wishes but stopped in place when they saw their commanding assassin standing at the opposite end.

"Idiots!" she snapped at them, "Buffoons! You will leave those gates shut! You know you cannot open them without express permission from our General!"

One by one, but in short order, each of the eight assassins quickly shifted to either side of the hall, pressing their backs against the cool stone, until four lined the distance between the General's Second and Reginald at the gate. This opened up the view of the violated oasis beyond the bars to Kitanah. And the large leather bladders that rested at the foot of the heavily barred gate.

"Let them stay... trapped... in..." Withermore's report about the farmers, particularly the woman, came to mind as Kitanah spoke, "Get out! Get out of there!"

Whipping her left arm forward, Kitanah's sleeve stretched and the hooks dug into Reginald's back. With a heaving pull, she pulled the man away from the gate just as flames ripped the metal bars apart.

The woman jumped to the side, pulling the nearest man standing against the wall down on top of her as she dropped onto the floor. Reginald's already dead body fell atop of the man on Kitanah as the shock wave of the explosion ripped scraps of the gate through the second man's torso rather than hers.

Even as the explosion subsided, the woman stayed still under the corpses. She heard men step into the hallway and she figured they had to be the ones that blew their way into the fortress.

The first man that she saw was old. Very old. But he was also flanked by over a dozen armed men. Judging from their unmatched armors, they were mercenaries.

Then a man in a long red coat stepped into view. He looked familiar but... he was supposed to be dead!

"Crichton..." Kitanah muttered under her breath.

None of the intruders heard her. They continued deeper into the keep, with the exception of two left at the end of the hallway.

One just happened to be standing so close to Kitanah hidden under the two dead bodies that she could reach out and touch his leg. Which made extracting herself and escaping all the more problematic.

The woman had to awkwardly stretch out her back to get to the dagger sheathed there without making the corpses serving as her hiding spot shift around noticeably. But when it finally came loose, the beginnings of a plan started to tack together in her mind.

Rearing her right hand back, Kitanah used her metal sleeve to push the bodies away from her. She made a show of it, too. The woman gasped for breath as she rolled onto her knees, giving the closest man her most pathetic look as if she was pleading for help.

Just as she expected, though, the heavily armored man turned toward her only to get a better position to swing his sword and kill her more efficiently. Any other way, his helmet and armor would have been a problem for Kitanah. But from this low angle, his helmet left the softest, most vital flesh wide open for her dagger as it leaped from her hand.

He dropped his weapon and groped for his neck. The dagger slipped through his airway, cutting off his warning to the other guard but the cuff of the metal sleeve was already lunging in his direction by the time the second guard noticed. It engulfed his head and continued until the hooks embedded themselves into the stone wall beyond.

It took a heavy grunt of effort from Kitanah to get the sleeve cuff to return, leaving deep gashes in the wall. She lifted herself to her feet, shaking the disembodied head of the second guard out of the sleeve. The process was both awkward and messy, the hooks not buried into the stone had lodged into the guard's head. It finally landed on the floor with a dull, squishy thud.

Even with as bold of an entrance as the farmers and Crichton had made, they were still going to have to rely on stealth to make their way deeper into the keep without attracting hundreds of assassins, all heavily armed, to their position.

That meant they would move slower than Kitanah, who had the opposite concern. She needed to get to the other side of the keep to rally the Al Razheem and ready a defense.

Crichton had to be the man in red from the last reports Kitanah received about the farmers. That meant that the little girl was his offspring. An impressive feat for a man who was supposed to have been dead longer than the child had been alive.

That also meant that their likeliest destination would be the dungeons. Crichton would have no idea that the cells no longer existed... would they?

Kitanah's emerald eyes opened wide as the realization came to her. Efreeti used the farmer's daughter as his prototype and was readying to use little Tilly as the next subject for his soul orb experiment that would make her nearly impossible to kill, like Ophelia.

Two enchanted assassins that just happened to have ties to the oh so helpful doctor? It was too much of a coincidence to ignore.

Kitanah rushed down the adjacent hallway in the opposite direction the intruders had gone. She knew the layout of the keep far better than even Crichton with his hopefully outdated intelligence.

She would warn the General and get enough Al Razheem stuffed into the hallway that held the entrance to Efreeti's lair that not even Ophelia could blink past all of them.

DEEPER INSIDE THE KEEP...

"This is the door that leads to the dungeons," Travus pointed down the hallway to the lone entrance mounted into either of the walls.

Their numbers dwindled down to ten, Travus, Perse, Alvin, Quisling and six mercenaries. The rest guarded what they hoped to be their way back out of the keep.

"Then what are we waiting for?" Alvin asked, "Let's get your girl and then we can get ours!"

Travus wrapped his hand around the handle of the door but did not pull it open. In fact, he stood motionless for far longer than anyone thought was normal before he shook his head.

"No. This is the only way out of the dungeons," he finally said, "We can't afford for all of us to get cornered down there."

Travus looked from one farmer to the other before focusing on Quisling, "Can you spare one of your men to go down with me while you continue on with them?"

The old mercenary nodded, "Todd. Go with Mr. Browder. Aid him, then retreat back to the oasis once he has found his daughter. Understood?"

The aforementioned soldier-for-hire stepped forward when his name was said. He was one of the lighter armored of the group, only wearing studded leather. He didn't have a helmet, either, but he did carry a sword on each hip, a bow over his shoulder with a quiver of arrows on his back, two daggers sheathed on belts wrapped around both his thighs and the handles of two more blades could be seen peeking out of the tops of his boots. He nodded his agreement and stepped away from the other mercenaries until he was leaning against the wall beside the door, just waiting for the Night Shield to pull it open.

Travus again looked over at Alvin and Perse, "Close this behind us and start after your daughter."

Perse frowned, "Don't you think we should at least wait here until you have Tilly?"

The Night Shield shook his head, "This is as far as I go. Tilly didn't ask to be part of this so I'm taking her straight out of here. You two have the harder job."

Perse wrapped her hands around her husband's thick forearm as they stood silently, "What do you mean?" she asked.

"Ophelia's been programmed to be one of the Al Razheem," Travus said, "Not only do you have to find her but then find a way to... persuade her to come back with you."

"We can be quite convincing when we want to be," the massive farmer smiled back, though there was no joy in the gesture.

"I'm sure you can," Travus sighed and turned his attention back to the door, "Good luck Perse, Alvin. I hope you get Ophelia back."

And with that, the man in the long red coat pulled the door open and he and Todd dove inside. The door closed behind them, just as instructed.

The logic was sound, at least to Travus. Any patrols that came by wouldn't immediately know that anyone had entered the dungeon and, if luck was with the Night Shield and the others, the guards would continue down the hall without a clue.

What greeted Travus and Todd, though, was not the dungeon. When the door closed, the torchlight from the hallway was cut off but the two men could still see each other as if it was midday and the weather was clear.

Looking around, the light came from what looked like a window off to the side. But outside was not the desert in the dead of night but in fact the midday sun hovering over the sand filled terrain of the desert. There was no way that much time had passed.

Even with all this light, neither man could make out any other part of the room. They couldn't see where the walls started, even around the very edges of the window. It seemed to simply be floating in the middle of blackness.

Travus turned back to the mercenary. "Something's not right. Let's get out of here."

He motioned back the way they had come but the door was gone. Todd scowled back at the Night Shield, pulling his bow from his shoulder.

"It looks like we've set off some kind of trap," his brown eyes narrowed as he scanned for anything that could be considered a target, "Do the Al Razheem have any kind of magicks that could do something like this?"

"I've never seen anything like this," feeling a shiver run through him, Travus endeavored to ignore the sensation by adjusting the leather on the grip of the sword in his hands, "Of course, it would help if I knew what *this* is."

"This, my good man, is my private residence into which you have trespassed in a most uncivil manner," a voice came from the shadows.

"Who's there?" Todd nocked an arrow and readied to shoot.

The two men suddenly felt the sensation as if they were moving but the window didn't change position at all. In fact, the only thing that did move was a marble table with a thin man standing beside it. While Travus and Todd didn't lift a foot, and the window still hung motionless to their right, the figure and the table came to be only steps away from them.

"Do you enter everyone's domiciles anticipating violence?" the unbelievably thin man said.

He was wearing a cloak made of tweed but he still looked little thicker than a skeleton. The white hair on his head only covered the back half and he had to round pieces of glass in front of his eyes tied together with what looked like wire that ran behind his ears.

"I came here looking for my daughter," Travus answered, raising his sword between him and the stranger.

"Your daughter? Your daughter..." The thin man's head tilted to the side, "I did overhear through the proverbial grapevine that the parents of the fair Ophelia were making their way here. Would you be they?"

Both men looked at each other for a brief moment. Neither could believe the question that was asked and they both wondered if he was making a joke of some kind.

"No, my daughter's name is Tilly, Tilly Browder," Travus answered back.

Todd looked insulted but he said nothing. He pulled back harder on the bow string so that the arrow would be loosed with more power behind it if the need arose.

"Ah, my apologies," the thin figure adjusted the circles of glass in front of his eyes, "You are both male specimens of your species. I have to admit a certain level of disinterest to look more thoroughly at the two of you.

"Although..." he continued, "The name Tilly does have an air of familiarity to it. If I recall correctly, she is to be the next subject of the procedure I developed."

"You're the one using the soul orbs to make assassins immortal," Travus felt a heavy dread fall over him when the realization hit.

The thin man tilted his head in the opposite direction until it was at an unnatural angle and would have been painful, if not fatal, to a normal human, "And how did you come to possess this knowledge?"

The Night Shield shook his head, "I have a better question. What use is there in making a child immortal?" he counter asked.

The white haired figure shrugged, "Apparently, the General feels she would be a resource to be exploited in his preferred trade. Or as a toy to play with that he wishes to not have outgrow his interests."

Travus had to tap down the rage that rushed over him at that answer. It wouldn't help to let his anger loose. Not yet, not when his daughter was still missing.

"I thought Ophelia was serving in that capacity for him," the Night Shield forced himself to sound collected.

"The General is a man of eclectic tastes," the not quite human stranger said, "Just as mortals do not enjoy ingesting the same meal back to back to back, the General does not like to slate his base urges with the same mates. I find it a waste of time, personally, but I am not one to judge."

Again, the paternal instinct to strangle the thin man had to be stifled. Out of the corner of his eye, Travus saw that the arm of the mercenary was starting to shake with the effort of keeping the arrow from launching at the target.

He rested a hand on Todd's shoulder to silently tell him to stand down. Travus still needed to find out where his daughter was and a dead body couldn't tell him that.

"What is the ultimate end of all this?" the Night Shield motioned to the darkness all around them, "I mean, an ageless harem would be nice and all but it seems a bit short sighted to me. Unless the General has gone through your procedure already."

The white haired man straightened up his head before shaking it, "He wanted a proof of concept first. That came in the form of Ophelia. Tilly, I believe she was meant to be used as leverage against... you. I suppose the General underestimated your resourcefulness and thought that you would not get here as quickly as you have," he smiled, the gesture only making him look more inhuman to the two men.

The stranger didn't even show the slightest hesitation at answering the questions posed to him by the Night Shield. That only helped reinforce the notion that Travus and Todd were indeed in a trap and were not expected to survive. What harm was there in sharing information with a dead man? Especially if answering his questions kept him where he was an easy target as long as possible.

Travus started scanning the darkness for any sign of pending attack. The thin man didn't move away from the table. He'd shown no sign of aggression at all during the entire conversation but neither man turned their back completely toward him as they anticipated whatever trap for them to spring.

"As I have answered all of your questions, perhaps you could answer mine?" the not quite human stranger said before waving his hand at Travus and Todd, "I appreciate that you are intruders into the keep but no Al Razheem will attack you in here. It is just us and it will remain so as long as I see a purpose to our discussion here."

"You didn't answer the last one," a leery Travus said, "Has the General undergone your procedure to become immortal?"

The thin man sighed, "Does turning your daughter against you sound like the plan of a man who does not fear death? I feel the answer is itself in the question. Now, answer mine."

That meant that the General was still mortal. That was good news.

"What question was that again?" the Night Shield remembered but he wasn't ready to let go of whatever leverage he had yet.

"How did you come to learn of my procedure?" the stranger asked without any sign of impatience, "Only a handful of humans know of the General's plot to turn those who serve him best into immortal beings. It is the closest those of your ilk can get to becoming, what is the term you use, a god? And only for those who prove their worth to him."

Travus weighed his options. If he told this... thing that was trying to pass as human about the Ferdinand being his source, he would also figure out that the leak of information was also plugged with Granger's death and there was no danger that anyone else would find out. That meant that both his and Todd's stay of execution would also be over.

"Ferdinand Malcolm de la Granger," the mercenary answered before Travus could speak again.

Travus heard the string of the bow again stretch to ready an arrow for shooting. This time, the projectile was aimed at the head of the Night Shield.

"This man stopped the Al Razheem assassin from killing him and then he and the farmers looking for that Ophelia woman interrogated the Ferdinand," Todd added.

Everything in Travus' posture, demeanor, the look in his eyes, even the way he was breathing was meant to convey to the mercenary how much of an idiot he had suddenly revealed himself to be. Everything short of saying it since Todd's likeliest reaction would be to shoot him.

"This would prove my usefulness to the General, right? Taking out the big head that planned the invasion of his castle?" the man with the bow asked the not quite human without looking away from his target.

The white haired man looked bored as he answered, "Considering that your own leader has already negotiated a price to thwart them, I doubt that you will curry much favor."

Quisling was planning to betray them? Everyone knew the chances of success, of finding and retrieving Ophelia and Tilly, were low but Travus thought he had won the mercenaries over to the high risk/high reward idea.

Admittedly, Travus had figured his chances of getting out with his little girl were better that the farmers. He also figured that they would likely rather die that leave without Ophelia.

He had been willing to let them die while he escaped with Tilly. Was there a tremendous difference between that and allowing them to be murdered by Quisling?

Travus cursed to himself when he decided that there was an immense difference. At least with Quisling's help, Alvin and Perse had a slim chance of succeeding at getting their daughter. With the old mercenary actively playing the role of turncoat they had none at all.

"You heard him," Travus turned and stared down Todd, his steel tipped arrow aimed directly between the eyes of the Night

Shield, "There's no reward waiting for you if you kill me. Why do you think Quisling didn't let you in on the deal? Because it was only for him. The rest of you are expendable."

The mercenary frowned, but he didn't immediately reject the other man's conclusion. Even as Todd calculated his own options, the thin man again spoke up.

"You had best mentally waddle to your decision now, bow-man," for the first time, his voice had an edge of irritation to it, "My patience is not infinite and I have to ready the various elements for the operation."

Another geyser of anger rushed through Travus, who took a sharp intake of breath to keep himself still. And with that still-ness, the trained interrogator inside the Night Shield noticed something. He learned that how a subject phrased an answer could be as important and sometimes more so than the answer itself.

Todd glared at the not quite human stranger before whipping the bow around to aim at the center of the tweed cloak, "You know our only option is to escape and try for your daughter again later, right?" the mercenary muttered at the Night Shield.

"Except that Tilly is near by," Travus kept his tone even and calm to keep the mercenary from attacking anyone as he looked over at the white haired man himself, "Isn't that right? That's why you mentioned preparing elements for the operation. You referred to it as a procedure while we were talking about the idea. Calling it an operation means that you are about to physically go through with it."

"Ah!" the unnaturally thin raised a hand to his narrow chest, "Hoisted upon the petard of my own words!" he practically sang with melodrama.

"Where is she then?" Todd scowled at the man in tweed.

"She's somewhere in this room," he chuckled back.

"Very funny," the man with the bow growled, "I'll make things simple for you–"

Travus tried to speak up to protest but Todd simply spoke louder to drown him out.

"Either give us the girl or I kill you and we find the girl anyway," he finished.

"That is a bold ultimatum, young man," the not quite human smirked back, looking as if the lower part of his face was completely separate from the top, "Especially considering that you do not know where it is you currently stand."

"Right now it's in easy picking range right in front of a target."

"Perhaps a non-subjective perspective on your situation will aid you in your decision making process," the man in tweed spoke as if he was discussing some mathematical equation rather than trying to save his own life, "I refuse to give you the little girl. You have noticed that this room is not what, from your perspective, would call normal. From where did you come in? How, pray tell, can you get out? And did you notice that the terrain outside the window has changed?"

The not quite human stranger motioned to the frameless window to his left. What had been the desert at the wrong time of day was now a snowy mountain peak, the clouds made it hard to tell what time it was supposed to be but it was still too bright to be the predawn hours that it was currently.

"Is that supposed to mean something?" Todd's eyes narrowed at the thin man.

"It means that this place is no longer connected to the Oasis," the stranger answered, "At least for the time being."

"That's impossible, we entered here from the keep!" the mercenary protested, pulled back harder on the nocked arrow, "What kind of game are you playing here?"

Again, irritation formed over the not quite human stranger's face, "It means that, if you are going to kill me just get it over with. But first..."

The thin man turned and reached for something behind him on the table. For a fleeting moment, Travus hoped it was going to be his daughter. Not realistic, he knew, but it was still a hope.

It turned out to be a long top hat with a red band around the base. The thin man placed it on his head, eliciting a quiet pop from it with a quick slap to the crown to show the action was finished.

"I have always felt that one should look their best before the end," the not quite human smiled broadly at the mercenary, "It is a shame that I cannot offer you a comb, or at least a wash cloth."

"Wait! We still don't know where Tilly is!" Travus protested, reaching out for the shaft of the arrow.

Before Travus could reach the weapon, the mercenary let the arrow fly. From this range, the arrow shot through the thin man and continued into the darkness beyond.

It took a few seconds before his body reacted to being shot and the man in tweed slumped back onto the marble table. He slouched forward, his hat hiding any reaction he might have had. It was as if he simply had poor posture, but his chest didn't make any of the familiar motions that came with breathing.

"You heard him," Todd faced Travus as his slipped the bow back over his shoulder, "She's somewhere in here. He wasn't going to help us so we'll find her on our own and get out."

The Night Shield didn't bother to hide his anger anymore, "And how do you expect to find her in a black room that doesn't have any walls or doors? He was the only one that knew how to maneuver around in here and you killed him before I could figure out how he did it!" Travus stomped over to the man slouched on the table and shoved at one of his narrow shoulders.

The tweed cloak collapsed into a pile of empty cloth on the marble table, the top hat spinning around as it landed on the flat stone before coming to a rest just short of the edge. Travus looked back at Todd. Both men were equally shocked.

Equally, that is, until an arrow suddenly struck the mercenary in the back. Then it was safe to say that his shock at the situation was greater.

Todd dropped to his knees. He tried in vain to reach back for the shaft that had, judging from its position, impaled his heart. It took only seconds for him to fall to the floor, lifeless.

Travus stood in the exceptionally empty room all alone. He rested both hands on the table, going through what just occurred in his head, trying to make sense of it all.

"That is the trouble with soldiers-for-hire," the disembodied voice of the inhuman stranger came through the air, "If violence doesn't solve the problem, they'd rather exacerbate the situation until it becomes the only option."

The Night Shield scanned the darkness all around him for any sign of the thin man, "How are you still alive?" he asked.

"Oh, it was merely a simple sleight-of-hand," the voice answered, "As you may have guessed, that was not my standard form. I simply shed it as easily as you would have shed the cloak before Todd released himself from this mortal coil."

Travus cocked an eyebrow, "Released himself?"

"Look at the arrow that killed him. It matches the others in his quiver, does it not?" the voice sounded on the edge of giggling.

Unable to see any trace of the not-at-all human stranger, Travus knelt down beside the dead mercenary and inspected the arrow that served the kill shot. It hit the small space between the edge of the leather quiver and Todd's shoulder blade, sinking between his ribs and straight into his heart, just as the Night Shield thought.

Pulling an arrow from the quiver, Travus inspected all the way from the sharpened head down the the nocking point at the base. The feathers that served as the fletching for the arrows, that kept the flight of the weapon straight and true, did indeed match the one in his back.

Straightening back up onto his feet, the Night Shield looked around aimlessly as he again spoke, "But how did he kill himself if he fired in the opposite direction that the arrow came from?"

"That is another question you answered yourself," the inhuman stranger's voice said, "There are no walls here. It simply continued on its way until it found something to strike."

"Without help changing direction?" Travus let the skepticism layer his words nice and thick.

"None. It simply continued on its natural trajectory," the voice answered, "I have to say that I am impressed by his marksmanship."

"So what you are saying is that this isn't a room as much as an entire world and that arrow just flew around it?" the Night Shield couldn't believe he was letting the words out of his mouth.

"Precisely. That is why you are still alive to converse, Mr. Browder," for the first time a hint of motion could be seen coming from behind the floating window, "You are far more clever than that dullard at your feet."

"But I came here to stop you from performing your soul orb procedure on my daughter," Travus focused on the movement, as it was still too vague to call even a shadow yet, "Why keep me alive at all?"

"Because you did not come to stop my operation. You came to retrieve Tilly," the source of the voice came closer as the inhuman stranger continued to speak, "I made my qualms known to the General that she was not my idea of an ideal candidate. With you in custody, it is likely that he will no longer need her and I can move on to a more meriting subject to become my next art in potentia."

"With me in custody?" Travus watched the shadow of the formerly thin man come closer and closer, a primal fear screaming at the back of his mind threatened to steal the organization of his thoughts and made speaking more and more challenging, "Wouldn't killing me solve all those problems in one fell swoop?"

Out of the shadows stepped a creature that was in every way a monster to the human. It was easily eight feet tall and that was before taking into account the two long gnarled horns that stretched from its head. They went one direction than another, like two rivers that had trouble keeping within their banks, with holes that Travus could fit his fists through. Still, they ended in sharp points that could rip through the meat and sinew of a mortal body.

Its eyes were beady, glowing red. The human had a feeling that the round pieces of glass merely obscured those back when the stranger was in its facade. There were no eyebrows above and no nose below the red beads. But that inhuman smile was still on its face, stretching unnaturally wide from one cheek to the other.

Fur grew down the thing's forearms, ending just at the wrists so that movement of the fingers with those black, curled claws would remain unobstructed. The same for its shins, the claws lightly scraping against the floor as it stepped forward.

"You are too welcoming of death now," the monster, its voice still as calm and pleasant as when it was masquerading as human, said, "I'd say that you have some kind of contingency plan that insures that even if you cannot attain your goal, the Al Razheem will be in real danger of being destroyed, yes?"

Travus didn't answer.

The creature turned to look out the window before again facing the human, "As we have some time before the Oasis comes back into synchronization, shall we have a conversation? We can speak of soul orbs, Ophelia and chocolate sauce. These are but a few of my favorite things."

It wasn't difficult for Travus to let the sword fall from his hand. His grip was tenuous on the weapon already as his nerves worked overtime.

"Okay then. Let's have a conversation."

To The General

Once she reached the top floor, Kitanah stomped past fellow assassins that gave her stranger and stranger looks as she walked. Her annoyance built with every look but she didn't have time to stop and discipline them while an emergency was befalling the Oasis, their home.

She marched straight to the General's quarters. The door was wide open as fellow Al Razheem rushed in and out to give their leader reports and then deliver his responses and orders.

Stepping into the doorway, ten scimitars suddenly found their way to her face to stop her from taking another step deeper inside. "I have to speak to the General. I have news he needs to hear!"

The swords fell away from the woman and the General came into view behind his desk. He motioned for Kitanah to come to him and she felt a wave of relief wash through her body as she closed the distance between them.

It wasn't until her thighs touched the edge of the flat stone surface that she noticed Ophelia standing with her sword drawn in the small space between the heavy bookcase and the wall. She was obviously meant to be their leader's last line of defense if the worse came to pass.

"Sire, I have encountered the enemy," Kitanah started her report before even being asked, "They used leather bladders full of some kind of explosive to breach your oasis. The explosion killed all the others, including Reginald. I barely escaped but I did see who they were. There were twenty mercenaries led by an old man, a gigantic man and a woman with brown and gray striped hair," the assassin's green eyes darted over to Ophelia to see if that stirred up any kind of reaction, "and, I know this will sound impossible, but it appeared that Travus Crichton was with them as well."

That last piece of news caused the General to straighten up in his seat.

"I believe they are headed for Efreeti's lair, Sire," Kitanah continued their report, "Either they think the girl is in where the dungeons used to be or they are rendezvousing with Efreeti to fulfill whatever machinations he may have."

The bearded man nodded as he took the information in. His mouth moved as he considered the words of his Second but he didn't say anything.

Kitanah struggled to stay at attention in front of his desk. She could feel herself shaking as she awaited word of whatever her part was to be in her patriarch's plan to counter the offensive against their family. After a few moments, though, the General looked up at her quizzically.

"Sire?" Kitanah asked, "What's wrong? I'm simply awaiting your next order."

The General rose from his desk. Stepping around it, he stepped up to the red haired woman. Again, his mouth was moving but no words came out. It wasn't until he snapped his fingers in front of her face that Kitanah realized what was happening.

"I can't hear," shock washed through her body and the older man kept her from tumbling to the ground.

Kitanah rested her head on the General's broad shoulder as he pulled her around to his chair. He bellowed for his personal doctor, the woman felt his chest stiffen, but what she heard of the command was barely a whisper.

It was only once she was sitting down that Kitanah realized how drained she suddenly felt. Even having a shield, the explosion had taken its toll on her.

The doctor arrived, wearing the same white mask that always concealed his eyes and nose. The idea was so that no one would know which of the corps of physicians under employ by the Al Razheem served their leader directly. That way they could not use the healer as a pawn in any kind of conspiracy against the General. Until this moment, the long pointed nose and the bejeweled edges of the mask had always given Kitanah a cause to chuckle. But not now.

After he turned her head from one side to the other, the woman thought she heard the words "ruptured eardrums". When she also heard the word "temporary", Kitanah breathed a sigh of relief.

The General wagged a finger at Ophelia, who obediently came up to him. Then he turned back to Kitanah, gently wrapping her chin with one hand.

"Supernal one, which way are they coming from?" his voice was gentle in tone but he spoke loudly to make sure she could hear.

"The quickest way from Efreeti's would be to go through the pens," Kitanah answered, "They are leaving guards to protect the way back to the oasis so I came up here through the servants' quarters."

"Excellent. Smart girl," the General nodded, "Ophelia take a company and go back the way Kitanah came to flank their support and kill them all on your way to Efreeti. Protect him only if his loyalty remains with us. Understood?"

"Of course, Master," Ophelia bowed and started for the door, motioning to several of the guards to follow her along the way.

Once she was gone, Kitanah spoke up, "Sire, if Efreeti is with Crichton, Ophelia may be as well. We can't trust her to stop them."

"I understand your concern, girl, but you know me better than that," he gave her shoulder a soft pat, "You are in no condition to fight so who do you trust to lead a company down through the pens to intercept Ophelia's parents?"

Kitanah didn't even try to hide her surprise that her patriarch knew who the intruders actually were.

"The old man you referred to," the General grinned down at her, "He warned me of this attack. He also mentioned that they were likely to split up. Ophelia will kill Crichton and your man will kill the farmers before they even get a chance to regroup. Who do you trust, girl?"

She looked around the room. One figure literally stood out among the rest. He was nearly as big as Ophelia's father. It was only after the arrival of the tattooed assassin that she'd come to appreciate that amount of muscle so intimately. Not only did it help pass long nights but, as he practically begged to share her bed, it also assured his loyalty.

The man now served as her First. The helmet he wore hid his short stubble of black hair and only gave a peek at his dark brown skin when he opened his mouth to speak and his chin dipped below the bottom edge. He had made the armorers work day and night to make plate mail that could actually fit him. Now he diligently stood guard beside the door.

"Hinder. He's the one that should go after the farmers. He may be the only one that can match that man's strength."

Again the General nodded, "Hinder, take a company down to the animal pens and kill the intruders. You are the main line of defense keeping them from getting here, lad. Show no mercy!"

"Yes, sir," the massive assassin nodded and started for the door. Half of the remaining guards followed him without a word.

Between him, Ophelia's company, the wargs, and the hell hounds. It was likely that this invasion was going to be over before there was any real risk to the General.

That is, assuming Ophelia's loyalties were indeed with the Al Razheem. And that she wasn't a tool of Doctor Efreeti herself. Otherwise, this situation was about to get a lot more complicated...

TWELVE

REUNION

"THESE GUYS WERE professionals?" Ophelia's voice had an air of disappointment to it.

The last of the mercenaries that stood guard, in this case at the intersection of the hallway that led to the entryway for Doctor Efreeti's living quarters, fell by Havarti's blade. He vibrated hard enough to shake the blood off his metal surface.

"Why could we not simply have taken them captive again?" the sword again protested in her mind.

Ophelia scowled, "The General ordered them all to be killed."

She didn't say it vocally, as Havarti's sentience wasn't common knowledge and Ophelia didn't need a reputation for arguing with herself. Their relationship had pretty much started in her head anyway, so telepathic communication was hardly unusual between them.

The assassins trailing behind her now numbered over a dozen. Most of them joined her company as she made her way down from the top floor.

Ophelia knew that many of them spread stories about her in the halls. Some referred to her as the "blinking horror", at least the few who had witnessed her ability to teleport out of the path of danger started calling her that and the name spread.

Whether it was an extolment of her abilities in battle or a mockery of the woman, it didn't fundamentally matter. She had killed enough of the General's enemies to attain the rank of his First Bravo, the one that he trusted above all others.

The assassins were all willing to fight and defend their home. Seeing whether or not the "blinking horror" lived up to her reputation was simply a bonus to them.

Ophelia motioned half of the group to fill the hall on one side of the door while the other blocked off the other side. The woman stood before the door, debating whether to try the handle or if she should just kick it in.

The former would be silent, likely keeping any of the invaders from realizing they were now not only being hunted but cornered. The latter was far more dramatic. Likely more fun, too.

She came to her decision and Havarti let out a quiet sigh that was partly annoyance but also a large part of amusement. Ophelia reared back to slam her boot against the doorjamb.

Just as the woman started forward, the door pulled open to reveal Doctor Efreeti. Ophelia didn't stop herself as much as force herself to spin off to the side to be caught by a lightly armored Al Razheem she thought was named Paddling.

"Oh my," the thin man in tweed chuckled, "I'm afraid I interrupted what would have likely been a truly spectacular rescue."

Ophelia straightened herself up, slipping Havarti back into his scabbard, "We were told that the intruders were heading this way."

"Indeed they did. Although only one saw fit to stay," Doctor Efreeti nodded as he pulled a man in a long red coat out of the darkness beyond the threshold of the doorway, "Technically, there were two but only one that survived. I only say this out of the interest of clarity, of course."

"Of course," Ophelia shook her head, letting out a quiet chuckle of her own as she stepped up to the newest arrival into the hall, "And who is this, Doctor?"

"His name is Travus Browder, milady," he answered, letting his clawed hand slip from the man's shoulder, "Apparently, he was the mastermind of this particular operation. Although his part in the plan only involved him taking young Tilly from our midst."

"Tilly?" Ophelia cocked an eyebrow... then had to hide the sudden twisting in her stomach as her memory didn't fail, "The little girl I brought a couple of weeks ago."

"You *are* the one who killed my wife," the man in the long red coat spoke up for the first time, his face flushing to match the color of his coat.

Efreeti hadn't restrained the man and now he took advantage of that fact. He punched Ophelia across her jaw with his left hand, causing her to upper body to twist away. The handle to her sword was easy to reach after that. He snatched the handle of the bastard sword and pulled.

Ophelia slapped her hand down on the cross-guard, not letting Havarti out of his scabbard. But the grip separated and Travus had the dagger concealed in the sword now in his hand.

The woman turned back to face Browder, the side of her chin turning dark pink. Over the man's shoulder, she saw Efreeti staring the man down angrily but not making any motion to stop him.

Paddling stepped between Ophelia and her attacker, swinging with both hands to lop Browder's head from his shoulders. Both hands were on the handle of his long sword to put maximum power into the strike.

Unfortunately, that also left his torso open. And Travus took full advantage. All he had to do was duck and shove the short blade into the young assassin's heart, not difficult considering the light leather the red sash wearing member of the Al Razheem wore.

Then he shoved the dying man into the rest of the group behind Ophelia to keep them from stopping his next move. The dagger and Browder's hand were drenched in Paddling's blood and it thrust for straight between Ophelia's breasts.

Both the woman and her creator had smirks stretch across their faces when they saw the man's intent, "Come on, then! Take your best shot!" Ophelia yelled.

Just as the tip of the blade was to slip through the fabric of the assassin's white top, she disappeared. The purple silhouette left behind was scattered as Browder's body rushed through where Ophelia stood just the moment before.

The woman rematerialized beside the man. She reared back then slammed the edge of her buckler into the side of his head.

Travus tumbled, his head slamming into the stone wall. He fell flat onto his rear but, after a quick shake of his head, he glared back up in Ophelia's direction.

"Blinking whore," he muttered and whipped his leg around to take the woman's out from under her.

Muscle memory saved her from the fall. Her hands found the stone floor and pushed her up into a quick back flip. Her heel slammed into the groin of the unluckiest assassin still pinned under the body of the now dead Paddling.

Even as that man let out loud groans of pain and last night's dinner, Ophelia freed Havarti from his scabbard, "Kind of hard to be a hero when you're dead, isn't it?"

The blade of the bastard sword started for the prone man's throat. Travus was just able to avoid Ophelia's first strike by pushing himself back until his head and shoulders were flush against the wall.

As her blade started its return trip, Travus rushed to get the next words out of his mouth.

"If you kill me, the General will have to be buried in the next grave over!" his brown eyes closed tight as the blade kept coming, "Just ask him about Travus Crichton if you don't believe me!"

When Browder didn't feel himself die, he risked opening one eye up. Ophelia wrenched the dagger from his hand and the blood fell from the weapon like a grisly little rainstorm.

She clapped the now clean smaller blade into the handle of the larger and stared down at him. If her pale blue eyes had been knives, Travus was sure that he'd have been in very small bloody pieces.

"Put him in irons," Ophelia's voice radiated a frustration that rushed through her entire body, "We'll take him to the General."

As assassins swarmed around the man in red, Ophelia started further down the hallway toward the animal pens rather back the way from which they had come. No one argued with her choice as they fell in line behind her with four men surrounding Travus, his arms and legs both wrapped in lengths of chain to keep him from being able to fight again.

"Why didn't you kill him, my dear?" Havarti's voice came into her head again, "Was that not what your General ordered?"

"If killing this Travus guy means that it would kill the General too, I can't let that happen," Ophelia replied telepathically, "The General will be able to figure out if he's bluffing or not so don't think you've gotten out of your job yet, either."

THE ANIMAL PENS

Alvin put a finger to his mouth as he opened the door. This room was supposed to lead into the warg pens. According to Travus what made them particularly dangerous was that the wargers, the men who shared some kind of link with the canine beasts, slept in each stall alongside their animal.

If the farmers and mercenaries were heard by the men, the wargers could release the beasts as well as fight themselves. For every man awakened, they would have two more enemies to fight in order to continue on.

Quisling left two more men outside the room to guard their escape route, leaving himself and the last three mercenaries alongside Alvin and Perse. As they quietly closed the door behind them, the group was finally able to take a good look at what lay ahead of them.

The Night Shield was wise to warn them. It was less of a room and more of a wide open chamber that filled out a good portion of what would have been roughly the center of the keep. It was also three stories tall and wide open with the newly arrived group on the second (that put the lowest level underground).

Above them was all open with the exception of some scaffolding and ropes tied up into some complex network of which none of them could make any sense. The pens were obviously below and all that stood between the invaders and the far side of the area were a series of bridges that ran along the tops of the walls that separated one open top pen from another.

They looked to see if there were walkways along the outermost walls. That way they could minimize their chances of exposing their presence to as few assassins and wargs as possible. Unfortunately, there were only the ones between the pens.

Any loud noise during their walk would be easily detected from below. At this time, it was so early in the morning that most would still describe it as the middle of the night, even nocturnal animals would be concentrating more on finding a comfortable spot to rest rather than scanning their surroundings for threats, particularly above them. That was the hope, anyway.

Perse started for the closest bridge, only to have her husband wrap his hand all the way around her shoulder to the nape of her neck. He shook his head and gently pulled her back. Her eyebrows pressed together at him. He shrugged. She pushed out her lower lip and he pointed at his own hazel eyes.

Perse finally let out a quiet huff and let him go ahead. His logic was sound. If he was able to get by without being seen, it was likely that all of them could get by. If he was spotted, he could at least hold their pursuers off long enough for the rest of them to get out. And that was if he just stood there without fighting.

Alvin's steps, particularly with him still lugging a heavy bag of drake oil over one shoulder, were remarkably light. The feat was even more amazing to his wife since he never made stealth much of a priority when he walked. He didn't even tip toe around during nap time when Ophelia was a baby.

The fact that the wood that made up the bridge was well maintained helped. It was polished with some kind of lacquer that kept the boards shining and the ropes tying them together were fresh. That kept them from creaking or making any other noise. But still, Alvin didn't just let his boots stomp and test the material's tolerance so... good for him.

He passed the first set of stalls without raising an alarm. Standing in the middle of the four way intersection of bridges, the farmer turned back toward Perse. She took her turn to start after him.

Looking down the right side of the bridge, the woman saw a man sleeping in a bed that was made with a straw mattress. A wolf, nearly twice as large as one she had ever seen before, slept curled up on the bottom end of it.

If she hadn't know that the man was an assassin and more than willing to kill her if she were noticed, the woman would have almost described the scene as touching. But the muzzle with the metal mask sculpted to look like a nightmarish version of the beast and the curved sword resting in the opposite corner spoiled the illusion.

Perse expected to see something similar on the left side but found a very different sight. Bones were lain about the packed ground and there was no sign of a bed that a warger would use at all. In the farthest wall, there was actually an opening to a small cave. The woman found herself wondering what, if not a warg, could possibly be in there.

Quisling started after the woman before she was even halfway across. His eyes locked on her back as she walked while his hands rested, wrapped around the grip of his sword on one hip and the handle of his dagger on the other.

The farm woman, of course, reached the intersection first. Her husband faced the old mercenary as he closed the distance. Quisling frowned as he stepped up beside them, turning his attention to the stalls below.

"Browder aforesaid that the Al Razheem exclusively bred wargs here," the old man gruffly whispered, "There is a least one other kind of animal amongst these pens. Perhaps more."

"What difference does it make?" Perse whispered back, "We can't let any of them see us anyway."

"The difference, my lady," Quisling answered, "is that there are animals with even finer tracking skills than the wolves that are trained to become wargs. If any of them are here, we could not help but be detected."

"They haven't seen or smelled us yet," Alvin's baritone voice softly interjected before he motioned for the other two to keep moving, "Let's not linger around to give them a chance."

There was only enough room at the intersection for the three of them, particularly since Alvin himself took up so much space (or the fact that the load he carried wasn't one they wanted to crowd around) so the remaining three soldiers-for-hire waited to start on their way across the bridges until the farmers and Quisling reached the second cross way. If they had been paid for their ability to move soundlessly, they would have been compensated handsomely.

The farmers and their tag-along past three more pens without incident. Always with Alvin going first and then watching his wife and the old man follow. Four more sections of stalls laid ahead of them before they were in the halls that led to the living quarters of the Al Razheem assassins, including those of their General.

Just as Alvin started across the next bridge the doors on the far side opened. Man after man spilled into the chamber, most of them wearing purple sashes and at least half of them carrying bows.

Last to come in was a man as large as Alvin. The farmer hoped that the plate mail armor he wore only gave the illusion that the man was that massive but he doubted it.

Not only the farmers but the mercenaries all froze where they stood on the two subsequent bridges. Each of the professional soldiers' eyes moved to the doorway behind them, calculating their chances of escape while the farmers looked ahead.

"Archers!" the big man in armor bellowed, "Fire at will!"

Alvin turned back and ran for his wife, tackling her down to the slatted wood of the bridge. His broad back completely blocked out everything above her as the thunks of metal arrow heads burying themselves into the wood all around them filled the woman's ears.

A few seconds later, an acrid, sour smell started to fill her nostrils. After the barrage of arrows stopped, Alvin lifted himself up to his knees. Perse sat up in front of him and that was when she noticed that his back and arms were completely drenched in drake gland oil.

Every arrow that would have struck her husband's muscular back instead embedded themselves in the leather bladder, causing the caustic liquid to trickle out. If it hadn't been thickened with the dried hops, the bladder would have sprayed its contents like a fountain and already be empty, coating both husband and wife, rather than slowly dribbling and just starting to slump against the farmer's back.

"Retreat!" Quisling drew his sword and waved back at his remaining mercenaries.

One lay on the bridge, filled with so many arrows that there was no way he was still alive. The other two started to obey the old man's order as best they could, although the one with an arrow through his knee struggled to keep up with the other whose arms hung uselessly with two and three arrows in each respectively.

"Cut them off!" the big assassin in heavy armor ordered.

Four assassins lit the ends of their arrows aflame and loosed them in a high arc into the air. They weaved their ways through the ropes, one actually catching fire as one shaft passed, and landed at the end of the bridge closest to the door through which they had entered.

The lacquer in the wood acted like ignition fluid and the bridge was quickly engulfed in flames none of them could get over. Still, it wasn't like there weren't other bridges…

"Infantry, you heard me, cut them off!" the armored man again bellowed.

Assassins charged down the four closest bridges toward the intruders. Unconcerned with stealth they quickly overtook every one of their targets.

Alvin knocked the first to come within arm reach over the side of the bridge with a single backhand. A howl that stood up the hairs on the back of the necks of everyone that heard it erupted from the pit closest to the newly burning fire.

It didn't sound like any kind of wolf the farmers were familiar with. No, it came from the other stall. The one with the bones.

A series of growls and yowling, as if whatever the creature was, it was speaking some kind of unearthly language, came from the pen along with scratching noises and what sounded like falling rock.

Finally, a black... it looked like a human hand except it was obsidian black, gripped the edge of the bridge, just beyond where it was burning. What followed after the hand, though, was decidedly not human.

The farmers couldn't decide if its eight foot long body looked more canine or like a panther. It had six tails whipping this way and that as it bound away from the flames on four paws that looked like human hands, only lacking thumbs.

The creature's eyes reminded Perse of a cat she had when she was a child but it had a long, canine looking snout, complete with the wet black nose. A mane of greasy hair, that had a color much like fresh bruise flaring on thin skin, spilled from the crown of its head, down along its neck to just between its shoulder blades.

It lunged straight for the mercenary who couldn't even raise his arms to defend himself. Its teeth ripped at the man's leather armor, exposing the pale flesh below before biting into his gut. It didn't kill the human but he screamed with such a searing mix pain and terror that it echoed through the chamber.

"A hell hound is loose!" an assassin in a red sash stopped just out of the massive farmer's reach when the thing came into view.

He looked as if he was ready to drop his sword and cower behind the shield hanging on his arm in fright. Neither Alvin nor Perse had ever heard of a hell hound and, seeing one, felt they knew too much about the thing already. They didn't want to learn any more.

As shocked as the infantry assassin was at the sight of the beast, the one just behind him powered through the fear and continued for the massive farmer. There was no space for Alvin to dodge. He readied himself for the coming cut, he just hoped he could get the attacker to hit somewhere non vital.

Quisling's blade knocked the charging assassin's scimitar away from the massive man, then proceeded to sever the attacking assassin's throat. He fell over the side of the bridge and the howl of a wolf thankful for the carnivorous equivalent of manna from heaven came up from the pit.

"Not even *your* meat hooks can stand up against a good swordsman, boy," the old mercenary growled at the farmer, "Now you two better figure a way out of here for all of us. Your daughter be damned!"

The gray haired soldier-for-hire glared back at Perse for a quick moment before striking down the shocked assassin and continuing down that bridge toward the next oncoming group.

"He's right. We need to figure out a way out," Perse said as her husband pulled her up to her feet without so much as a grunt of effort, "To get to Ophelia."

She took a turn to glare at Quisling's back as he fought. Another sickening scream came from behind the woman and she realized that meant that there was nobody left between them and the hell hound that clawed its way up onto the bridge.

The second man tried to come to the defense of his armless compatriot. The hell hound wrapped the long digits of its forepaw around the sword arm of the mercenary with the wounded knee. It didn't take much effort to pull him off balance and make him fall down onto the bridge.

It did take a special effort, however, to position the man's elbow at just the right position against the edge of the slatted wood to snap it back so hard it bent back in the opposite direction that nature had designed. The mercenary's sword clattered into the pen below and the beast stomped the human's other arm, snapping the bone hiding under the bicep in half.

Then it flipped the soldier-for-hire onto his stomach and chewed on the hamstring of his unscathed leg until it severed apart, leaving the man so that he couldn't move from that spot. The hell hound was going to eat well today but at its leisure. It wasn't hungry just yet...

Its nose found a new scent, that of another human but different. Female. The beast had not had one of those in some time.

The man the animal had gutted groaned, his voice getting weaker and weaker with each utterance. The newly resting piece of meat the hell hound had just prepped for storage whimpered. But it was already moving on.

Alvin snatched the metal shield from the corpse of the assassin that was overcome with fear. "Our only chance is a hard charge before they launch another volley of arrows at us." He looked back over at his wife as he slipped the shield onto his own arm.

Perse nodded, consciously making an effort not to look back over her shoulder. The farm woman did pull a small vial from one of the pouches around her waist. Pulling the cork, she dumped the contents behind her. Little gel-like crystals scattered onto the polished wood and she tossed the empty container away.

Taking a deep breath, the woman turned to her husband and rested either hand on his hips. Giving him a light slap in the side, he started forward using himself as the human shield/battering ram.

The shield that covered a large portion of the man it previously belonged to barely covered most of Alvin's torso. At least now he had a way to block the curved blades that each and every assassin seemed to carry.

Perse struggled to keep up, that is until Alvin hit the three assassins that tried to stop him at the end of the network of bridges. He started swinging his thick arms around like a mad man, knocking even more men away from the couple.

While her husband fought to make a path to the door, the woman looked back to the bridges. The hell hound reached the intersection where Perse had dumped the crystals. It stopped, practically mid-step, just as she had hoped.

The beast sniffed at the ground, then let out a retch of disgust at the smell of the crystallized herb, rue, it found in front of it. Instead of pouncing forward, as it had intended, the black fur covered animal turned and sped along down the same bridge the old man fought along.

"Perse, get back!" Alvin's voice snapped her attention forward again.

Her husband raised the metal shield over his head as the equally massive armored assassin joined the fight, bringing his sword down on Alvin with both hands.

It hit the shield, sounding like a cathedral bell tolling, and even dented the defensive piece of metal. The farmer had to step back to brace himself or he would have easily fallen over.

The armored assassin reared back for another strike. Alvin didn't let him have it that time. Instead the farmer dashed forward and tackled the equally large man to the ground, flat onto his back. The simple farmer straddled the professional killer's broad chest, pinning him down.

When the Al Razheem tried to swing his sword to get the other man off of him, Alvin used the bent piece of metal that had been a shield to slap it out of the other man's hand. Twisting like that, though, whipped the bag of drake oil hanging on his back forward and pulled the farmer to the side.

The assassin took advantage, pushing the man even further off balance and then rolling away himself. He scrambled onto his feet, lifting his hands and readying himself to fight without a weapon.

Alvin let the strap keeping the leather bladder on him slip from his shoulder as he stood up. His attention darted to his wife, who blew a powdered mixture into the faces of a group of assassin who were rushing to the aid of their armored leader. They all stumbled back, so blind that one even tumbled down into the pen below.

Then he set his focus fully on the armored assassin. Even with the metal covering his opponent's body, Alvin couldn't help but smile. Hand to hand just happened to be his specialty. Although what happened next did surprise him.

"I am Hinder, First Bravo of the elegant Kitanah Baynette," the assassin said, his voice nearing cordial in tone, "What is your name, that I may properly honor you as the next sacrifice to my goddess?"

Alvin scowled at the other man. He couldn't believe what he was hearing. Finally, though, the farmer shook his head.

"The only thing you need to know about me is that you are keeping me away from my daughter," his hands balled up into mammoth fists, "And I will not let that stand any longer!"

Alvin stepped forward and slammed his hand across Hinder's face, his helmet tumbling off and down into the stall below from the force of the attack. The other hand flew up and smashed into the assassin's chin, whipping his head straight up. It would have looked as if Hinder was getting up on his own if his eyes weren't spinning around faster than that of a dizzy man.

He stumbled back, the armored man's massive arms wrapping around either side of his head. Hinder glared between his gauntlets at the farmer, rage quickly replacing the disorientation that came from the attack.

"You have no honor," the assassin grumbled as he and the farmer circled each other.

"I don't care about honor. I care–" he had to duck to avoid Hinder's steel glove enhanced punch.

The farmer opened his hands (hitting where he was aiming with fists would have only broken his own knuckles) and repeatedly slammed the heels of his palms into the metal covered abdomen of the assassin, hitting so hard that the armor dented and pressed harder and harder against the vulnerable skin underneath.

Hinder smashed his elbows into Alvin's broad back but the farmer didn't go down. He simply wrapped his thick arms around the assassin's waist, burying his face into the blue sash hanging there.

Then he straightened up, intent on throwing his opponent into the pit below. Hinder, though, twisted around and both men tumbled to the ground. Again, Alvin found himself atop the assassin.

This time, the farmer dropped his forearm onto Hinder's throat with his whole body weight behind it, "I care about my daughter and I swear in holy Juna's name, I am getting her back from you monsters," he declared.

Hinder died only seconds later, his windpipe crushed. Not that Alvin cared what kind of response the man would have had. As he finally straightened up, the man thought he might have a moment to recover but he saw his wife rushing for the door that led deeper into the keep... and the four men chasing after her.

Before Alvin could even get up to one knee, the black hell hound burst through the pursuing assassins and they tumbled to the ground in four separate heaps. It lunged for his wife and its teeth ripped through Perse's long skirt, just missing the back of her thigh.

It tore the fabric away as its long fingered paws again found the packed earth. Perse fell and rolled on the ground, curving away from the doorway and back toward the pens.

The beast spat the meatless mouthful out and lifted its nose. It picked up the sweet smell of the woman's sweat. She was afraid. It could tell. That only served to make the meat all the more succulent.

He also sensed... a drake? No, the scent was off. It reeked of drake spittle. Surely whatever that happened to be was already soured. That was of no interest to it. So it again lunged for the sweet smell of the woman.

Alvin wrapped his hand around his wife's arm and roughly pulled her out of the path of the hell hound. Her now exposed leg and other arm was scraped and bleeding but she was otherwise untouched by the monster.

It took Perse a moment to realize that she was still alive. When she opened her eyes and saw her husband, she let out a soft laugh.

Quisling was suddenly on this side of the chamber, plunging his long sword into the chests of the four men who had been chasing the farm woman before they had a real chance to get back up. His face was a mask of rage as he looked over at the married couple.

"You tried to feed me to that– thing!" he started to berate them but then saw the hell hound turn and again lunge toward all three of them.

The drake spittle was drowning out the smell of the woman. It made her harder to find. The beast leaped for where it last sensed her. Then the scent of aged leather appeared again.

It showed up back on that other bridge, sounding just as loud and obnoxious as before. The hell hound ignored it then and decided to do so again.

Alvin looked down at himself, specifically his oil drenched clothes. It wasn't a stretch to figure that the monster was hunting by scent and his smell was drowning out that of his wife.

"I think it's blind, Quisling. It's hunting for Perse by smell!" Alvin wrapped his arms around her and scrambled to his feet.

The hell hound whipped around, snapping its jaws right where the farmer had been just before. It let out a growl of displeasure when it came up empty again.

"It hears just fine, though," the old mercenary answered back.

He kept his blade between him and the black furred beast. Quisling had expected the creature to turn and attack him when he spoke as well. Every line in his face seemed to appear as he tried to figure out why it didn't.

The sweet smell was almost completely gone. The hell hound growled as it sniffed the air. The last time he caught it strongly was when it was moving toward the drake spittle. Whatever that was, it was hiding the tasty meats the woman was made of from the beast.

But now there were... two piles of drake spittle? Its quarry was clever but it was only a matter of time before the sweet woman was his.

The hell hound lunged for the leather bladder of drake oil. Landing on the billowy surface, the creature stumbled but stayed on its paws until they again found solid earth.

Oil had spurt from the holes in the pouch and coated the beast's entire left side. It turned its head away from the reeking stench that had attached to its body.

Disgusting! He was covered in the acrid secretions of that loathsome reptile! They were clever, yes, clever indeed. But this would not keep the beast from her.

The thing that drenched him didn't move. As long as it kept its head turned to the right, the beast would still be able to center in on its quarry.

The hell hound snapped at Quisling's leg as it stalked away from the still half full bladder of oil. It sniffed at the air, pointing its nose straight at Alvin, who pulled his wife behind him.

The farmer readied himself, "When it comes, run for the door," he hurriedly whispered to Perse, "I'll hold it down until you and Quisling are out."

"Are you crazy? That thing will kill you!" his wife snapped back, "Just run!"

The argument became moot almost immediately. The hell hound lunged for Alvin and Perse reflexively started for the door as her husband wanted.

But the beast landed short of the massive farmer. Horror washed through Alvin as the truth of what happened revealed itself: it was a feint.

He dove for the monster but it was too quick. The beast already pounced for its true target.

Perse reached out for the handle to the door when the hell hound's teeth sank into her calf. She fell to the packed earth and watched the door draw further away as the creature pulled her back.

The monster whipped its head back and forth, throwing the farm woman from side to side. Pain surged up from the farm woman's leg to all through her body. As she reached for the dagger on her belt, she felt her knee snap.

Whether what happened next was a matter of panic or a moment of clarity, the result was the same. Perse sank the blade of her knife into one of the green eyes of the beast.

With one last whip of its head, the woman fell free from the creature's jaws, momentum rolling her away from the hell hound.

Her entire body was shaking and shuddering and sweat drenched every pore of her body.

Looking down, Perse realized that she hadn't escaped with just a bite wound. Her entire leg had been ripped off at the knee.

She looked over at her husband, who was lifting himself from the ground and just starting to understand the consequences of what had happened. Grief twisted his face when he saw the extent Perse's injury.

The hell hound used its human-like fingers to pull the dagger from its eye. It took a moment to regain its equilibrium but it obviously wasn't going to let the woman escape unpunished.

"Get Ophelia out of here," she pleaded to her husband, "Bring our daughter back!"

She started crawling for the still leaking bladder of drake oil. A trail of blood from the bottom of what was left of her thigh followed her.

"No! Perse!" Alvin scrambled up to his feet.

"Get him out of here, Quisling!" her voice was shrill but only because it took so much effort for her to get the words out, "He's covered with oil. He'll burn if he stays!"

The growling beast was already sniffing at the air to find the woman again. Her blood made it so much easier to find her now. It started stalking where the woman stopped crawling, making sure to give the moving pile of drake spittle a wide berth.

The farmer again protested but the old mercenary stepped in front of him and blocked Alvin's view of his wife. He rested a hand on the larger man's broad shoulder.

"She is doing this to give you a chance to save your daughter," Quisling said, "Otherwise that thing will kill us all and Ophelia will stay with the Al Razheem."

"Please, Alvin," Perse looked as if she was about to pass out as she pulled the bladder with the nozzle free from the strap on her shoulder, "Get my little girl back."

"I will, baby. I promise!"

Quisling shoved Alvin in the direction of the door as the hell hound dashed for the woman. The mercenary pulled the door open and forced the farmer through before slipping through himself.

"I love you, Perse!" Alvin yelled as he turned to look back at his wife one last time, "I love–"

As the hell hound landed on the farm woman, she made sure the beast's weight found the bladder filled with the igniting solution. The nozzle sprayed the liquid onto the larger leather bladder of drake oil and everything exploded in a blast of light and heat.

The force of the blast pushed the door shut before the flames could reach it but that didn't stop the wood slabs from instantly starting to smoke. Silence replaced the chaos almost immediately after, to the point it was almost strangling to both men.

The farmer slammed both fists into the wall as silent sobs gripped his barrel chest. No tears came, those would be freed once he and Ophelia were free of this place. Alvin swore that silent vow to himself.

Quisling wiped the blood from his spattered sword and slipped it back into the scabbard on his hip. His hand drifted to the handle of his dagger as he looked over at the farmer's quaking back.

He stepped closer to the larger man, "It is an utmost necessity that we keep moving, Alvin," the mercenary said, "Honor your wife's memory by finishing the job."

The farmer nodded, pushing himself away from the cold wall and turned to go deeper down the torch lit hall, "I'll make sure Ophelia knows about her mother's sacrifice. I'm just glad that she'll never have to see Perse like that."

A SHORT DISTANCE BEHIND...

The second of the two mercenaries that guarded the entryway into the animal pens fell without much effort on Ophelia's part. She didn't even have to blink to strike either one down.

Pulling the door open, the General's First was surprised to find a fire burning at the end of the closest bridge. The rest of the assassins filed in after her, including the four surrounding her prisoner in the long red coat.

"Put that out," Ophelia ordered, motioning to the fire, "Our guest and I will take the long way around."

And she walked over to the next bridge. The woman was surprised to see that there was more smoke billowing from the far side of the chamber.

As she and the four guards with the prisoner got closer, they could see that not only had there been a fire but something exploded with such force that it destroyed the barrier between two of the warg pens.

The fact that such destruction was right next to the door that ultimately led up to the General's quarters worried Ophelia. There was obviously a battle. She just had to figure out which side won.

Once on the packed earth on the far side of the chamber, Ophelia immediately saw the armor clad corpse of Kitanah's First, Hinder. He'd been sent down here to guard this entrance, obviously. His failure was equally obvious.

Several surviving Al Razheem assassins nursed various wounds as they either lay on the ground or sat leaning against the wall. Ophelia pointed toward them as she walked.

"Find one that can talk," she ordered.

All four men that had taken up the duty of guarding the man in the long red coat look at each other for a moment. Ever helpful, Doctor Efreeti tapped the shoulder of one of the guards standing behind Browder and volunteered to take his place.

The rest nodded back at him. With a look only the slightest confusion, he split off and started toward his wounded compatriots.

Closer to the door were two smoldering bodies. The closer was of one of the General's prized hell hounds, a gift from the Xaviour Tribe of svartalfar, if Ophelia remembered the story correctly. The entire front half of the animal was gone, the assassin was only able to recognize it by what was left of the six tails and its distinctive paws.

The guard returned with an Al Razheem whose eyes were bright red with irritation. His hair was wet, apparently from dumping the entire contents of his canteen on his head. He gave the General's First a quick, slightly unsteady bow.

"Don't leave me in suspense. Tell me what happened," Ophelia said, giving the dead animal's rump a light poke with the toe of her boot.

"We met up with the enemy here," the lower ranked assassin said, "The big man killed Maester Hinder, then left with the old mercenary.

Only a couple of steps away was the upper torso of a woman. Ophelia nodded over at the body.

"Who is that?" she asked.

"She was with the big man," the assassin answered, blinking his eyes heavily, "She set off some kind of explosion to kill the hell hound and let the others escape."

Ophelia knelt down beside the deceased woman to get a closer look. She was a couple of decades older than Ophelia. Her soot caked hair had thin streaks of gray running all through it and her lifeless eyes were that shade of jade green that Ophelia found so... haunting.

The assassin found herself wondering if she would look anything like this woman when got older. This woman looked so familiar...

"Oh, Perse," the assassin heard Browder mutter quietly behind her.

Ophelia frowned, feeling as if some... moment of importance had passed but unable to identify it. Shaking her head slowly before rising back to her feet, Ophelia let out a heavy sigh.

"Did any others escape with them?" her face was stone hard again when she turned back to the lower ranked assassin.

"No. Just the big one and the old man," he answered.

"That door still open?" she stepped up to the smoldering threshold that led to the living quarters of every member of the Al Razheem.

The assassin used his red sash to dab at his irritated eyes, "None of us have tried yet, Mistress."

Ophelia shrugged and kicked in the scorched doorjamb. It crumbled into the hallway beyond.

"The General is this way," she looked back at Travus, then motioned for him and his guards to follow.

ON THE STAIRCASE TO THE UPPERMOST FLOOR

Neither the massive farmer nor the old mercenary said much as they ascended the spiral stairs, not bothering to stop at any other floor until they reached the top. As the doorway to their destination came into view, Alvin reached out and grabbed the other man's arm to stop him mid step.

"Why are you still here, Quisling?" he asked before letting out a heavy sigh, "You had a perfect opportunity to escape when the hell hound was attacking me and Perse."

The old man's forehead crinkled into more lines than could easily be counted, "I acknowledge that I've expressed my incertitude about this venture. Holy Juna knows our probabilities of success have only worsened since we've arrived. But I am a professional. I will see this undertaking through until there is zero potentiality of procuring your daughter," he gave the farmer the closest he could to a reassuring smile (from a face that didn't do it much, it was quite a feat).

Alvin let out a quiet grunt before answering, "Thank you," he said simply.

Quisling stepped up to the closed door and pressed one of his over sized ears to it, "Don't thank me yet. We haven't even seen Ophelia," he whispered.

It took only a few moments of listening for the old mercenary to figure out that there was a guard standing on each side of the door in the hallway beyond. He relayed his information to the farmer by holding up two fingers and then pointing to each end of the doorjamb.

As Quisling pulled his dagger free from its sheath, Alvin stepped up to the door himself. The farmer rested a bulbous shoulder against the wood, wrapping his hand against the door handle. With his free hand, Alvin pointed to the side of the door opposite the hinges. Then he pointed to himself and the other direction.

Quisling nodded, then mouthed the words "in three". Alvin took a deep breath and held it. "Two", the old man continued. The heavily muscled man squeezed down on the handle.

"Go!" the command came out as a coarse whisper.

Alvin pushed his full body weight against the door to make it open as wide and fast as it possibly could. The mercenary darted out through the threshold and slit the throat of the still surprised guard before pulling him back into the tower with the spiraling staircase.

The other guard was sandwiched between the door and the stone wall. He let out a yelp of shock that was stifled by the farmer's broad hand. Then Alvin snapped the assassin's neck.

It didn't feel right to the man. He had been in a fight to the death with the armored man, Hinder, below. Kill or be killed. Even though this young man was an assassin that would have surely stabbed him just for stepping into his sight, it felt wrong that he didn't even have a fighting chance.

Like his grief for Perse, Alvin forced himself to put those feelings aside. He had to focus everything he had into finding his little girl.

According to the information Travus had given them, the General's living quarters were to the right. In the event of an emergency like this, he would have been evacuated there if not already inside and the rooms fortified and filled with guards.

Alvin pulled a small leather packet from his pocket. One of the last little surprises concocted by his wife.

Even with his tremendous advantage in size, there was no way he would be able to stand up to a room full of armed assassins. This was what Perse made to even those odds.

The corner came up after a short walk. Quisling peeked around and held up two fingers.

Leaning back against the wall, he pulled a thin tube from some hidden pocket in the leg of his pants. Two small darts with small puffs of feather attached to their rears came from another.

The old man pressed one dart into the tube then the tube to his mouth. He then leaned around just enough to aim the tube down the hall. After a quick exhale, Quisling quickly stuffed the next dart into the tube and then launched that one short order.

Several agonizingly slow seconds later, the sound of two men tumbling to the ground came to the farmer's ears. When there wasn't any sound of alarm, he looked over at the old mercenary, who motioned for him to follow.

They both rushed down the hallway as silently as they could. The more experienced of the two (at least in matters of subterfuge), Quisling chose just the right moment to dash to the far side of the open doorway without being seen by any of the assassins standing guard inside.

Alvin chanced peeking inside.

The man in the white uniform with the long beard and bald head was the likeliest candidate to be the Al Razheem General. Guards were all around him, either pacing around or standing in place.

The only other standout was a red haired woman in some kind of a black vest that also seemed to double as a corset and almost impossibly tight pants. The odd metal sleeve she wore on her left arm struck the farmer as familiar.

The assassin that ambushed him and Perse several months ago mentioned that he was under the command of a woman with a sleeve like that. What was her name? Kitanah?

Unfortunately, Ophelia was nowhere to be seen. If she was as precious and mighty as the "blinking horror" was supposed to make her, both he and Travus figured that she would have been standing right beside the General as his last line of defense. Kitanah appeared to be filling that role, though.

Still, Travus gave the farmers a contingency plan in case something like this happened. They would take the General and ransom him for Ophelia. Of course, that was when they figured they would have Perse's chemistry expertise to keep the General compliant and the Al Razheem from trying a foolhardy rescue with a well placed trap.

Still, assuming Travus got out with his daughter, Alvin may just be able to enlist the Night Shield's contacts to do something very similar. He held up the leather packet so that Quisling could see it.

The old man nodded, closed his eyes and covered his ears. Alvin tugged the little string hanging off the side and tossed the leather into the room, also slapping his hands over his ears.

"Bomb!" one of the assassins noticed just before the explosion.

It wasn't strong enough to kill anyone not right on top of it but the smoke that now filled the room knocked one assassin after another unconscious. After everyone both men counted inside had fallen, Alvin and Quisling pulled kerchiefs from their pockets and wrapped them around their heads to cover their nose and mouth.

While the smoke made their eyes water, the cloth they now breathed through countered the agent Perse had used to create the gas. They stepped over one sleeping guard after another, finally reaching the desk of the General.

To both their surprise, the man looked up at them from his seat. His eyes watered, just like theirs but his chest didn't move. He was holding his breath.

The General stood up behind his desk, coming up to just below the farmer's blonde hair covered chin. It was impressive, really, not only did he think to hold his breath to counter the gas but also that he had held his breath this long...

The smoke was already a lot thinner in the air than when the farmer and mercenary entered. The rest of the assassins would stay unconscious for some time yet but the General could put up a fight. Fights take time and the intruders didn't have much left to spare.

"If you come along quietly, General, you won't be harmed." Alvin hoped, prayed that this would work.

The man with the braided beard looked unmoved, "I find myself quite comfortable here, sir. I will not allow you to bring harm to my family by taking me away as part of whatever petulant plan you've concocted," he leaned back in his heavily cushioned chair, crossing his arms over his broad chest.

Alvin dropped both fists onto the flat stone surface of the desk, "Petulant? I am undoing the harm you have done to my family. Now get up from the damn chair or I–"

The feeling of cold steel slipping into his back made the farmer freeze mid sentence. After a few moments, he started to wonder why he wasn't dead and risked cocking his head to look back over his shoulder.

It was Quisling's blade in his back and the old man was still holding the dagger, "Do not move, Alvin. With a flick of my wrist your spine will be severed and you're legs will become useless."

"Why... now?" the heavily muscled man's words came out hesitantly as he stayed as still as possible, "You could have... betrayed us... downstairs."

"I told you that I would see your contract through until there was no chance of success," Quisling answered, "Once we hit that point, my new contract came into play."

"And that would be mine," the General motioned to the red haired woman to the side of the desk opposite the mercenary and the wounded Alvin, "Kitanah, my supernal, you are awake, yes?"

The woman with the metal sleeve let out her long held lungful of air. After a few deep, filling breaths, she nodded at her General.

"Of course, Sire, I was just waiting for your word," and she rose to her feet, the ring at the end of her armor sleeve starting to spin slowly, "Shall I dispose of him now?"

The General shook his head, "No, Kitanah. This is the part where both of our worries are either confirmed or put to rest for good."

THIRTEEN
THE TRIAL AND THE KEIAN

Ophelia gripped Havarti's handle tightly before stepping around the threshold and into the General's living quarters. The woman's gray eyes narrowed at the sight that greeted her. Every guard that had been left behind was just starting to lift themselves up off the floor. That alone was enough to cause her worry.

Then she saw the General behind his desk, unharmed, with Kitanah standing at his left. To his right was... the gigantic man and, just behind him, the old mercenary that had intruded into the Oasis. She didn't even bother to try and hide the fact that she was confused at the scene.

"Are you alright, Master?" Ophelia asked as she stepped up to the desk then pointed at the two men off to the side, "They didn't harm you, did they?"

At the word "Master" she heard a quiet groan come from the massive blonde man. Her attention stayed on the man behind the desk.

"No, not at all, my dove," the General smirked up at his First Bravo, "But I am surprised to see that you seem to know who these men are."

"They are why I came back up here, Master," Ophelia said, "I was afraid I was going to be too late to stop them from attacking you but, it appears my worries were thankfully unjustified."

"But how did you know that they were going to be here at all?" the General asked, leaning back in his seat as his fingers intertwined.

Ophelia sighed, "They went through the animal pens to get here. I'm sorry to have to be the one to tell you this, Master, but they killed one of your hell hounds."

The General's cheek twitched. Ophelia figured it had to be from restraining whatever disappointment or anger he felt at the news but it didn't look right for it to be that. His face looked, for lack of a better term, colder when he was displeased and he didn't seem that way for some reason.

"But do you know who this man is?" Her Master pointed to the large blonde man.

Ophelia turned her attention over to him, crossing her arms over her chest. Her gray eyes scanned him up and down. He was dressed like a farmer, which was odd for someone attacking a group of professional assassins. His nose looked familiar...

"He's the one who killed Hinder," she answered the General, "At least, that's what one of the red sashes said downstairs."

"And you know nothing else of him?" the General let a fleeting glance shift over to Kitanah.

Ophelia shook her head, "Including why he's still alive. He attacked us in our home. He was intent on killing you, Master. Why haven't you killed him and why are you asking me all these questions?"

Any hope that had been left in the farmer fled from him in that moment. He knew that she'd been brainwashed. He and Perse had prepared for that eventuality, even figuring that they would have to drug Ophelia to get her out of the Oasis. But she didn't even show the slightest hesitation at the death of her own father. Was there really none of his little girl left?

"You are right, of course," the General turned and nodded back at Quisling, "It is time that he died for his crimes against us."

"No! General, don't!" Travus tried to rush forward but the two guards in front of him both slammed their elbows into his midsection and he doubled over in a fit of coughing.

Not seeming to notice the Night Shield's outburst, the old mercenary pulled the dagger that was already resting in Alvin's back out and then plunged it back in, higher this time into the back of his chest, right into the heart. Alvin fell to his knees, his hazel eyes staying locked on his daughter even as the life drained from him.

"still... love... you..." he muttered with his last breath, falling forward as his lungs forgot how to take air in again.

The General watched the entire event with great interest, as did Kitanah, who watched every reaction that came from the woman who took her position as the General's First Bravo. She waited for even the slightest hint of regret or concern or even being too interested in what was happening (a common tactic for those who tried to hide duplicity).

Ophelia did watch as the farmer fell but turned her attention back to her Master before he spoke his last words. But it wasn't as if she trying to protect herself from something unpleasant. More like she had what she felt were more important matters to attend.

Even the heavily muscled man's last proclamation brought out little more than a cocked eyebrow from Ophelia. She didn't even turn back to the now dead intruder in confusion.

But, once the deed was done, the General did notice the crowd behind Ophelia. Particularly the man in red who tried to interrupt things.

"Who is this man, Ophelia?" suspicion actually itched at the back of his mind for the first time, "Did I not order you to kill all the intruders?"

"You did, Master," Ophelia motioned for Browder to be brought forward, "But he said that if I killed him, you would somehow be joining him shortly after. I couldn't risk endangering you if it was true."

"Is that all it takes to thwart you woman?" Kitanah chimed in, "Someone to invoke the name of the General and you just have to bring him up and endanger our leader?"

Ophelia only spared the briefest of malignant glances at the other woman before answering her questions... to the General, "He said the name Travus Crichton would prove that his words were true. Does that mean anything to you, sir?"

"Crichton," all the color drained from the face of the patriarch of the Al Razheem, "I know the name," the General lifted himself to his feet and walked over to the man in red.

He inspected the prisoner closely, even pulling the claw holding a shield pendant handing around the man's neck up for a closer inspection, "A Night Shield," he muttered and dropped the trinket as if it somehow burned him.

Travus cleared his throat. He had to before he could speak after coughing so hard from the double strike to his stomach.

"It's been awhile, Kraven," his voice was more hoarse than usual.

"Be silent!" the General snapped at the prisoner, "I presume you have some failsafe in place for the moment of your death."

Browder nodded, "If you want details, you know where it's going to have to be," the look of smug satisfaction on his face was enough to convince the leader of the Al Razheem that he wasn't bluffing.

"You were very wise to bring him, Ophelia," the General's eyes stayed locked on the Night Shield even as he spoke to his First Bravo, "He has proven that he at least warrants a hearing in the Keian," his entire focus shifted to the other man, "Until then, Night Shield, it would behoove you to keep that pit you call your mouth closed. Any *gossip mongering* and I will take my chances with whatever trick you've concocted. Understood?"

Again, Travus nodded, "As long as you don't do anything to my daughter. Especially whatever you were going to have him do."

He quirked his head back at Doctor Efreeti, who was picking grime out from under one claw with another. He looked completely oblivious to anything that had happened in the room since his and Ophelia's arrival.

"Fine."

"And I want to see her, Kra-" as Browder spoke, the look on the General's face leaned enough toward the homicidal that he edited himself, "-General. I want proof that she is still alive, unharmed and unaltered."

"Big demands for someone being held at our mercy," Kitanah said.

Ophelia actually found herself agreeing with the General's Second Bravo; a rare occurrence to say the least. Both women were practically floored when their leader agreed to the demands.

"Kitanah, see to it that our guest is isolated from seeing or even being able to hear or be heard by another Al Razheem," he turned away from Browder and started back for his desk, "Bring his daughter. You and she are the only ones with which he will have contact once he is situated."

Instead of sitting back in his chair, the General snatched a piece of parchment from the desk and held it up over his head. "Efreeti!" his voice was loud enough that everyone in the room could hear his voice, then the tearing of the document clearly.

For the first time, the man in tweed looked up from his efforts at grooming, "Oh, pity. Perhaps a more willing supplicant will reveal themselves in the meantime," he said, smiling wide in the direction of a certain recovering assassin.

"As for me, I am going to bed," the General said, "Kitanah, get everyone out of here and do as I instructed. Ophelia, you will join me."

KITANAH'S LIVING QUARTERS

The darkness of her room was almost like a security blanket to Kitanah now. The fire lightly crackled in the fireplace. The cushions of her chair cradled her like a supportive lover. And no one disturbed her. She knew that because the woman had been staying up and waiting more than actually sleeping of late.

Her palm still carried scars from the last glass that had kept her company through a long night. So the glass she sipped from now had a small handle spun off from the side just big enough for her forefinger.

The liquid she poured into her mouth gave her entire body a warming sensation as she mulled over the events of the last few days. The last few months, really.

Kitanah had been so focused on enemies within that she was so sure that those from without were merely puppets. But the one Kitanah thought was truly her enemy, Ophelia, showed no hesitation when it came to the safety of the General.

Nor did she show any concern for those who had invaded the Oasis. Kitanah thought for sure that Ophelia would have somehow betrayed her feelings for her father when the woman saw his life threatened.

No one was that good of an actor. Ophelia truly did not know who that farmer was. Efreeti really did make a truly loyal soldier.

Kitanah may never be close with Ophelia but the action she was considering, it was a point of honor now. The woman had to go to the General's First. She had to apologize for her doubt and show Ophelia at least some belated respect. It was the Al Razheem way.

Ophelia had slept with the General every night since the attempted incursion. This was the first night that Kitanah knew Ophelia was actually back in her own quarters.

It was only natural. He would have to actually rest some time and Ophelia was not one to make such a feat easy. Kitanah shivered at the memories of the General's lessons that the two women had to share.

It was a long, long walk down the corridors to get to the room that served as quarters for the General's First. Kitanah had second thoughts every step of the way but the woman continued until she finally reached Ophelia's door.

It took a few minutes for the door to open after Kitanah knocked. When it did, Ophelia was wearing only the sheet from her bed and running her fingers through her hair to tame the tangles from her slumber.

She didn't bother to hide her surprise, although irritation may have been a better word at the sight of the woman in the metal sleeve, "It's the middle of the night, Second. What could you possibly want now?"

Kitanah didn't expect a warm welcome. She was familiar with the old adage that bad news came at all hours while the pleasant waited for the sun. Still, this was the only time the woman was sure that neither their duties, nor the General himself, would get in the way of them having some time alone together.

Still, being treated like an underling, that *irked* Kitanah. But the assassin wouldn't let that stop her from doing this.

"May I come in?" she asked.

The Al Razheem way didn't mean that she had to do it in public.

Ophelia looked back into her room as if someone said something to her, something Kitanah couldn't hear. It must have been that sword of hers, Havarti.

The auburn haired woman with the braids shrugged and stepped to the side. Kitanah took it as an invitation and entered. Finally inside Ophelia's room, the assassin was surprised to find it so... sparse. At her rank, Ophelia could have had anything she wanted brought in to make the place more comfortable for her in any number of ways.

She didn't have anything up on the walls. There was only a mirror on one wall and next to it was a single dresser. On top of it were some vials of makeup, all scattered around without any real sense of organization, and a pitcher of water with an empty glass beside it.

A torch in every corner lit the room, when they were all burning, that is. Ophelia had only kindled the one closest to her bed to be able to see well enough to get to the door when Kitanah knocked.

The First's bed was, of course, luxurious. A puffed comforter was all bundled to one side, presumably the side Ophelia didn't sleep on. Kitanah furrowed her brow when she saw the blue grip of Havarti's handle protruding from under the pile of blankets, the hilt resting on a pillow like someone's head.

"I do apologize for the lateness of the hour," the red haired woman said, stalling to find the words that she truly wanted to say, "I just wanted us to be able to speak without any interruptions."

If Kitanah hadn't been standing in the middle of her room, where she had control of the environment, Ophelia would have thought that she was being set up for another ambush. As it was, now she was just perturbed that she was awoken for no important reason.

"And what do you want to say?" Ophelia stepped around the other woman and sat down on the side of her bed, "Did you have a really good insult you just couldn't wait till morning to use?"

Kitanah forced herself to not get angry. Ophelia had just described how their relationship had pretty much been up to this point.

"No. No, nothing like that," this was harder than Kitanah thought it would be, "I've been doing a lot of thinking since the incursion. Not being able to hear clearly for two days removed a lot of distractions."

"Alright. Yeah. So you weren't distracted," Ophelia dropped down onto her side, her elbow digging into the mattress while her head rested in the palm of her hand, "What does this have to do with me?"

Ophelia unwrapped the sheet from around her torso with her free hand. She, barely, kept the front of her body covered while the shifted the fabric around so that it was no longer touching her back. Then she looked back at Kitanah, still waiting for an answer.

"I realized that the way I have been treating you was unjustified," the older woman forced the words out of her throat as quickly as they could come out, "I've always been suspicious of Efreeti's motives and that suspicion carried over to you when he brought you into the Al Razheem."

Ophelia seemed, if not interested, at least slightly curious for the first time, "Why don't you trust Efreeti?"

The calculating side of Kitanah's mind went into overdrive. Could Ophelia be trying to set her up for something? Could she tell Efreeti and have him try to use this to discredit Kitanah for some reason in the future?

While her paranoia had served her well in the past, Kitanah realized that her distrust of the doctor was well known. Particularly after Ophelia came to join them. Ophelia was not about to gain new information from this conversation.

"He's not Al Razheem," Kitanah said, "He came to the General several years ago, promising to deliver the perfect assassin. Lethal, unkillable and completely, perfectly loyal to the General. I always thought it sounded too good to be true."

"But you let Doctor Efreeti experiment on you," Ophelia pointed at the metal sleeve the other woman always wore.

Kitanah lifted the cuff of the sleeve, as if presenting it as evidence, "It wasn't like you came to us the next day. Efreeti also promised various, he called them upgrades, for those chosen by the General until he could deliver. He gave me this but never did anything to my mind or memories."

"Your memories?" Ophelia cocked a thick eyebrow, "Are you saying that he did something to mine then?"

Kitanah cursed at herself. She had come so close to violating her oath to the General. He made her promise never to reveal what was exactly done to make Ophelia into the perfect soldier she was now.

The woman shook her head, "No, that isn't it at all. That he would manipulate my mind somehow was my worry. Back then."

"Okay. That makes sense to me," Ophelia rubbed her eyes as a yawn overtook the next sentence, "Let's get back to that point you were going f-or th-en."

Most of Ophelia's sheet slipped off as she yawned. It only tenaciously stayed in place around her hips. She didn't seem to notice, or care, though.

Kitanah did and had to turn away from the woman to continue to speak, "After hearing about how you tore through every mercenary they brought just to get back to the General before he could be harmed and how you and Efreeti captured that Light Bringer so that he could face the Keian. That assuaged whatever doubts I had about you."

"About me," Ophelia pushed herself back up to a sitting position, "But not Doctor Efreeti?"

"That," the paranoid side of Kitanah's brain kicked in again, "is a completely different set of issues. You may have come from Efreeti but you are not him."

Ophelia nodded, then something else clicked in her mind, "What is a Keian, anyway?"

"You don't know? The General never explained it to you?" Kitanah actually turned back to face the woman in shock.

"When we're alone he's," Ophelia bit down on her plump lower lip for a moment, "not a big talker."

Kitanah felt another shiver run through her body. Shaking her head, she forced herself to keep talking.

"The Keian is a communal trial that punishes traitors to the Al Razheem. They are brought into the audience chambers and questioned by the quorum," Kitanah explained, "We ascertain how widespread their conspiracy is among us and then gather the guilty and kill them."

"Wouldn't it be possible that the traitor would have friends in the group that would try and save him?" Ophelia asked, "It sounds like something the General would do more efficiently on his own."

"That is precisely why, in his wisdom, the General set it up as a communal trial," Kitanah felt herself grinning wide as she spoke, "The traitor's guilt isn't in doubt. Anyone trying to save him only reveals themselves to justice."

"But it sounds like a big waste of time if there's no secret combination of people to kill," Ophelia said.

"Every Keian is guaranteed at least two deaths," Kitanah hadn't felt this pleased with herself in a long time, "The traitor and the one who recruited him into the Al Razheem. That way, any possible root of corruption is cut off."

"Even if the recruiter wasn't part of the conspiracy?" Ophelia was, surprisingly, actually finding this interesting.

"Even if," Kitanah agreed, "If their judgment was faulty enough to bring a traitor into our midst, we don't want him or her to have another chance."

Again, Ophelia nodded. Then she decided she was thirsty. She slipped out of the bed, leaving the sheet behind, and strode over to the dresser where the pitcher of water rested.

"So this Light Bringer guy was a member of the Al Razheem then?" she asked.

Kitanah cleared her throat, "Yes, from back when I first earned my azure sash. I knew him to be called Travus Crichton then. Apparently his surname is Browder now."

Ophelia suddenly felt as if the water she just swallowed was going to come right back up. The image of Inara, the life draining out of her as she lay pleading for the life of her daughter, came to Ophelia's mind. Setting the glass down, the woman rested both hands on the dresser to steady herself.

"It's taken longer than usual to set up this Keian," Kitanah continued, not noticing Ophelia's reaction, "But when he does, I'd wager the little girl will be joining him on the gallows."

The naked woman quickly downed another glass of water to try and weigh down the last one, "Even though the General wanted her to go through Doctor Efreeti's process?"

"That was until..." Kitanah's crimson eyebrows pressed together, "until Browder was captured."

"I doubt it would be as effective on the girl anyway," Ophelia spoke barely loud enough for Kitanah to hear, "Can you imagine what it would take to erase the memories of her parents? Of everything that happened to bring her here?"

Kitanah stopped herself from laughing at the other woman's words. Instead, she stepped up beside the thickly cushioned bed, picking the crumpled sheet up from the cool stone floor.

Ophelia forced a lopsided smirk onto her face as she turned to look back at the other woman, "I doubt even Doctor Efreeti could do something like that."

"You're right, of course," Kitanah gave Ophelia, for the first time, her most genuine smile back, "How could even he remove a lifetime of memories?"

Kitanah lifted the sheet up to her face, giving the cloth a quick sniff before tossing it back onto the bed. She turned and walked over to Ophelia, who could see her hips sway with every step in the mirror as she closed the distance.

"Anyway, all of this distracted from my main point of coming here," she leaned in close to the auburn haired woman's ear, her voice a soft whisper, "I wanted to let you know that I trust you, Ophelia. I truly believe you belong among the Al Razheem."

"Even after all the trust exercises the General made us do together," Ophelia turned her entire body around to face Kitanah, "It took an invasion to get you to believe in me?"

Both women stood only inches away from each other. It was quiet for a long moment, with only each woman's breathing able to be heard.

"That is the difference between reality and training," Kitanah's emerald eyes stared deeply into Ophelia's slate gray ones, "If it makes you feel better, though, we can go through those exercises again now."

Ophelia felt Kitanah's hand glide up her bare thigh and the General's First suddenly wished that her blinking wasn't just for lethal attacks. Instead, she stepped around the red haired woman and started toward her bed.

"I don't think that's necessary right now," she said as her hand slipped under the soft comforter, "I think it's time we both went back to bed."

"Are you sure that mind reading isn't among your abilities?" Kitanah smirked as she started after Ophelia.

"I meant in our own *separate* beds," Ophelia wasn't happy when she had to bend forward to reach.

"Are you sure? I mean," as the other woman feared, Kitanah's hand found its way to the glowing runes on her back, "it can get so cold in these windowless rooms."

Ophelia's entire body shuddered and she had to stifle a bunch of small gasps before she found what she was looking for. Again she spun around to face the other woman. This time, the bare length of Havarti's blade stretched between them.

"I'm afraid I'll have to insist," the naked woman scowled.

Anger finally found its way back to Kitanah's face along with a dash of, was that disappointment? Regardless, she slowly backed away from the General's First and even gave her a deep, courteous bow before retreating from the room altogether.

When the door closed behind the older assassin, Havarti finally decided to speak, "I think I liked her better when she hated us."

SOMEWHERE UNDER THE OASIS, SEVERAL DAYS AGO...

"Daddy!" the little girl twisted her entire body to get out of the grip of the red haired assassin.

She rushed straight for Travus, who had been sitting on one of the only two pieces of furniture in the room, a wooden chair. It rested right in the middle of the room. Judging from the imprints in the carpet beside it, there had been a small table just beside it but it must have been removed when it was decided this room was going to be the man's prison.

The father met his daughter halfway between the doorway and where the chair now teetered, threatening to fall onto its side. Tilly buried her face into her father's shoulder and the Night

Shield wrapped his arms around his little girl so tightly that she squeaked at him.

It took everything he had to let her go enough to look her in the face and ask,"Are you okay?"

She nodded, although tears started welling up in her big brown eyes, "The one with the purple marks hurt Mommy."

Travus pulled her back into him when Tilly started sobbing. Seeing his daughter in so much pain caused his own chest to tighten, particularly the left side of his chest.

"I know, sugar blossom," he gently kissed the side of Tilly's head, "I found Mom."

"This really scary man touched me in my no-no place," the little girl sniffled.

Travus glared back up at Kitanah, who threw her hand up, the sleeve arm mirroring the gesture, "That was Efreeti. He was checking to see if she'd had her first period or something. It was why he had to wait to perform his procedure on her."

The father stifled the urge to become violent but only because he wasn't willing to let his daughter go yet. They kept holding each other for a long time but when Tilly finally started pulling away, it still didn't feel like long enough to her father.

"So what happens now?" Travus asked as he straightened up.

"You saw your daughter," Kitanah pointed at the little girl with her metal sleeve, "You've seen that she's unharmed. That fulfills the agreement you had with the General."

Tilly slowly sank more and more behind her father as the woman spoke. Travus squared himself up, ready to resist the assassin if she tried to come for Tilly.

Kitanah seemed to notice it, too, "But you two seem a little attached at the moment. Personally I don't want the headache of having to beat you down just to take her back to her cell. So, I'll make you a deal," she leaned back against the wall, resting her bare right arm against her flat stomach.

"I'm listening," Travus said back.

"Your Keian will be in the next day or two," The woman grinned, her metal sleeve swaying with each condition, "If you don't try to pull anything, especially any kind of escape attempt that uses your daughter in any way, I'll let her stay in here. If I even suspect that something is off. I'll kill her, cripple you and, just because I'd be annoyed I'll send a garrison to kill what few Light Bringers are left in Paimae. Reasonable?"

"Not exactly the word I'd use," Travus answered, "but I can agree to not try and escape."

"Good!" Kitanah used her shoulders to push herself away from the wall, "I'll have Ophelia bring your breakfast first thing–"

"NO!" Tilly shrieked, dropping to her knees and burying her face into the back of her father's leg, "Don't let her come near me!"

The corner of Kitanah's mouth twitched into the briefest of smirks before she nodded, "Fine. Only she and I have the sufficient rank to even be in the same room with you so I'll bring you breakfast. After I've had mine."

The assassin turned and started to open the door when Travus spoke up again, "Aren't you at all curious why he thinks I'm so dangerous that only his First and Second Bravos are allowed to even be around me?"

"Not particularly," Kitanah said as she was halfway through the door, "But then, I don't really put too much thought into the motivation of traitors."

And with that, the woman closed the door, leaving father and daughter alone together. Travus guided Tilly to the chair, then he started to ask her questions. Most were to see if she was truly unharmed.

THE NEXT DAY...

Travus sat on the wood chair backwards, resting his arms on the top of the backrest. The seat rested just beside the bed where his daughter now rested. Their conversation had started with Travus comforting his little girl but had since moved on to him trying to find any kind of information that could aid them in the here and now.

The dishes that had made up their breakfast sat forgotten on the floor beside the mattress. He hadn't dared try to take the plate toward the door. While the room itself looked normal, there was a deadly trap that could only be deactivated outside the door. The lack of visible security helped sell the euphemism that prisoners were actually "guests" of the Al Razheem.

His red leather coat had been taken from him just before he was put in this room. It was mostly meant as a precaution due to the fact that the scabbard to his sword was sewn into the lining. They must have suspected that he may have had other surprises hidden inside, as well. So now he was in a simple white shirt and gray pants, the last change of clothes he had before the assault on the keep.

Tilly, she explained, had been given a new dress to wear every other day since she had been taken captive by the Al Razheem. She was given the one she wore now, made from dark green silk (quite fancy for what amounted to a prison uniform), just before she was brought into this room to see her father.

"So you were there when I encountered Efreeti," Travus said.

Tilly nodded, "I yelled and yelled but you didn't hear me. The thin man's place was weird. Not even that window seemed to work right."

"How do you mean?" her father asked.

"Well, um, I was there for over a day but it never became night in that window," Tilly lightly scratched at her cheek, looking as if she was struggling to make sense of what she was about to say herself, "The landscape always changed from desert to mountains to plains to forest and then back to desert. But it always stayed daytime. The only time it changed was when the thin man looked annoyed. It got cloudy then."

"That is weird," Travus agreed with his daughter.

The way that made sense to the man was only in a theoretical sense. Like when a wizard in the Light Bringers tried to explain how he was able to fit a pole arm into his coin purse.

If Efreeti's quarters or lair or whatever they wanted to call it was in some kind of alternate dimension, it could possibly make some kind of sense that time was somehow measured by distance rather than its actual progression of events. That would explain why the conversation he had with the man masquerading as human took what felt like hours but only minutes had passed back in the Oasis.

But then that would mean that when the sky changed in that dimension that it was somehow connected with Efreeti's emotions for state of mind? Travus felt the veins in his head thumping with the effort of trying to keep all those off the wall ideas straight. So instead of making his head hurt more, especially since that didn't seem to be of any help to their current situation, he changed the topic.

"You mentioned that they wanted to keep you from hurting yourself while they were holding you in the room down the hall," Travus poked his thumb back at the door that led to the hall, "Why did they care?"

"It was at the thin man's instructions," Tilly gulped as she answered, trying to keep herself distracted from the memories that popped up as she spoke, "If I was injured in any way before the procedure he wouldn't be able to do it."

Her father tapped his chin for a long moment, "So what did you do then?"

Tilly didn't want to answer at first, "First, I tried to make the woman with the purple marks cut my arms but she was too quick."

"She used the blade restraint technique on you to force you to come here?" he pantomimed having a sword stretched across his back with his arms pulled back over the blade.

"I was so scared I... I wanted to be with Mommy," Tilly focused the entirety of her attention to the mattress as she wrung the blanket in her hands.

Travus reached forward, draping his hand over those of his little girl, "It's okay, Tilly. I'm glad you weren't hurt. What happened next?"

"They, they put me in the room down the hall," The little girl was so relieved that her father wasn't mad, "I remembered that you were still out there and I knew that you would come looking for me. But I didn't want the thin man to touch me again..."

Travus' cheek twitched. Otherwise, he concentrated on listening to his daughter's story.

"...so I still tried to hurt myself," Tilly continued, "Not seriously. He made it clear that even a little cut would keep him from being able to do anything to me. But they were able to stop me from even doing that."

"How?"

"They brought this weird candle into the room," she answered, "While it was lit, it was like however fast I tried to move, I went slower and slower. I tried everything from trying to use my silverware from meals to give myself a cut to even trying to skin my knee on the wall or floor. No matter what I did, though, they were able to come in and stop me because I was moving so slowly."

"And you think it was because of that unusual candle? Why didn't it affect your guards?" Travus asked.

"I think it was because of the chokers they were wearing. I knew I was moving slow but I couldn't do anything about it. They could still move normally and once one of them had a hold of me, one would put the candle out and I was normal again, too."

"Then they would relight the candle and you would be slow again while they stayed normal," her father finished for her.

She nodded in agreement as a knock came at the door. It opened, without waiting for permission, and Kitanah stepped inside with a tray of food resting on the upturned cuff of her metal sleeve.

"Dinner time," she announced.

Pushing her shoulder forward, the sleeve whipped ahead of the woman. The tray landed on the mattress with a small bounce right beside Tilly. Then the sleeve retracted and hung at Kitanah's side like it did usually.

"You two aren't trying to plan anything that would make me unhappy, are you?" the assassin's emerald eyes scanned around the room.

Travus shook his head back at her, "Just catching up with my daughter, learning about how she was treated before I arrived."

"With kid gloves, I assure you," Kitanah smirked as she turned back toward the doorway.

"I'm getting that impression," the man agreed, "Things sure have changed since I was the Second Bravo to the General."

That gave the woman with red hair only the briefest of pauses before she stepped out of the room completely and closed the door behind her. Travus grinned. It was subtle, barely a reaction at all, but it was a start.

Tilly reached over and tugged at her father's sleeve, "Daddy, the choker she was wearing was like the ones that the guards watching me had."

TWO DAYS LATER...

"I swear on my pretty, flowery bonnet that you will pay for that!" Travus blew the pink piece of cloth up so that it didn't block his view of Tilly.

He chased his daughter around the room. She was getting quick, too. He wasn't even slowing down on purpose like he did when she was in her single digits.

She laughed as she ducked under his arms when Travus tried to put his daughter into a bear hug. Then she poked him in the ribs again before running off in the opposite direction.

It was good to hear her laugh again, even if it was just to temporarily forget the situation they found themselves in at the moment. If he had known that all it would take was a raucous game of blind tag (the bonnet from her latest dress was serving as the blindfold), they would have started playing much, much sooner.

"Cheater cheater pumpkin eater!" Tilly said in a silly sing-song voice, "You're supposed to be blind!"

"And you're not supposed to poke the one who's 'it'," her father jested back.

A knock came at the door, interrupting their fun. Kitanah came in, again carrying a tray on her metal sleeve's cuff but, unlike every time before, she had a bundle wrapped in parchment under her other arm.

Tilly stepped out from between Kitanah and the bed before the woman launched the tray onto it. The assassin made a show of it, impressing the little girl enough that she even gave the older woman a round of applause.

Once dinner was delivered (and Kitanah took her bow), she turned her attention to Travus. Stepping up to him, she placed the package in his hands.

"The Keian will be happening very soon now," she said, "I thought you might want a change of clothes. Not that I'm an expert or anything but I think these are a little more," she nodded up at the bonnet still wrapped around the man's head, "butch."

"Thank you," Travus pulled the pink piece of cloth off his head with his free hand, "I can't imagine that this came as an order from the General. Or from Ophelia. She treats every word from his mouth quite literally, doesn't she?"

Kitanah started reaching for the bundle to take it back but stopped herself. Instead, she quickly spun around and marched out of the room with the door closing with a much hardier slam than usual.

When Travus turned to his daughter, he noticed that his words not only elicited a reaction out of the assassin but Tilly as well. Her chocolate colored eyes dug daggers at him while her lower lip twitched with the effort to keep from bursting into tears.

"I'm sorry, sugar blossom. I'm trying to get us out of here and to do that," he motioned to the door, "I have to get her to do something she wouldn't want to do under normal circumstances."

"What does that have to do with *her*?" Tilly stomped toward the bed.

"Ophelia took Kitanah's position as the General's First Bravo," her father knelt down beside the mattress as he explained himself, "I wish I could explain in more detail, Tilly, but they could be listening to us right now."

The little girl rolled onto her side in the bed, with her back to her father, and pouted into her pillow. She shut her eyes tight, not giving the tears a way to get out and pretended to go to sleep.

AFTER A WEEK…

"Want to play 'I spy' again?" Tilly let out a quiet sigh, or stifled a yawn, both were starting to happen with regularity lately.

Travus shook his head, "It's the door, or the handle of the door. You always pick the door."

"No, I–" his daughter started to protest but she just let herself drop back to lean against the wall again. "Fine. I was going to pick the door again."

Both father and daughter were sitting on the floor with their backs against the wall. To their right was the bed and the doorway stood almost directly across from them.

"Shouldn't Kitanah have been here with breakfast by now?" the girl asked.

The man scratched at his chin, which had a good coating of scruff by now since he was denied a razor at every turn, "I think so. She's never been overly punctual but she hasn't let us starve yet."

"You know, for an assassin, she's not so bad," Tilly idly picked at a lose strand on the hem of her burgundy dress.

"Only because you don't know what she had to do to get as high of a rank as she has attained," Travus leaned his head toward his daughter, "That sleeve she wears isn't there so that she can play waitress, you know."

The girl puckered her lips up at the man, "I know that. I'm just saying we could have had someone a lot worse guarding us."

That *worse* was Ophelia. One thing Travus had noticed was that everything that his daughter hated and feared was now embodied in the woman that had been the beloved daughter of the farmers Alvin and Perse.

The Night Shield found himself wondering how much of the original Ophelia was left in the assassin that Doctor Efreeti made. Was there even any of the real Ophelia in there at all?

His musings were interrupted by the door opening. No knock like usual, the slab of wood just swung open to reveal the General's First standing on the other side of the threshold.

As Ophelia lifted a foot to step inside, Tilly let loose a piercing scream and scrambled over her father to escape under the bed. The assassin's foot froze for a moment but then she continued her way inside.

"Sorry for the delay, Browder," she said with one hand resting on her round hip and the other resting on the grip of her bastard sword, "But your Keian is ready to begin now."

Stepping off to the side, Ophelia motioned for Travus to go out the door. Instead, he knelt down beside the bed and lifted the blankets to check on his daughter.

"I'll be back in a bit, sugar blossom," he said in as gentle of a voice as he could manage.

"Don't go with her, Daddy," the little girl whispered back, "She'll kill you like she did Mommy."

Travus looked back at the woman, who now stood with her firm arms crossed over her chest. Judging from the tapping of her boot, her patience was already starting to wear thin.

"No she won't, Tilly," he looked back at his daughter, "She can't for the same reason I'm still alive now."

The little girl looked at her father quizzically from the darkness under the bed. Without asking, she realized that it was another one of those things he couldn't explain to her at the moment. A lot of his work had been like that when she was growing up but it was only since their capture that the idea started to upset her.

"Let's go," Ophelia spoke up (and Tilly cringed deeper into the shadows) again, "No one will disturb her while you're gone. I promise."

The promise of a murderer. Did that actually hold any weight with anyone? Travus sighed as he lifted himself up to his feet.

He had already changed into the clothes that Kitanah had given him several days ago. They were very much like what the lowest tier assassins wore around the keep, minus the sash, of course. A gray shirt made of a sturdy but fine cotton and brown pants that were a little more form fitting than he was used to.

Since he didn't have much room to move around and he wasn't a sloppy eater they were still, at least mostly, clean. However, they did have their fair share of wrinkles and creases.

The Night Shield started for the door. "I'll be back soon, sugar blossom." He said as he walked by the assassin.

Once in the hallway, Ophelia closed the door behind them and pulled the key out of the lock once it was secured. Travus didn't see what happened to the key after that.

"Why did you come to collect me instead of Kitanah?" Travus kept his tone that of casual conversation.

"I was busy doing other things for the General," Ophelia stayed behind the man as they walked and talked, "so Kitanah was given the job of guarding you. But, from what I'm to understand, it always comes down to the First to collect the prisoner for their Keian."

Travus looked back over his shoulder at the woman, "From what you're to understand? I figured you'd know everything about how the Al Razheem does things by now."

Ophelia's pale eyes narrowed, "By now? What do you think you know about me?"

Travus turned, continuing to walk in the same direction only backwards, "That you've been with the clan for a few months. That's usually plenty of time for indoctrination."

"I've never really been one for doctrine," she snapped back.

"And how would you know that?" he asked, "What were you up to before you became Al Razheem?"

Rage slowly engulfed the woman's face. The only thing she physically did, though, was to point straight ahead.

"Walk," she ordered, her voice a coarse growl.

"I have to wonder," he turned around and kept walking as the assassin ordered, "Street walker, maybe? Nah, you have the wardrobe but not the air of desperation. I know, a carriage driver! No, wait, are you any good with horses? I got it this time. You had to be a farmer, right?"

He looked back to closely watch Ophelia's reaction to his last suggestion. He had to know for sure if there was any of Alvin and Perse's daughter left.

Not even a quirk of the eyebrow, a twitch of the eye, a hint of a frown, nothing. How could someone be *erased* so completely? She would never care who her parents were. She was nothing but a tool for the Al Razheem and the General's insane wish to somehow become immortal.

And she was the one that murdered his wife. Now, if he could figure out a way to negate those runes on her back, Travus could kill this Ophelia for her crimes free of guilt. Free of the idea that he was killing an innocent girl under mind control and the child of people he had come to respect. They surely wouldn't want her to continue living like this.

As his mind raced for any kind of method of killing that those enchanted tattoos couldn't counter, Ophelia ordered Travus to stop walking. They stood on a wooden platform about twenty feet wide. He had been so preoccupied that he hadn't even noticed that they had left the hallway.

At each corner of the platform was a wooden pillar with a system of ropes and pulleys attached. On the pillar that Ophelia approached was a hose with a cone on the end. The end was almost as big around as her head.

She lifted the cone to her mouth, "We're ready down here," she said.

After almost a minute, the roof above them pulled away, revealing a room that was lit far brighter than the one the Night Shield and the assassin now stood within. After the opening became as wide as the platform, the wood square that he and Ophelia waited on rose.

It finally filled the open spot in what was now the floor, just as it was designed. The two were in the middle of what looked like a circular arena, complete with benches of seating lining the walls all around them.

Travus felt a series of thumps under his feet. Someone or something was under them, where he and Ophelia were standing alone just moments ago, and reinforcing the floor so that it would stay in its upper position securely.

Ahead of them, in seating that was built to be separate and more opulent than the benches all around, sat the General and Kitanah. He was slouched forward in his seat, resting his bearded chin on the back of his intertwined hands. To his left, on the other hand, the red haired woman looked uneasy. She sat uncomfortably straight with her arms crossed over her chest.

Travus wondered what could be so unsettling to her. As he looked around, he got what may have been an idea: there were no other Al Razheem assassins anywhere in the arena. Not one other on any of the benches or even in what, if Travus recalled correctly, were called the "Maester Seats" that only currently held two but were capable of holding up to five more.

Ophelia stepped toward the General, giving him a deep curtsy, "Here is the accused as requested, Master."

He smiled back at her, "Very good, Ophelia. Please feel free to come sit up here," he motioned to the seat on his right.

She did just that. Not giving Travus a second glance, she walked straight into the box seats and sat beside her beloved Master. Ophelia lounged back in her polished wooden chair, leaning in closer to the General.

"Isn't a Keian supposed to be a public event, General?" Travus spun around to make a show of the emptiness of the immense room before focusing on the man to which the question was directed.

"Usually, yes," the General agreed, "But I wanted us to have a little talk first. Call this a little pretrial conference if it makes you feel better."

It really didn't. The Night Shield rested his hands on his hips as he looked from face to face to face of only other people in the room.

"And just how long were you planning this little preamble to last?" he asked.

The other man let out a soft grunt, "I guess that depends on you, really. I want you to explain to me why I've kept you alive this long. If it's for as big of a bluff as I think. You'll be dead before I have a second thought about you."

Kitanah's eyes snapped over to stare at her leader. Her head stayed looking straight ahead. That was what was bothering her. The General wasn't following his own rules.

Travus chewed on the inside of his cheek for a long moment. Finally, he nodded to himself and started talking.

"I'll tell you why I'm still alive, Kraven," he started, and felt a hefty shot of ego when he saw the General wince when the Night Shield used his given name, "I have a secret you don't want to be known. That is why you only have the two closest to you in here. So that you can claim the Keian was fair but still trust that they won't let your secret slip."

The General started to reply but Travus spoke over him to continue. That made face of the bearded man flush with rage.

Travus smirked, "But I'm also alive because you know I'm a man who attacks his problems from multiple angles and you know that I have a ringer in the case of my murder. You want to know what it is?"

The Night Shield unbuttoned his shirt and pulled it open. On the left side of his chest was a circle about the size of his palm that looked the same color as bone. Inside of that was a ring that looked to be attached to what could be best described as a cap. The skin around it was irritated, a practically glowing ring of red around whatever the mechanism was.

"You remember what this thing is, Kraven?" he asked the General but continued without the other man answering, "It's a heart plug. The highest ranking member of the Light Bringers gets this implanted as an alert system. If he is injured or killed, all Light Bringers know immediately where he is and rush to his aid."

"I remember," the General scowled, running a hand over his braided beard, "I also remember that your little *panic button* is only attuned to the Light Bringers in the city which it is implanted and, if memory serves, Paimae is running a bit thin at the moment."

The leader of the Al Razheem took a moment to be pleased with himself before Travus could speak again. The moment, though, was fleeting when the smile on the other man's face didn't falter.

"When it is properly tuned, you're absolutely right, Kraven. Sending your blinking whore there," the Night Shield nodded toward Ophelia, "did decimate our numbers in Paimae. It left me the highest ranking member of what was left in Paimae. It also kept the surgeon from having the time to localize the signal of this heart plug."

Travus continued, "You remember that old defect in these, right? An injured leader's plug would send an emergency signal to the entire continent and every Light Bringer would come rushing to their aid. It was nearly impossible to get an all clear signal sent via courier to get everyone to stand down."

The man stood in the middle of the empty arena, the room filling with silence for a long, long minute. The General had inadvertently pulled the left braid of his beard loose as he tried to contain his fury. Ophelia took a moment to be insulted but her face was again passive after her slate colored eyes took one big roll around her head. Kitanah, however, was taking the same moment to be amused by Travus calling Ophelia a whore, though she hid her smile behind her hand by pretending to be in deep in thought.

"I think I see our solution then," the patriarch of the assassins rose to his feet with a heavy grunt, "I'll have you taken away from the Oasis and fed to the rocs that fly around at night. Or perhaps the fire ants. They could use a warm meal."

"You might be able to stop me from manually activating this," Travus lifted a hand to fiddle with the ring that rested in the middle of the bone plug, "but what about when my dispatches start circulating?"

"Dispatches?" the General's shoulders shot up next to his hairy jaw.

"Didn't I mention those?" the Night Shield playfully slapped his own cheek, "You still use those hidden compartments to distribute kill orders like the one to kill the Ferdinand de la Granger that I intercepted. I just happened to place messages into each and every one that I know about to tell every one of your little hirelings who it was who recruited this vile traitor," Travus motioned to himself, "into your beloved Al Razheem in the first place."

The General turned and slammed his foot through his chair, shattering it into splinters. He erratically paced around in a circle between the two still sitting women, huffing and puffing without anything coherent actually coming out of his mouth. He'd completely lost control of himself.

The patriarch let out a vehement curse but only loud enough for his First and Second Bravos to hear. Finally noticing that his facial hair was messed, the General undid the braid on the left side just so they matched.

After taking a moment to smooth out the tensed, curled hair on his chin as best he could, the middle aged man turned back to face his prisoner, "Then it appears we are at an impasse, Travus. What is it you propose to rectify our predicament?"

"Let me take my daughter home and we can all get on with our lives like nothing ever happened," the chances of this working were just about zero but there was no real harm in trying, now was there?

"And count on the word of a traitor that he wouldn't sic his Light Bringer paramilitary force on us once he was clear?" the other man shook his head.

"Hey, I didn't start this, Kraven!" gor the first time, anger flared up in the words of the Night Shield, "I left your bloody little cabal years ago. I started a family. I left the region to make sure I didn't even chance a run in with one of your mooks!

"Then, all of the sudden an idiot in a red sash tries to stab me in the back while I'm walking in the market with my wife and child," Travus continued, his eyes stinging as his voice continued to rise, "I was forced to come back to Paimae so that the largest contingent of Light Bringers in the region could watch over my family. Then she happened."

The man shoved a finger in Ophelia's direction. The woman looked as if she was about to be sick. She clutched at the hilt of her sword, pressing the tip to the ground and using it to brace herself upright.

"She killed dozens of good men and women, Kraven. She murdered my wife! She kidnapped my daughter! Until then, I was willing to let you keep on doing your work despite my oath and everything I stood for as a Light Bringer," Travus clutched for the ring on his chest, "You want a war? Just remember that you brought this on yourself!"

Kitanah jumped to her feet, pointing to a door the Night Shield couldn't see from inside the arena in which he stood. "You do that, you sacrifice your child!"

Tilly was dragged into the Maester Seats section by an assassin in a blue sash. Blood trickled from the little girl's nose and her cheek practically glowed from the earliest stages of a bruise forming.

Still, she struggled against the grip of the man until she caught sight of Kitanah. For a moment, Tilly looked hopeful that the red haired woman would come to her aid, until Kitanah snatched the child by the collar of her dress and pulled until her head was only inches from the golden cuff of the metal sleeve of the assassin.

It started to spin, slowly building speed as the loose bladed hooks whipped through the little girl's brown hair, snipping strands with each pass. The little girl stared into the middle of the cuff, stunned into silence and petrified.

Ophelia also leaped to her feet at the sight of the child. She wasn't supposed to be here. Kitanah must have gone around her and had Tilly snatched from the holding cell after she collected Travus for this trial.

The tattooed woman's first reflex was to start to pull Havarti free from his scabbard, and he was more than willing to come out, but *something* stopped her. If the prisoner activated the heart plug, the General would be in danger. She… she couldn't have that.

Havarti protested in her mind but Ophelia didn't move toward Kitanah or the little girl. Instead, she wrapped a hand around the General's broad shoulder and pulled him away to place herself in between him and the scene of the standoff.

Travus hesitated at the sight of Tilly in Kitanah's hands. He played every edge he had. It had only gained him a week's reprieve, but it was a week with his daughter he wouldn't have had otherwise. Perhaps it was time to think of the greater good?

If Tilly was killed, Travus was going to activate the heart plug for sure. The best he could manage now was to keep them both prisoners in a castle full of murderers. It was only going to be a matter of time until the assassins found some way to counter this one advantage he had left.

If he and Tilly died here and now, at least the Light Bringers would have the location to the Oasis. In the years since he faked his death to leave the Al Razheem, he could never figure out how to explain how to find the keep. Nor could any other Light Bringer he brought back after showing them the location. At least now they would have a beacon to follow…

Kitanah was able to see the resignation that suddenly fell over him and she threw Tilly away, whipping her sleeve straight for the prisoner to stop him.

The little girl screamed in unbridled terror as she stumbled for Ophelia, who was still holding the grip of her bastard sword. She knocked the assassin off balance as Ophelia reflexively reached out to catch the girl.

Tilly's shriek distracted Travus long enough to not notice Kitanah's cutting sleeve flying straight for him. The hooked blades dug into his hand and arm, causing his hand to shudder and drop the ring. She pulled back with all her strength to keep him from getting his grip back on the plug's trigger.

Travus fell, spinning onto his back as his arm was tugged around by Kitanah's sleeve. The woman didn't wait for her weapon to pull him back to her, she ran out into the arena and pounced on the man to keep him from using his other arm to activate the device.

She stomped on his left hand to do just that. The assassin felt bones crunch under her stiletto heel as it dug into the man's left palm. As Kitanah stood over him, keeping him immobilized, Travus had to look up to see what happened to his daughter.

Ophelia was holding the little girl in a tight bear hug while Tilly kicked and squirmed with everything she had. Oddly enough, the full grown woman was taking hits to her shins and knees that she didn't have to in order to keep from injuring the girl.

She had already killed Inara, Tilly's mother. Why not just kill the little girl now that he was restrained and couldn't trigger his only failsafe?

Travus heard the General mutter a very similar question to Ophelia. While he wasn't able to hear the answer, he did see the woman's patriarch eventually nod in agreement. Then the older man rested his hand on the back of Tilly's neck and she slowly lost consciousness.

The Night Shield was right behind her. Kitanah dropped her hand onto the neck of the Night Shield in a similar manner to what the General did to his daughter but, unlike how it seemed for Tilly, the assassin made sure that his loss of consciousness was as painful as possible...

FOURTEEN
THE ONLY REAL OPTION

A COUPLE OF DAYS LATER...

"The sun is long since down, my dear," Havarti said, "Shall we begin?"

Ophelia tied down the largest flap of the backpack and lifted herself off of her knees, "I guess it's now or never," she answered.

The woman snatched her sword off the bed and tucked it back into the scabbard resting on her hip. She started for the door to her room, picking up the pack and slinging it over her shoulder.

The hallway was empty when she closed the door behind her. Not that she was expecting much of a crowd. That was why she picked this time of the night to leave, after all.

Ophelia only walked past a couple of other Al Razheem along her way. Over the months that she had been a part of their ranks, it had become common knowledge not to ask the General's First where she was going, what her business was, or why she was carrying whatever was on her at the time. That came to her advantage now.

As she neared the room that held Travus, the blue sash wearing assassin that took Tilly up into the arena during the Keian was standing guard beside the door. Shortly after, she learned that his name was Soren and was now taken position as Kitanah's new First with Hinder's death.

He was tall, muscular and had short, spiky black hair. Despite the difference in skin tone (He was very, very pale compared to Hinder) it was obvious that Kitanah had a type.

Soren looked at the woman questioningly, obviously not expecting her. She set the backpack down on the floor, leaning it against the wall opposite the door.

"Mistress Ophelia," he gave her a welcoming, of somewhat hesitant, bow, "to what do I owe the pleasure."

The woman smiled back, "I just wanted to see how you were doing down here. It is my fault that you are stuck with this duty, after all."

Soren shook his head and smiled back, "No, not at all, Mistress. The fact that you requested I take this post was a great honor."

"Oh? That's good to hear," Ophelia rested one hand on her hip and her right hand on the grip of her bastard sword, "I've been meaning to talk to you and it's been so hard to get you alone and in private."

"What about, Mistress?" Soren's high eyebrows betrayed his curiosity.

"To thank you, really," she answered, "Havarti and I haven't been seeing eye to eye on a lot of things lately. You are the first thing that we have agreed on in the longest time."

"Havarti?" Soren's head tilted at the unfamiliar name.

"My sword," Ophelia answered, stepping up to him and finding him about half a head taller than her, "You managed to upset both of us by dragging that little girl up into the arena the other day."

"I was just following Mistress Kitanah's orders, M-Mistress," on reflex, Soren pressed himself back against the cold sandstone wall.

"I know. But I can't really go after her right now, can I?" the woman twisted the handle of the bastard sword and pulled the hidden dagger free from Havarti's hilt.

The thin blade quickly slashed across the throat of the heavily muscled assassin, then pierced one lung, and finally bored a hole into the man's liver before tugging the azure length of silk from around his waist.

Soren slid down the wall as Ophelia wiped his own blood from the dagger's surface on his shirt and tucked it back into the hiding place in the sword's grip. He couldn't cry for help because is vocal cords were slashed. He couldn't breathe due to the blood now filling his chest cavity crushing the air out of his lungs.

And the pain in his side... The pain was excruciating! He knew that he wouldn't have to bear it long, that each and every cut that the General's First inflicted on him were in a race to see which would end his life first. At least, the stabs into his throat and chest were competing for that honor.

Perforating his liver, that would have killed him on its own but slowly, painfully. That was a kill shot used if the assassin wanted the victim to suffer...

Ophelia crouched down in front of the dying man, "You punched her to get her to come with you, right? I know from personal experience that she can be a handful. But I promised that the girl wasn't even going to be disturbed, let alone hurt. You made a liar out of me, Soren."

The woman stood up and opened the door into the room Travus awaited within, "Not that I'm a pinnacle of honesty or anything but that was one promise I meant."

She wasn't sure whether or not Soren heard that last remark or not before his body finally gave out. In keeping with the theme of honesty, Ophelia didn't really care. She stepped into the room, already fumbling with the keys from the guard's sash.

It was the same room that Travus and Tilly were held in before the Keian. This time every piece of furniture had been removed and the little girl was being held back in the room down the hall she'd been in previously.

Travus sat on his knees, his arms locked in manacles attached to chains that stretched to the walls on either side of him. There was to be no chance that he could activate the panic button on his chest so his arms were pulled so that he looked as if he was a child pretending to be a bird with its wings outstretched.

The captured Night Shield still wore the gray shirt that had been given to him wide open like when he revealed the existence of the heart plug to his captors. His right sleeve was rolled up and the wounds from Kitanah's sleeve bandaged.

He was looking straight down, either asleep or moping, the woman figured. She gave the top of his head a rough tap with a fingertip to get his attention.

Ophelia crouched in front of him much like she had Soren outside, "Travus Browder. You and I need to have a talk."

The man looked up at her, his brown eyes full of so much contempt that he didn't need words to tell the woman how badly he wished she was dead. He tried to use some of the most colorful pieces of syntax that came to mind but the gag in his mouth obscured every one of them. It took a bit of time before he realized that Ophelia was holding a key up just in front of his face.

"I am willing to unlock your cuffs and get you out of the Oasis," she said, "But, in return, I need your help to save the General."

Travus laughed so hard that his head hurt. He sound was muffled, sure, but the tears rolling down his cheeks betrayed how much the very idea amused him.

"Did I mention that your daughter would be leaving with us?" Ophelia added.

And he stopped laughing.

"I take it that means you understand," the woman untied the gag from around his head and tossed it away.

"Tilly's still alive?" Travus asked after spitting the taste of the untreated leather out of his mouth.

The General's First nodded, "Back in the room she was held in before you came."

So much of the tension that had been holding him upright suddenly washed away from Travus' body. Ophelia thought she heard him mutter "thank you, Juna", which she figured was some kind of prayer but she didn't bother to ask about it.

He looked back up at the woman and asked, "How could I possibly save your General? Save him from what? I'm already bound up like a roast for the feast. What could he possibly have to worry about?"

"You know the rule that the one who recruited a traitor is killed with them after their Keian, right?" Ophelia asked the question even though she already knew the answer.

"That particular bylaw was what I was counting on to keep me alive if our rescue plan didn't pan out," Travus looked from one manacled wrist to the other, "I think it's safe to say that the plan was a bit of a letdown."

The assassin waved off his last comment like an errant belch and continued, "But the General was the one who recruited you in the Al Razheem, wasn't he?"

"Not that he even chanced anyone hearing that the entire time I've been here," Travus pouted.

"I think Kitanah figured it out," Ophelia said, "or she will soon, at least. That's why I need to get to Paimae and negotiate a deal to get protection for the General."

Skeptical was a muted way of describing how the Night Shield felt at that moment. "Protect the General. From the Al Razheem. In exchange for what?"

"He's run the clan since its inception, right?" Ophelia lifted herself back to her feet, "What if he shared everything he knew about the Al Razheem's operations? That would warrant saving his life, right?"

The disbelief Travus felt was unmoved, "He would help the Light Bringers take down the very organization he spent his entire lifetime building? Pull the other one, lady."

"I don't give a damn about the Al Razheem, Browder," Ophelia snapped back at the shackled man, "and why would he protect the very people who are going to mark him for death?"

A little hobgoblin scratched at the back of the Night Shield's mind, "He doesn't know that you're doing this, does he?"

"The real question," the General's First tapped the end of the key against the metal of the cuff around Travus' right wrist, "is whether or not you are going to go straight for the plug in your chest if I cut you loose."

"Only if I think you're playing me," he said back, "Like if you're lying about my daughter being alive like you said that she'd be left alone before."

Ophelia felt her chest tighten and the urge to punch the man in the face. Havarti had to remind her (mentally of course) that, from the perspective of the Night Shield, she didn't keep her word. He didn't know of Kitanah circumventing Ophelia and taking the girl as leverage.

"We'll make a deal of our own then. Just between us," Ophelia slipped the key into the lock of the shackle but didn't turn it quite yet, "You don't trip your little widget trap thing at least until after I prove that your daughter is alive and well. Personally, I'd prefer if you held your wad until we were all within sight of Paimae."

"I'll hold off pulling the plug until after I've seen my daughter," Travus agreed, "I'll promise up to that far. Since I keep my word, I won't promise anything beyond that."

A little underhanded jab at Ophelia because of what happened with his daughter. Again, Havarti had to remind her that the man didn't know the whole story.

The General's First turned the key and Travus' right hand fell free. It immediately shot for the ring implanted on the left side of his chest.

Ophelia snatched a handful of the Night Shield's hair and wrenched his head around until he was looking straight at her. "You can pull it now. Then I'll snap your neck like a twig and your daughter will be fed to the remaining hell hound along with your corpse. You want that?"

She was likely lying, he told himself. This was some kind of ploy to get him away from the Oasis so that triggering the heart plug wouldn't reveal the location of the Al Razheem home base. After all, everything Ophelia was offering was far too good to be true.

But what if this was the most unlikely of scenarios, that everything was as the assassin said? That would mean that the most powerful guild of assassins on the continent could finally be taken down. Travus wouldn't have to look over his shoulder again. His daughter, assuming she wasn't really dead, would be able to life the rest of her life in peace.

"I want my daughter back," he groaned as he lifted himself to his feet and shook the chain still attached to his left wrist, "Even if it's a one-in-a-million chance that you're telling the truth and she's still alive, I'll take it."

His finger never left the ring on his chest as Ophelia unlocked the second manacle. He was tempted to take a swing at her, to knock her out and go find his daughter on his own.

As if reading his mind, Ophelia smirked back at Travus, "Go ahead and try it. Just remember how well it went for you when you were actually armed."

He dropped his hands and rubbed his aching left wrist that was chafed by the metal cuff, "Alright. Let's go then."

"I'm starting to wonder about your track record when it comes to keeping your word," she couldn't resist a little verbal jab of her own back at the man.

He shrugged admitting (at least to himself) that his honesty wasn't exactly one hundred percent but it was up there. A solid ninety, er, eighty-five, eighty-two...ish percent of the time.

They stepped out into the hall. Travus actually had to stifle a yelp of surprise at the sight of Soren's corpse lying on the cold floor. His face twisted into a scowl when he recognized who the man had been when he was living.

"He was the one who took Tilly," Ophelia confirmed what the Night Shield was thinking as she picked the backpack up from the floor, "He didn't have my permission to do that. Kitanah sent him behind my back."

She tossed the heavy leather bag to the still living man. Then she held up the azure sash that had belonged to the now dead man and offered it to Travus.

"If no one looks at you too closely you can pass as my attendant," she explained as he tied the length of silk around his waist, "And button up."

Travus did as he was instructed while they made their way down the deserted hall. After a few steps, he looked like an Al Razheem that was a little worse for wear.

"We are heading for my daughter, right?" he whispered, just in case there were any guards patrolling around corners unseen.

Ophelia nodded, "Just as I promised. She just a couple of doors down," she spoke normally, not acting as if she was worried about any kind of discovery.

That made the suspicious hobgoblin in the back of the man's mind start to scratch again. He undid a couple of buttons on his shirt to make getting to the ring on the plug easier if this was indeed some kind of set up.

Ophelia again pulled out the keys she took from Soren as they neared a nondescript door. She pushed the key into the lock and twisted. With a push of the handle, the door came just away from the doorjamb.

"You might want to go in first," for the first time, the confidence that the woman had been radiating faltered, "I don't think she'll be overly pleased to see me."

The hobgoblin jumped up and down, scratching at the fight-or-flight instinct in Travus's mind. He scanned all around the door for any sign of a tripwire or other kind of trap. The man couldn't see one but that didn't mean that they weren't there.

"You go ahead," Travus gave her a mocking, gentlemanly curtsy, "I insist."

Ophelia eyed the door for a long moment but then sighed and nodded back at him, "Okay, but don't say that I didn't warn you," And she pushed the door open.

A scream so piercing that Travus instantly had a headache exploded through the air. The man dashed into the room after Ophelia, shoving her to the side until he saw his daughter.

He rushed over to Tilly, wrapping his arms tightly around her, "Shh, shh, shh, it's okay, sugar blossom. I'm here. I'm here."

He buried his face in the little girl's hair as they refused to let each other go. She was really there. She was alive. She was alive!

"I hate to spoil the moment," Ophelia groaned as she picked herself up off the floor, "But we really do need to get going."

Both father and daughter glared back at her. Travus, though, was surprised to see Ophelia rubbing her shoulder. The woman must have hit it against the wall or floor when he forced his way past. So... did that mean that she wasn't invincible?

Again, Ophelia picked the backpack up from the floor. Travus didn't even realize that he dropped it. She rifled through one of the pockets until she pulled was looked like a crystal brooch out and tossed it to the Night Shield.

"Put that on her," she ordered and then held out the backpack, "And take this back. You're acting like the worst attendant ever."

A shade of that arrogance she had before they entered the room crept back into her voice but it wasn't there as strongly. Travus took the brooch and looked at it curiously.

Again, as if she were reading his mind, she answered his unspoken question, "You can pass as an Al Razheem. She can't. That will obscure her from everyone's sight as we walk out. As long as they don't look at her directly."

"What's that supposed to mean?" the man actually did ask.

"It was the best Efreeti could do on short notice," Ophelia answered, "Apparently, invisibility requires several days notice with the tools he has at his disposal."

"The thin man made that?" Tilly's entire body radiated with such worry that she could have been the poster child for it.

"I figured you wouldn't want to see him again, either," again, the arrogance slipped from the assassin as she spoke.

The little girl nodded in agreement. The first interaction she had with Ophelia that didn't involve screaming in terror or swinging her limbs around in a rage.

"It's okay, sugar blossom," Travus said as he fastened the crystal to the little girl's collar, "I'll keep an eye out for you."

"Just don't stare at her the entire time," Ophelia stepped over to the door and looked down the hall one direction and then the other, "Someone might wonder just what you're looking at and spot her."

Travus used the bed that Tilly clamored out of at the sight of the assassin to help push himself back up to his feet. He glared back at Ophelia for one more brief moment before looking back down at his little girl.

She was gone! His daughter had been sitting on the floor right in front of him literally three seconds ago!

"Tilly!" Panic rushed through his body as he started searching for her.

"I'm right here, Daddy," his daughter tugged at his right sleeve, the one with all the little tears from Kitanah's sleeve weapon.

He looked down in the direction of his child's voice and it was like she suddenly appeared in front of his eyes rather than having been standing there the whole time. That stood as proof that the crystal did in fact work.

Ophelia turned to face back into the room again, leaning against the side of the doorjamb, "Hey, kid, since no one can see you now, would you mind going to the end of the hall and checking if there are any patrols wandering around?"

Tilly was about to say something that was not going to be overly kind when her father's hand came to rest on her shoulder. The father gave his little girl his best comforting smile as he nodded to her.

"It's okay, sugar blossom," he said, "Just go to the next intersection and wait. I'm sure we won't be long."

His daughter nodded and, seemingly without moving, shimmered and disappeared from sight. After an *accidental* shove against Ophelia's hip, the girl was out of the room.

Ophelia tossed the backpack the man kept ignoring into his arms, "If you're thinking of triggering your thingy now, I wouldn't."

Travus slipped the straps of the bag over his shoulders, "And why is that?"

"You know that Efreeti gave that heart plug thing of yours a good going over," the woman explained, "He said he wasn't able to deactivate it but he did tell me how it worked."

The Night Shield wondered what the point to her story was. He didn't interrupt, though, figuring that it would make itself plain soon enough.

"When you pull on that ring, it sends out some kind of signal that makes the bones of the inner ear of any Light Bringer vibrate," Ophelia shrugged, unable to resist a little aside, "I didn't even know that there were bones in the ear!

"That vibration draws them to the location of that thing," she pointed at the plug on the man's chest even though it was covered by his shirt, "Until they find you, the Light Bringers would be drawn to this place like moths to a flame."

There was a little more to it, of course, but Travus had to admit that was a pretty accurate description of how the heart plug worked to warn the Light Bringers of leadership in danger. Still, he felt that she hadn't made her point yet and said as much.

"The point," Ophelia gave the hallway a quick scan before continuing, "is that Efreeti also taught me some interesting things about crystals, too. Like, for instance, did you know that they could shatter with the force of an explosion when exposed to certain high pitched sounds? Even ones we can't actually hear?"

And there it was. The hobgoblin in the back of the mind of Travus cursed and stomped around in an exceptionally private tantrum.

What Ophelia was implying, or he was at least supposed to infer, was that if he activated the signal from the heart plug that it would also cause the crystal he just pinned to his daughter's chest to explode and kill her. Another blasted failsafe to protect her beloved General.

If all these little surprises and traps weren't being directed at him, Travus would have been impressed. The woman was covering as many angles as he would have in her position.

Travus stepped out into the hallway, "I presume that taking off the brooch will have the same effect as pulling the ring?"

"That would be logical," Ophelia nodded, "But I'll take it off when we get to Paimae. Promise!"

Great. Another promise from a professional liar and killer. What possible down side could there be?

IN ANOTHER PART OF THE OASIS...

There was a knock at his door that Doctor Efreeti was not expecting, "One moment!" he bid the unknown visitor.

Wrapping the tweed cloak around himself, he was again the thin man that everyone in the keep had come to recognize. With a jaunty gait to this step, the being in human...ish guise stepped up and unlocked the wooden portal.

Then, like realizing he'd missed a point on a checklist, Efreeti reached out and pulled the door open. The visitor was revealed to be the General's Second, Kitanah Ursa Baynetta, the seventh daughter of Camilla Diynne Kitherun, who was, in turn herself a seventh daughter. Not that Efreeti kept such information available to himself at the notice of a single whim.

The woman looked uneasy. Having shared the history of their interactions, the thin man could hypothesize as to why. She has never trusted Efreeti all the while he had been taking up residence in the home of the Al Razheem. She had often gone through special effort to keep her commentary just short of accusing him of treachery but still make the General doubt the motives of the human-like man. And now she was standing at his door.

"To what can I attribute this pleasure?" Efreeti smiled oh so wide.

The woman's eyes darted one way down the hall, then the other before she again looked at him, "May I come in?" she practically whispered.

"Oh please do," Efreeti stepped aside to allow her entry into, as Kitanah had so eloquently dubbed it in the past, his *lair*.

When he closed the door behind the woman, Kitanah visibly jumped. The sunlight had had been pouring through the window without a frame suddenly sank away to be replaced with a night sky, filled almost to overflowing with shimmering stars. It was almost as bright as it was before but now the quality of the light was... colder.

Silence filled the space. Efreeti stood unnaturally still, like a statue that had yet to be put into the garden or graveyard for which it had been commissioned. Kitanah was breathing like a novice swimmer struggling to stay afloat in water deep enough to go over her head.

Finally, though, she did find the gumption to speak, "It was not an easy decision for me to come to you, Efreeti. But there's no one else I can talk to without word getting back to the General."

The thin man arched the skin where an eyebrow would have been. This was getting tastier already and the conversation had just started.

"When Ophelia's parents came for her, I was so sure that you and she were conspiring with them to destroy or usurp the Al Razheem," she hesitantly turned to look at the thin, human-like man as she spoke, "After what happened, I know I was wrong."

"Indeed you were, dearie," Efreeti tapped a clawed fingertip along his lower lip for a moment, "but it was not a conclusion without merit. After all, you know nothing of me or my interests. None of which go to the political leanings or control of the Al Razheem or any mortal organization, just to be clear.

"But as you are so thoroughly trained to be suspicious, I do understand why you did not come and speak to me before," his finger moved from his mouth to push his round glasses up higher along the bridge of his narrow nose, "But, for the life of me, I cannot hazard a guess to why you seek my council now."

"Will our conversation stay in confidence?" again, her emerald eyes darted around for any sign of danger.

Efreeti nodded, "Indeed, it will, my good woman. While I am in partnership with your General, I do not owe him any special fealty that I cannot hold a new found friend's words in trust."

Saying that Kitanah relaxed at his words would fall under the category of overstatement but her insides didn't shake quite so much after hearing that. Still, she hadn't come for reassurances but for a cause she felt vital to the survival of the soul of her family.

"It's about the General, you see," the words didn't want to come out of her mouth but she forced them, one by one, "I think he's no longer the watching over the Al Razheem but his own interests."

Efreeti let out a quiet grunt, "Were you not the one who told me that the General and the Al Razheem were one and the same?"

"I thought so," Kitanah's eyes closed tight as she shook her head, "But that was before Ophelia came to us."

Dark clouds started to form in the sky at the edges of the window floating behind the woman. The thin man seemed to become even taller as he stepped closer to her.

"Surely you don't blame Ophelia for whatever troubles you with your General," his voice sounded like how cold stone felt.

"I wanted to. I so, so wanted to," Kitanah took a moment to try and rub the tension out of her face before she continued, "But she proved herself unflinchingly loyal to the General during the incursion. But I came to realize that the Al Razheem may have outgrown the General."

"Oh?" the clouds in the window quickly drifted away as amusement seemed to refill Efreeti, "How so?"

"I went and spoke to Ophelia afterward," the woman said, "She didn't know anything about how a Keian worked. And you do know that she has never picked a Second Bravo, let alone a First since she was given my old position with the General?"

"And what does that tell you?" the thin man asked.

"That the General, the man who taught me everything I know, he has never taught anything about the Al Razheem to Ophelia," she answered, "Then I realized that if he had really wanted her to know, he would have had you program our tenets into those runes you put on her back."

Efreeti nodded, looking impressed, "Indeed, I put all the information and skills he asked for into Ophelia. He did not provide me with the tomes that contain your bylaws and procedures."

"I think he's been using her to hide his crimes against the Al Razheem," Kitanah's unease disappeared when she spoke aloud the very idea that troubled her so, "After you gave Ophelia to the General, I noticed that pockets of my brethren were being killed in a systematic fashion. I suspected her but the General told me not to investigate further."

Efreeti stood and nodded reassuringly. He struggled so hard to keep his excitement contained to within his cloak.

"But I didn't stop," Kitanah confessed, "I later learned that the strangers killed with our men were Night Shields. All the assassins Ophelia killed were betraying the Al Razheem by feeding information to the Light Bringers!"

"Then it sounds to me that the General was simply skipping the step of your Keian and moving straight to sentencing and killing those who were betraying your people," Efreeti only said what would have been apparent to a less devious mind.

"That was what I thought at first," the woman agreed, "but then Travus Crichton showed up. Only now he was calling himself Browder. I checked into it and every assassin that Ophelia had been sent to kill was recruited by Travus Crichton. Travus was a Light Bringer plant from the start!"

"That does beg the question of who recruited this Travus Crichton or Browder or whatever into the Al Razheem in the first place," the thin man pointed out.

"And that was erased from the records," Kitanah continued, "I was hoping to ask him during the Keian, which would have been my right there, but the General picked a fight with Browder and I had to subdue him before I could ask the question."

Indeed, Efreeti was impressed at the woman's deductive reasoning, "And you feel that this lack of allowance to even ask the question was, in itself, the answer."

"I think the General recruited Travus himself," the woman concluded, "But I don't want to... do what I have to do without being absolutely sure."

Efreeti guided the woman to the marble table, as it was the only place he had where she could sit down, "It sounds as if Mister Crichton/Browder would have been a more logical destination than my uninformed self," he said as he slipped onto the marble slab beside her.

"Any access to him has to go through Ophelia now," Kitanah sighed, "She's even co-opted my new First to stand guard. And before you ask, no I can't use him to get in. He feels that being chosen by the General's First Bravo was a great honor and a step up from serving under me. Soren won't betray Ophelia's trust on his first duty assignment."

"I take it that means that you already tried," Efreeti chuckled.

The woman nodded in agreement. She looked so hopeless, like everything she had lived, fought and killed for was suddenly revealed to be a lie.

"I have a way that could perhaps reveal the truth to you, if you are willing to give it an attempt," Efreeti decided it was time to be more than a sounding board to the assassin.

"How?" she asked.

"Many of my skills revolve around the manipulation of energy. To do so effectively, I must be able to identify those energies with a high degree of accuracy," Efreeti's pride was obvious as he spoke, "With the project that created Ophelia, it was necessary for me to master those energies that mortals share among each other be they familial, relational or organizational."

Kitanah narrowed her eyes at the human-like man, "What do you mean *organizational*?"

"When one joins an assemblage of like-minded individuals, oftentimes oaths are taken," the man explained, "Those oaths link that subject to the energy for which that association stands."

"So you can detect what groups a person has sworn fealty to," she said back.

Efreeti nodded, "And the strength of the bond reflects the amount of time and energy one has devoted toward that oath."

"So if you looked over Browder's energy, you would be able to tell if he was a member of the Light Bringers before he took the oaths to infiltrate the Al Razheem," it looked like hope had returned after all.

He nodded again, "If I had something of his to be able to tap into his energy signature."

"What about his blood?" Kitanah held her metal sleeve up, displaying the sharpened hooks with dried ichor still clinging to them, "I haven't really had a chance to give it a good cleaning yet."

Efreeti leaned in close to the lifted cuff, inspecting the offered samples for viability, "Yes... yes, I believe that could work. To evaluate his connection to your General, I would need something of his, as well."

Kitanah's red lips pressed tightly together in thought for a moment, "He gave me this as a memento when I left to assassinate the old Xaviour Vizier. Would this work?"

She pulled a small metallic vial from the inside of the black belt wrapped around her waist. The family crest of the General was etched into the surface of the vial. The workmanship was skillful but hardly of a professional grade, it was likely that the patriarch of the Al Razheem had inscribed the vial himself.

Efreeti wrapped two claws around either side of a hook on Kitanah's cuff, scraping the offered blood sample, with one hand while the other took the vial from her hand. He brought both hands close to his mouth, muttering something so quietly that the woman couldn't make out anything he said. She wasn't even sure the sounds coming from the man-like creature were even really words.

A puff of air escaped from between his flat lips and two sparks of light, one crimson and the other gold, leaped away to rest in the air in front of the thin man and the General's Second. After a few seconds, the red light changed into a shape that roughly resembled the shape of Travus Browder. The gold light changed to look like the General laying in his bed, although the piece of furniture wasn't visible.

"So how do you reveal their connections?" Kitanah asked, her eyes locked on the two figures hovering in front of her.

To answer her question, Efreeti poked the sharp tip of his forefinger into the head of the gold figure like one would to dip their finger into soup for a taste test. When he pulled the curved claw out, thin streams of light followed.

Thin strings of gold whipped out every which way from the likeness of the General, each of varying thickness. Each ended with little simple silhouettes of other assassins in the Al Razheem.

The thickest, though, took the the longest to reach its destination. It dribbled almost straight down from the General until it finally pooled near the black floor, taking the shape of Kitanah sitting down on the unseen slab of stone beside the equally nonexistent Doctor Efreeti.

"These are all the still living mortals that the General had a personal hand in bringing into your fold that have taken the oaths required to join your Al Razheem," the thin man said.

One gold string stretched further than the others. Other than Kitanah's, it was easily the thickest. It buried itself into the red blob of light that was Travus Crichton's likeness.

"That proves conclusively that this man has taken the same oaths as you," Efreeti reported, "If he had followed the Al Razheem's tenets, it is likely that his bond light would have been even stronger than yours."

The woman scanned through every light as best she could, "Where is Ophelia? Am I just missing here in all of this?"

"Apparently, you were correct when you said that the General had no interest in Ophelia being Al Razheem," Efreeti shook his head, "She has not taken the required oaths."

Kitanah looked personally insulted when she heard that. Then disappointment washed across her face but only for a moment. Her demeanor changed into a way that the man would have described as focused.

"What about his bonds to the Light Bringers?" she pointed to the red light.

Efreeti didn't even bother to hide his smile as he dipped his claw into the crown of the little semblance of Travus Browder. A geyser of crimson flowed from the little man away from the interwoven matrix of golden lights. Each and every one were thicker and stronger than the gold stream that connected Crichton to the General.

"That conclusively shows that Travus Browder has not only served the Light Bringers longer than his oaths with the Al Razheem but has also gone through great pains to live by their rules and traditions," the man-like creature in tweed concluded.

Efreeti did not expect the reaction to come from the woman. Kitanah leaned forward, wrapping her hand around her mouth as if she was attempting to keep herself from vomiting.

"The General did recruit Travus," she finally muttered.

"It is so," Efreeti agreed.

Something else caught Kitanah's eye, "The General looks like he is sleeping, so are these likenesses in real time?" she asked the thin man.

"They are."

"Then why doesn't Browder look bound and gagged?" she again pointed at the blob of red light, "Where is Ophelia now?"

"I told you, dearie, that she has not taken the oaths of an Al Razheem assassin," Efreeti answered.

"You said that you could track people interconnected by relations. What did you mean by that?" she asked.

"Typically, those with family bonds or those with an intense emotional connection or have had, shall we say, intimate relations with the target could have bond lights that can be tracked," Efreeti explained slowly, as if he was speaking to a small child.

"Track Ophelia," Kitanah ordered.

"In order to perform that type of bond search I would need the General himself, or at least a sample of his body or blood," Though it took all of his control to conceal it, Efreeti was almost ready to dance in giddy jubilation.

The woman scowled, "You have to have someone she's been in bed with physically here to perform the search? Take what you need from me then."

"You? But you are not of the opposing gender... oh," the man in tweed would have doubled over laughing if it wouldn't have gone against his purposes, "One of the General's extracurricular activities, I take it. A waste of time, if you ask me, but I am not one to judge."

Efreeti reached over to Kitanah's shoulder and sank the claw of his forefinger into her pale flesh. The woman winced but otherwise didn't make any noise.

The man-like creature pulled out his claw, now coated with her blood, and dipped it into the simulacrum of Kitanah that floated beneath the rest.

Blue lines of light shot to various spots in the castle, some of them overlapping with the likenesses of assassins already represented in gold light. One bond line, though, shined violet (coincidentally the same shade as the runes tattooed on Ophelia's back?) and swept up beside the crimson silhouette of Travus Browder.

Kitanah let out a thick curse, "Where are they?" she growled.

"Did you not realize, my dearie, that not only are the people represented in real time but also geographically accurate?" Efreeti asked.

"You mean that where everyone is here is where they actually are in relation to each other? To us?" she looked down at the wound in her shoulder, the metal sleeve making her unable to cover it so all she could do was let it bleed.

"Indeed, if you will not judge me too harshly..." with only a couple of steps the door rushed up to the man in tweed even though the marble table didn't move any further away.

A disgusting noise came from Efreeti. The sound that came from usually lower class men when they were violently forcing mucus from their sinuses and into their mouths. He pursed his lips as if he were about to whistle but instead loosed a sickly yellow glob of slime that struck the door and slowly started to roll down the surface of the wood.

He turned and pointed at the myriad of lights and a transparent model of the castle, made from green wire work of light built itself around the gold lights. The red and purple lights representing Travus and Ophelia stood at the edge.

"She's taking him from Oasis," Kitanah started for the door but, no matter how fast she walked it never got closer.

The table, though, didn't get any further away, either. Her emerald eyes locked onto Efreeti who simply shrugged.

"There is no way you can get to them in time, Kitanah," the words came out as if he was stating fact, "Instead, focus on why would she be taking a traitor away?"

Kitanah wanted to rant. She wanted to force Efreeti to let her go so she could hunt Ophelia and Browder down. But, and this only further enraged her to admit it, Doctor Efreeti was right. They were already at the main gate. Ophelia and Browder would be long since gone by the time she could even raise the alarm.

She couldn't go after them now anyway. The rocs were getting ready to take flight and go on the hunt. It was why no assassin was ever to come to or leave the Oasis at night. Ophelia was likely counting on her blinking to counter an attack by the giant bird, if it happened upon her and her charge.

But why? Why would she set the Night Shield traitor free? There were only two possibilities. Either the General was trying to get Browder away from the Oasis so that his heart pump would not betray the location of their home. Travus seemed to be going along of his free will, though, and he would not give up that advantage for nothing.

That left the second reason and it tore Kitanah's heart apart. Ophelia was taking the Night Shield back to Paimae to negotiate a deal to turn the General against the Al Razheem.

She would speak to the General first thing in the morning. He deserved a chance to explain himself, at least. Besides, there were too many safeguards for Kitanah to counter during the night.

He left the woman only one real choice. The General's reign would end tomorrow. The only question would be if his reasoning left him remembered as a martyr or a betrayer...

THE MAIN GATE

"Daddy, why can't we just leave her behind and run?" Tilly asked, shielding her face from the blowing sand as father and daughter stepped outside of the sandstone keep.

It took Travus a couple of glances around to find her but, finally, he focused his attention down to his little girl, "It's complicated, sugar blossom. But please trust me when I say that we need Ophelia with us for now."

He didn't have the heart to tell his daughter that he had personally pinned a crystallized explosive to his little girl's chest. It surely had safeguards against removal, which meant that Ophelia was likely the only one that could do it.

Once they were well away from the keep, it was the only means Ophelia had of forcing Travus to keep his word to take her to Paimae. That also meant that all the leverage the Night Shield had in exposing the headquarters of the most powerful ring of assassins was gone, as well.

It was more important to save Tilly now. He always had another shot at taking the Al Razheem down later.

The heavy wood door kept pushing out further into the sand, opening wider thanks to Ophelia's effort at the wheel that controlled the mechanism to that door. The entryway to the Oasis was engineered so that it forced itself closed if there was no one at the wheels to keep the doors open. That was only natural considering the natural dangers of sandstorms and the not so natural danger of enemies at the gates.

The assassin could open the doors on her own and they would close behind her automatically, leaving no one in the keep any wiser that she was gone. Ophelia had an idea of about how fast the doors pulled themselves shut so, after Travus and Tilly stepped outside, the woman kept turning until she felt that she enough of a margin of error to get out without any real risk to herself. After all, the runes on her back protected Ophelia from fatal wounds but she didn't want to test whether they would keep a limb from being wrenched off between doors that weighed more than a ton.

The moment she released the wooden wheel, Ophelia dove off the platform down for the sand covered ground of the main court-yard. Tucking Havarti's hilt against her stomach, she rolled as she hit the sand until she found her feet. The woman wasted no time sprinting for the steadily closing door.

It seemed to be closing faster than usual. It didn't matter. She was committed now. If she didn't get through now, Travus and Tilly would not wait for her to try again and everything she had done would have been for nothing.

Ophelia had to turn her body sideways to get through the shrinking gap. She was about to breathe a sigh of relief when she heard a terrified scream.

"Keep going! Keep going! I don't want to die!" Havarti yelled.

That was when she noticed that while she was past the almost sealed entryway, the scabbard of her sword was still in harm's way. Havarti was about to be mutilated!

The woman stepped forward while pulling on her bastard sword's handle to swing his scabbard, with him still inside, out of the path of the door. The gold filigree on the end of the sheath was scraped off but the sword himself got out unscathed.

"I am so sorry," she said breathlessly.

Havarti harrumphed.

Ophelia would have argued with him about his attitude but Travus and Tilly (she presumed, because of the smaller tracks being left in the side beside the man) walked up to her. The man had a confused look on his face as he looked around.

"Who were you talking to?" he asked.

"Perhaps now is not the best time to make introductions," the sword spoke into Ophelia's mind.

"Fine, but please don't dwell on what almost happened with door, okay?" she telepathically replied while physically saying, "No one. It was just a close call."

The answer appeared to appease the Night Shield. He focused his attention on the dark, sand strewn landscape ahead of them.

"We should get as much distance between here and us as possible before sunrise," the man said before looking up, "Without drawing too much attention to ourselves."

"What do you mean?" Tilly spoke up, though neither adult could spot her immediately, "It's too dark for any sentinels to see us, right Daddy? You taught me that."

"It's not the guards on the keep walls I'm worried about." he knelt down in front of his daughter as he explained, "It's the rocs. Giant birds that live in the desert that only hunt at night."

"He's right," Ophelia said, stepping behind Travus and digging into the backpack he carried.

She pulled a small brown cloak from the largest pocket. Unfurling it, Ophelia held the garment out as far as her arm could reach.

"This is yours, Tilly. You may not need the camouflage but it'll protect you from any sandstorms we stumble into," the cloak stayed in the assassin's hand without any sign of moving, "Kid, if I could see you I'd just throw the thing to you but now you just have to take it, okay?"

The little girl let out a harrumph that almost put Havarti's to shame. But the cloak finally disappeared from Ophelia's hand. Tilly was visible for only a quick moment as she wrapped the earth colored cloak around her shoulders.

Ophelia started digging again. Out came another cloak, tan colored this time.

"This one is mine," the woman said to no one in particular and, after draping it over her shoulder, she continued digging, "And here's yours."

Travus turned his head enough to see a familiar garment made of red leather. He honestly thought that he wouldn't see it again. But, another thought did occur to him as he took his long coat from the woman.

"You know this doesn't exactly blend into the landscape," he said as he slipped the pack off to put the coat on.

"Protection from the sandstorms is more important at the moment," Ophelia answered as she put her own cloak on, "Besides, you know that rocs are colorblind."

"No sword, eh?" he asked as he patted the back of his coat.

"It was locked up and I didn't have time to go around stealing keys," the woman tugged the hood of her cloak up, hiding her face in shadow.

Travus nodded but then felt a tug at his sleeve. He looked down and his daughter shimmered into his sight.

"What does one have to do with the other, Daddy?" she asked.

"Hmm?" Travus seemed confused by his daughter's question.

"Sandstorms and rocs," the little girl clarified.

"Ah. The reason sandstorms are so prevalent at night is because of the rocs, Tilly." he explained, "Their wings cause such a downdraft that the sand whips around whatever is caught in the storm, giving the bird something to target and dive on."

"But I don't even see a hint of any storms all the way out to the horizon," Tilly disappeared from their sight as the three of them started walking.

"Rocs are so massive, Tilly, that they can cover great distances in only a couple of wing beats," her father slipped his hands under the straps of the backpack as they went along, "They also have such sharp eyes that they can spot something shiny like a silver coin from miles away."

Travus found himself smiling. He was reminded of trips he had taken with his family from one town to another for various assignments. Tilly would ask questions about everything from the animals they saw to trees they rode past while in a coach or walking along the road.

The Night Shield figured out pretty early on that he had to make himself very familiar with the region he commuted through with his family in pretty short order. Like him, Tilly never took "I don't know" for an answer.

Despite what was an inquisitive start, the talk became almost non-existent shortly after. That also reminded Travus that his family was severely damaged. His wife and the mother of his daughter dead, apparently killed right in front of Tilly by the very woman who enlisted his help. And was using his little girl as leverage so that he would cooperate.

Thankfully, while the wind sprayed sand in their faces there wasn't any sign of a sandstorm for the four hours they had been walking. Travus felt a tug at his sleeve that had become a familiar signal.

"What do you need, Tilly?" he asked after she appeared in his field of vision.

"Daddy, I'm hungry," she said.

Travus chewed on his lip thoughtfully for a moment. Ophelia had stopped several steps ahead of them and turned around. Pulling off her hood, she looked as annoyed as someone who wasn't accustomed to having to pause to at least hear out a child's demands.

The man motioned to the pack on his back, "You didn't happen to pack any food, did you?"

The woman sighed, "Yes, but I was hoping to at least keep going until dawn. Distance is our best friend at this point."

While Travus agreed with the sentiment, he started pulling the backpack off anyway. "Tilly isn't a soldier, Ophelia. She hasn't trained to do a hard march through rough terrain," he pulled back the flap to the largest pocket only to find it empty.

When he looked back up at the assassin, she rolled her gray eyes and pointed at different pockets, "The two on the left.

Don't expect gourmet cuisine. It's just some scraps I scrounged from the kitchens."

He pulled out a small burlap bag and pulled it open. Inside was a couple of handfuls worth of ground nuts. They were easy to identify because the shells typically had two bulges, one for each nut it held inside.

"Why don't you start with these, sugar blossom," Travus looked up to throw the bag to his daughter but couldn't find her.

He resigned himself to holding the pouch out so that she could come and get it. Once the bag disappeared in a shimmer, he resumed his search into the pockets.

He didn't notice the echoing screech at first. In fact it wasn't until Ophelia tapped his shoulder to take his attention from the bag that the distant noise occurred to him.

"That isn't what I think it is, is it?" the woman asked, her pale eyes narrowed and scanning the horizon.

The screech came again, louder this time. Travus suddenly wished that he had his sword at this particular moment.

"It's a roc," he confirmed Ophelia's worry, adding his own to the mix.

"We had better find some cover," the woman said, still searching for any sign of the beast.

A swirling cloud of dust rose on the horizon. Within a matter of seconds it doubled in size as it got closer.

"Are there no blasted boulders in this cursed country!" Travus spun around, searching for any kind of landscape that wasn't sand.

There weren't any. The small group could feel the wind start to pick up and grains of sand starting to scrape over their skin. The cloud was only seconds away now.

"Pull your hoods up!" Ophelia yelled, doing the exact thing she just ordered.

The man didn't have a hood on his coat so he pulled his collar up over his head. The sand was building up around their legs like the water of a river starting to flood.

"Duck down and don't move!" again, the assassin followed her own advice, "Let the sand bury everything except your head! The bird may not notice us!"

The sandstorm overtook them. Ophelia could barely see Travus who was only a handful of steps away from her. He was doing as the woman said and was already covered in sand up to above his waist.

"Tilly! Do what she says!" the man yelled over the wind.

He looked around as best he could but having the jacket over his head wasn't as flexible as having a hood, his field of vision was too limited to find his daughter. As the sand started building over the assassin's thighs, she couldn't help but start looking for the little girl herself.

Tilly shimmered into Ophelia's vision. She was just standing there, holding her cloak tightly around her body with one hand while the other pulled her hood down over her face with a white knuckle grip. The kid was scared. She didn't know what to do so she did nothing. She froze.

The knife like shriek of the roc was unmistakable now. Ophelia looked up, finally able to tell where the beast was in the sky.

It was diving straight for them! What could possibly be attracting it? Travus was buried up to his chest now. Even Tilly was... where was Tilly?

The woman looked back where the little girl had been moments before and Tilly again shimmered into Ophelia's sight. The woman looked back up at the bird and the child disappeared. She looked back down in Tilly's direction and the little girl reappeared.

Ophelia started rattling off a trail of curses as she started pulling herself free of the sand. The giant bird was after the girl! Something about the crystal that made her hard to see for people was attracting the roc straight to her!

The roc lowered its open talons to scoop the girl up (although the animal was large enough that one was more than enough to take her). Ophelia couldn't reach Tilly, but she could reach the end of the child's cloak as it whipped around in the speeding winds. She just hoped that Tilly had as good of a grip as she thought.

Ophelia grabbed the brown fabric and pulled with everything she had. Tilly landed face first in the sand right in front of the woman with a dull thud just as the talons of the roc sliced through the soil where she had been the moment before.

The woman grabbed the girl's shoulders and flipped Tilly onto her back. Ophelia pulled Tilly's cloak open, searching for the crystal pinned to her chest.

When Tilly saw Ophelia standing over her, though, she started to scream and cry. She swung punches and kicks at the woman with such ferocity that Ophelia actually had to block them to keep from taking a knockout blow or being blinked away before finding the brooch.

The roc shrieked again. It was coming around for another pass!

Ophelia wasn't going to be able to find the crystal in time. She fell on top of the little girl just as the bird's massive talons snapped down again.

Pain ripped through the assassin's shoulder, making the woman scream. When the world came back into focus around her, Ophelia realized that her own cloak was gone, ripped off. But she wasn't airborne so the sharp talon must have just grazed her. Otherwise she would have been sliced in half.

Travus made his way through the sand as best he could, "I thought those runes on your back made you invincible!" he yelled over the winds as he finally reached them and started inspecting the wound.

He brought his hand down in front of Ophelia's face to show her that she was, in fact, bleeding. The Night Shield told her the cut went from the bottom of her right shoulder blade to the peak of that same shoulder.

"My runes! Are any of the tattoos cut?" she asked as she pulled herself off the still struggling girl.

"No!" Travus shook his head, "But they are glowing! Is that normal?"

"Get that damned brooch off her!" Ophelia ordered as she pulled Havarti free from his scabbard, "I'll distract the roc!"

"I thought it would explode if I took it off!" he yelled.

"I was lying, you idiot!" Ophelia lifted her sword straight up in the air, spinning Havarti around to catch whatever light there was within the whipping windstorm.

Ophelia trudged away from father and daughter. She wasn't looking to be a hero. The bird had just successfully pissed her off.

She had no idea what she was going to do next. Ophelia wasn't even sure if Havarti's blade was going to be enough to get the giant bird's attention. The assassin didn't have to wait long to find out.

The beast gave up swooping down on the targets. They were too small for it to get a good bead on. So it slammed into the ground right in front of Ophelia.

At forty feet tall, it towered over the woman. It was so big that it could snap Ophelia up in its curved beak without any of her limbs hanging out. Its long tail pummeled the sand behind it, whipping up more and more sand all around. The sand was so thick in the air that Ophelia could barely even see the massive beast before her.

That was, of course, what it counted on. What it didn't realize was that, too, was what the assassin was waiting on.

The thing's head dropped, the ax like beak reminding Ophelia of an executioner's preferred weapon of his trade. She pressed her arms tightly against her sides, holding Havarti so close that the cold steel of his blade caused goosebumps on her bare thigh. The woman held her legs together, wanting to make sure that the bird got a good mouthful.

The beak of the roc snapped together, the sharp tip intent on drilling through her back and stomach. It lifted its head to swallow the first course of his snack.

Ophelia reappeared standing on top of the curved beak. It was too narrow for her feet and she slid down the smooth surface, straddling the beast's bone mouth.

This wasn't exactly where she expected to pop back up but it was time to make the best of it. Grabbing a handful of feathers in her right hand to keep herself stable, Ophelia brought Havarti down right at the crown of the monster's head.

Some of the gray and red feathers were suddenly shorter but no blood was drawn. This thing had a hard head. Ophelia tried driving the tip of her sword through the thing's crown.

It reared back, trying to shake her off, but there still was no blood. The woman braced herself as the bird shook, digging her heels into the ridge where the top and bottom of its beak met.

"This is not a creature we can kill in one blow, my dear," Havarti's voice was calm as he spoke, despite Ophelia holding on for her life, "May I suggest an alternate target?"

Again, the woman raised her sword but this time she used the beast's own shaking against it. She held Havarti out to the side and when the beast whipped its head around, the blade of her sword slashed into the right eye of the roc. This time there was blood and... other viscous fluids.

Ophelia couldn't hold on anymore. As she dove toward the ground, the vengeful roc went for one last snap with its beak. It would have impaled her, maybe even severed her into several pieces but she again blinked out of the way of the attack and into a face full of sand.

The wind buried her in seconds, hiding her from the wounded monster. When it lost any sign of the one that hurt her, it turned back to look for the shimmering thing that had caught its attention in the first place.

It was gone, too. Shrieking with rage, the roc launched itself into the air to search for its quarry. Meager as it was by roc standards.

It didn't take long for the pain from its now useless eye to convince it to fly and find some sanctuary to try and make itself feel better. Besides, it couldn't see as well as before so the animal decided to cut its losses and flee.

The sandstorm followed as the beast flew away. Travus was the first to lift himself from under the sand, Tilly cradled inside his long coat with him.

The roc was gone as quickly as it arrived. The now clear horizon revealed the first changes of color in the distance, dawn was preparing to make its presence felt.

He pulled his coat back so that the collar again rested against the his neck. Pulling his daughter out of the sand so she was again standing atop it, Travus followed her out of the hole. He scanned the landscape all around them. There was no sign of Ophelia.

"Is she dead?" Tilly asked, "Did the roc eat her?"

It was a good question. If he hadn't seen the woman actually sustain as serious a wound as the talon that slashed her shoulder dealt, the Night Shield would have said that it was unlikely. But there was no sign of her now. Did that mean that Travus and his daughter were finally, truly free?

As quickly as the hope was birthed inside him, it was dashed. Ophelia suddenly appeared a short distance away in a pop of violet... the man hesitated to describe it as light but he didn't really have another word for it.

The assassin gasped as she took a deep breath. She acted as if she'd been deprived of air. The sand she was laying on collapsed but she stayed on top of it.

It had filled a sudden cavity that had formed below. Apparently, she could blink away from being suffocated, too.

Travus weighed his options. Neither had any real leverage against the other now. The crystal laid buried somewhere in the vicinity without any real clue to its resting place. But this far away from the Oasis, the Night Shield had long since lost the advantage that his heart plug had given to keep him alive back in the Al Razheem home base.

Ophelia had revealed that she wasn't invincible. But she bested him handily when he had the dagger hidden in the hilt of her sword. He didn't have a weapon at all now.

He started toward the assassin despite his daughter's protests, "I need to check something," Was all he told her.

As he closed in on Ophelia, he looked for the wound the roc gave her. Was it covered with sand? He couldn't see it now.

Within arm's reach of the woman, he saw that it wasn't due to sand being caked in the slash or anything else hiding the wound. The cut itself was gone without even a scar in its wake. Her tattoos weren't glowing anymore, either.

Was her blinking ability somehow linked to healing as well? That would indeed be a fearsome enemy to face. And he was facing it without any kind of weapon while she held tight to her bastard sword.

He had to take it, it was as simple as that. He had to get the one advantage he could take from her and that was her weapon.

Ophelia lifted herself up to her hands and knees and Travus slammed his boot into her midsection. She fell onto her side and then rolled onto her back, coughing.

He stomped his foot down on her left arm so that she couldn't raise her weapon. He bent down, keeping his weight on her arm, and pried Ophelia's fingers of the grip of her sword and took it for himself.

"Get up," he growled, lifting his foot away from her but pointing the blade at the assassin.

Tilly cheered for her father a short distance behind him. Ophelia didn't appear impressed as she again lifted herself to her knees.

"Oh, no!" a completely new voice to the man said, "I will not stand for this."

The sword suddenly started vibrating. The shaking got stronger and stronger until Travus just couldn't hold on anymore.

Ophelia launched herself to her feet and snatched the sword out of the air before spinning around and laying a back kick into the stomach of the Night Shield, driving him down to his knees.

"Don't make me turn your daughter into an orphan, Browder," Ophelia rasped at the man, too quiet for the little girl to hear.

She rested the cold, sharp edge of Havarti's blade on the back of the man's neck. The small hairs stood on end but the assassin didn't put enough pressure down to slice the flesh.

"All I want is to get to Paimae so I can save the General," she said, "Do that and both of you live. As an added bonus, we won't have to see each other again. Deal?"

Ophelia pulled the sword away. She tried tucking it back into her scabbard but found it full of sand. After shaking out the most of it, she looked at the blade.

"Any more in there?" she asked.

Then she nodded and slipped Havarti inside successfully this time. She offered her hand to the man, to assist him onto his feet. He did so under his own power.

"Who were you speaking to?" the Night Shield asked.

"Havarti," she answered, patting the hilt of her bastard sword, "I was going to introduce you earlier but we were too busy trying to play each other at the time."

The woman stepped around the man and started back toward Tilly, who had fallen deathly silent. Before she was close enough to the little girl for her father to protest, Ophelia looked around and didn't look happy.

"Where's the pack?" she asked.

Both Travus and Tilly shrugged. It was buried, to be sure, probably even deeper than the crystal that the little girl had been forced to wear.

"There goes all the food," Ophelia pouted, but only for a moment before she turned and pointed at Travus' chest, "Does that thing actually alert every Light Bringer on the continent?"

The man looked down at the front of his shirt, knowing that she of course meant the heart plug. He chewed on his lower lip thoughtfully for a moment, wondering how honest he really should be at the moment.

He shook his head, "That was a bit of an... overstatement," he confessed, "It has the range to reach Didact Keep, the Valen Court and what forces we have left in Paimae."

It may not have been the numbers he threatened but those were the three closest and, coincidentally most key areas controlled by the Light Bringers. Valen Court was the closest the organization had to a capital, even controlling a small area of territory around it to sustain at least an air of neutrality when they were called into any kind of negotiations between nations. It was also where they held their tribunals.

Didact Keep was where they trained their newest recruits. Between those two places, the Light Bringers would surely be able to assemble a force that could take the fight to the Al Razheem on their own turf. But, still, it wasn't all of them.

"You should probably call them in now," Ophelia slowly spun around in a circle as she took in everything all around them.

"And why would I want to do that?" he asked, folding his arms across his chest.

Her face turned stern as Ophelia stared the man down, "Any food we had is gone. Water, too. Paimae is still over a day away on foot through a burning desert. You think that you can make it that far once the sun is beating down on us at full strength? How about her?"

She nodded at Tilly. The little girl looked insulted that the woman evoked her name to reprimand her father.

Travus nodded, reached into his shirt and pulled the ring out of the plug, "You really think you can negotiate some kind of deal for your General?" he asked, "You did kill an entire outpost of our brothers-in-arms, you know," he tossed the ring away to show her that there was no turning back now, figuratively anyway.

"Everything I do is either at the General's order or for his benefit," Ophelia glared down at the hilt of her sword as if it had said something not so kind about her comment.

"Which of those two categories did murdering my wife fall under?" Travus stomped toward Ophelia.

The woman swallowed hard, her breathing becoming quick and shallow, "It was the General's order," her voice came out so weak that the man almost didn't hear it.

"You realize the '*I was just following orders*' defense hasn't worked in a war crimes tribunal yet, right?" Travus had a smile on his face that was almost predatory.

"I'm here to save the General. That's all," her voice hadn't regained any of the confidence it had before.

"Even if it leads to the death penalty for you?" he stepped over to his little girl and wrapped his arm around her shoulders, "Assuming they can find a way around those runes, of course."

"It's the only real option. For the General," Ophelia she said and then frowned down at her sword again.

"We should get moving. The Light Bringers should have dispatched a team with horses by now," Travus said, "You lead the way."

Ophelia nodded and started in the direction of the nearest city. Travus had an ulterior motive for making her walk ahead. He wanted to see if her runes were glowing again. And they were. Brightly. Particularly the one on the lower left that bore a striking resemblance to the General of the Al Razheem's family crest.

"Well, looky here," Ophelia bent down and slipped her hand into the sand.

She pulled out her mostly forgotten cloak. It was definitely the one she was wearing before. It even had a rip in the shoulder where the bird's talon tore through it. After a few shakes and the dissipation of a woman-made cloud of dust, Ophelia slipped the garment back on and pulled the hood on again.

With some luck they would be back in Paimae before midday. That was, of course, assuming that there were no more surprises between here and there.

FIFTEEN

CHANGING OF THE GUARD

PAIMAE (AFTER MIDDAY)

Whoever cleaned up the holding cells in the Light Bringer outpost deserved a medal. The fact was that all the blood from the woman's earlier assault had been cleaned up very thoroughly. But signs of her attack still remained. Every door that Ophelia had kicked in still had shattered frames. There were patches carved out of the wall where Havarti or another weapon had pierced the wood.

Upstairs wasn't in quite as repaired shape. The blood was all gone, like below, but the walls were still caved in and the furniture in every room the woman had passed was still flipped over or busted.

The thought about whoever cleaned the place was meant to be a joke, even if somewhat macabre, but it did more to turn Ophelia's stomach than lift her mood. The door to the cell closest to the wall was still smashed in from where she used the armored Light Bringer as a human battering ram.

The bedding that had been the last resting place of Inara Browder was gone, likely taken out along with the victim. Ophelia had been provided with a chair in her cell and sat on it, patiently waiting for whoever was in charge to come and talk. Both her arms and legs were crossed as she sat silently but hardly without conversation.

Ophelia was already looking at the door that led out to the hall before it opened. Travus was the first to enter, looking about as happy about coming into the room where his wife was killed as one could expect. Behind him came another man, quite a bit taller and built thicker. Not muscle, really, but it was as if his bones were larger than they needed to be, even for a man of his height.

When the second new arrival came in he removed his hat to reveal a head of hair was completely gray. It was cut short enough to stay out of his way but it wasn't truly styled, except he did have unusually long sideburns. They reached all the way down to the bottom of his jaw.

His skin was weathered as he looked over at Ophelia, like one who spent most of his time outdoors. That conclusion was supported by the way he walked, like one who rode horses quite often. The woman wasn't sure if any of this information would be useful but she filed it away anyway.

"Ophelia, this is Investigator Doniphon," Travus said as he took up space against the wall and planted his feet, "He will be talking to you about why you've come here."

The Investigator gave the woman a shallow bow in greeting. He wasn't wearing armor but he did have the insignia of the shining sword that symbolized the Light Bringers embroidered on his chest. He didn't say anything.

The room stayed quiet until a page brought another chair into the room. The gray haired man gave the young man a thankful smile, an old man's relieved smile, and sat on the offered piece of wooden furniture.

"Thank you, Calvin," he finally spoke as the page turned to leave, "And my joints thank you, too."

The barely grown man bowed and closed the door behind him. Only then did Doniphon turn his attention to the woman in the cell.

"So you're this blinking horror I've heard so much about?" his eyes, a dark metallic shade of blue didn't waver as they looked at Ophelia.

"Apparently that or the blinking whore, depending on which side of the blade you are," She replied.

Doniphon didn't even bother to stop himself from chuckling at that, "You've a lot of gumption to come back here after what you did in this very building. You know that?"

His tone wasn't accusatory as he poked down on his own knee to indicate the place in which they stood. It was more like he was stating something that was common knowledge.

Ophelia concentrated on controlling her breathing, "It was necessary."

"For your General," he didn't say it like a question.

"For my General," Ophelia agreed.

The Investigator's eyes narrowed as he watched her. Again, the room fell silent. Ophelia didn't let it stay that way for long.

"Why is he here?" she nodded at the Night Shield, "I figured I would be the last person he'd want to see now."

"You mean Travus here?" Doniphon made a show of groaning as he turned around in his seat to look back at the man in the long red coat, "Travus is here to corroborate anything you tell me that he had a hand in or witnessed. And that's going to be your job with what he told us, too."

"I think I can save us all some time then," Ophelia turned her attention back to the gray haired man, "He already told you everything and the only thing he got wrong was that I was never going to blow up his daughter."

The Investigator cocked up a gray, angled eyebrow, "You heard all that, did you?"

Ophelia shook her head, "No, but it was all relayed to me."

"By your friend Havarti here?" Doniphon reached back over his shoulder and pulled Ophelia's sword away from his back, scabbard and all.

That only made the man seem bigger to Ophelia. He was able to have an entire bastard sword on his back and look as if he had no weapon at all on him.

But Ophelia nodded in answer to his question.

"So that explains why your sword wasn't exactly being forthcoming with us," the Investigator said, "He was busy having another conversation."

She was tempted to try and correct his interpretation. It wasn't that he was completely wrong but more... off. But she didn't.

"Still, that gels with that piece of intel he gave us," Investigator Doniphon handed the sword over to Travus with the ease a smaller man would pass a dagger before smiling at the man in red, "You may just get out of this yet, partner."

There was more going on here than just Ophelia's interrogation and the old man was letting her know that in an only kind of subtle manner, "Just what does Browder need to get out of?" she asked.

"Oh, caught that, did you?" Doniphon let out a quiet grunt, "You may or may not have realized that the little assault that Travus led wasn't exactly a sanctioned L.B. Operation. Did you?"

Ophelia shrugged. Honestly, she hadn't given it any thought.

"Well, depending on what you have to say," the old, heavy boned man leaned back in his chair, "Travus may be imprisoned for deserting his post and misapplication of Light Bringer property. Namely the heart plug, what we've come to refer to as a *panic button*, that got us running you down out in the Akshar Desert."

Ophelia's pale, granite hued eyes snapped over to the man in question, "He was getting his daughter back. That's against Light Bringer rules?" she turned her attention back to the Investigator.

"He did get results," Doniphon nodded in agreement, "That's why he wasn't clapped in irons right beside you when you were brought in town," Then he let out a heavy sigh, "But he did get every last man and woman who went with him killed. From what I understand, a couple of them were looking for a daughter of their own, too."

That was news to Ophelia, "There was a man who looked like a farmer. And a woman who blew up one of the General's prize hell hounds. I don't know about any other children beside–" she motioned to Travus without actually saying his little girl's name, "I don't think that he can be held responsible for them acting on bad intelligence."

For the first time the Investigators face was no longer passive. He actually looked... disappointed?

"I guess you're right," he looked from the man against the wall to the woman in the cell, "Their daughter wasn't there after all."

Again, no one spoke. But this time it was Doniphon to break the silence by making a popping sound with his tongue against his teeth.

"Then I guess we should get onto the subject of your General and that deal you want for him," he said.

Ophelia nodded, everything in her feeling relief that they were finally getting onto that subject, "Travus told you of the Al Razheem bylaw that kills not only a traitor but the one that recruited the traitor into the fold, right?"

The old man nodded, "And that your General was the one who recruited Travus when he went in undercover with your people."

"When he went into the Al Razheem, yeah," Ophelia agreed.

"You don't count yourself as an Al Razheem?" the heavy boned Investigator looked confused.

"I serve the General so, I guess that counts," the woman flinched when Havarti started speaking so strongly that he shook in Travus's hands.

"I guess Havarti has some opinions of his own on that one," Doniphon observed.

"It doesn't matter," Ophelia shook her head to get her focus back, "I'm here to help the General."

"You do keep saying that," the Investigator again nodded, "He does realize what coming here means though, right? He would be destroying the very organization that he spent a lifetime building."

"He'll die otherwise," Ophelia replied.

"Men are funny that way," the gray haired Investigator said, "Especially us older ones. A lot of times we'd rather die so that everything we cared for, everything we built with our own hands can keep standing."

"What's your point?" she honestly didn't see it.

"I guess it all comes down to this, doesn't it, Miss Ophelia?" the old man leaned forward, resting his elbows on his knees, "You're obviously very loyal to your, you call him Master, right?"

Women of blue sash rank were called "Mistress" while men were referred to as "Maester" within the Al Razheem. But this was different. This was as much a pet name as it was an acknowledgment of his dominance.

"Yes. So?" she felt her patience start to wane.

Again, the man's metallic blue eyes locked on the woman, "So does your Master know that you came here to trade his people in for his life?"

THE OASIS

"What's that smell?" the General was still groggy as he fastened the last golden button that rested at this collar.

He stepped into his office from his bedchamber to find Kitanah sitting at his desk, a plate of blood sausages and toasted bread along with a steaming mug of coffee. His favorite breakfast.

"I took it upon myself to welcome you to the land of the living this morning, Sire," the woman smiled widely as she rose from his cushioned chair.

The General's brow furrowed together tightly, "That was very kind, Kitanah but hardly necessary."

"It was my pleasure," she pulled a chair up along the side of the desk opposite the man in white.

"I get the feeling that a delicious breakfast wasn't the only reason you wished to greet me this morning," he said as he slipped into his soft seat.

Taking the fork resting beside the pewter plate, the General chopped a piece of sausage down with the edge of the utensil. Never taking his eyes off of the woman, he speared the piece of meat and started chewing.

"It has been far too long since we have simply sat and shared a meal together. Don't you think?" Kitanah rested her elbow on the desktop, smiling sweetly.

"I do not see a plate for you, my supernal one," he ripped a chunk of bread away from the rest of the slice and swallowed it down.

"Oh, I ate several hours ago," Kitanah waved her hand at the minor issue, "I had several duties and errands to perform around dawn. Right now, I wanted to take the opportunity to enjoy your company before the day starts its full swing."

"Take the opportunity?" the man took the folded napkin on the side opposite the utensils and dabbed at a stray bit of blood from his last bite of sausage, "Have you felt as if I've been denying you my attentions?"

"Oh, nothing like that, Sire," Kitanah shook her head, "It was just, with Ophelia leaving the Oasis, I thought you might have been lonely."

"And how do you know whether or not Ophelia is here?" his head tilted as he asked the question.

"As you've often told me," the woman fiddled with the unlit candle that rested on the desk between them as she replied, "the source isn't as important as the accuracy of the information. And I am positive I am correct." She kept the same sweet smile on her face as her green eyes trained back on her patriarch.

The General took another bite of sausage. His eyes narrowed but he otherwise showed no reaction.

"This rivalry you've built up between yourself and Ophelia is getting tiresome, Kitanah." the bearded man sighed, "I thought things had changed between you and her."

"Indeed, they have, Sire," Kitanah was most sincere as she spoke, "That was part of why I wanted to speak it you. To assure you that I now know that her loyalty is unquestionable."

"Then why wait until she isn't around to come see me?" the General finished off the first piece of toast and then leaned back in his most comfortable seat.

"That wasn't my aim," Kitanah picked up the little piece of flint, rolling the finger sized piece of well used stone between her fingers, "It was simply a coincidence."

"One of which you just happened to be aware ahead of time," the man ran his fingers over the braids hanging from his chin.

Bringing the smooth stone to a stop between her middle and forefinger, she looked a little pained by what the General said, "Why does it worry you so that I know that Ophelia is gone? Like I said, I have no doubt where her loyalties lie."

Was that worry she saw on his face? It was only for the briefest of moments but Kitanah was almost positive it was there.

"That was some masterful control of phrasing," the patriarch of the Al Razheem leaned forward, intertwining his fingers and resting his hands on the desk, "Twice now you've mentioned that you do not doubt her loyalty but you never said that her loyalty was to the Al Razheem."

He was starting to understand. Something about that revelation relieved the guilt that had been threatening to shake her insides apart. It would have been a shame if he didn't understand what was about to befall him. A condemned man should always know why his doom meets with him in its chosen manner.

"You're right, Sire," the smile faded from the woman's ruby lips, "I realized that when I was the one who had to explain the Kaien to Ophelia."

His eyes flicked in the direction of the dagger that he kept strapped to the underside of his desk. That mote, that tiny sliver of doubt about her conclusions died right there.

"I don't see what that has to do with Ophelia's loyalty to our family," he argued.

"All these months you've kept her to yourself," her metal sleeve rose above the surface of the sandstone desk, the cuff hovering only inches from the flint in her right hand.

The General stiffened. Kitanah would have said *jumped* if he'd actually moved at all. Instead he was now doing a very skilled imitation of a marble statue. Perhaps the kind one would find in a graveyard.

"Did I do something to startle you, Sire," the crimson haired woman gave him a look of utmost concern.

He shook his head and, clearing his throat, said, "Please, by all means, continue."

The assassin nodded and did just that, "You've made frequent use of her body, to be sure. But you never took any time to teach her anything of being Al Razheem. Yet, she did everything you ever told her to do. To the letter."

"I'm still not seeing your issue, Kitanah," the General said.

"When I stopped figuring Doctor Efreeti for a traitor, I decided it was time to actually have a conversation with him," the woman said back, carefully gauging the increasing worry in the eyes of her patriarch, "I felt it was the only proper thing to do. Since you are my father in spirit, if not body, I wanted to understand the full potential and limitations that he had given your First. To figure how I could be as complementary to her skills in defending your life as possible if something like that incursion should happen again."

"And what did he tell you?" the General's hand shifted toward the fork resting beside the almost forgotten plate.

"About Ophelia's abilities?" the General's Second Bravo answered, "Nothing I didn't already know. But how subjects like Ophelia are chosen, about how energies interconnect, I found that very interesting."

One of the hooks from Kitanah's metal sleeve lightly tapped against the flint in her bare hand. She let that sound of steel on stone be the only noise in the room for a long moment before speaking again.

"He showed me everyone I had slept with in the castle, including our beloved First Bravo," she grinned, "and the veritable army you've built out of the Al Razheem. Absolutely everyone who has sworn the oath to you and that you personally have recruited."

"So you know," the General said, his voice flat.

"I know," she nodded.

Her patriarch again leaned back in his seat, letting out a long, slow sigh, "So what happens next."

"You wrote every principle I live by, Sire," Kitanah's eyes started to sting, "You made it very clear that you were never, ever exempt from the consequences of every law you taught me to hold dear."

He nodded back, "That's right. I did. I made the Al Razheem what it is today. Does that not earn me any kind of special consideration?"

"What price avarice?" the precious words spoken previously by Kitanah's leader flowed from the woman's mouth without her having to even think of them, "At what point do the scales of justice and my personal worth balance out so that I may become righteousness itself? This is the question mere men ask of themselves. We Al Razheem, we brothers and sisters in holy creed, we must be above such small sentiment. Ours is a mission of purity and, in such, impure thoughts cannot color our edicts. The law is sound. The law is absolute. Carry it out without pity."

Kitanah wouldn't let a single tear roll from her eyes. Though her vision was clouded by the conflict within her, she looked straight into the man who violated his own writ.

"All I can offer you... father," the woman's throat was painfully tight as she spoke, "All I can offer is that you can be remembered with honor. If you answer my next question truthfully. Please speak the truth and not what I want to hear. Please."

The face of the General was an unmoving mask that took a wrenching effort to get the words out, "What is your question?"

"Did you order Ophelia to take Travus Browder back to Paimae to negotiate a deal of protection? A deal to betray us to the Light Bringers?"

The General's eyes dropped down to the surface of the desk, "When I learned that Travus was still alive. I knew what would happen if anyone else found out. I did everything in my power to make this all go away so that no one would find out that I was the one who let the wolves into our beloved family of sheep.

"I had Ophelia kill every man Travus brought to me, as well as the agents to whom they reported. She purged the Light Bringers from our halls," the man continued, "But Browder went into hiding. When I learned of the location of his family, I thought I had the answer. I had Ophelia kill his woman to tell him and take his daughter as a message to remain silent. Then Efreeti was going to make the girl mine and she was going to find and kill Browder and all would have been as it should be again."

"But she wasn't mature enough for his operation with the soul orb," Kitanah interjected.

Again the General nodded, "Browder reacted faster than I thought he was capable. He even somehow came to gain the aid of Ophelia's birth parents."

"Why didn't you just have them killed when you had your men take Ophelia?" the woman asked.

"They needed to be alive in order to manipulate the bond Ferdinand Granger informed us about," he answered, "As farmers, they should never have been able to afford travel across an entire continent."

"But they did," the General's Second Bravo added an answer of her own, "And dozens of my brothers, as well as a hell hound, the symbol of the Xaviour Tribe, our subterranean allies, were killed. All payment for your lack of forward thinking."

The General bristled at that. Ultimately, though, he could not argue the point. Instead, his hand slipped on top of the resting fork.

"But you still did not answer my question, Sire," she rose from her seat, the flint in her hand pointed directly at the candle's unlit tip, "Did you give Ophelia the order to betray us on your behalf?"

The patriarch of the Al Razheem took the fork and lunged for Kitanah. She ran the sharpened hook on the cuff of her sleeve along the flat surface of the flint. Such a thick shower of sparks flew that it was impossible that the wick of the candle wouldn't catch and make a bright little flame flare into existence.

And the General froze in place. Well, not exactly froze but he was moving so slowly that his Second Bravo was able to take his choice of improvised weapon from his hand, place it back on the pewter plate, and walk around the desk to stand beside him before it even looked like he was doing any more than raising his hand to make an energetic point during their conversation.

Kitanah bent down to whisper in his ear, her soft lips brushing over his earlobe as she did, "You did everything to hide it but you were the one who recruited Travus Crichton into our family. You even killed every Al Razheem who had any meaningful contact with him just in case they were also plants from the Light Bringers. Thank you for that, by the way."

She reached out, taking the man's hand and pressing it down to the surface of the desk. Then she lowered her patriarch back into his seat. Although, she did lean him forward deeper than he would usually sit. It made him look as if he was in a deep stupor of thought... or had fallen asleep in his chair again.

"I know that you are surprised," Kitanah again pressed her lips to the man's ear, "But who was it who set up the magick countermeasures to protect you from assassination in this, your sanctuary?"

The question was, of course, rhetorical. It was Kitanah, years ago when she had just become his First Bravo. Before the General supplanted her with Ophelia.

The candle was the same security measure Kitanah had set up to keep young Tilly Browder from harming herself. Before the General reversed his decision about making the girl another slave like Ophelia. And Kitanah was the owner of the very choker upon which the counter to the enchantment on the candle flame was based.

"Before you die," her voice only slightly shook as she spoke to the man who raised her, "know that I will recover Ophelia. I will make Efreeti turn her loyalty to me and she will serve as my First."

She cradled her right arm across the man's chest and shoulders, giving him one last embrace. The cuff of her blade started to spin, quickly gaining its full speed.

"Please, Sire, my love, take comfort that your secret shame will die with you. I will never tell anyone," and the razor sharp hooks dug into the man's back.

The enchantment filling the room kept him from reacting, outwardly anyway, as his spine and ribs were shredded, followed in short order by his organs. Kitanah did not stop until her sleeve would no longer spin.

With a heavy pull, she finally removed the weapon from her General's back. Not a drop of blood covered the metal as even his life fluids were under the spell of the candle. They did not have the ability to move fast enough to cover the device of murder, even for the short time it was stuck.

Kitanah sat him back in the chair as he would sit normally. She pushed his half eaten breakfast off to the side and pulled some papers from a drawer in his desk. The woman put the documents in his hands to make him look as if he still lived.

He still did at the moment. But it was only a technicality that lasted as long as the candle's light.

"I will leave you like this," she said after gently kissing his cheek, "After Ophelia returns, I will tell everyone how you died peacefully at your desk, working diligently to serve us as you always did. And when Ophelia becomes a fully realized Al Razheem, we will wage a war on the Light Bringers that will leave all of Honua in awe of our name!"

With that, the woman strode out of the room. She gently closed the door behind her. The General could still hear her speak clearly in the hallway. It was one of the security countermeasures that were meant to protect him from being assassinated. But it continued as if it was mocking him.

"Do not disturb the General, he is deep into one of his stupors of thought," she told the guard who stood by the door in the mornings, "Any and all Al Razheem business is to come to me, just as usual when he's like this. Understood?"

"Yes, Mistress."

PAIMAE

"Tell me again, Ophelia," the old Investigator rested his hands on the bulge of his stomach as he leaned back in his chair, "whose idea was it for you to come here to barter for the General's life?"

Ophelia groaned, rubbing the bridge of her long, straight nose with her thumb and forefinger, "Making me repeat myself is just wasting time the General doesn't have!"

"Then he really should have come himself, don't you think?" Doniphon spoke as if the conclusion was obvious.

"He couldn't," the woman answered, "It would have aroused too much suspicion if he had disappeared in the night. It was also too dangerous for him to cross the desert in the dark. We had our own troubles getting across last night," she motioned back to Travus, who still held Havarti by his scabbard.

Doniphon looked over at the member of the Night Shield. He didn't even ask a question but Browder started to answer anyway.

"The roc," he said. "It would have eaten all of us if Ophelia hadn't driven the beast off."

"Well, isn't that heroic?" the old Investigator grinned as he turned to look back at the woman.

She disagreed, "It was necessary. You wouldn't have listened to me at all if I showed up without one of your Light Bringers."

"Even one that's been relieved of his duties?" Doniphon asked.

"There was no way I could have known that," Ophelia frowned.

"That's true," the gray haired man nodded, "Still, that is a lot of trouble to go through for the small chance that we'd be willing to give your General clemency."

"It's the only way I can save him," she insisted.

"Forgive my lousy memory, my dear," the Investigator said, "Whose idea was it for you to come here again?"

"I wouldn't have been able to come here without the General's order, Doniphon," the assassin answered... again.

"So you said," the older man agreed... again, "But was turning state's evidence his idea?"

An exasperated Ophelia leaped from her seat, stomping toward the bars closest to the two men. It was the first time she'd left the chair during the entire length of their conversation.

"What difference does it make?" she growled, "I'm here now!"

"It's kind of in the title of Investigator," the older man looked more kindly at the woman after her outburst, which was the opposite of the reaction she was expecting, "Details matter to me."

"It was an idea that... evolved," She turned to look away from both men, the Night Shield in particular, "I went to the General to beg him to let me kill Browder. He was too afraid of the heart plug giving away the position of the Oasis."

"That has always been a problem for us," Doniphon muttered, "We haven't been able to figure out how to get any sized group out there in the desert. Only one or two at a time and they could never explain how to get out there to anyone who hadn't been there already."

"The only other alternative I could think of to save him was to get him to come to the Light Bringers for protection," Ophelia continued, "I may not be able to die but I couldn't protect him all day, every day fr-from every assassin in ahh the Al Razheem."

"So it was your idea," the Investigator rose from his own chair, watching the woman intently.

"I- guess– so," the woman felt as if her back was suddenly burning.

She pressed her hand on the small of her back and another surge of heat rushed through her, making Ophelia feel as if she was going to throw up. The cold bars of the cell pressed against her forehead, telling the woman that she was still on her feet somehow.

"My only nng concern was, was his sssafety..." Ophelia's knuckles turned white when her hands wrapped around the bars to keep herself upright, "Even though the bastard deserves to die in every new and more violent way I can think of!"

Doniphon and Travus looked at each other. The man in the long red coat pointed to his own back and the older man nodded as he stepped up to the woman in the cell.

"That was quite a change in tone, young lady," Doniphon said, leaning down so they were even in height.

The Investigator was even larger close up. Ophelia swallowed hard, trying to control her suddenly erratic breathing. She didn't notice that Travus moved for the first time, toward the cell where his wife died.

"The General used me in every possible way," Ophelia slowly straightened herself up, "I did everything he asked of me, no matter how dirty it made me feel or how much I didn't want to. Even Havarti was starting to hate me for all those *innocent* people I killed."

"His crest is gone," Travus spoke up, pointing at the woman's tattooed back, "I think the General is dead."

"That's a logical conclusion, I suppose," Doniphon folded his arms across his wide chest. "Especially with how sudden the change was. It looks like you failed in your mission here, Ophelia," his cobalt eyes stared deeply into the woman's, "How do you feel about that?"

"I'm just sorry I wasn't the one to do it," she replied.

"So you would have gladly killed the General," the Investigator said, "But you regret others, like Inara Browder."

"What makes you say that?" Ophelia again rested her forehead on the cold steel of the bars.

"The fact that you haven't even looked in the direction of the cell you killed her in," the older man pointed out, "The entire time you've been in here, you have kept your back to that space."

Ophelia closed her eyes tight, "I didn't want to do it," she whispered.

"Excuse me?" Investigator Doniphon motioned for Travus to return to his position by the door to the hallway.

"I couldn't stop myself," she shook her head as she spoke, keeping her eyes shut, "The General told me that I had to kill her in front of Tilly. As a warning to keep her from resisting when I took her away to be leverage to keep Travus quiet."

"That didn't exactly go as planned," Doniphon jibed.

Ophelia opened her eyes to glare at the Investigator. That was when he noticed another change in the woman. Her eyes were a different color. They used to be the same shade of gray as granite but now they were blue, pale blue like the sky after a storm.

"Another side effect of that enchantment being released?" Doniphon asked Travus as he pointed out the alteration to the Night Shield.

"Likely," the man in red sighed, "But now what do we do with her? Could she still stand trial after everything she did? Could she still be loyal to the Al Razheem?"

"I don't think you're loyal to an organization where you're willing to kill the one who represents everything it stands for," the Investigator shook his head, "And there is standing against prosecuting victims of mind control. Her standing trial then, I feel would be unethical, son. Even if we passed the death sentence you said yourself that there doesn't seem to be anyway to enforce that on her while those runes are on her skin."

"She could be hurt," Travus scowled, "That blinking of hers can heal her but if she sustained enough minor wounds..."

"That would be tantamount to torture," Doniphon scowled back at Browder, "For a horrific crime, to be sure, but one that she did not choose to commit. She was forced. She's just as much a victim as your wife was, Travus."

"I am no victim!" Ophelia slammed her fist against the bars, "What I am is the highest ranking member of the Al Razheem and, if the General *is* dead, Kitanah will be sending a party to come and recover me."

"Are you threatening us, assassin?" the Night Shield's entire attention focused on the woman.

Ophelia shook her head much like the Investigator did moments before, "No, I'm saying that if you're going to keep me here, give me Havarti and let me fight. Kitanah doesn't realize that the rune on my back made me loyal to the General is gone. She'll assume that my loyalty will be hers now that he's dead," the look on her face showed that the idea was distasteful to the woman, to say the least.

"She's right," Travus reluctantly agreed, "Kitanah will assume that Ophelia will want to go back to the Oasis but that we're holding her to stand trial for her attack on the outpost. She won't let her unkillable assassin languish in prison when Ophelia could still be useful to the Al Razheem."

"With her being so important," the Investigator started, "they will send their best to get Ophelia. What can we do to hold them off?"

SIXTEEN

STRATEGIC WITHDRAWAL

LIGHT BRINGER OUTPOST

"Mistress Ophelia," a voice whispered.

On the mat of straw in the cell, Ophelia lay with her glowing back facing the rest of the cells. She wasn't asleep so she opened her pale blue eyes to let the new arrival know they had been heard. Regimen stared back at her, resting on one knee on the other side of the bars.

When the Investigator figured they would be sending the best of the best of the Al Razheem, he wasn't wrong. Regimen was a part of the elite team of Fidai. They were handpicked by the General for their cunning and ferocity in battle.

They were the most expensive of the Al Razheem to hire because they only worked as a team while most other assassins were hired out singly or in pairs. They were so skilled at manipulating the tides of full blown battles, often infiltrating behind enemy lines to turn what would have been a hopeless situation into a great victory for the noble willing to pay the price (a first born child to become Al Razheem but still maintain their right of succession to the noble family's title and assets).

While it was the General who selected the members, Ophelia was the honorary leader thanks to her rank as the General's First Bravo. She had only served on one mission with them in her time with the Al Razheem (the cost was steep) but it took all her abilities just to keep up with them once the fighting started.

And Regimen was one of their best. He wore flowing black robes, his head and face wrapped in the same material to hide his features, along with a scimitar on each hip. He had a skill to be able to draw out one of his blades, cut his target and slip the blade back into the scabbard before the person even realized they had been killed.

Ophelia sat up on the mat, wiping pretend sleep from her eyes. "How many are here?"

"Three here, Mistress," Regimen answered dutifully, "Suqoar and Phantoom are watching the hall. The rest are going after the secondary targets."

The rest? There were six members of the Fidai if you didn't count Ophelia. That meant that the three others, Meedial, Coloron and Theta were unaccounted for.

The woman rose to her feet, "Who are the secondary targets?" she asked as she stepped up to the door of the cell.

Regimen stuck close to the outside of the cell as he followed Ophelia to the locked door. He pulled a couple of short lengths of metal from somewhere and started to pick the lock.

"Travus and Tillyria Browder, Mistress," he answered and swung the door open for her to exit.

"I thought they'd have left town by now," Ophelia stepped around Regimen and, instead of walking straight for the door, she headed for the one window that was far too thin to be able to get out through, "Where are they?"

The Fidai, who already had a hand on the handle to the door leading into the hall, was surprised by her question. As well as her turning in the wrong direction.

"Why do you care, Mistress? They are being disposed of for their crimes against you as we speak."

"Are you saying that you wouldn't want to watch the finale of a play you've attending from the beginning?" Ophelia said.

She slid her hand along the side of the narrow window's frame. It was too narrow, in fact, to have glass in it so it served as the room's only means of ventilation. An important issue when the buckets in each cell were full, the woman was sure.

"They are two buildings to the north, Mistress. I can take you to see the bodies, if you wish," even though his black eyes were the only part of the man clearly visible, they did show how confused he was, "What are you doing, Mistress?"

"Two buildings. North. Got it." Ophelia muttered, then stepped back from the window with Havarti in her hand, still in his scabbard, "I'm getting ready to kill you, Regimen. Since I'm pretty sure the Light Bringers have already taken down Suqoar and Phantoom."

"Mistress?" Regimen's hands crossed in front of his body and wrapped around the grips of his two swords, "You're betraying us?"

Ophelia slipped her bastard sword free from his sheath, "You can't betray what you never believed in the first place," she declared.

Ophelia was glad she kept hold of Havarti's scabbard. It blocked Regimen's first strike while his second blade blocked her own attack.

It was hard to maneuver around with long blades in such a limited space. Regimen's scimitars being thinner gave him the advantage and Ophelia was forced against the wall where the window rested.

Then the door burst in to reveal Investigator Doniphon wielding a long sword of his own. He was flanked by two other Light Bringers in heavy armor but there was no way they would fit in the room with Ophelia and Regimen still inside as well.

"They came just as you said they would," the old man announced to Ophelia before pointed his weapon at the man in black robes, "Surrender is still an option, son."

Regimen didn't even take a split second to think. He drove both blades for Ophelia.

She was only able to block one and the other slid through her flat stomach. Or, at least where her stomach would have been.

Ophelia's view of the room was suddenly limited to a narrow sliver. Regimen already turned his back to her and slashed both of his blades through the torso of the old Investigator.

Then the woman was falling. She had blinked to just outside the second story of the building. She wasn't even able to get a full curse out before she landed hard on the dusty ground.

Picking herself up from the dirt, Ophelia looked down at herself. No stab wound in her gut. That was good. Her arms and legs were scraped up from the rough landing but she was otherwise not badly injured.

Rising to her feet, she had to take a moment to orientate herself. Regimen would have to wait. North was to the left. She dashed in that direction, worried that she was already too late.

Nothing but a short white fence separated her from the house that Ophelia's would be rescuer indicated. She saw Theta through a window on the first floor. She was standing over something that was below the area Ophelia could see. But Theta had one of her daggers out. She was going in for the kill.

"Throw me!" Havarti demanded.

Ophelia didn't argue, she did as her sword ordered. Spinning around to give the heavy sword extra momentum, she loosed the blade like a javelin at the closed pane of glass.

Havarti crashed through the glass, hurling shards all over as he continued through the air. The tip of the sword blade shot through Theta's chest and continued until he hit her shoulder blade. The force of the hit shattered the bone.

Ophelia ran after the sword, not even bothering to mind the glass as she pulled herself up and through the destroyed panes. She unexpectedly landed on a soft bed and bounced off, landing on the floor next to the member of the Fidai as Theta fought a losing battle to keep gasping for breath.

When she looked back up at the bed, Ophelia saw Tilly staring at the assassin as she lie dying. The former assassin thought about telling the girl to look away, to try and protect her from watching something like this at her young age. But she didn't.

This was going to be Tilly's life for the foreseeable future. She'd best get used to the idea of people having to die around her to keep her safe. Again, though, Ophelia wished that she didn't have to be the one to keep teaching the little girl all these unpleasant life lessons. Still, the child was safe for the time being at least.

"My dear, I must insist you clean and wrap your hands before you handle me again," he said.

Ophelia didn't even notice her hands were bleeding until she reached out to Havarti and heard his protest.

She wasn't sure if he spoke mentally or physically because Tilly seemed to laugh at what he said. But then, the girl could have just been reacting to the realization that she had just survived an attempt on her life. The timing of both was so close that it was hard to tell.

"Sorry, Havarti, we don't have time," she wrapped her hand around her sword's grip, "Meedial and Coloron are still around here somewhere."

Havarti shuddered in her grasp when Ophelia took hold but otherwise didn't try to get away. He begrudgingly agreed that she was right.

Ophelia turned to look back over her shoulder at Tilly as she strode for the door that led deeper into the house, "You should probably hide."

The little girl nodded and quickly shuffled out of her bed. The former assassin closed the door behind herself, not bothering to see where the girl went.

Blood trickled down Havarti's handle as Ophelia held the sword up, as well as the sword's scabbard in her other hand. The pain was finally starting to register but she pushed it into the back of her mind as she struggled to listen.

"Any ideas?" she whispered to her sword.

"I would wager that Travus would not want to be far from his daughter. He is probably down here somewhere," Havarti replied.

Ophelia nodded in agreement and started toward the front of the house. The hallway opened up into the foyer after only a few steps. The front door of the house was barely open. The lock had been picked so that the Fidai could enter without alerting anyone inside.

She raised her sword as she went down another hallway. The sound of struggling told the woman that she was on the right track. The noise was coming from the door that rested in the end of the hallway.

Ophelia pushed the door open with her shoulder just enough so that she could peek inside. Rushing headlong into a fight was a sure way to get someone, typically the one you're trying to help, killed.

The door opened into the kitchen and three figures were darting this way and that around the counter in the middle of the room. Ophelia recognized one silhouette as Coloron thanks to the mohawk he wore. The figure he was attacking with his hatchet must have been Travus. The long coat looked right even in the darkness.

That meant the other shadow must have been Meedial. His weapon of choice was a clawed gauntlet he referred to as a *cat claw*.

Travus seemed to be fighting bare handed. He was slapping the Fidai's weapons away with his open hands, all the while trying to create some distance between them.

Ducking under the swipe of Coloron's hatchet, Travus threw himself over the counter. Then he ran for the door Ophelia was behind.

She pushed herself back against the wall as Travus pulled the door open and rushed past. He didn't even notice Ophelia as he ran. The assassin with the mohawk threw his hatchet. Ophelia slapped it out of the air with Havarti. The small ax embedded itself into the ceiling.

"Coloron, Meedial, stand down," the woman ordered as she stepped into the kitchen.

"Mistress Ophelia?" both men looked confused, "What are you doing here?"

"What? You thought I was going to miss killing the Night Shield that brought me here?" she asked, lowering Havarti to keep from looking threatening.

The assassins didn't speak again until Ophelia stood across the counter from them. It was Coloron, who motioned to the hallway.

"Why did you stop me from killing him? Why didn't you kill him yourself as he ran by?" the Fidai asked.

"One, I only saw a hatchet flying for my head. I reacted accordingly. Two, how was I supposed to know that he was going to come waddling through the door?" she folded her arms across her chest (which also brought Havarti up to a better position from which to attack). "Three, I want you out of here so that *I* can kill the bastard. Understood?"

The two Fidai looked at each other. Finally, though, they nodded.

"We'll just collect Theta are retreat to the rendezvous, Mistress," Coloron said, "Regimen and the others are already there, I assume?"

Ophelia nodded, "You go there and wait. I'll kill the Night Shield and meet you there later," she ordered.

"Mistress, are you sure that this Browder is a Night Shield? Our sources never mentioned that," Meedial spoke up for the first time, "That would mean that he's likely connected to some informant within the Al Razheem. We should capture and interrogate him together."

"Just follow my orders," Ophelia rolled her eyes at the two men, "Thinking at this level is above your pay grade."

Both men reluctantly turned for the back door of the house. After only a few steps, though, Coloron jumped as if he realized that he had forgotten something.

"What about Theta, Mistress?" he asked... then suddenly pointed behind the woman. "Incoming!" he yelped.

Ophelia turned just in time to see Travus charge at her and drop his blade down between her eyes... and she found herself suddenly standing between Coloron and Meedial. She looked back and forth between the men before shrugging.

"Ah well," she sighed, "I wasn't really planning on letting you leave alive anyway."

The woman spun in place as she lifted Havarti. Coloron was slashed across his chest but he stepped back just far enough to avoid the worst of Ophelia's attack. Meedial had already charged at Travus and smashed the man's blade against the counter top with his cat claw, bending the length of steel into an awkward curve. One that made it useless as a weapon anymore.

Coloron reached for the dagger in his belt and his fingers met the hard edge of Havarti's scabbard as Ophelia slapped it down on his hand, using the scabbard as a weapon. As the assassin reeled back from the painful hit, the woman brought her bastard sword down on the nape of Coloron's neck and he fell to the ground.

Havarti's scabbard again took the role of a weapon. This time a projectile that hit Meedial on the back of the head.

"Browder!" Ophelia threw her sword with handle forward so that he could catch it.

And catch it he did, followed by removing Meedial's head along with a couple of fingers from the hand that had been cradling the bump that Ophelia caused. Travus's brown eyes darted toward Ophelia and he tightened his grip on the bastard sword. Just as he started around the table, stalking what would be his next target, Havarti started shaking in his hands.

"Oh, no you don't, sir!" the sword protested, "You will not use me to attack the woman who just saved your life!"

When the man stopped moving, Havarti stopped shaking. Travus squinted in the faint light at the woman and let out a quiet groan.

"Oh, it *is* you," he grumbled, "How did you get out of lock up?"

"Well, hello to you, too," Ophelia stepped over to a pile of small towels that had been knocked over in the ruckus and started wiping her hands clean, followed by the scabbard, "One of the assassins split from the group to get me, just like I figured they would. He mentioned that you and Tilly were also on their to do list and I came running."

"How heroic of you," Travus rolled his eyes, "What about all that rigmarole about you wanting to kill me yourself?"

"Didn't you ever lie to an assassin while you were undercover?" Ophelia grinned back as she held her hand out to the man.

"You were taking advantage of the fact that they still thought they were here to rescue you," Travus handed Havarti back to the woman who started wiping blood from Havarti's hilt.

She nodded in agreement, "Good thing, too. Theta would have stabbed Tilly in the heart while you were busy getting killed by these two here."

Panic suddenly rushed through the man's face, "Is Tilly okay?" he rushed out of the kitchen again.

Ophelia followed, slipping Havarti into his scabbard and actually taking the time to place him back onto her belt properly before she actually reached the little girl's room. When she reached the doorway, Travus was already pulling his daughter out from under the bed.

Ophelia entered the room, stepping over the corpse of the woman who had been Theta, "You're okay, aren't you, kid?"

The smile left the woman's face when she saw the look on the little girl's face. There was the hatred that had been there since... Ophelia took Tilly to the Oasis. That was expected but the child also looked as if she were about to break into tears, or vomit, or just yell at the top of her lungs. That was a lot of expression for a face so small.

Ophelia looked for something, anything to say when the wind blowing the curtain beside the broken window caught her attention and she let out a loud curse. "Regimen is in the outpost!"

The woman rushed past father and daughter and poked her head out the window. The Investigator and the two Light Bringers who were following him before were already walking down the road toward the house. That was more than a little surprising to Ophelia. Last she saw, the old Light Bringer got two sword slashes across his not overly small gut.

"Are your hands better?" a little voice came from behind Ophelia. She looked back to see Tilly, her head resting on her father's shoulder as the two embraced, actually addressing her. The woman looked down at her perfectly uninjured hands and even showed them to the little girl.

"Good as new," she said.

"Ho there!" the Investigator called as soon as they were outside the fence, "Is everyone alive and well in there?"

"In better shape than I thought you were in," Ophelia called back, "Want to tell me how you're not dead?"

"Think we can do that inside?" the older Light Bringer asked.

Travus, with Tilly clinging around his shoulders with her arms and around his waist with her legs, went and opened the front door to allow the other Light Bringers inside. Once they came in, the two armored Light Bringers were ordered to make sure the house was now secure.

Investigator Doniphon, Ophelia, Travus, and his daughter each took up seats in the living room just past the hall that led to the kitchen. The old man let out a relieved groan as he took the load off his boot wrapped feet.

"So you saw your old pal chop me down but you came here anyway, eh?" Doniphon asked.

Ophelia shrugged, "You had those two," she motioned to the armored Light Bringers elsewhere in the house, "backing you up. They didn't have anyone."

"How did you get out of the lock up, anyway?" Travus again asked the question the woman earlier ignored.

"Regimen stabbed me and I blinked. Outside the wall," Ophelia said.

Doniphon grunted, "I know I can't speak for Mister Browder here but, on behalf of the Light Bringers we thank you for coming to the rescue of one of our most experienced officers."

"Gratitude does seem a little lacking," Ophelia again folded her arms in front of her chest, "He even tried to stab me in the back in the kitchen."

That piece of information came as a surprise to the older man. When the Investigator looked at the man out of the side of his eye, Travus scowled.

"It was dark! I thought she was that Coloron guy," he protested.

"Coloron is a man and has a mohawk," Ophelia sneered back, "In what way could we possibly look alike?"

"I told you," Travus's voice went gruff as he spoke, "It was dark and all I saw was the purple glow. His back glowed, too."

"You're saying that he could blink, too?" the woman obviously didn't believe him.

The Night Shield shook his head, "No, I got too many good shots in on him. He couldn't blink."

It was Ophelia's turn to scowl, "Then what did the runes do?" she lifted herself from her seat and started for the kitchen.

The two armored Light Bringers were in the kitchen when she stepped inside. They had lit the two lanterns that were on either side of the room, making it so everything could be seen easily.

The back door was wide open. Ophelia stepped up to the counter and looked down at the floor on the other side. There was a puddle of blood on the floor but no body.

Streaks of blood led to the open door that led outside. The former assassin cursed loudly enough that the Investigator came in.

"Those runes must have had healing abilities," Ophelia frowned, her pale eyes locked on the floor.

"You're saying that one of the Fidai escaped?" Doniphon stepped up to the puddle of blood that lacked a corpse with it.

The woman nodded, "It looks like it. That means that Kitanah will know that Travus is still alive and I'm not on her side anymore."

"Travus said that you almost decapitated Coloron and at the very least severed his spine," The Investigator stepped up to the back door, looking outside for a long moment, "How could he have recovered from something like that so quickly?"

"I sliced my palms up climbing into the house through Tilly's window," Ophelia held up her uninjured hands to show the older man, "When Travus attacked me, I blinked. Now I don't even have scars where the glass was in my hand. Although I do need to get new wrapping for Havarti," she added the last part as an aside for her sword.

Investigator Doniphon had the woman follow him back into the living room, "So what do you think Kitanah's next move will be?"

"To cover her tracks," Ophelia answered, "You said that she's already stopped every Al Razheem from using all the dead drops so no assassin has come across any of Browder's letters. That only leaves me and Travus as the ones who know about the General's betrayal. She'll keep sending more assassins until Travus is dead and I'm back under her control."

"We don't have the manpower to stave off a steady stream of Al Razheem attacks," Doniphon frowned, scratching at one of his long sideburns, "But we're obviously not going to let them have Travus or you, Ophelia."

"We're going to have to leave Paimae," Travus spoke up, "Tilly and I can head west, get out of the area the Al Razheem has the most influence in."

"Where would you go?" the Investigator asked.

The Night Shield shook his head, "I think it would be better if you didn't know, sir."

"I overheard something when we were separated that I haven't had a chance to tell you, my dear," Havarti said in Ophelia's head, "Apparently, a man named Connelly and an Al Razheem named Marque attempted to go into hiding when Marque turned on the guild. They were killed before they even made camp on the first night out of Paimae."

"The Light Bringers have an Al Razheem plant in their midst," Ophelia said out loud.

"And how do you know that?" Doniphon asked, although both Light Bringers eyed her suspiciously.

"Havarti just told me about Connelly and Marque," the woman replied, "Did he leave any official word on where they were going?" she asked the Night Shield.

Travus shook his head, "I told him not to leave any paper trail."

"Our numbers were well decimated by," the investigator's gaze flicked over to Ophelia for the briefest of moments, "the assault the General orchestrated. Our suspect list should be short."

"The culprit would be the one person that Connelly would trust to give word to that he was leaving," Travus tapped his chin thoughtfully, "Briggs. It has to be Briggs."

"I'll question him," the Investigator started for the front door, "In the meantime, I suggest you pack."

"We have to leave again, Daddy?" Tilly looked up from her father's lap.

"I'm sorry, sugar blossom," he kissed the crown of her head, "I'll find some way to make it up to you."

"We should take Ophelia with us, Daddy," the little girl said.

Both her father and the former assassin were surprised to hear her say that. His daughter didn't look like she liked the idea which just begged the question...

"What makes you say that, Tilly?" ...to be asked.

"The bad guys will keep coming here if she's here, right?" the girl started, "She was with them so she might recognize some of the ones they send after us," she continued, "Plus, we can keep an eye on her to make sure she doesn't do anymore bad stuff."

Travus hugged his daughter tightly. Pride wasn't anything physical but he knew that was what he was feeling at the selflessness his little girl just showed. Despite watching what Ophelia did to her mother, she was still willing to protect other Light Bringers by having Ophelia come with them rather than remain behind as a target.

"That's probably for the best, Ophelia," he looked up at the former assassin before rising from his own seat with his daughter, "We'll pack some things and then get on the road."

"If Briggs is the traitor, it should be safe to tell Doniphon where we're going," Ophelia watched as father and daughter walked back to Tilly's room.

"If the Al Razheem do come back here, it's better that the Light Bringers don't know for their own protection," Travus said before disappearing from the hall.

"I believe your cloak was tossed into the refuse shortly after we arrived, my dear." Havarti chimed in, "So leaving will not be much of an issue for us as much as surviving when we get to wherever Travus has in mind to go."

"I am going to need new clothes," Ophelia looked down at herself.

Her vest and skirt were caked with blood. Even though she wiped down her hands most of her skin was still tinted with red or otherwise covered with crimson specks. She needed a bath as much as new clothes. Hopefully, Travus had a plan that could give her both by the time they were in the next town...

SEVENTEEN
BREAKING BONDS

THE OASIS

Another knock on the door. Efreeti was again taken by surprise (not really). Slipping into some tweed, the man-like doctor opened the door for his unexpected visitor.

Crimson hair, black leather wardrobe, metal sleeve on her left arm with razor sharp hooks attached to the cuff, it was indeed General Kitanah Baynette. Unlike the last time she came to visit, Kitanah seemed far more at ease.

She stepped into Doctor Efreeti's room, surprised to see a cauldron with what appeared to be chocolate sauce on the marble table. It was simmering without any visible heat source.

"To what do I owe the pleasure of your company tonight, fair General?" the almost human-like figure stepped back over to the table, "Could I interest you in some?"

He dipped one of his curved claws into the sweet liquid concoction then brought it up to his lips. Kitanah walked up beside him, scanning around the table.

"What are you dipping into it?" she asked.

Efreeti quirked a fleshy brow at the woman, "You can dip things into chocolate sauce? General, you have opened a whole new world of culinary delights to me!" he grinned with a little dollop of chocolate clinging to his lower lip.

The woman didn't know whether to be amused, confused, or perhaps disgusted by the not-quite-a-man's reaction. So she chose to ignore it.

"Coloron has returned from Paimae," the Al Razheem's new matriarch informed Efreeti.

"I trust the mission was successful?" Efreeti said, "Should I expect Ophelia back on the table in short order?"

Kitanah shook her head, "Ophelia almost killed him. She had a hand in killing the rest of the Fidai, too, I'm sure."

Efreeti's thin lips pressed together tightly for a moment, "I was afraid something like this would happen when the General's crest was deactivated."

The woman's brow furrowed at the not-quite-a-man, "What do you mean?"

"I believe I mentioned that the General had me program Ophelia to be loyal to him, not the Al Razheem?" He said the words as a matter of review, "When the General met his unfortunate fate, that destroyed the rune that controlled that loyalty to him. One cannot be loyal to a dead man."

"But why would she attack the Fidai?" Kitanah wrapped her arm around her metal sleeve, "Even if she's not loyal to the General any longer, she trained with them more than any other Al Razheem. Why didn't she trust them to bring her home?"

"Do not misunderstand," Efreeti leaned against the edge of the marble table, "Life here in the Oasis is the only one she has known but the General did force Ophelia to perform acts that were *distasteful* to her. She is, as you would put it, confused. Everything about how she understood the world has been thrown into upheaval. Ophelia does not know who to trust at the moment."

"So you're saying that she just lashed out?" the new General frowned, "Doing that added a new complication. Before she killed her brothers-in-arms, it was just a simple matter of getting her in here for you to put a new rune on her back. Now, I have to figure out a way to get her back under my service that satisfies our laws. Especially since killing her isn't an option."

"Neither is, I'm sure, allowing her to stay under the influence of the Light Bringers," Doctor Efreeti added.

Kitanah didn't bother to stifle a curse, "You're right. We need to get her back sooner rather than later. Can you still track her?"

"You mean using your particular bond?" Doctor Efreeti smirked back at the woman, "Of course. There is nowhere in the world of Honua that your bond with her cannot reach. I will need a new sample from which to initiate the search, though."

Efreeti brought his hand up and tapped the woman's bare right shoulder with the tip of his claw. Kitanah nodded back at him and the curved talon sank into her flesh.

He pulled the digit out and flicked blood from it into the air in front of him. Kitanah scowled. That wasn't how he did this last time.

But Kitanah's likeness, about the size that could fit into the real one's palm, came into existence in the air before her. She was glowing gold, as brightly as the General did before. Also just as before, blue streams of light again streamed from the golden similitude to blossom into likenesses of all those with whom she had been intimate.

The violet light was the last to emerge. It stretched a much further distance than the blue ones that were focused around the keep (which was invisible at the moment).

As the light kept stretching further away, Kitanah looked over at the almost-human. He simply started walking after it. The woman followed suit.

Efreeti's lair was always disorienting to the woman. While the marble table moved away behind them, that frameless window stayed in the same place. Always showing a daylight scene even in the dark of night.

Finally, the violet light came to a stop. As Doctor Efreeti and Kitanah neared, Ophelia's similitude came into being. She was wearing clothing very different from when she was under the previous General's control but the back of the shirt was still opened to reveal the intricate runes covering her back.

"Where is this, Efreeti?" the new General asked, her emerald eyes glued to the image of the other woman.

The not-quite-a-man looked back at the gold and blue lights in the distance then pulled his glasses off his face. His eyes were already closed. Muttering some words, Kitanah caught a few to be numbers, he slipped his glasses back on and the faint dots of red reappeared behind the round frames.

"She is currently in hiding in the city of Middlemount," he declared, "The northeast quadrant, the area the locals refer to as "squatter's lodge". I believe it is referred to that due to the, shall we say, lower economic climate of the neighborhood."

Kitanah tapped her plump lower lip thoughtfully for a moment, "Who could I send that she wouldn't kill on sight?"

The sun suddenly started shining more brightly through Efreeti's window, "If I may be so bold, perhaps you should be the one to go and collect your precious sister-in-arms?"

"Me?" she looked doubtful, "We haven't had the most trusting of relationships, Efreeti."

"That is true," the thin almost-man didn't even pretend it wasn't, "However, you do have a strong bond. If you speak to her honestly, there is a strong chance that she would return with you willingly."

"Hmm…" Kitanah nodded, "I'll need some insurance to make sure I make it back if the worst should happen. I am responsible for the whole clan now, after all."

"What is it that you are cogitating?" Doctor Efreeti asked.

"The healing runes that you gave Coloron worked perfectly," she said, "Could you give me something like that?"

"You do realize that the ones I gave your Fidai were temporary, correct?" he replied, "A rush job at your request. If the leader of the Al Razheem were to have my runes displayed about her body, I would insist on the higher quality, permanent inks."

"What do you mean by higher quality?" her attention was piqued.

"I can make you unable to be killed as well," he slowly strode around her, as if giving her a quick inspection, "But also, I can make your cells regenerate until you are again at your optimal state."

"Cells? What are cells?" Kitanah furrowed her brow at the doctor.

"Forgive me, General. I meant that your skin, your hair, your muscles, all would return to a state when you were at your finest form," he answered.

"You're saying that you can make me young again?" the woman was suddenly aware of the pain from her still bleeding shoulder, "and I would be able to blink, too?"

"I can restore you to your body's optimal age," he agreed but then Efreeti shook his head, "Blinking, however, that procedure would have to have been done, er, earlier in your development in order to take root."

"But you *can* make it so I can't die?" her eyes narrowed at the thin almost-man in tweed.

"Absolutely!" he grinned back, "The procedure will take some time, though. I suggest you delegate your responsibilities to your subordinates until you've had time to recover."

The hairs on the back of the woman's neck rose, her old paranoid suspicions reemerging, "And how long would that be?"

"Two weeks at most," he answered, "And, I assure you that I will make sure that Ophelia does not move on from Middlemount in that time."

Her doubts started to strengthen, "You can do that?"

Efreeti waved his hands, as if he were surrendering, "My apologizes. I phrased that poorly. I meant to say that I will watch Ophelia to make sure that she does not move on before you are ready to face her."

He motioned to the lights still hanging strongly in the air. Kitanah's suspicions stepped back... slightly.

"Very well, I'll undergo your procedure," she said the words as if she was announcing them to a room full of soldiers, "Afterward, I will bring Ophelia back to us and you'll give her loyalty to me."

Doctor Efreeti smiled wider than he ever had in his time living in the Oasis.

MIDDLEMOUNT

During her time among the Al Razheem, the only alcohol Ophelia drank was different types of wine. When she arrived in this city with Travus, he introduced her to beer. Ever since then, she had come back to this pub to try different flavors.

But this one, this one was easily her favorite. It tasted sweet, like honey but the barkeep told her that there wasn't actually any honey in it, even though it was called honeybark ale. Would that be the definition of ironic?

It was a shame that this was going to be her last glass of honeybark, though. It was apparently the last of the last barrel that the pub received from the bar in Paimae. While the two bars still traded, the one who actually made honeybark ale left for some reason. A shame really.

So Ophelia made sure to take small sips, staying back in the shadowy corner like Travus insisted. With the other flavors of beer and mead, she wasn't shy about downing as much as possible as quickly as she could. It almost made her forget that she was a terrible person, at least for awhile. But the honeybark ale... that just felt so... familiar... and comforting.

The Night Shield insisted on her keeping a low profile after she brought a man home for some... recreation. He said that it drew too much attention even though the woman was sure he wasn't an assassin. The stranger was a former mercenary with a limp from an arrow wound to his knee and a cute butt.

She supposed that Travus did have a point, after all. He was trying to protect what was left of his family.

Still, this was the first time that Ophelia was able to make decisions for herself. No enchantment from the General, no Light Bringers to shove her into a cell and continuously ask the same questions over and over, just her mind and what she wanted... she wasn't going to waste that.

Ophelia was so caught up in thinking, trying to decide what to do next (until Travus tried to hit her with a curfew, at least), that she barely noticed the woman sit down across from her at the table. When she did look up, a quiet groan escaped her lips.

Pale skin, bright green eyes surrounded by too much dark make up, short red hair, a low cut black leather top with one long sleeve down her right arm with burgundy painted nails to match her equally painted lips and a posture that just screamed narcissism. Add to that a bronze sleeve on her left arm, there was no doubt. It was Kitanah.

"It's nice to finally see you again, Ophelia," the woman smiled.

The former assassin took a long pull from her mug before replying, "You came all this way just to see what I look like in pants?"

Ophelia kicked a leg out from under the table to show off her long leg wrapped in form fitting gray cloth. They were tucked into leather boots that came halfway up her shin and on her waist was a thick belt where Havarti was resting comfortably in his scabbard with new strips of blue leather wrapped around his handle.

Her shirt was white with long sleeves and thick cuffs. There was no sign of the buckler she wore almost constantly in her time at the Oasis. And her torso was wrapped in a cherry colored vest made of thin, treated wool. The front was loosely laced up, which made Kitanah wonder...

"Do you have the back cut out of both of those?" she curved to finger to suggest that she was pointed behind Ophelia, "Your tattoos were always so sensitive."

The former assassin frowned. She didn't like that the other woman knew her so well. All that held the vest together in the back were a couple of lengths of cloth, only just touching her skin when she leaned back in a chair.

"What do you want, Kitanah?" Ophelia took another long sip of her drink, leaving only a few drops of liquid behind, "I'd offer you a drink but I just drank my last coin."

"Oh, that's no issue," the red haired woman grinned, "I was hoping that we wouldn't be staying here," as she looked around the pub, her expression changed to one who was looking at something that wasn't only unpleasant but maybe even revolting.

Kitanah took Ophelia's mug and drained the last of the beer, "Ugh, I thought that I had taught you better taste than this," she tossed the pewter cup over her shoulder and it clattered across the floor.

A few of the other patrons glared in her and Ophelia's direction angrily but didn't make a move to complain. That was when Ophelia realized what should have been obvious from the start. The new General (it was a logical conclusion considering that *her* General was dead) wasn't here alone.

"All you taught me was to keep looking over my shoulder, Kitanah," Ophelia leaned back in her seat, her right hand wrapping around Havarti's grip where he rested on her right hip, "Have a look around." she added telepathically to her sword.

"And still I get the drop on you," she had such a sweet smile on her face, "Every time."

"I'm not going back," Ophelia made the statement a definite declaration, "And you know you can't take me in a fight."

"I didn't come here to fight," Kitanah motioned to the young man who had served Ophelia her beer to come to the table, "Bring us two glasses of your finest wine. I assume you do have some actual, decent vintages here somewhere?"

The waiter was visibly shaking but he nodded back to the matriarch of the Al Razheem. She shewed him away and he ran to fulfill her request. Then she turned her attention back to her former compatriot.

"I came here to bring you home," Kitanah continued as if she hadn't paused the conversation, "With the General's unnatural control over you gone, I thought we could put our old rivalry to bed, so to speak. Come back to the Al Razheem, take your place as my First Bravo, and I'll teach you everything about your family that my predecessor neglected to give you."

Havarti interrupted into his wielder's mind, "I count at least three assassins for sure, maybe one or two more behind Kitanah that I can't get a good angle on."

While Ophelia kept facing the other woman, her blue eyes scanned the room slowly, in the directions her sword indicated, "No more killing innocent women and children? And I wouldn't have to make a return visit to Efreeti?"

Kitanah arched a crimson eyebrow back, "What's wrong with *Doctor* Efreeti?"

"What's wrong with him? You were the one who was convinced that he was trying to steal control of the Al Razheem out from under the General," Ophelia snapped.

"I realized I was wrong. Doctor Efreeti has been nothing but helpful since I was forced to take command," the other woman answered.

Kitanah didn't make any sound or movement to acknowledge the waiter when he placed two glasses with long stems in front of either woman. Ophelia sat silently for a long moment, giving the waiter a glance that was, perhaps, a little longer than she had intended. The Al Razheem General didn't seem to notice.

"You glossed over the first question there," the former assassin said.

Kitanah lifted her glass to her lips, "What question was that?"

"If I would be used to kill more innocent women, children, you know, bystanders," Ophelia answered.

The other woman seemed confused, "Even with our former General's *extracurricular* missions that he sent you on, who did you attack that wasn't an enemy of the Al Razheem?"

"Inara Browder for one." Ophelia felt herself tense just at the sound of the name, "And her daughter. I didn't kill her but I kidnapped her and took her to the Oasis. Remember?"

Kitanah set her glass back down on the table after taking a sip, "They were hardly innocent, Ophelia. They were part and parcel to the spoils of Crichton's treachery. The only proper punishment for a traitor is destroying everything he gained before killing him."

"Oh," Ophelia's attention shifted to the waiter still standing beside the table, "He'll be relieved to hear me not only reject your offer but tell you that I intend to kill you for what you just said."

"He? Who's he?" Kitanah looked up at the waiter who was still standing beside the table.

It wasn't the same scared kid from before. It was Travus Browder, holding the tray under his arm and glaring straight back into the assassin's eyes.

He didn't have his red trench coat on. His shirt looked a little too loose and his pants a little too tight. If Kitanah didn't hate him with all she had and more, she would have enjoyed the view.

"You never were one to give the help a simple thank you, were you?" the man practically growled.

Kitanah didn't even have to speak for the first assassin to charge at Travus. He took a face full of tray for his trouble, the Al Razheem tumbling to the wood floor without his consciousness for his efforts.

Kitanah reared back her sleeve to attack Travus herself when she felt a sudden pressure on her chest. No, not *on*, more *in*, or even more accurately, *through*. Looking down, she saw the familiar looking handle of the bastard sword between her breasts, pressed against the black leather of her top, just below her sternum. But the handle looked too short.

Then it came to her... Havarti had a dagger hidden in its grip and that was the blade that was in her heart. She tried to say something but only a spray of blood came out of her mouth.

"Thanks for saving me the trouble of coming after you," Ophelia said as she pulled Havarti's dagger out of the other woman.

The sword shook Kitanah's blood from his blade as the woman with the braids lifted herself to her feet. Ophelia looked down at the Al Razheem General quizzically for a moment before speaking again.

"You really didn't think that I'd stab you?" She chuckled, "You may or may not have meant all those insults and jibes but I *know* I meant every last one of them."

That old spark of rage that the woman had before (when Ophelia first joined the Al Razheem) in her green eyes returned as Kitanah slumped out of the chair. Falling to the floor, she rested flat on her back. There was surprisingly little blood but, now that she was laying prone, it would likely start pouring out.

"I would be lying if I said that I had not been looking forward to that," Havarti said before adding, "Perhaps a tactical retreat would be in order here."

Everybody in the pub was staring at Ophelia and Travus. Even the two left that were pointed out to be assassins by the woman's sword didn't make a move to attack them.

"Anyone who doesn't want to get chopped, skewered or sliced by my friend here," Ophelia put Havarti together, pulled him free of his scabbard and into a position he was ready to fight again, "Had best get out of the way between us and the door."

The people in the pub were quiet and very efficient. The path to the door out to the street left plenty of room for Travus and Ophelia to walk across the room, even if she decided to start haphazardly swinging her sword around.

It led the woman to wonder why people in a crowd couldn't be more polite and let her through without being bumped into, groped and slurred at like when she came in earlier. Havarti agreed, his handle having been molested by several different people when they arrived.

"And you two," Ophelia pointed her blade at the two Al Razheem, "you keep doing what you're doing. A whole lot of nothing."

The Night Shield and the former assassin made their way through the aisle between the two crowds of people as a discomfited quiet filled the building. They reached the door but just as Travus pulled the handle to open it...

"This was my favorite top!" Kitanah shrieked as she bolted straight up to a sitting position on the floor.

The not dead woman jumped to her feet and turned back toward the table. Reaching for her glass, she lifted it to her dark lips and drained it completely before putting it down, taking the glass meant for Ophelia, and drinking it all, too.

Only then did Kitanah turn in the direction of Travus and Ophelia. She covered the hole in her top with her hand but there wasn't even any blood.

"You can run now. But you know I will find you. Again and again," she said between deep, enraged breaths, "You will be mine again, Ophelia. And you," she lifted her bronze sleeve and pointed the hooks at the Night Shield, "will be so dead that your little girl won't even remember she had a father!"

Travus looked straight at Ophelia, who mirrored the gesture, "Time to go?"

"Most definitely," she agreed.

They both dashed through the door and down the street as fast as their feet could carry them. After a few twists and turns down this street and that, Ophelia finally spoke up.

"How did you know I was in trouble?" she asked.

Travus answered between winded gasps as they kept running, "I didn't. I was coming to find you... and tell you that we were all packed up and ready to move on... I told you that I thought we had stayed here too long."

Ophelia nodded, "But I really liked that honeybark ale."

She saw Travus grin at what she said. But at the same time his brown eyes looked so... sad.

BACK IN THE OASIS

"Efreeti!" Kitanah bellowed as she opened the door, slamming the door against the unseen wall.

The thin, human-like figure that was the subject of the hollering stepped out from behind his window and into the woman's field of vision, "Is there a problem?"

Her laugh was as dry as the desert outside, "You can say that. Ophelia stabbed me in the heart!"

Her hand fell away from her severed top (the ride home was rough on her wardrobe), exposing her chest to the not-quite-a-man. The only reaction from Doctor Efreeti was for him to adjust the brim of his top hat. He had put it on in a hurry and it wasn't quite straight.

"It was a real possibility," he said without any emotion in his voice, "I did warn you that she did not know who to trust."

"She seemed pretty chummy with Crichton to me," Kitanah scowled.

"Likely an unfortunate side effect of several weeks of continuous contact," Efreeti explained, "Surely you did not expect a single conversation over a glass of alcohol would be sufficient to turn her loyalties back to your particular little cult, did you?"

"Yes, actually," the woman propped her hand on one hip and the cuff of her metal sleeve on the other, "I thought that was your whole damned point of me going out there!"

"My *point*," clouds started to make the light from the window cold and colorless, "Madame General, was that of all the Al Razheem your bond with her was the strongest. That did not mean that she would come to you like a lost pet."

"Then what would you have had me do, Efreeti?" she asked though her tone did not suggest that she expected an answer.

But answer he did, "For an assassin, you do not practice the art of subtlety often. Perhaps it would have been more beneficial to visit her over a series of nights, to build her trust and counter the influence from the Night Shield and Light Bringers on her. Ophelia is too strong willed to bend to an ultimatum."

"You made her subject to the General's will," Kitanah snapped back.

"With a personally designed rune, time to properly inject the solution and extract various levels of luminosity from her essence for implantation into the soul orb," the red glow behind the lenses of the not-quite-a-man's glasses flared brighter, "Due to such effort, he never had the need to give Ophelia an ultimatum."

What Efreeti had to say only upset the new General more. She paced back and forth in front of the man, her pale skin flushed as her expression vacillated between rage and almost pleading.

"I want to kill her so badly!" the woman fumed, "She stabbed me as if it was nothing to her. Like she was protecting that Night Shield bastard!"

"Unfortunately," the faint sound of thunder came from the overcast mountainside on the other side of the window, "her death is neither tenable nor amicable to your needs or those of the Al Razheem."

"How would you know about my needs?" the new General glared at him.

"There is a severely limited supply of soul orbs with which to build an immortal sect of demigods from the Al Razheem," Doctor Efreeti removed his top hat and placed it on the marble table that appeared in the most timely manner, "And thanks to Ophelia and your adept skills in the art of murder, specifically of Squire Trelaine, it will be impossible to create more within the span of this generation of mortals or the next. This was, of course, as the General intended."

Kitanah let out a curse so vile that even Efreeti thought it would be appropriate to blush. He didn't but he did think it would have been an appropriate response.

The fire that had been carrying the woman so intensely quickly faded. Suddenly feeling drained, Kitanah walked over to the marble table and sat on the cold, flat stone.

""What was the General's ultimate plan for the soul stones, Doctor?" Whether her tone was exhausted or depressed, the effect was the same.

Efreeti shook his head, "Every contingency he had in mind involved him being alive so I can assure you that they are all null and void."

"Why didn't he tell me any of his plans?" she had moved on to despair, "I thought he trusted me implicitly. I, I loved him, Doctor."

Though the clouds outside the window parted, the thin man rolled his eyes behind his thick lenses, "Your General was a man who relied heavily on control. Anything he could not influence through love, he manipulated through fear. Even himself. Both feelings can either fade with time or become stronger."

The not-quite-a-man lifted himself onto the table beside the woman. He kept his hands inside his tweed cloak, making him look more like a life sized doll than an actual living being.

"The fear overtook him. Every decision he made that went against your professed beliefs was a direct reflection of that fear controlling him," Doctor Efreeti sighed, "In this case, the fear of his own mortality."

Kitanah didn't want to believe it but his words made sense. The General could have known that Travus Crichton was out there for months. Feeling that the Night Shield's very appearance could have been a death sentence, he started indulging every whim as if he were about to die all while taking every step, no matter how outlandish, to ensure that he would (in this case literally) live forever.

He undoubtedly intended one of those orbs for himself. But the new leader of the Al Razheem knew that he was a man whose trust was hard to gain. Ophelia was the proof he wanted from Efreeti that the soul orbs functioned as promised.

"The question then becomes," he started speaking again, "what do you want to do with the nineteen remaining immortals en potentia?"

That wasn't the question that Kitanah had in mind, "After you proved the procedure's success with Ophelia, why didn't the General use one of the soul orbs on himself?"

Efreeti's cheek twitched, the only sign of annoyance he gave at either his question being ignored or being asked a question in return, "Your General was unwilling to relinquish control of the day to day operations of the Al Razheem. I can only presume due to the worry of Travus Browder being discovered."

"So he was going to undertake becoming immortal once the coast was clear," the woman sat in thoughtful silence.

But the not-quite-a-man didn't want to give her too much time to do so, "Again, my General, what do you want done with the remaining nineteen soul orbs?"

Kitanah slipped from the table and back onto her feet. She slowly strode toward the door as she considered her response.

"I was planning on going to war with the Light Bringers to avenge the General," she turned around to face Efreeti before she reached the door, "Rebuilding the Fidai into an immortal force would have made it a short campaign. But now I don't think that is in the best interest of the Al Razheem."

"What, pray tell, do you mean?" the almost-human grinned back.

"Ophelia's a wild card." she answered, "I can't have her out there, able to take my immortals out of play. I'll need to use our bond to track her down again. Then I need to either bring her back or figure out another way to neutralize her since death isn't an option."

Efreeti's hand emerged from under his coat to lightly tap a fingertip against the end of his chin, "I'm afraid that tracking her via your bond is no longer possible."

Kitanah's green eyes narrowed, "What do you mean?"

"I mean that the energy to heal your wound had to come from somewhere," he responded, "Since it was Ophelia who dealt what would have been a lethal blow, your new runes pulled the energy from your bond to reverse the damage. Just as it would have done with any attempted killer."

"You mean that your runes can only protect me from people I already know?" she growled, the cuff of her metal sleeve starting to spin around.

Efreeti shook his head, no longer acknowledging the woman's anger, "That would be ineffective. The act of murder creates a bond between two people, just as taking oaths and other *physical* activities together do. Usually, though, the bond is almost immediately severed upon the death of the target. In your case, that newly forged bond keeps death from claiming you."

Kitanah's hand reflexively rose to cradle where Havarti's dagger had pierced her chest, "You didn't mention that it would still hurt."

"That is why blinking is such a boon to whomever has the prerequisites to receive it," Efreeti answered, "It not only keeps a killing blow from landing but moves the target out of harm's way."

It took a conscious effort for the woman to stop the cuff from spinning, "You said that I couldn't get blinking. Why?"

"I can only bestow that ability upon mortals within a certain age range, among other factors," he answered, hopping up onto his feet himself.

"You've made me as young as Ophelia again," Kitanah said, "Could you make me able to blink now?"

"I'm afraid not," Efreeti said, "Restoring youth and blinking sap their energies from the same tributary of energy. You can have either one or the other but who wants immortality if eternal youth does not come with it?"

The woman's eyebrows pressed together, "But Ophelia will be young forever and be able to blink."

"Recovery and maintenance are different," the almost-human explained, "That is why there is an age restriction."

Kitanah loosed a frustrated little grunt, "Fine. But with her and Travus scattering to who knows where in Honua, how can I find her before she gets it in her head to come back after me?"

Efreeti nodded, his head making his chin tap against his fingertip rather than the other way around, "Each of her runes radiates a different spectrum of energy that can be tracked with varying levels of success."

Her eyes locked on the almost-man, unmoving, "In a language I can understand, please."

He let out a disappointed sigh, "One of her runes radiates energy strong enough that I will be able to find her most anywhere."

"Why didn't you tell me before?" a spark of anger reignited in the woman's voice, "I would have rather you done it that way than make me confess to sleeping with Ophelia!"

"You did not ask," Efreeti answered simply, "And the methodology we've been using was most effective up to this point."

"You can still find her. Wonderful," Kitanah didn't look as pleased as her words would have suggested, "But I still can't kill her. You said that you can help with neutralizing Ophelia?"

He nodded, "Indeed. Shall I introduce to you my new pets that I have been training since I lost my poor crinotaur?"

THE MENAGERIE OF DOCTOR EFREETI

"MADAM GENERAL, ARE you wearing that special eye wear the way that I showed you?" the voice of Doctor Efreeti echoed through the open space of the arena.

The very same arena where the former General held that mockery of the Keian for the traitor Travus Crichton, or Browder when he wasn't lying. Kitanah, First Bravo Spacek and Coloron, the last remaining member of the Fidai, stood in the middle of the darkened space. Doctor Efreeti was feeling theatrical for the latest demonstration.

If asked, Kitanah would have grumbled her annoyance at such a spectacle being made when a simple introduction to her latest weapons would have sufficed. If she were honest, mostly with herself, that the ache of the anticipation, the uncertainty of whether the thin not-quite-a-man could deliver on his promise, the new leader of the Al Razheem would have to admit that she did enjoy these brief moments of release from having to be practically omniscient.

Despite Doctor Efreeti's assurances, Kitanah came dressed in attire ready for battle. Her bladed metal sleeve hung at her side like always, a black leather corset wrapped around her athletic frame was loaded with an assortment of daggers and throwing knives, and her pants held several flasks of various compounds in hidden pockets.

Her red hair was pulled back into a tight ponytail with two crimson ribbons cascading down her back. It was the only hint of decoration to her wardrobe this evening.

What was not a part of her usual wardrobe were these things Efreeti referred to as "goggles" that were wrapped around her eyes. They made her usually emerald green irises look more pastel. She was finding them uncomfortable but was assured that they were necessary for the demonstration.

Since his return from Paimae, Coloron had taken to wearing a short black cape with a hood. He had always been so proud of his physique before but now that a massive scar, courtesy of Ophelia, ran from his shoulder and down through the middle of his chest, he kept it hidden.

He had already replaced his hatchet lost in the failed rescue mission with two that hang from his hips. His hands rested on the butts of the blades, the handles slipped through loops attached to his belt.

Spacek had just been appointed the new General's First mere days ago. Her head was shaved and her brown skin smooth. She wasn't as athletic as Kitanah, relying more on her knowledge of alchemy and arcane energies in her rise to power within the Al Razheem hierarchy.

The azure doublet she wore had a tall collar and pouches full of different ingredients rested between each button that held the jacket shut on her lithe frame. The silk sleeves wrapped around her hands even as she flexed and stretched her fingers... just in case.

Again, the disembodied voice of Efreeti fell on the trio of assassins, "Tell me, oh wise leader of the Al Razheem, her newest First who is strong mind and sharp in wit, and the elite member of the Fidai who knows no limit to guile, do you see anything amiss among you, around your immediate area?"

He sounded as if he was enjoying himself. By now, Kitanah had learned to keep her overly paranoid thoughts at bay around Efreeti. Not completely ignored, mind you, but to keep her guard up around the not-quite-human would have drained her in short order, especially with how much time they've spent together of late.

The other two, however, were ready for battle. Coloron had his weapons in hand as his dark eyes scanned the dim arena around them. Spacek pulled a pouch out of one of her many pockets with one hand, as well as a thin stiletto dagger in the other. She started chanting something under her breath and her chocolate colored eyes started to glow a soft amber.

"In the third row of benches," the smaller woman motioned to where an audience would usually be sitting to watch the proceedings.

"Very good!" Efreeti giggled.

A woman sat deathly still right where Spacek described, resting her head in her hands and, in turn, her elbows on her knees. The way her legs were bent, though, didn't look right.

Then Kitanah noticed that the stranger's hair was moving, as if she had snakes coiled around her head. The new General was tempted to tear these goggle things off her face. The color of everything wasn't quite right and the lenses, that was what the thin man called them anyway, apparently distorted what she was looking at so that her vision was easy to trick.

The sitting woman stood up. She wasn't wearing clothes but she didn't look like a naked woman typically would. Her chest was, to put it indelicately, her breasts were missing their nipples. Light glinted off her shoulders, arms, hips, and thighs in an odd way, as if her body was covered with scale mail armor. No, they were literally scales.

As the odd woman stepped onto the lower bench in front of her, the assassins could see that her legs seemed unnaturally long for her body. Then her leg bent like the entire body of a snake rearing back. Once her legs weren't obscured, they watched each limb take turns slithering more than stepping as she made her way down into the arena.

Kitanah realized that the goggles weren't playing tricks with her vision after all. The stranger's hair was indeed writhing around as if it was a nest of vipers on her head. Headless vipers. There were no eyes at the end of any of the scaled tendrils. The new General had to contain a shiver when she did see the end of one open to reveal a pair of fangs in the lower, for lack of a better term, jaw.

"You found young Sesklo!" the still missing Efreeti's voice echoed, "But what of her two sisters?"

"Sisters?" Spacek and Coloron asked at the same time.

"That would be Euryale and Stheno," Efreeti answered from wherever he was, "They are in the arena somewhere, I assure you."

"So you're showing me fighters that can hide well?" Kitanah looked up as she spoke since Efreeti seemed to be hiding himself.

"You have stumbled upon the most exquisite point of this, Madam General!" he answered, "They are not hiding. They are simply standing still."

Kitanah's eyebrows pressed together and she started to look around again.

"The scales covering the sisters make them blend into most any environment," Efreeti explained, "They are not hiding as much as they simply have a natural camouflage. You can come out ladies!"

At the not-quite-a-man's word, two figures suddenly appeared like they stepped out of the shadows. Like Sesklo, they had slithering hair and no clothes. Their legs also curved rather than bent at the knee like human legs, giving the impression that they were sliding on their shins as they approached the three assassins.

All three of the female monsters lined up in front of Kitanah, Spacek, and Coloron. Just to the side of the group, the very air beside them opened like a door. On the other side was darkness and out of that came Doctor Efreeti.

"These, Madam General, are my gorgons," he said proudly as he closed the... air behind him, "The tallest is Euryale, she wields a crossbow. She also has special, shall we call them loads, of bolts she creates herself for her weapon."

The female monster standing across from Kitanah responded with a polite bow at the sound of her name. The crossbow and quiver, both resting on her scaled back, were visible for a brief moment before she straightened back up.

Euryale was slightly shorter than Kitanah. Thinner as well, not that Kitanah was at all fat of course, the gorgon was thinner even than First Spacek who always seemed to nearly malnourished looking to the General

"Next is Sesklo, whom you saw earlier," the man in the tweed cloak continued, "She prefers two scimitars. They are typically dipped in a neurotoxin that is derived from the venom sacs in the hair tendrils of herself and her sisters."

Sesklo stood before Spacek, and over her, although she wasn't as tall as her sister Euryale. She stood much like Coloron did when he arrived in the arena with her hands wrapped around the hilts of her swords resting on her round hips.

"And ultimately, but certainly not least, is fair Stheno," Efreeti concluded.

"And what is her weapon of preference?" Kitanah asked.

The answer was presented by a flick of motion and a curved dagger was suddenly at the base of Coloron's throat. He didn't even have a chance to raise his hatchets in defense. And he'd been prepared to fight.

"Ja, daggers, Mistress," Stheno nodded politely toward the Al Razheem General.

"You can speak," the assassin General said, "Why haven't you before now?"

"Ja, you had not inquired anything of us, Mistress," the gorgon answered.

Kitanah nodded, "Very well, Stheno. What other skills do you and your sisters possess that should convince me to use you for this coming undertaking?"

Stheno turned her attention to Doctor Efreeti, who nodded. Then the woman looked back toward the new General.

"Do you value this one, Mistress, ne?" she asked.

"Coloron?" Kitanah quirked an eyebrow, "Not really. Show me what you have in mind."

At "not really", Stheno's legs spun around under her while she stayed in place, whipping the man's out from under him. Coloron fell to the dusty ground of the arena, spreading his arms and legs to disperse the force of his landing. It was a move he'd used in training hundreds if not thousands of times to keep from having the breath knocked out of his body.

He threw one of the hatchets at the monster, who dove under the flying weapon like a swimmer diving into a pool. The gorgon slid between Coloron's legs even as he tried to scramble away from her.

The assassin brought his other small ax down at the woman, who wrapped her free hand around his wrist to stop the strike. She didn't appear to expend any effort as the hatchet stopped between them. With just a squeeze of her fingers, the assassin expelled a curse in his native tongue as pain washed through him and his wrist crumbled. The gorgon was unnaturally strong.

"Ja, look at me, my love," Stheno whispered to the man, laying down on top of him.

She released his broken wrist, resting her hands in the dirt on either side of his head. After a quick series of pops, Coloron's wrist was suddenly whole again, thanks to the tattoos Efreeti had injected into his back.

He slipped his arms under the monster's shoulders, lifting her away from him. The assassin started to twist his body to throw the gorgon away from him, to give him a moment to recollect his weapon, when she again spoke to him.

"Ja, look at me, my love," Stheno said again, her voice as calm as it was before.

Coloron's dark eyes looked in the direction that he was planning to toss her. Then he looked up at her, readying a scorching remark at her expense.

But then his face went blank as if he'd forgotten what he was doing. His hands immediately dropped back into the dirt as his entire body convulsed. Then they went cold.

He couldn't move his gaze away from Stheno, who had taken to sitting on his well defined stomach. She smiled down at him wickedly, bobbing the blade of her unused dagger up and down as if to wave goodbye as his vision faded.

After only a matter of seconds, the assassin couldn't see anything. His teeth ground together as the freezing feeling spread up into his arms. Coloron's feet went numb and his legs followed suit.

Moments later, the assassin went from being the last of the elite Fidai to the Fidai becoming a team of elites with no members. Coloron was no more and all that remained...

"He looks like a statue," Spacek observed, her voice quiet with either awe or fear, maybe both.

"Essentially, he is," Efreeti answered, "Come now, your predecessor told you the stories of the magical beasts of his home land, did he not? Stheno, Euryale and Sesklo are of the most storied species of his people."

"She petrified him," Kitanah slowly walked around the man who was laying on the ground now made of what appeared to be obsidian rock, "Just by looking at him."

"By him looking at her, if you desire a more accurate specificity," Doctor Efreeti corrected her.

Something occurred to the new General. Their moving hair was always the first thing she noticed but, when her attention moved lower, it always skipped straight to their bodies.

"Is whatever did that the reason I instinctively moved my attention past their faces?" Kitanah looked toward Stheno, who was still resting upon Coloron.

"Very good, Madam General!" Efreeti's face almost split in half, his smile was so wide, "Most would not have noticed that reflex to not look directly at a gorgon."

The thin man ushered Kitanah over to Stheno. After bidding the monster to rise, again, the gorgon was standing before the Al Razheem leader.

"Now, do realize that the only reason you are about to perform such an exploit as looking upon the beauty of the divine eye is due to these," Efreeti tapped the side of the goggles on the woman's face before turning his attention to the gorgon, "Please look directly at the Madam General, dearie."

"The divine eye?" Kitanah questioned the thin man as Stheno looked up at the taller woman.

The gorgon's face could be considered exotic to these lands. Her eyes were angled, with her eyebrows curling up at the outside tips. She had what was often referred to as a "button nose" and, while her lips were plump, particularly her lower one, they didn't look out of place. When the monster smiled, though, long pointed teeth, more than just fangs but not enough to fill her entire mouth, poked out to rest on her lower lip. It reminded Kitanah of a set of darts resting on a pillow.

"The divine eye is the true defining characteristic of a gorgon," Efreeti began to explain. "A gorgon's physical structure is a mutation of naga and lamia lineages. Nagas, as you know them, are those "snake heads" that your Al Razheem often contended with during the days of the construction of this Oasis. Lamias fair from the lands of your former patriarch and their serpentine characteristics more often evolve around, let's say, their locomotion."

The new General scowled back at the thin not-quite-a-man, "Mutation? Locomotion? I'm afraid you're losing me, Doctor."

"Ah, my apologies, Madam General. Your mind is so sharp that I often forget that you've not received training in the fine sciences," the thin man removed his hat and pressed it to his narrow chest, "Lamia's snake halves often manifest themselves in the lower portions of their bodies rather than human legs. As for the explanation on mutation...

"As you can see, gorgons like Stheno and her sisters do not have, "snake heads" like the naga, though their hair has retained the serpentine characteristics of their ancestors. You will also notice that Stheno's legs move much like a snake's body but look like a human's. That is, of course, also recognizing that they have two legs instead of one long tail," Efreeti leaned in close to the new General, the curved tip of his clawed forefinger pointing to the various characteristics to which he referred.

"But all of this is window dressing," the Doctor continued, "Nagas and Lamias do occasionally exhibit one or two of these recessive traits as well. No, to be a true gorgon, you must, indeed *must* have the divine eye!"

"But what *is* the divine eye?" Kitanah felt her patience start to slip.

"Ahhh…" the sound escaped Efreeti slowly, almost like a hiss, as his smile didn't so much widen as much as change to a sharper angle, "Look closely at Stheno's face, dearie. Really, really look!"

The woman did as Efreeti, well, she took it as a request anyway. She leaned in close to Stheno. The gorgon's slithering hair reared back but the Doctor admonished the monster to stay still.

Stheno's eyes looked, as far as the General could tell, normal. She couldn't detect anything "divine" about them. Then she noticed as odd, for lack of a better term, *swirling* on the gorgon's left cheek, just under her eye. Kitanah reached up to point at the area, her hand floating only inches away–

"Ah ah ah ah ah, Madam General!" Efreeti snatched the woman's hand away from the strange *thing* on the gorgon's face with a speed that surprised even her, "While the sisters will indeed serve you well they have a, shall we say, a bad history with people whose hands have enveloped their throats. They reflexively lash out in defense if anyone's hands get too close."

Kitanah let out a quiet grunt, "Fine, Efreeti. Just tell me what that swirling I saw was."

"The swirling, as you described it, was the goggles protecting you from the effects of Stheno's divine eye," the thin man answered, "If you did not have such protection, you would have suffered a fate like poor Coloron."

"So it's what petrifies people but you still haven't explained what it actually is, Doctor," the annoyance in Kitanah's voice was hard to miss anymore.

"Indeed, you are a sharp one, Madam General," as always, Doctor Efreeti didn't appear to notice, "The divine eye is what marks a gorgon as either blessed or cursed, depending upon whether they are born to the nagas or the lamia. Those who view it as cursed due to its petrification abilities have hunted any known gorgon to extinction on this continent.

"But those, like many in your predecessor's homeland, viewed gorgons as oracles. They believed that they had a direct connection to the spirits beyond this world. They would seek the gorgons to learn what fate their lives held. Those worthy would find great fortune. Those found wanting, well…" he looked down at the black stone shaped like the last member of the Fidai.

"How do they determine worthiness?" Kitanah shook her head and instead redirected her attention to Stheno, "How do you determine worthiness?"

"Ja, Mistress, I have never had anyone look upon me and not return to the earth," the gorgon answered, "Except you."

The General turned back to Efreeti, "Return to the earth?"

"Petrify," the thin man answered, "The divine eye drains all living energy from those who look upon it. In fact, its gaze is so powerful that anything immediately touching the victim is also petrified be it clothing or even the ground itself."

The Doctor tapped his foot beside Coloron where his hand met the sand that coated the arena floor. Black sand expanded beyond the former member of the Fidai's palms for about another foot.

Kitanah looked down at the petrified man's feet but didn't see the same effect. She looked at Efreeti questioningly.

"Boots or sandals are often thick enough to insulate the ground under them from the effects of the divine eye," he answered the unspoken question.

Kitanah chewed on her lower lip, wearing away the lacquer coating it, "You said that in the legends some of the people who've looked into the divine eye have survived. How?"

"Those who seek to look upon the divine unprepared do find their fates," he said, "Indeed, they seal it by their own shortsightedness. It is those who have demonstrated a wisdom to approach the gorgon prepared," he tapped the side of his own glasses and then pointed at the goggles on Kitanah's face, "that have fed the portion of the legend that it brings much fortune upon the survivor. I believe that great fortune would have met one who can think ahead and prepare for any situation like that regardless." Efreeti shrugged, "But who am I to judge?"

Kitanah's mind began to race with possibilities, "And there's no way that your runes could spare Ophelia?"

The thin not-quite-a-man again looked at Coloron, "They did not save him."

The new General suddenly smiled a smile that could have rivaled the good Doctor's, "Send them out at once."

"Indeed, Madam General," Efreeti answered, although he didn't have the usual enthusiasm in his voice.

Kitanah sighed, "What's wrong now?"

"As you know, Ophelia is well outside of the territory controlled by the Al Razheem and continuously on the move," the Doctor said, "While the sisters could indeed make chase, I feel their abilities would be better suited for laying in wait for her."

"And how do you propose to do that?" the hairs on the back of the woman's neck rose, "We never know where Ophelia is going."

"While they are out of your direct reach, Madam General," Efreeti replaced his top hat onto his balding head, "They are not beyond the reach of your allies. Perhaps you can reacquaint yourself with some old friends within the svartalfar tribe of the Xaviour?"

Kitanah tapped her lower lip thoughtfully for a moment, "I could send Spacek to visit. She's always had a good relationship with them. What do you say, Space– (svartalfar word for the bastard children of cursed elves and the goats that love them. There isn't a direct translation).

The bald woman stood still before Sesklo. Deathly still. Her cocoa brown skin now more closely resembled granite.

The sword wielding gorgon bowed and begged for forgiveness from Doctor Efreeti and General Kitanah Baynette, "She was so intent to inspect my divine eye that she refused to heed your warnings!"

The assassin waved as if she was dismissing an unpleasant but hardly damaging odor, "The only complication will be finding someone to take the post after it's been vacated so quickly as many times as it has lately."

EIGHTEEN

WILDEVALE

"HEY, OPHELIA, CAN I ask you something?" Tilly asked after she poked her head into the older woman's room.

The former assassin was surprised to say the least. In the weeks since they fled Middlemount the little girl had barely said a word to her. Ophelia lifted herself from her bed, keeping the sheet wrapped around herself (she already had to sit through a lecture about modesty from Travus the morning after they arrived here and didn't want another).

Wiping the sleep from her pale eyes, she nodded back at the girl, "What do you need, Tilly?"

The young woman fidgeted as she slipped into the room, her hand shaking as she pushed the door closed. Whatever she wanted, it wasn't going to be something simple, at least to her.

"I... need some advice," Tilly said as she stepped before Ophelia, who was still sitting on the side of her bed.

The woman cocked an eyebrow, "Advice? From me? Is there something wrong with your father?" Ophelia looked back in the direction of the room that usually housed Travus, as if she could see him through the walls.

Tilly shook her head, "No, nothing like that. I just don't think that he would… understand."

Ophelia suddenly wished that she could put on some pants, "Understand what? It has to be something really weird if you're willing to come to me."

The little girl bristled at the woman's words but she shrugged back, "I need to talk to *another woman* and you're the only one I know within a hundred leagues of here."

"Another woman," Ophelia's cocked eyebrow rose even higher, "Even if it is because we're the only two allowed to talk to each other, I do fit your prerequisite. Ask away, I guess."

"It's about boys," Tilly looked as if she was fighting either the urge to giggle or pee.

"Oh, good. A subject I enjoy," the former assassin laughed.

That seemed to calm the young woman, at least a little, "How do you know if a boy likes you?"

"Usually they tell me that they like my breasts," Ophelia wasn't joking as much as her tone may have suggested.

Tilly looked down at her own mostly flat chest then at Ophelia's, which was decidedly not, "You mean boys will only like you if you have big ones?" she pointed.

The woman shook her head, getting a lot more uncomfortable than she thought she was going to, "No, that isn't what I'm saying. You asked how I can tell when they like me. By the time they get to me, the boys I'm around have already drank quite a bit of alcohol," Which sounded very comforting to Ophelia right now.

"So you're saying that I should get the boy I like drunk and then ask him?" Tilly looked confused with a splash of disgusted.

Ophelia let out a loud groan, "Stop putting words in my mouth! I was just talking about me."

Tilly scowled back, "We're not talking about you! I want you to help me!"

And Ophelia scowled right back, "I'm trying to but you keep saying that I'm telling you things that I'm not telling you!" she hid her eyes behind her hand, massaging her temples.

It took the long, long moment of silence that hung between the two for the still drowsy brain of Ophelia to realize something. She looked up at Tilly over the little flap of skin that connected the inside of her thumb to the side of her hand.

"Wait a minute," she said, "A boy you like? You like a boy here in town?" she screamed internally, hoping in her heart of hearts that Travus would show up and take over the conversation.

Tilly nodded, her forehead, cheeks and neck all turning beet red, "He's the one who hands me the bag of groceries every morning."

Ophelia knew who she was talking about. He was cute but too young for the former assassin's tastes. But when he matured up...

The woman shook her head and looked back at Tilly, "He's a couple of years older than you, isn't he?"

The girl's brown eyebrows pressed together, "So?"

"Some older boys expect a little more *physical* loving from their girlfriends than the experience level you're at, Tilly. That would be none, right?" a shiver suddenly ran through the woman.

No one had ever said anything like this to her but she was definitely feeling as if this was something she heard before. This wasn't even advice she'd follow herself so why was she giving it? Her eyes snapped to the corner of the room when she heard Havarti laughing in her head.

"By physical you mean sex, right?" Tilly raised her hand to her mouth as if she'd just said something naughty, "But how do you know if he's the one that you're going to marry so that it's okay to, um, do it?"

"I don't know about marriage but for me *doing it* takes about four or five strong beers," Ophelia snickered but then raised her hands defensively, "It was just a joke! Just a joke!"

Tilly huffed, crossing her arms in front of her thin chest, "This isn't funny!" she protested.

Ophelia shook her head, letting out another groan, "Listen, kid, you're way too young to be thinking about marriage at this point. Especially never having had a guy between your legs before."

"My Mom said that the only guy I should have sex with should be my husband," Tilly said back.

"Really?" the former assassin was genuinely surprised by the idea, "Then how would you know if he's good in bed or not before tying the knot?"

The question was meant to be to herself but, judging from the disgusted look coming from the little girl, Ophelia must have said it aloud. She suddenly wondered if there was something handy with which she could stab herself and hopefully blink out of having to have this talk anymore.

"Listen, Tilly," Ophelia let out a heavy sigh, "I'm not the one to talk to if you want to figure out if this boy you like is the one for you. I pick my boys based on a ratio of handsome versus how drunk I am. I've met a couple of guys I wouldn't mind talking to again, I also know a couple I wouldn't mind making their heads inside out."

"Can't you just think back to when you were my age then?" Tilly practically pleaded, "What did your Mommy tell you?"

Ophelia stared at the girl blankly, "I don't know."

Now it was Tilly's turn to look genuinely surprised, "How can you not know? You're a grown up, that means that you had to be my age once!"

The more Ophelia tried to think back, the heavier the pit of her stomach became. Her shoulders tensed as she glared back at the girl.

"I never was your age," the former assassin spoke very slowly, very clearly as the sheets started to tear in her grip, "I don't have a mommy. I never had a mommy. If I did, I sure wouldn't have pestered her like this!"

Tilly stepped back from the older woman. She looked ready to bolt for the door but she forced herself to stay, her little hands balling up into tight fists.

"Well, you're the one who killed my Mom!" Tilly snapped back, "You should take some responsibility and at least try to help me since you made sure she couldn't!"

"Fine!" Ophelia felt the sheet shred between her fingers. "Fine. Fine! FINE!"

The woman leaped to her feet, leaving the sheet behind as she stomped up to the girl who just barely came up to her chest. Havarti stopped laughing in her head.

"Please remain calm!" the sword pleaded, "She's just a child. She's confused and dealing with feelings she's not had before, my dear. It is a natural thing."

Ophelia turned her back on Tilly and glared back at her bastard sword, "I never went through anything like this. I see someone I want to have sex with, I do it. Then I figure out if I even like them or not."

"You don't really think I should do that, do you?" the little girl looked as if she couldn't decide whether to scream in anger or cry.

Again, Ophelia didn't realize that she was speaking out loud. She let out a growling groan that almost shook the room.

"Why not?" she shrugged, stomping over to the door, "It works for me. Maybe it will work for you. At the very least you won't be here anymore!"

With that, Ophelia yanked the door wide open. The main entryway was just outside, the late morning light pouring in through the network of small windows put together in the far wall. The entryway half full of people just arriving in town to check in or leaving after staying for at least a night.

Tilly's anger found its footing and she made sure to loose it as she stepped out of Ophelia's room, "I'll never inconvenience you again! I'll also make sure to warn every other mother in town to stay away from you so their kids don't become orphans!"

"Thank you!" Ophelia screamed and slammed the door shut.

"Murderer!" Tilly screamed just as the doorjamb and the slab of wood met, though it wasn't quite loud enough to drown her out of Ophelia's ears.

"I'd say that is likely the end of this town," Havarti said, his voice calm in the woman's frenzied head.

"I was never her age," Ophelia wrapped her hands around her ears as she slid against the door down to the floor, "I never had a mother. I never had a father. I never had a family. I never went through puberty. I never fell in love. I never had a first date. I never was a virgin..." she muttered to herself, closing her eyes tight.

"That isn't possible, my dear," Havarti's soft voice came again, "You had at least some of those things. Efreeti must have somehow... taken them from you."

"I have only ever been a killer," the realization came to the woman not as a thunderbolt, but as if it had been an overdue message slid under the door, "I have only ever been a killer."

"That is not true, Ophelia. You are my friend," Havarti protested, "You have been ever since you saved me from Trelaine. You are my savior. You have protected Travus and Tilly from every threat that has found us since the Al Razheem lost their control over you. You are their guardian."

"Some guardian," Ophelia sniffled, "I just drove Tilly out who knows where."

"Then I suggest you dress and that we go and find her," the sword answered.

Shaking her head, the woman continued to sink until she was lying on the floor. Then Ophelia broke down. Tears streamed from her eyes as sobs rocked her body.

"Ophelia, please. There is no need for this," Havarti tried to sound comforting, "Tilly needs us."

Ophelia kept shaking her head, her cries keeping her from being able to talk. Havarti kept trying to calm her but she didn't even acknowledge anything he said. She was just *gone*.

LATER...

"Thanks for telling me about all this, Tael," Travus dropped a couple of coins on the desk before stomping over to Ophelia's room.

He slammed his fist against the slab of wood a half dozen times, much like he did when he arrested hiding criminals. A long silence followed where the elf that stood behind the desk pretended that he wasn't watching what was happening. He was not a very good actor.

Just before the Night Shield racked his knuckles across the wood again, a voice came through the door, "Please come in," it was a man's voice.

That only made the blood already boiling in his veins turn into figurative steam. He threw the door open and marched straight in, closing the door hard behind him but just short of slamming it. There was enough of a scene in public this morning.

"I am sorry, Mr. Browder," the voice spoke up again, "I'm afraid Ophelia is *unwell.* I don't know what to do to help."

Travus didn't see any other man in the room. Then he remembered that the sword, Havarti, could talk. Judging from the poncy accent, it had to be the bastard sword.

He pulled the sides of his long red coat back to rest his hands on his hips. He looked around for Ophelia, wanting to make sure that his vitriol shot in the right direction. She was in bed.

And she was naked. A torn sheet barely protected her modesty, at least around her full hips. The position she was lying in couldn't have been comfortable.

Ophelia's skin was covered with sweat, her breathing ragged. One of her braids was half unraveled. Travus had flashes of an old case he worked on where a mercenary had forced himself on an unwilling bar girl. Ophelia's condition was almost identical to how the girl looked then.

The anger that was ready to launch came to a stop in the throat of Travus. It was quickly replaced with confusion, perhaps with a slight portion of concern.

"What happened in here, Havarti?" he spoke into the air since he couldn't immediately see the weapon, "Was she attacked?"

"Not physically," the sword answered, "Are you aware of what happened this morning?"

A deep frown overtook the man's face, "The blow up between her and Tilly? Yeah, Tael told me."

"I think that their argument made Ophelia come to some... realizations about the extent of whatever it was that Efreeti did to her," Havarti explained.

"What do you mean?" Travus stepped around the bed to look at Ophelia's face.

Her eyes were closed tight and puffy. She'd been crying. For a while from the look of it. He couldn't tell if she was conscious or not. The way Ophelia was breathing suggested she was awake but she could have just been having a nightmare or sleeping uneasily. The man was familiar with the latter, particularly when he was undercover among murderers.

"She cannot remember anything of her life before waking up in Efreeti's chambers. She cannot remember whether or not she had parents or any other family, anything from her childhood like her first talk about the proverbial birds and the bees," Havarti said to Travus, "Her entire life as she knows it has been lived in the Oasis as a toy for the General."

Ophelia showed a reaction to that, not much of one but her mouth definitely curled into a tight scowl, "Traitor," she muttered.

Slowly, her pale blue eyes opened and focused on Travus. The man felt himself tense. What if this had caused some kind of relapse or activated some kind of failsafe that remade the woman into an assassin again loyal to the Al Razheem. It all depended on what she meant by "traitor" and to whom it was directed.

The woman pulled herself up to a sitting position on the bed, not bothering to cover herself. She rubbed her eyes with the heels of her hands before she spoke again.

"There's no reason for him to know any of that." she was glaring at the corner of the room just past Travus.

"I apologize, my dear," Havarti replied, "I was worried and if he were to be any help he would need to know what I do."

"Which is nothing, you bastard," she growled back, "sword. You don't know me."

The sword let out a throat clearing noise like a harrumph. Apparently she hit whatever the steel equivalent of a nerve was.

Not that it seemed to please her. Ophelia turned her attention back to Travus, her eyes bloodshot.

"You shouldn't be here," she said, "You should be finding your kid."

"You mean the one you drove off?" he turned his back to the woman, stepping over to where Havarti rested.

"That's the one," Ophelia pulled her undone braid in front of her face and started weaving it back together.

"Get dressed," Travus ordered, "This is your mess, you're helping me fix it."

The woman shook her head even as she stayed very, very focused on her braid, "I've never been one of her favorite people. She's even more likely to run at the sight of me now."

"Then why in the name of blessed Juna did she come to you to talk?" the man snatched Havarti up by the scabbard and turned to face Ophelia.

"Because you forbade either of us from talking to *anyone* else and I'm the only other female in our little troupe," she kept her eyes intently staring at the string she was wrapping around the end of her braid, "If you'd let her out of the inn alone she probably would have found a passing bag lady to talk to. Probably would have turned out better, too."

"Is that what this is about?" Travus's entire face tightened, "You've finally gotten around to loathing yourself? And after killing dozens of innocent people, all it took was yelling at a little girl?"

"You don't understand a damned thing," she tossed her now retied braid away so that she could stare him down without distraction.

"I don't understand? Don't understand what?" Travus pulled his long coat off, switching Havarti to either hand when it came to the sleeves, "Having your whole life taken away? You killed my wife! The mother of my child! She *was* my entire life! Why I kept coming home every night!"

Ophelia looked as she she'd been punched in the face, "More reason to leave me alone," Her voice was barely a mumble.

"Or did you mean I didn't understand having to do despicable, terrible things at the General's whim?" He kept going, "I was undercover with the Al Razheem for *years*! I had to do things to innocent people just so they wouldn't kill me for being lazy! I was trying so hard to make up for all that, and I finally thought whatever gods that kept track of this stuff finally handed me a break when I found Inara. Then you came!"

Ophelia's eye twitched but her head stayed bowed. Her fingers twisted together, her knuckles cracking as they intertwined far too tightly.

The reaction was coming, he could feel it. She just needed another push. And he was more than willing to give it.

"Oh, woe is me!" Travus pressed the back of his hand to his forehead, laying the melodrama thick in his voice, "Your life is nothing but pain! You're such a terrible person that you let yourself be violated by an old hairy man. You killed good men trying to stop assassins from killing innocent people! You are probably responsible for Tilly lying dead in a ditch somewhere!"

"What would you have me do, huh?" Ophelia sprang from the bed even faster than the man had anticipated.

Her bare chest bumped into his, throwing him off balance. Even as he righted himself, the former assassin stomped toward him again.

"If I could die for all of that, I would!" she yelled, "I've already tried half a dozen different ways just today! I can't bring any of them back!"

This time Travus was ready and he stood his ground, "That's exactly my point, woman! They're gone because of the General. If you hadn't been put under his control, he would have killed every last one of your targets another way. He had you under some kind of spell that you couldn't break. You had no choice then!"

She had expected a physical blow, perhaps even trying to use Havarti to cut her. Ophelia didn't know how to react to what he was saying now. So she stood like a shaky statue.

"But you have a choice now!" he continued, "My girl is out there. Get dressed and help me find her! Help me keep her safe from the Al Razheem. *They* are the ones who screwed all of us!"

The woman slowly turned back to the bed. Digging through the sheets, she finally pulled a piece of gray cloth out. It turned out to be her pants. As she started pulling them onto her legs, she looked back at Travus over her shoulder.

"I don't have a shirt anymore," her cheeks actually flushed pink as she softly spoke, "I used it for kindling to try and set myself on fire."

Travus tossed his leather coat at her. She caught it in her left hand while her right kept her still unbuttoned pants mostly up.

"Buckle that up and we'll buy you a new one after we find Tilly," he said as he started for the door.

Tossing Havarti onto the bed, he wrapped a hand around the handle to the door. After a moment of standing still, he looked back at her with a wry grin on his face.

"You know, you're the first woman I've seen naked since I married Inara," shaking his head, he stepped out of the room.

IN THE DEAD OF NIGHT...

Ophelia wandered down the street, keeping an eye on every building as she passed. Most of them were restaurants and about half of those had outdoor seating. There were couples at a good percentage of the tables outside the windows but they didn't obscure the view of the interior.

The woman stopped at the intersection at the far end of the block. There was no sign of Tilly or her date, inside or out of the buildings.

A few seconds later, Travus strode up next to her. His face was passive but his skin was pale. Ophelia knew him well enough now to tell that meant that he was worried. To be honest, she was join-ing him in the feeling.

"This is where the boy's father said he usually takes his dates," he turned back to face the row of cafes.

"If Tilly was the one he brought," Ophelia said.

She pulled the belts that wrapped around the left sleeve of the long red coat to tighten it around her arm. The former assassin was tired of it slipping down over her hand. It made it hard for her to get to Havarti.

"The father's description sounded like Tilly to me," Travus replied, "But they must have moved on. It has been a few hours since they left the grocery stand together."

The man spun around slowly, taking in his surroundings as he considered their next move. It was then that he realized that he had no idea what to do. It was a sensation unfamiliar to him and... and he didn't like it.

Ophelia, on the other hand, turned her focus onto one well muscled teen who was sitting alone at his table outside the cafe on the corner nearby. Judging from the way he was dressed, he was a local.

Most of the men in Wildesvale wore form fitting cotton vests over their shirts. Apparently, it was a local fashion that paid hom-age to the founder of the town.

It was a style that this young man wore well. He had black hair and piercing blue eyes that the bright red of the vest and dark blue, almost black of his shirt made stand out even more. Not to mention that he had enough in the way of muscles that Ophelia wouldn't have minded having to make a topographical map.

"Give me a second," she patted Travus on the shoulder and started in the direction of the young man, "And pretend you're not with me."

"You would laugh if you could see his face right now," Havarti chimed in Ophelia's head.

The woman smirked as she slipped into the chair across from the aesthetically pleasing young man. She folded one long leg over the other and leaned back in her new found seat, making herself comfortable.

"I'm not intruding, am I?" she batted her eyelashes.

The teen sat dumbfounded for a moment, staring at Ophelia. It took a few seconds but, after a quick shake of his head, he found the ability to speak.

"No, not at all," he smiled sheepishly, "Although... I wasn't really expecting any company."

"Really? I find that hard to believe," the woman smiled sweetly, "But it's quite an argument for fate."

He tilted his head at her, "Fate? What kind of fate?"

"That we had to meet tonight," Ophelia answered, "I wasn't planning on being out here tonight but here we are."

"Here we are," the young man repeated, "What did you want to with our fated meeting then?"

The woman smiled wider as she leaned forward, resting her elbows on the table then her chin in her hands, "Well, first, I think we should introduce ourselves. I'm Ophelia."

"I'm Klark," he grinned back.

"Klark. That's a good, strong name," she reached out and wrapped one of her hands around his on the table, "Tell me, Klark. Is there someplace we could have a bit more privacy?"

The young man's breathing was already sped up just from Ophelia touching his hand. It took a great effort for him to look away from her so that he could clarify his thinking.

There weren't many people at the few tables that were occupied in front of the restaurant but it was still in public in the strictest sense. He wondered what she had in mind as he turned back to her hand shrugged.

"My house isn't far from here," he said.

Even as the words came from his mouth, it was apparent that he didn't like the idea. While it was technically private, he probably had some other family that lived with him that didn't give him as much privacy as he would have liked to have with Ophelia.

"That's a bold move for a first date," she chuckled, "How about a little more of a *neutral* territory. There has to be a place for a couple of young lovers to be alone out here, right?"

He audibly gulped at the word lovers. Pulling at his collar with his free hand, the handsome young man nodded.

"Well, there's the Smitten Bluffs just outside of town," he said, "A lot of us go out there when we want to be alone together."

"Where is that?" Ophelia asked, "I'm new here, remember?"

"I, I can show you," he started to lift himself from his seat.

The woman pulled on his hand, keeping him in his chair, "You could. And I would love to follow you out there. Believe me."

That part was true. She did want to see how well he filled out those pants he was wearing.

"But I wouldn't want to cause any rumors that could damage your reputation," she spoke fast, "I mean, how would it look having a good boy like you walk out to those bluffs with a strange girl that no one around here knows?"

Klark chewed on his lower lip for a moment (a gesture that only made him more attractive) before answering, "I guess it wouldn't be the best first impression for you in town, either. Going out there before anyone knew anything else about you, huh?"

"But we can meet there?" Ophelia smirked, "Just tell me how to get to these Smitten Bluffs."

Again, the young man looked thoughtful, "Go south down this road," he pointed toward the intersection where Travus was still standing (and not looking happy about it), "turn left in four blocks and keep going until you leave the buildings behind. The bluffs aren't far after that."

"Thank you, Klark," Ophelia said, rising from her own seat, "I'll start there now. Why don't you wait here for, oh, half an hour and then follow?"

She gave him a playful wink and turned away. The woman gave her hips a healthy sway that couldn't be missed, even though the leather of the long red coat she wore.

Ophelia turned back just as she stepped back into the road, "Oh, if we do somehow miss each other, I have a room in the Manticore Inn."

Klark waved back and the former assassin walked up to Travus, who had already started down the road that the younger man had pointed out. Ophelia had an extra spring to her step as she caught up. Not to mention an encouraged, or perhaps predatory, grin on her face.

"You're pleased with yourself?" Travus shook his head as they continued down the road, "Leading on a guy swimming in hormones on like that?"

"It got us an idea of where to look next, didn't it?" She answered, "And who said I was leading him on? I told him where my room was so that we could play after we found Tilly."

"Does that really make you happy?" The man asked, "Having a different man in your bed every other night?"

Ophelia shrugged (to be honest, she was shocked she didn't get scolded for revealing where she was staying to a stranger), "I haven't really thought about it. They have fun, I have fun, it seems like a mutually beneficial situation to me."

"And what happens if you get pregnant?" Travus answered, "Or if one of them has some kind of disease or infection?"

"I can't get pregnant," she said back, "I remember the General asking Efreeti that very same question. And if a guy had some kind of *infection* my blinking would make it like it never happened."

"So no bad consequences for you?" that didn't seem to please Travus, "A mutually beneficial situation. Is this the kind of advice you saw fit to give my daughter? She doesn't have blinking to undo her bad decisions, you know."

Ophelia lifted an eyebrow, "We didn't really get that far. Sure, she would have to be more careful than me but what's wrong with her bedding a guy she likes? Surely, your wife wasn't the first woman you took to bed."

"As a matter of fact, she was," Travus replied.

His face, no his entire body ran through a whole barrage of different emotions. He had a grin that Ophelia could only guess had to do with some memory he had of Inara but his shoulders shot up past his ears as tension bound them up. Annoyance or even anger at Ophelia could explain that. But there was still the worry over his daughter and other... reactions that the former assassin wasn't sure how to read.

Ophelia figured he had to be telling the truth. Most of the men she knew exaggerated the number of women they had actually been with, not the other way around.

"That's the very idea we have been trying to teach Tilly," Travus said when he finally found his voice again, "That she should wait until marriage to have sex like we did."

"Why?" Ophelia pointed to the left as they reached the block Klark described.

As they changed direction, their conversation took up so much of the duo's attention that neither noticed the figure dart from the shadow of one building to another. Even Havarti was so engrossed in listening that the unexpected tag along slipped past his notice.

"Mostly, to avoid any unnecessary drama," the man answered, "She doesn't have sex, she doesn't have to worry about getting pregnant before she's ready to have a child. She doesn't have to worry about getting sick. It just makes life easier."

"Sounds lonely to me," the woman replied.

"Romantic relationships don't have to be built on sleeping together," Travus fought the urge to glare back, "Inara and I dated for a year before I got the nerve to ask her to marry me."

"How did you know she was the one if you didn't know whether you two were compatible in bed or not?"

"Compatibility comes with time and," Travus stopped himself and shook his head at the woman, "I'm not getting into the story of my love life with you, Ophelia. Let's just go and find my daughter."

The rest of the walk out to the cliffs was in silence. The buildings were replaced by trees after only a few paces but they weren't so closely bunched together that the duo couldn't see their destination in the distance.

They walked along the carved out dirt road until it started to curve away from the Smitten Bluffs. Then Ophelia stepped over some shrubs that marked the outer edge of the path and into the trees.

Travus was right beside her after a few steps. The grass under their feet began to slope upwards sharply as they neared the edge of the length of cliffs.

Havarti thought he saw a shadow move between some brush and a tree trunk. There had to be plenty of animals living out here. Warning Ophelia at the first sign of a spooked vole wasn't going to do anyone any good so he didn't say anything. Although the sword did decide to keep a tighter look out.

The grass hung over the side like a tourist trying to get a better view of the valley that stretched out beyond. While the rock face was sheer, it was only about twenty feet above the ground just beyond and, even then, the terrain rose until it matched the height of the Smitten Bluffs after only a few hundred paces.

The trees mostly stopped growing past the cliffs but the long grass swaying in the breeze, reflecting the pale moonlight, gave the impression of staring out over a beautiful lake. The shrubs and other plants dotting the landscape were like little islands of greenery.

They had arrived but there was still a lot of territory to cover to find Tilly. Shrubs and trees lined up and down the cliff's edge. This was why this was such a popular getaway spot with teenagers enamored with each other. Privacy behind the plant life while also hiding their whereabouts from prying parents.

"We'll cover more ground if we split up," Travus pointed to the south, "I'll go this way. You go that way."

"Yes, sir!" Ophelia rolled her eyes as she started walking northerly along the edge of the cliff.

"I do hope she is around here somewhere," Havarti said as he and his wielder weaved between the bushes.

"Tilly's young but cute," Ophelia replied, "The boy has brought her here. The problem will be whether or not he takes no for an answer."

"How do you mean?" the sword asked.

"There's no grownups to stop him from trying to force himself on Tilly," the woman answered, "That's a big part of why they come here. To not be caught."

"That is not comforting," Havarti said, "I was expecting to, at worst, have a disappointed girl on our hands. Not a potential fight."

"Why do you think I didn't mention anything to Travus? He probably already knows but he didn't need the remind–" Ophelia's attention snapped to her left.

Voices were coming from behind some bushes. As much as she wanted to pull him free, Ophelia kept Havarti in his scabbard on her hip. But she crept, very slowly, toward the bushes. If it wasn't Tilly and the grocery boy there wasn't any need to interrupt, after all.

But there they were, Tilly with her lips locked together with those of the thin grocery boy. They both seemed to be enjoying themselves, with little moans escaping their lips when they took the time to take a quick breath, until the boy's hands wandered up to Tilly's underdeveloped chest.

"Chod, no!" Tilly pulled her mouth away from his and slapped his hands down, "We're not going there tonight."

"Oh, come on, Till!" Judging from his reaction, this wasn't the first time the girl had stopped his advances, "You can't expect to work a guy up like this and not give him a little relief!"

Tilly huffed and crossed her arms over her small chest, "I can't believe Ophelia was right about you," she muttered.

The former assassin stiffened at the sound of her name. For the briefest moment, she thought that Tilly had spotted her from behind the tree she was standing behind.

Chod frowned and looked confused all at once, "Who's Ophelia?"

Oh, this was too good to pass up.

"I am," the woman said, stepping into the small clearing in which the two teens were hiding, "And she did say no, Chod."

Both of the youths looked dumbstruck at the sight of Ophelia. But when Tilly saw what the former assassin was wearing...

"Who invited you, Ophelia?" she snapped, "What I'm doing here with my boyfriend is my own business."

Both the woman and the boy looked surprised by that statement, "*Boyfriend*?" they both said at the same time but there was as much disdain in Ophelia's voice as there was fear in Chod's.

"Give us our *privacy*, Ophelia," the girl practically sneered.

"You don't really want that, Tilly," the woman pulled her long coat back and rested her hands on her round hips, "I just heard you."

The former assassin noticed that Chod's eyes were lingering on her rather than the younger woman he had brought up here. Something about that really annoyed Ophelia.

"You weren't listening right, like always," the daughter of the Night Shield replied.

She reached out and grabbed the thin boy by the collar of his green vest and pulled him into a deep kiss. The whole time, she was staring at Ophelia. The anger in her eyes only got brighter as Tilly pushed her tongue into his mouth.

Ophelia sighed. She had hoped to avoid this.

"You misunderstood *me*, Tilly," she said, "I came here to take, er, Chod for myself."

The boy pulled away from the girl and looked back at Ophelia in disbelief. The rage Tilly felt made her entire body flush.

"You heard me. Everything you told me about him made me want him for myself," Ophelia shrugged, "I would have been here sooner but there's a lot of shrubbery around."

"I never told you anything about him!" Tilly protested.

"Sure you did. The way you described how his hard arms made lifting even the heaviest of loads look so easy," the woman scanned the boy up and down with her pale blue eyes, "Even how well you said he filled out a pair of pants. It was all true."

"You harpy!" Tilly growled.

"Come on. Do you really think he'd want to play with those," Ophelia pointed to the girl's mostly flat chest then at her own well developed one, "when he could do whatever he wanted with these?"

Chod gulped, "Really?" he asked, staring in a way that made Ophelia feel dirty.

"Let's leave the kid and find our own little hideaway," the former assassin motioned for the boy to follow her.

Chod scrambled to his feet. Tilly was shocked but, even more so, insulted. She lifted herself to her feet and stomped right behind the boy as he practically ran toward Ophelia. His hands immediately started reaching for the woman's chest, only to be intercepted by the woman's own wrapping around his wrists.

"Just a second, lover," Ophelia grinned back at him before motioning back over his shoulder, "I think she has one last thing to say to you first."

Chod turned around just in time for Tilly's foot to slam right between his legs with a ferocious kick. The boy collapsed to the ground with a not at all manly sounding squeak. Then he proceeded to vomit whatever it was that he and Tilly had for dinner.

The girl glared at Chod for a long moment before darting up to glare at Ophelia. The rage was intense but it quickly drained from her to be replaced with tears threatening to roll down her face.

"You did that to prove a point, didn't you?" she asked, trying to keep herself from sobbing.

"Only that he didn't care about you," Ophelia answered, "Not yet, anyway. His only concern was getting his own pleasure taken care of," she idly kicked Chod's shin and he cowered into a tight ball on the ground.

"How did you know?" Tilly wiped at her nose with the back of her hand.

"Easy," Ophelia said, "If he really cared about you, he wouldn't have kept groping you. You save that until the other one's ready."

"But you," everything about the girl said that she didn't understand, "you have sex with guy's you only met an hour before."

"I was only looking to get my pleasure taken care of," the woman chuckled, "I never said I was a role model for healthy relationships. I've never been in a real one."

"Daddy's going to be so mad at me," Tilly rushed over to Ophelia and broke down.

She sobbed into the older woman's chest, her arms wrapped tightly around the former assassin's waist. Ophelia had no idea how to react.

"Wrap your arms around her shoulders, my dear," Havarti advised, "She needs some comfort at the moment."

The woman nodded and did as the sword suggested. It worked. Even though she was still sobbing, Tilly seemed to relax, at least a little.

"He may be angry later," Ophelia said, unsure if this was the best thing to say but she couldn't think of anything else, "But he'll be a lot more relieved to see you first. Milk that for all its worth."

The little girl couldn't help but giggle at that. They stayed that way, ignoring Chod's groans of pain, until a familiar voice caught the girl's ears.

"Tilly!" the voice of her father traveled through the air, obviously still some distance away.

"Speak of a devil," Ophelia looked back over her shoulder in the direction from which she had come, "Let's go have that reunion. I'm betting he won't hit angry until at least the next town."

Tilly nodded in agreement and the two women left the small clearing and Chod behind. They were out of the clump of trees after only a dozen or so steps and the moon light bathed the grassland all around them in its silver light.

"He's going to kick himself for going the wrong way first," Ophelia let out the comment as they followed the lip of the cliff.

"There was no way he could have known where I was," Tilly said, looking a little guilty, "I was so angry at the two of you."

Ophelia cocked an eyebrow, "At the two of us? I can understand me but why your dad?"

"Because he's not Mommy," the girl looked sullen admitting that.

"No one else could be," Ophelia wasn't exactly speaking from experience but it seemed logical, "But he's made a point of always being there for you, hasn't he?"

Tilly sniffled, "He has."

"That's got to count for something," Ophelia scanned ahead, "It's my fault everything's harder now. On both of you. And I'm sorry about that, kid."

She spotted a silhouette that moved a lot like Travus coming their way, "Tilly!" his voice came again.

"Over here!" Ophelia called back, waving both arms over her head.

"Daddy told me about how you had a mind control spell on you," Tilly said the words so softly that the woman barely realized that she'd been spoken to, "I didn't want to believe it. Especially with everything I watched you do..."

The girl almost broke down again. Ophelia again wrapped her arms around the little girl's shoulders.

She couldn't think of a thing to say this time. Any words that came to mind sounded so hollow.

"Ophelia!" Havarti's voice snapped into the woman's mind, "There's someone trying to conceal himself behind Travus!"

Ophelia muttered a curse that tugged Tilly out of her grief with a sharp dose of shock. The former assassin pulled the little girl behind her with her right hand while her left wrapped around the handle of the sword.

One thing that Ophelia noticed was, now that Travus was only three paces away, was that he was very quiet. Not like when he was yelling for his daughter just moments ago. And he hadn't rushed to Tilly when he knew where she was. So Havarti was right. Now she just had to find out with whom they were dealing.

"Okay, that's close enough. Come out where I can see you!" Ophelia ordered.

"How did you know I was here?" a man that only came up to Travus's shoulder stepped out from behind the Night Shield.

He had dark gray skin, white hair, though his skin was smooth, a nose like half an ax blade and pointed ears. He was also quite a bit thinner than the other man. He was a svartalfar, a race of elves that lived underground. He wore a brown leather tunic with matching pants. The legs were just a touch too long, bunching up around his ankles and hiding most of his shoes from view.

He had the long sword belonging to Travus in his right hand but his left hand was curled up tight as if it was holding something very small or thin. The confident way he stepped away from the Night Shield surprised the woman.

What was even more surprising was that Travus didn't even try to move when he was out of the reach of the svartalfar. Something wasn't right.

Thankfully, Tilly realized this as well and didn't try to run to her father. She stayed behind Ophelia, doing to her best to watch what was happening without doing anything to make herself a target.

"Who are you?" Ophelia asked, "What do you want? You know, all the standard questions."

"I am Anga Scaram, my lady," the svartalfar answered, "You are aware of me, yes?"

Scaram. He was one of the Fidai from before the time Ophelia was with them. He had taken some kind of leave from the Al Razheem with the General's blessing. She was never told the reason and there was never even a whisper about him returning but apparently that had changed.

But he was dangerous, to be sure. Coloron and Phantoom described facing the man as the most frustrating experiences they've had to trudge through. A portion of that has to do with his unusual weapon of choice. It took the woman a moment to remember it.

And that was when she saw it, a faint reflection of moonlight in the middle of the air between Scaram and Travus. He called it the Thread of Fate. It was nearly invisible and while it could be handled safely, a hard tug somehow rendered the line razor sharp... and it was wrapped around the neck of the Night Shield.

That is why Travus wasn't making any move to escape. With a flick of the Scaram's wrist, Tilly would officially be an orphan.

"I know who you are," Ophelia said to the svartalfar.

"Then you know what I want," the svartalfar replied, "You will come back with me to the Oasis. Without a fuss, of course."

"Just me or all of us?" Ophelia asked, motioning from herself and Tilly to Travus.

"Just you," he said, raising his left hand to his shoulder level.

Havarti whispered even though Ophelia was the only one who could hear him, "I have an idea, my dear, but I need to be in our opponent's hand to make it work."

"What happens to these two?" now she had to stall to figure out a plan for her sword to execute his plan.

"Why do you ask questions to which you already know the answer?" Scaram gave the Thread a playful tug.

That elicited a grunt of pain from Travus. It wasn't enough to kill the Night Shield, he was still being used as leverage, after all, but the assassin was making it clear that father and daughter were not going to get out of this alive.

Ophelia shook her head, letting out a soft sigh, "The only thing I can't figure out is how you got him to call out to us. I thought he valued the life of his family even over his own."

Scaram smirked, "Oh, don't judge him too harshly. Apparently, you have not been told of all the Thread of Fate's abilities, including," he lifted his right hand to his throat and opened his mouth wide, "Tilly! If you kill yourself by running off that cliff over there, I might just spare your father!"

Those words sounded like they were coming from Travus but out of Scaram's mouth. The line allowed him to mimic the voice another person touching the line. Great.

"Listen, I don't have a lot of time for negotiating or playing cat and lawn gnome," Ophelia unbuckled the belt around her waist and pulled Havarti free, scabbard and all, "I'll come along willingly."

She tossed her bastard sword over to Scaram, Havarti landing at the feet of the svartalfar. Scaram looked down at the weapon then back up at the woman with a wry grin on his face.

"Just like that?" he didn't sound convinced, "No last minute plea for the lives of your comrades."

Ophelia shook her head, "Wouldn't work, would it? In fact, my only request is that you keep my sword in good condition until we return to the Oasis. I'm quite attached to it, you see."

Scaram let out a thoughtful grunt. Slipping Travus's sword back into his belt, he picked up Havarti and inspected the sword where the hilt met the scabbard.

"It is a fine weapon," he said, "Very well, I will give your sword proper care on our trek back east. I suppose that means that this one's use has come to an end."

"No!" Tilly screamed as the assassin pulled his left hand back.

Havarti suddenly started shaking, leaping free of his sheath and hitting Scaram's left hand. The sword started falling to the ground as the svartalfar reeled but Havarti stopped in midair. He was tangled in the Thread of Fate!

Travus tumbled forward, trying to keep his head from being separated from his shoulders. As the Night Shield got closer to the sword, Havarti dropped and his blade sank into the grass covered soil. Scaram finally righted himself and pulled back on the thread. Havarti shifted in place but Travus didn't react at all.

"Pull the Thread off! Havarti's keeping him from using it on you!" Ophelia yelled at Travus as she charged at the assassin.

The Night Shield didn't have to be told twice. His fingers skimmed around his neck for a way to loosen the line at this throat. Travus pulled the Thread up over his head, inadvertently snipping a tuft of hair from his head with the motion, and tossed it away. Then he ran to his daughter.

Ophelia tackled the assassin to the ground. He screamed in pain but not from the landing. At least not directly.

His fingers fell into the grass, completely severed from his hand as the line went razor sharp in his palm. Even before he could cradle his bleeding appendage, the woman started pummeling him as she sat on his chest.

Scaram lifted his good arm to block at least some of her blows. Then his knees launched into her back, hitting the glowing runes hidden by the red leather. That sent a shock through Ophelia's body that let the assassin push her off of him.

Scrambling to his feet, he pressed his bleeding hand into his tunic while his good one wrapped around the collar of Ophelia's coat. He pulled her to the woman up and quickly switched arms around her neck. Then his good hand drew Travus's sword free from it scabbard.

Resting the blade against the base of Ophelia's throat, the svartalfar realized that she, like the Night Shield, was taller than him, making the woman lean back into him awkwardly. Scaram quickly shuffled backwards, getting as much distance between himself and Travus as possible before the man took Havarti into his hands.

"You stay back!" the assassin ordered, "You stay away or I'll slit her throat and throw her over!"

Travus, with Havarti in one hand and his scabbard in the other, looked at Scaram quizzically. Tilly was already running toward the city, presumably at her father's command, so that she could not be used as possible leverage or become a casualty of the situation.

Ophelia hadn't realized how close to the side of the cliff the assassin had dragged her before she was fully cognizant again. But after hearing Scaram's threat, she was just as confused as the Night Shield.

"Scaram, you do know who I am, right?" she would have turned back to look at him but then the blade would have sunk into her throat.

Then she would have blinked. The woman would have to kill the assassin and stay confused instead of getting some answers. Travus seemed to have the same idea. He even slipped Havarti back into his scabbard as he walked over to Ophelia and Scaram.

"You are Ophelia, General Kitanah's First Bravo. She wants you back," the assassin answered the woman's question, "So that she can undo whatever brainwashing the Light Bringers did to you to make you turn. I received word that you were in Wildesvale and orders to find you," he motioned to Travus, who shrugged.

"He has some of it right," the man said to Ophelia before turning his attention back to the svartalfar, "Did they mention anything else, like special abilities, weapons, anything like that?"

"That the bastard sword could talk," Scaram's eyes darted this way and that, "But not that it could move on its own!"

He was trying to figure a way out of the situation. Answering questions was his way of stalling for time.

"Anything else?" Travus looked at the other man like he was an idiot, "Anything at all?"

Scaram said a word in the svartalfaran language. Ophelia didn't have to be a linguist to realize that it was a curse. It was really the only part of the language that she knew.

"It said to report your position but not confront."

Judging from how his body was starting to slump, he couldn't come up with a plan to get out of this or he had just lost too much blood to be so tense. Either way.

"But you thought you could take us and get a promotion or something else out of this," Travus concluded the thought process for him.

The bitterness in the assassin's face told the Night Shield that he was right, "If I'm going to die anyway, I'm at least taking one of you with me!" he pulled back on the sword to slice Ophelia's throat.

She disappeared, leaving a purple fog in her shape behind. Scaram had already turned to throw her body over the side before he realized she was already gone. He struggled to understand what happened as he stared over the side of the cliff.

Ophelia reappeared behind him. She didn't bother to say anything witty. Ophelia simply planted a foot in the svartalfar's backside, throwing him over the side of the cliff.

The scream of the assassin was cut short by the ground. Travus stepped up beside Ophelia to check the final result.

Scaram laid in the middle of a field of long grass and rocks that ranged in size from his fist up to his head, at least when it was still in its original shape. There was no doubt that the man was dead.

"How in all the green lands of Honua did he recognize us from a written description?" Ophelia asked the Night Shield.

"Not sure. We still haven't figured out how Kitanah found us in Middlemount, either," he frowned, "Let's get back to the inn. I want to make sure Tilly's okay."

Travus was short a sword but he did take the time to wind up and take ownership of the Thread of Fate of which the former owner was so proud. After that, both the father and Ophelia ran back into Wildesvale.

Back in the inn, there were many revelers drinking at the tables that had been set up for the weekend. The two weaved their way past and into Travus's room.

They both stepped inside without knocking to see Tilly, already in a new dress, tucking the rest of her and her father's clothes into a leather bag. The girl smiled wide when she saw her father enter. They rushed to each other and hugged. When they finally let each other go, there was a smudge of blood on her cheek and a worried expression on her face.

"Daddy, your neck's bleeding," she pointed to the wound.

"It's nothing, sugar blossom," he grinned back, dabbing his hand against the cut, "It's just superficial."

"I'll get the medical kit." Tilly declared, hopping into the toilet room.

Before he could protest, Ophelia rested a hand on his shoulder, "I'll leave you two to your triage."

She started for the door. Travus cleared his throat to get her attention before she reached for the door handle.

"You do realize we have to leave in the morning, right?" he said.

Ophelia nodded, "All the more reason for me to have a party tonight. I'll sleep in the carriage."

Travus let out a soft laugh. Then he waved goodbye to her without saying another word.

Ophelia stepped back out into the common area of the inn, taking a good look around. A familiar red vest and blue shirt, being worn by a man with piercing blue eyes, caught her eye.

"Klark!" She grinned, "I'm so glad you found me."

NINETEEN

RUBENESQUIRE

The city of Riverbelt

The carriage came to a stop in front of the wide open city gates. The granite wall was at least twenty feet high, giving it an imposing visage but it wasn't thick enough for soldiers to walk along the top let alone mount an attack.

Ivy grew all along the surface of the stones. The only area that anyone seemed to trim it back was immediately around the black iron gate. That was likely just to keep the plant out of the hinges so the entryway could be closed off at night.

One of the city guard came up to the vehicle, the horses leaning away from the man in his loud, squeaking armor. He wasn't wearing a helmet, so his face was fully visible. He had long blonde hair pulled back into a ponytail and a tan that betrayed that he was out in the sun for long stretches of time.

He had a wide, friendly smile on his face as he waved up at the driver, who was letting the reins hang loose in his hands. "G'afternoon, Earl! What have you brought us today?"

"A couple of Light Bringers, Tristan," the driver answered, "Just stayin' the night then movin' on."

The guard stepped up to the door mounted in the side of the carriage. Pulling the door open he gave the two inside a salute, though not an overly formal one.

"G'afternoon to you as well, Light Bringers," Tristan greeted the occupants inside the cabin, "What names shall I put in the record?"

Travus leaned forward in his seat in the back end of the cabin, giving the guard a polite smile in return, "Lieutenant Weston, Michael Weston. This is Scout Gabby Union," he motioned across to the front seat.

Ophelia, again wearing Travus's long red jacket, leaned forward and gave the guard a quick wave. Her hair was pulled back into a tight, long ponytail. Her braids were undone and she did not look happy about it. After her terse greeting she dropped right back into the shadows.

Tristan's lips pursed tight for a moment, "Long trip, eh?"

Travus only had time to give the woman a quick glare before nodding and grinning back at the other man, "You have no idea. It will be nice to be back in a town after being out in the bush for so long."

"Had to pull ranger duties, eh?" the armored guard nodded back, "Get to protect and serve the wildlife and direct the flow of river traffic?"

"With nothing out there as wild as her," Travus, er, Lt. Weston pointed at Ophelia, "She saw a griffin cub about to get eaten by a bear and she rushed in to save it yelling *Cute and cuddly isn't on the menu!*" the lying Night Shield laughed, "Craziest thing I've ever seen in my life."

Tristan chuckled himself, "And only funny because she wasn't mauled instead, right?"

Travus pulled a bear claw from his pocket and tossed it to the other man, "And we didn't have to hunt again the rest of the time we were out there."

The guard whistled, obviously impressed, "That's some lady you got there. Welcome to Riverbelt and enjoy your rest," Tristan held the claw out to the other man.

Travus tucked it back into his pocket and gave the other man a quick salute. The blonde guard closed the door and patted the side to signal the driver that he was able to enter the city.

"Where did you get that thing?" Ophelia asked once they were moving again.

"The story was true," Travus couldn't stifle a yawn as he leaned back in his seat, "I just traded my wife for you in it."

"You wife killed a bear?" Ophelia was pretty sure he was still lying.

The man nodded, "I should also mention that it wasn't a griffin cub but Tilly when she was a toddler."

Travus reached up and knocked on the baggage compartment that stretched the width of the carriage. The thin door slowly opened and the aforementioned child poked her head out.

"You remember that story, don't you?" Tilly's father grinned up at her.

The little girl nodded the exact same way her father did, three little dips and a smirk at the end, "Yes, Daddy. You and Mommy told it a *lot*. Like every time I did something wrong."

Travus chuckled and turned his attention back to Ophelia as Tilly climbed out of her hiding place. The former assassin pulled the curtain aside just enough to catch a narrow view of the buildings lining the main drive of Riverbelt.

"You never explained why you wanted to sneak in here as Light Bringers," Ophelia said without looking back at the man, "It seems to me that the Al Razheem would be checking the records and descriptions from transfers like this."

"The names are a signal to the Light Bringer commander in this town," he explained, "Colonel Dende and I came up with the distress name Weston years ago when I was working a sting operation in this neck of the woods."

The sound of the horse hooves changed as the carriage went from rolling down a packed dirt road to cobblestones. It made the equine footfalls louder and a sound more hollow.

"Besides," Travus continued, "we're well west of the lands the Al Razheem has a foothold in."

"Although I doubt that will stop them from continuing their search," Havarti chimed in.

Ophelia agreed, "And the description that the guard sends will inevitably get intercepted and they'll know where to look for us. Again."

Tilly frowned up at her father, worry making her young brow wavy (she was too young for lines yet). The fact that the Al Razheem kept finding them in each of the three cities since leaving Wildesvale was why she was hiding in the luggage bin.

Her father explained it to the former assassin, "They're looking for a Light Bringer, a woman with your braids and a little girl. Not two Light Bringers returning from extended duty out in the woods. That's why she," he wrapped an arm around the girl's shoulders, "had to stay hidden.

"Kids traveling aren't uncommon but it is for them to be escorted by two Light Bringers. Add to that Lt. Weston and Scout Union are going to leave tomorrow..." Travus shrugged.

"We're going to leave?" The fake Light Bringer asked.

He shook his head, "Two others who will match our general descriptions. I chose here for a very specific reason and I think it'll take some time to do what needs to be done."

Ophelia quirked an eyebrow. She must have thought that he picked Riverbelt, the largest city on the west coast of the continent, at random like everywhere else they had gone since leaving Paimae.

"I think they're tracking us by one of the runes on your back," Travus explained, "I know a cleric that should be able to figure out which one and hopefully remove it."

"If you're right," Ophelia replied, "your little ruse with Weston and Union would be for nothing and they'll find us in no time anyway."

"I have that covered," he said back, "It'll be clear as soon as we check in."

The carriage slowed down and then finally stopped. Both Ophelia and Travus peeked out the window to see a single story stone building with a sign in front of it that read:

LIGHT BRINGERS
RIVERBELT OUTPOST
#1701

"Okay, Tilly, just like how we got in the carriage before," the man instructed his daughter.

With a little fuss and awkward positioning, the much shorter girl positioned herself in front of Ophelia, wrapping her arms around the taller woman's waist and tucking her knees up, forcing the fully grown woman to walk bow legged.

Ophelia wrapped the coat closed and fastened it so that it couldn't fall open, "Just because it's baggy on me doesn't mean that people can't tell I'm hiding something in here."

It was a concern she voiced before. It fell on similarly deaf ears this time.

Travus grunted with effort as he handed the former assassin a massive sack that had been resting on the floor between his and her seats. She took the bag of heavy, awkwardly packed gear with an obviously sarcastic grin, knowing what he was about to say.

"With you carrying that, anyone watching would attribute your weird gait to the load." It was the exact same speech he gave back in Rekale, the last city they had left, "And it doesn't matter if you're a woman. You're the lower ranked officer between us and grunts get to carry the luggage."

He chuckled, as did Tilly inside Ophelia's coat. Then Travus pushed the cab door open and stepped out, holding it open for the woman.

"Next time you are the grunt," she muttered at the Night Shield as she stepped past him.

Thankfully the walk wasn't a long one from the road to the main entrance to the outpost. Without anyone around to gawk (that they could see), Ophelia was inside the building in a matter of seconds. Again with Travus holding the door open for her.

Her relief was short lived. The foyer was much like the one in Paimae, a small room with a raised window in the far wall where a clerk wearing a tunic with the Light Bringer symbol embroidered on his chest sat, scribbling something on an unseen desk.

The differences here were, first, that the door into the building was in the same wall as the window, just to the right and, second, that there were two men in armor standing guard between the window and door. That meant that the woman couldn't take a moment to rest without making this charade and smuggling in Tilly all pointless.

The Night Shield stepped up to the window, "Lieutenant Weston to see Colonel Dende," he announced.

The obviously new Light Bringer shuffled through a bunch of papers on his desk, growing more and more confused with each passing sheet, "I, uh, don't have you listed on the duty roster or the relief lists, Lieutenant."

Travus nodded, expecting this, "We're just returning from ranger duty assigned in Middlemount. As the patrol ended, this ended up being the closest outpost."

"I'll have to write to the Middlemount Outpost for confirmation," the clerk said.

"Of course. In the meantime," the Night Shield pulled a patch of cloth from the same pocket that housed the disembodied bear claw and laid it out on the desk that stood just at his shoulder level, "I still need to check in with the commanding officer."

Travus flattened out the piece of cloth, making it a long rectangle that was about a foot long but only about four inches wide. Various symbols were sewn into it up and down the entirety of its length.

The clerk leaned down to look at the cloth, recognizing it as Light Bringer credentials. Looking satisfied by the information represented on the cloth, the young man leaned forward so that his head came into the foyer.

"Allow them entry," he said to the guards.

Both armored Light Bringers nodded and one knocked on the door. *Knockknockknock knock knockknockknock* and the heavy wood slowly pushed out to reveal the interior of the building.

"After you Gabby," Travus grinned and motioned to the door in a gentlemanly way.

"Gee, thank you, sir," the sarcasm practically dripped from the woman's lips like honey.

It was a walk down a long hallway to get to the Colonel's office. By the time they reached it, Ophelia's breathing was ragged and sweat was dripping into her eyes with effort.

Looking up and down the hallway and seeing it empty, the Night Shield finally took pity on the former assassin, "Tilly, you can come out now," he said as he took the heavy bag from the woman's shoulders.

"I'm sorry," Travus said as he knocked on closed door, "I didn't remember the walk being so far."

"Enter," a muffled voice came through the polished wood.

Tilly, with the help of Ophelia undoing buckles on the coat, finally found her way out from under the red leather and reached for the handle of the door. Pushing the door open, she led the way into Colonel Dende's office before either adult could say anything in support of or against the idea.

The office itself was spacious with bookcases lining both sides of the room. There was a wide window opposite the entrance but the thick drapes (complete with the shining sword symbol of the Light Bringers on each curtain) were drawn closed. Short potted plants and trees helped make the space smell fresh and also feel more inviting than it could have been otherwise.

A man with sharp features and dirty blonde hair that went off in several different, pointy directions looked up from behind his desk as the three of them entered. His head tilted to the side as an only partially suppressed look of surprise came across his face.

"I was told that only two Light Bringers were coming and three show up?" the Colonel grinned, "What did you two do between the entrance and here?"

"She dropped about eighty pounds," Travus motioned to Ophelia, who was still wiping sweat from her brow, "And it decided that it couldn't wait to see you any longer."

Tilly charged around the desk. The man behind it was just barely able to get to his feet before the little girl ran right into him, wrapping her arms around his torso.

"Uncle Rassilon!" she said with a big smile on her face, "I'm so glad to see you!"

"By Juna have you grown, Tilly!" he huffed as he recovered from the impact, before turning his attention back to the Night Shield, "What's the problem, Travus? Has to be pretty big for you to invoke Weston."

Ophelia had already closed the door and Travus set the heavy bag down on the floor in front of it. The Night Shield nodded at the other man and stepped over to one of the two chairs that rested in front of the Colonel's desk. He motioned for the former assassin to do the same.

"I'm afraid it is, Rass," Travus said as he sat down, "We're being tracked and hunted by the Al Razheem."

The other man's brow furrowed, "All the way out here?"

"They've found us in every city we've stopped in since we left Paimae," Travus answered.

"How do you think they're tracking you?" the Colonel asked.

"She was under their control for awhile," the Night Shield pointed at Ophelia, "They tattooed some runes on her back and I think one of them is acting like a beacon."

"Runes? May I see them?" Rassilon turned to face the now sitting woman.

Ophelia had just let out a sigh of relief at getting off her feet when the Colonel made his request. Her pale eyes shifted between the men, hoping that the Light Bringer wasn't serious. When it became apparent he was...

"Fine. My back has been itching anyway," she snapped.

With a grunt of effort, the woman lifted herself back to her feet. Pulling the long coat off, she tossed it onto the chair and then turned so that she was facing away from the man behind the desk. Then she pulled the back of her green shirt up until the material was bunched up under her arms and everything from the small of her back up to her shoulder blades was exposed.

"They're glowing," the Colonel observed.

"Typically they get brighter the more pissed she gets," Travus chuckled.

"Then this is definitely a job for Urehara," the other man said, gently pushing the little girl away before patting her on the shoulder, "I'll inform him to receive you after we get you settled in."

The Night Shield rose from his seat as well, "I also need you to send Weston and Union away tomorrow."

"Classic decoy maneuver, eh?" the Colonel shrugged, "I need a new grizzler pelt anyway. Looks like it's back into the bush for Axesam and Fiona. They can play the part of your dynamic duo."

"Thanks, Rass," Travus said before hoisting the heavy bag back onto his shoulders.

Trying to say it after would have been awkward, considering how out of breath he was from the effort of that one action. Ophelia tucked her shirt back in, not sure what was going on.

"Who's Urehara? Where are we going? And what are we going to do with her?" the questions rolled out of the woman, the last adding a pointed finger at Tilly, "I didn't go through all that effort to hide her just to prance her around now."

"Not to worry," Rassilon said, "My quarters are through here."

He pointed to a different door in a different wall that neither Travus nor Ophelia had noticed. It was pretty effectively obscured by a bookcase and a thin potted tree without actually making it look like it was trying to be hidden.

"Tilly can stay in there until we come back. Provided you don't mind, young lady," the Colonel turned to the little girl.

"It's okay with me," the girl shrugged.

"We'll figure out more permanent arrangements once Urehara's done his magic on her," the Light Bringer pointed at Ophelia.

"Then let's stop talking and get to doing," Travus let the pack fall from his shoulders with a thankful look on his face that turned toward the woman, "Scout, put your coat back on and let's move!"

A SHORT TIME LATER...

The carriage belonging to the Colonel came to a stop in front of the already massive but still only half finished stone building. The carriage itself was covered in metal that looked purely decorative but also served a dual purpose of a layer of armor protecting those inside. Not that they needed it at the moment.

A man in black robes with a long red ribbon draped over his shoulders rushed out and opened the door to the vehicle so that the passengers could disembark. First was Colonel Dende.

His blue eyes scanned the area around them. When he was satisfied that there were no immediate threats, he stepped down onto the cobblestones and held out his hand.

Ophelia took the offered gesture of politeness and stepped out of the carriage. Once her feet hit the street, she looked at the building quizzically.

"What's this?" she asked.

"This, my dear," Rassilon answered, "will be the grand cathedral of the goddess Juna. She leads people to knowledge and protects those who ask with that knowledge."

Ah, so Juna was an actual goddess. Ophelia thought that the people who said that around her were just cussing. Havarti had a good, silent laugh at her realization.

"No matter whether they are a follower of hers or not," a new voice chimed in, "And you missed services yesterday, brother Dende."

A man in black robes much like the one who still held the door to the carriage made his way down the steps from the large archway that served as the cathedral's main entrance. His though, had a ribbon that was wider than the apparently lowered ranked member of the religious order that also had pictographs of several symbols that no one outside of his religious sect would recognize.

He was taller than Ophelia and Rassilon, and Travus as well once he was out and standing beside the new arrivals, with short graying hair that had only started to recede. His square jaw and bulging physique belied a man that sat inside a church and simply preached all day. To Ophelia, the way he carried himself was as a man of action that would be more comfortable in a life of labor.

"Sorry, Father," Rassilon gave the other man a quick bow of his head, "I was stuck out on a boat with a sea sick son all morning."

"Squall still hasn't gotten over his fear of the ocean yet, eh?" the man in black robes smirked back in a way that was quite charming to the woman, "With a name like his, you'd think he would be a natural."

"Ironically, that honor goes to the kid we named *Rocky*," the Colonel laughed, "In fact, he should be taking his little brother out as we speak."

"Let's hope he has better luck," the other man replied, wrapping a hand around the forearm of the Light Bringer leader, who returned the gesture, in greeting, "Is this the lady you referred to in your missive?"

He motioned to Ophelia, who suddenly and inexplicably felt flattered. Rassilon nodded and motioned that they should start for the entrance to the under construction building.

"This is Scout Union," the Colonel said loudly, but not so as to be too obvious about it, "She's leaving tomorrow but I wanted to introduce her to you, Father Urehara, and give her a little tour of your site of worship."

"Well, we can give her a status report on the construction, at least," Father Urehara said as they worked their way up the steps, "It will still be at least another ten years before our beacon of knowledge and hope can be declared complete."

Ten years? On a building?! Ophelia had to have heard wrong.

"This is quite the common practice, my dear," Havarti chimed into her head, "Many sects build as impressive an edifice to their deity as possible for a myriad of reasons."

"Do gods and goddesses really care what kind of place their followers flock into to worship them?" Ophelia silently asked her sword.

"Typically, no," Havarti answered.

"Then why–?"

Havarti interrupted her question to answer it (he already knew it was coming), "Many believe that their god, or in this case goddess, are pleased by a building that they could use as a literal sanctuary on Honua in which to abide. Others erect the massive walls to protect the things which their deity holds dear. To be honest, I am not familiar with the goddess Juna so I do not know under which philosophy this shall be constructed under."

"Not that it fundamentally matters," Ophelia replied, "Thick walls are only built to keep people out, no matter how pretty they make them."

Regardless of Ophelia and Havarti's unspoken conversation, Urehara and Colonel Dende walked side by side and spoke among themselves while Ophelia and Travus trailed behind them. The Night Shield didn't say much as they walked deeper and deeper into the wide building, leaving the woman free to converse with her sword.

It opened almost immediately into a wide meeting hall area that had two columns of long benches on either side of the hall for worshipers to sit upon during these services like the one that the Colonel missed. In what was the back of the room but the direction that everyone faced was a raised platform with a stand where Urehara or someone like him addressed the assembled crowd.

In the wall behind that was a single door, much smaller than the one that let the group in here in the first place. As they all made their way toward that entrance, Ophelia looked up.

The ceiling was a much simpler affair than the ornately decorated walls and windows with stained glass. It was little more than a scattering of planks held up with makeshift wooden columns that dotted all around the room, some of them among the benches. It was obviously temporary as the rest of the cathedral was built around and above it.

As Urehara ushered the group through the door that, apparently, led to the Father's aforementioned rectory, he addressed Ophelia and Travus for the first time, "You will find yourself quite safe in here, Miss Ophelia. The reason this site was chosen for the cathedral was that a ley line rests right under it. It sends out so much spiritual energy into the air that any other messages get drowned out."

"Whether you want them to be or not," Colonel Dende added as they stepped, one by one, through the door.

"Meaning no one or anything will be able to track you here," Urehara added, "Please have a seat."

There wasn't a desk like Ophelia was expecting, figuring that a rectory was something like an office. There was a long couch with cushions wrapped in treated leather that stretched the width of a broad fireplace where flames were already crackling between half eaten logs. Heavily cushioned chairs flanked the couch on either side and the father stood next to one, claiming it but waiting for everyone else to sit down before doing so himself.

The Colonel claimed the chair on the opposite side and Ophelia and Travus each took a seat on either end of the couch. The Night Shield closer to the Light Bringer while the former assassin sat near the religious leader.

"So what use is having a cathedral on one of these *ley line* things?" the lone woman asked, "Especially if you can't get your own messages out?"

Urehara looked over at the Colonel who nodded. It didn't seem like the Father was asking permission as much as, Ophelia wasn't sure, seeing if time permitted answering? She was guessing, of course.

"Ley lines are concentrations of the planet's energy, like arteries in our own bodies," the religious leader explained, "The way we are making use of the energy is to be a beacon to believers of Juna so that they can find us on their pilgrimages, no matter where in the world they start."

"And this beacon will keep the Al Razheem from sensing whatever is guiding them to me?" Ophelia's tone was skeptical.

Urehara nodded, "You could have the highest spiritual energy a mortal can tolerate without literally burning to fuel your runes but even that cannot match the planet's energy. Trust me, you are undetectable here."

The former assassin leaned back against the leather couch. The logic seemed sound. However, she couldn't help but doubt anyone who said "trust me". Call it a quirk.

"Now do you mind if I ask you a question?" the Father leaned toward Ophelia.

She shrugged back.

"How much do you know about the runes tattooed on your back?" he sounded genuinely curious, rather than worried or paranoid.

"They protect me from lethal danger, glow when I get angry," her pale eyes flicked over at Travus on that one, "and, as far as we can figure, they've made me forget my whole life from before they were on me."

Urehara quirked an eyebrow on that last one, "Everything? But you can still talk, walk and everything else that you learn in childhood."

Ophelia shrugged again, "Don't look at me, I was just the canvas. I didn't get the full tutorial."

"Why, pray tell, would the Al Razheem be so intent on getting her back that they would follow you across an entire continent?" the robed man asked.

"She used to have a rune that kept her completely under the control of the Al Razheem's leader. During that time, she was able to kill an entire outpost of Light Bringers trained in combat without getting a scratch," Travus answered.

Ophelia felt herself flinch when the man brought up when she killed his wife. She didn't say anything to argue or agree with the Night Shield.

"If they get her back, they'll put another rune on to make her loyal to their new leader and they'll have an unkillable assassin again," Travus finished.

"A veritable one woman army," the Colonel chimed in.

Judging from his voice, this was the first he heard of the atrocities Ophelia committed during her time with the assassin clan. The woman's stomach tightened and threatened to make her vomit.

"May I see these runes?" the Father requested before his attention shifted to the other men in the room, "Unless you would prefer some privacy first."

The woman already had her coat draped over the armrest and shirt halfway up her torso. She looked over at the Light Bringer and Night Shield for a moment before pulling the garment over her head.

"They've already seen them." She said.

Turning around on the couch, Ophelia rested her knees on the cushion and leaned over the back of the piece of furniture. She kept the green fabric of her shirt over her chest, more for the Father's benefit than her own embarrassment.

Urehara lifted himself to his feet and step over to her. When she felt his fingertip brush over the skin of her back, she couldn't help but jump.

"Careful, they're sensitive," the woman smirked back at him.

"It's very intricate work," he said with a hint of admiration in his voice, "It will take time to figure out which of all of these is the culprit responsible for your problems. Unless you want us to remove them all."

This was the first time Ophelia had even heard, let alone considered that idea. That meant that she should be able to get memories of her old life back. The idea was *interesting* but it didn't excite her.

She likely had family. Wouldn't they like to see her again? But even if she did go back to whomever missed her, it was likely that the Al Razheem would keep up their hunt for her, only then they would be able to kill her. She would be more of a danger to anyone who knew her before than now, completely ignorant of their admittedly theoretical existence.

"I want to keep them," she looked back over her other shoulder at Travus, "I'm the only one that even has a chance against anyone else the Al Razheem puts these things on."

The Night Shield wanted to argue. In fact, his mouth opened to start. Then Travus remembered the *conversation* he had with Doctor Efreeti during the failed assault on the Oasis. The thin almost-man told him that the assassins had at least twenty more of those "soul orbs", giving them the ability to recreate killers with Ophelia's abilities that many times over.

The thin not-quite-a-man also said that he had no interest in mass producing so called *super assassins*. At least not yet. But he did also insinuate that Ophelia was the benchmark by which every other recipient of runes would be judged.

The Light Bringers couldn't stand a chance against another assassin that was enhanced with those runes. Not without Ophelia's help. If she was powerless, she could easily be killed by even normal assassins. If she kept the power of those runes, though, that meant that Ophelia could be recaptured. That meant that she could be brainwashed again and forced back into their ranks.

They had no guarantee of the former assassin's help, or even her success if they had it, but if she didn't have those runes there was no chance of the Light Bringers, or anyone really, being able to stop the Al Razheem. There was no good choice here but he did have to make one.

"She's right," Travus reluctantly agreed, "She's our best chance of taking down these enchanted assassins if and when they show up."

"How long did you figure we have to search out the tracking rune?" Urehara asked.

"Axesam and Fiona are heading out tomorrow under their aliases," the Colonel answered, pointing at Travus and then Ophelia, "We're hoping that will get the Al Razheem off their backs for a little while."

Urehara let out a thoughtful grunt, "She will not be able to leave the cathedral until we remove the offending rune then. Doing so will undo all your misdirection. They'll come straight here and neither the town nor this building is in a condition to repel a full scale attack."

"Oh, don't worry about me leaving, Father," Ophelia winked back at the man in black robes, "Did I mention that these runes also keep me from getting pregnant?"

THIRTEEN DAYS LATER...

The next night, Urehara and Ophelia had a pleasant dinner and conversation that didn't quite make it into the bedroom. The next day, his examinations of the runes on her back began. She hadn't been up to any bedroom activities beyond sleeping since then.

Every day he would inspect a different rune and inadvertently make her blink much of the time but, after every session, Ophelia was exhausted. Even his promises of showing her his souffle' (she was pretty sure that was a euphemism) but she hadn't been able to gather up the gumption to do so yet.

But this had been the longest Ophelia, Travus and Tilly had gone without being discovered by the Al Razheem since they started running. The Father was telling the truth that the signal from the ley line was drowning out the one from the runes on her back.

Havarti in particular reveled in not having to fight, cut or stab anyone for almost two weeks. Ophelia wanted to get her gumption back to give Urehara a proper thank you. But that day wasn't likely to be today. Not with another, non-fun probing.

Ophelia scowled as she lay face down on the table that was a long as she was tall and barely wider. It was especially designed to be rested on this way, complete with a hole for the woman to put her face. All she was wearing were her form fitting gray pants, just as she had every morning for the last twelve days, and was waiting. Again.

She had to wait longer than usual this time. Didn't they realize it was chilly in the rectory when the fire wasn't going?

Then Urehara stepped into the room, the long sleeves of his black robes rolled up past his elbows to expose his well muscled forearms. He had a leather bound book in one hand, with a feather pen and glass ink well with a stopper pressed into the mouth between his fingers. In the other, he had three metal instruments.

They each looked like steel sticks with different ends. One was curved, like a flat spoon, the other was square and dull while the last had a sharp blade that was only about as big as her forefinger from the top knuckle to the tip.

That book was what he was keeping the notes about her tattoos in. The religious man hadn't been lying. This was taking awhile. In his defense, there were quite a few tattoos on her back.

But he never entered alone. He always had another priest with him to "assist and ensure that there is no improper contact during the inspection". The woman had the distinct impression he was more worried about any *improper contact* she had in mind rather than his.

What was his name? It sounded something like tomato... toboggan...

"Tommaso," Havarti chimed in from his resting place inside the long red leather coat hanging in the corner, "Where is he, anyway? The Father has never come without him before."

"That's a good point," Ophelia said aloud.

"What's a good point?" Urehara asked, "I haven't said anything yet."

The religious leader stepped up beside the prone woman, resting the book on the back of her thighs as he always did. He pulled the cover open and flipped the pages until he found the one for which he was looking. Then he placed the inkwell, pen and instruments on the parchment to keep it open in the proper place.

"Havarti and I couldn't help but notice that Tommaso didn't come in with you," Ophelia turned her head to face the man, resting her cheek on her overlapped forearms.

"I waited for him as long as I felt was appropriate," the man answered, "Tommaso left on an errand earlier and something must have held him up. I didn't want you to shiver to death so I came without him."

Urehara turned his attention to the fireplace, which had a fresh layer of logs waiting to be lit inside along with the stone and metal strikers waiting on the mantle. He bent down, started muttering a prayer that Ophelia couldn't understand (It was part of his morning ritual. That was why she didn't just light the fire herself.) and then he struck the piece of flint against the steel bar into the mound of kindling and the fire was officially burning.

After a quick rap on the door Tommaso stepped into the room. While he was late, the more unusual thing was that Travus came in right behind him.

Neither appeared uncomfortable, the priest with his tardiness nor Travus showing up at all. During all the sessions where the Father inspected Ophelia's runes the Night Shield had never come to watch. The latter fact was not lost on the Father.

He arched an eyebrow at the two other men. "What is going on here?" Urehara asked.

"I apologize, sir," Tommaso answered, "I'm afraid the interruption was unavoidable."

Behind the newly arrived priest and the man with the flattened nose stepped in an obsidian skinned man. He had silver hair, pointed ears and long green robes under armor that was equally black as his skin.

While he smiled at those already in the room, it radiated no kindness. In fact, it gave the man the impression of a predator having located his favorite prey.

"I'm afraid it is all my fault, Father," the man in the armor said, "It took me some effort to find Mr. Browder here. Tommaso was kind enough to wait before guiding me here."

Ophelia slipped out from under the book on the back of her thighs. Ink dribbled over the edge of the little jar, pooling onto the page but not onto any part of the sketches mapped out on the parchment. The former assassin recognized the man, not who he was specifically but with whom he was affiliated.

The newest arrival was a svartalfar, like Anga Scaram. The new arrival was from the underground territory of the Xaviour Tribe, if Ophelia wasn't mistaken.

The gold stylized symbols of hell hounds embossed on his armor suggested that (she had seen them from time to time in the Oasis). They also said that he was a cleric of whatever god or goddesses they worshiped down there. Ophelia never cared enough to find out.

The cleric noticed the woman move, "Please, Ophelia, don't leave on my account. The Al Razheem asked me to confirm that you were still within these walls. I would hate for you to make a liar out of me by leaving before they have a chance to retrieve you."

"You don't look like an assassin," Urehara said, "And why would you have thought she was still here?"

The svartalfar looked insulted, "I can assure you, *sir*, that I am no assassin. I am a servant of the *true* goddess Lleuad. Our allies intercepted a pair of Light Bringers who told us that Ophelia was hidden here somewhere. They asked me to confirm."

"So you *are* here on behest of that nest of assassins," the Father frowned.

"These *assassins*, as you call them, merely asked us to find their errant daughter," the cleric sniffed as if he smelt something unpleasant, "In there a nobler goal than wanting to reunite a loving family?"

Ophelia stepped toward her long coat hanging in the corner. As she reached out, the cleric let out a loud hissing noise.

"If you value the lives of either of these men you will stay away from your weapon, woman," he snapped.

Travus pulled the sword from the scabbard hanging on his hip. While he didn't move his body, and the way he held his weapon, made him look ready to pounce on anything deemed a threat by the cleric.

Her hand still hanging in the air halfway between her and the red coat, Ophelia asked, "What have you done to them?"

"My goddess has given me the gift of turning men to obey her word and my will," the svartalfar cleric proudly explained.

He wasn't like Efreeti, some being from a land that wasn't even physically in their own world. Svartalfar are mortal. He didn't appear to have whatever it took to create runes on the bodies of victims and make them slaves so whatever kind of enchantment the cleric wielded was likely temporary. Hopefully more temporary the stronger the willpower was of the victim.

"You mean you've hypnotized them to do what you say somehow," the woman turned to face all the men, crossing her arms over her chest.

"At least let her put her shirt on," the Father protested, "There's no reason to make her parade around exposed like that!"

The obsidian skinned man quirked an eyebrow, "You find a woman's natural state to be unpleasant somehow? How far you on the surface have fallen," he muttered.

Ophelia couldn't stop her eyes from rolling, "Spare me the commentary on surface to tunnel nudity admiration and tell me what you were planning to do here if I wasn't on the menu."

"I had only planned to look for you and leave. Now, you have given me an opportunity to turn these infidels to the word of the *true* goddess," the cleric answered as if it was obvious.

Again, her eyes rolled in a most unmistakable way, "You know I'll kill you before I let you tell them where I am, don't you? Kind of hard to convert new followers in that condition, don't you think?"

Ophelia marched around the table toward the cleric, her hands balling up into fists. Again, the svartalfar hissed.

"Another step and the priest is dead," he threatened.

Travus added the punctuation to the statement by pressing the sword into the other man's chest hard enough to puncture the fabric with a quiet rip. Oddly enough, young Tommaso didn't raise a word in protest or even pull away from the blade so Ophelia stopped, the three intruding men still out of reach.

"Alright. Fine," Ophelia said, "Cleric (vile svartalfar insult that doesn't have an equivalent in any other language), you mind if I call you (same insult)? You might as well just turn around and leave. Right now. Any leverage you think you have dies with them and I have a sneaking suspicion I can rip your head off without needing my sword or even these."

She turned her body enough to display the glowing tattoos up and down her back to the silver haired, pointy eared man. She was obviously angry but, even if she had tried to hide the emotion, the runes glowed so brightly that they betrayed the feeling.

"You may call me Rubenesquire. You cannot make me angry, girl, with your petty insults nor childish threats," he nodded, then seemed to come to a realization, "But you are right. Their value as hostages is greatly limited," the svartalfar cleric sighed, "Since you have, admittedly, caught me off guard I will put them to a much better use as I make my exit. Travus, would you kindly kill the false witness they call Urehara."

The Night Shield nodded and marched straight for the Father without a hint of hesitation. The older man in black robes picked the book up from the table, pressing it closed. Whether he wanted to flee with it or somehow use it for defense, the woman couldn't tell.

"Tommaso," the cleric pointed in Ophelia's direction, "Keep her from interfering with the disposal of the infidel leader of this morbid cult."

Without hesitation the young priest pulled a small silver dagger that was only meant for use during ceremonial functions from the folds of his robe slashed at the former assassin, "You know he can't kill me, Rube. I doubt he'll even slow me down, really."

Ophelia dashed back for her long red coat. Twisting Havarti's handle, she pulled the hidden dagger free from the hilt and threw it in the direction of Travus. Tommaso tried to jump in the way but wasn't fast enough.

The blade flipped through the air, the red jewel in the pommel hitting Travus on the side of the head. The man let out curse as he stumbled but didn't fall.

"My dear, you really do need to learn how to throw blades more effectively," Havarti huffed.

"Alight, fine, I admit I was trying to stab him in the side or arm," Ophelia huffed as she hurriedly pulled the long red coat out of the corner, "But I'm glad I didn't impale his head! You want to explain that one to Tilly?"

Ophelia suddenly blinked, landing directly behind Tommaso. Still holding the leather coat in one hand, the former assassin grabbed the priest by the back of his loose fitting robes with the other. Pulling him the off balance priest around, she whistled for the cleric's attention.

"Hey, Rube! Incoming!" Ophelia hollered before throwing the priest away.

Tommaso flew over the top of the temporary table. It tumbled onto its side, dumping the man onto the stone floor and bowling over the armored svartalfar.

Pulling the coat around her shoulders, Ophelia charged straight for Travus. He was already recovered from the glancing shot to his head and rearing back to slash at Father Urehara.

Ophelia dropped a now leather covered shoulder and rammed it into the waist of the Night Shield. Both the man and the former assassin tumbled into the wall beside the fireplace mantle. Travus groaned in pain as his sword fell from his hand.

"Do you think that was enough of a shock to knock Travus out of whatever trance he was put in?" Havarti asked.

Before she could answer, the woman's mouth was punched shut with the back of Travus's hand, "Apparently not," she thought as she rolled away, landing flat on her back beside the thin, upended table.

"Get off me!" Rubenesquire growled at the young priest.

The cleric pushed Tommaso away even as the man in black robes struggled to do as he was told. As the svartalfar scrambled to his feet, he glared back at the youthful human.

"You are no longer of any use to me. Remove yourself from my concern," the man in green robes and black armor ordered.

Tommaso nodded, raising his head and opening his mouth wide. He slipped the silver blade of his dagger between his teeth until the jeweled hilt pressed against his lips. Then he stirred the knife around.

Blood gushed from his mouth and he fell onto the ground flat, gurgling as he exhaled his last breath. The Father let out a scream of disbelief that quickly changed to agony at the sight.

Ophelia didn't have that luxury as Travus jumped on top of her and started pummeling her with his fists. The Night Shield knew that if he tried anything that could kill her, Ophelia would blink so he was obviously trying to beat her to unconsciousness so that he could get to Urehara unmolested.

Ophelia blocked his blows as best she could, that is, until his hands found her braids (she started putting them in again around day four of their stay). Travus wrapped the tied lengths of hair around his fists and pulled her head up and away from the stone floor.

"This will all be over when you wake up," He muttered at her before thrusting her skull back into the flat stone floor.

His voice didn't sound like a man eager to get the job done. It reminded Ophelia of Paimae when she kept reminding herself "The General asked me to find Inara Browder and I will do it. For him". It was a mantra that she repeated again and again to keep her moving forward, to perform the General, her master's will. Travus was doing something very similar now.

Ophelia's vision flashed white with the first hit against the smooth stone floor, then it blurred and it looked like there were two Travuses hovering over her. She clumsily reached up and wrapped her hand around her attacker's throat.

Just as she started to squeeze, the man lifted Ophelia's head and again slammed it to the floor. This time, though, the woman disappeared and left only that violet silhouette behind. She reappeared several paces behind Travus, still on her back.

It took her a second of looking around to get her bearings. She was immediately thankful that there was no pain in the back of her head.

But that gratitude was short lived when she saw that Travus was already back on his feet. He bent down, scooping his sword up from the floor and immediately swinging the blade at Urehara.

"Don't do this, Travus!" the Father jumped out of the path of the attack, "We're friends. Colleagues! You can fight whatever this control is!"

That didn't even slow the Night Shield down. He stabbed at the religious leader.

Urehara used the heavy tome to knock the sword out of the other man's hand, "I didn't want to do this!"

He swung the book in the opposite direction, slamming the leather spine against Travus's chin. The man with the already flattened nose reeled back, lifting his hands in front of his face defensively.

The Father dropped the book to the floor before landing a crushing punch down on the other man's ear, "I was the one who taught you how to box, Travus. You can't beat me!"

Despite Urehara's declaration, Travus straightened up. He was met by another fist to his flattened nose, causing blood to start rolling from his nostrils.

Another punch, this time to the ribs, caused Travus to let out all his breath in one hiccuping gasp. It was sheer luck that Urehara's next strike hit the Night Shield's forearm instead of his eye. It wasn't until Travus ducked under the other man's next punch that Ophelia saw the handle of Havarti's dagger sticking out of the top of the Night Shield's boot.

"He has my dagger in his–" the woman started to yell, scrambling to get back to her feet in a race that she was sure to lose.

And Travus sank the blade into Urehara's chest before Ophelia could even get the next word out. The dagger sank in under the man's solar plexus, where the two halves of his rib cage met.

Travus didn't look overjoyed that he'd succeeded. The hypnotized Night Shield didn't even try to stop the Father from wrapping both his hands around his head. He pulled Travus's face down so that they looked each other straight in the eyes.

Urehara's entire body started to shake as his life slipped away, "You didn't do this, Travus," his voice came out in weak, unsteady gasps, "This isn't your... fault."

The religious leader slumped to the ground, Havarti's dagger slipping out of his chest, blood drenched as Travus kept a grip of the weapon. Travus didn't look horrified by what happened. If Ophelia didn't miss her guess, it was because he hadn't been told that he could. He was awaiting his next command. He didn't have the luxury of having a standing order to "return home" when the job was done like she had.

"Oh, very good, Travus." the almost forgotten cleric didn't bother to hide the delight in his voice, "I'm quite pleased with your effort. You are now free to remove yourself from my concern."

"What the hell? He did what you wanted!" Ophelia grabbed the wrist of the Night Shield to keep the dagger away from his open mouth, "Why are you doing this now?"

Rubenesquire shrugged as if, again, the answer was obvious, "Your family wants you back. They also want him dead. While I cannot give them the first, it is my pleasure to grant them their second wish."

Ophelia would have taken the moment to at least shout a curse at Rubenesquire to express her frustration and disgust at the man but Travus pulled her hair and she went down again. This time she took him down to the floor with her.

"Havarti, why didn't you stop him from using you like that?" the woman let out a guttural whisper as she struggled with the man for control of the dagger.

"I couldn't get free of his grip. Travus is very driven by that cleric's orders!" the sword said back.

She couldn't help but agree. Ophelia wasn't physically weak by any stretch of the imagination but Travus was still winning at the contest of shoving the dagger's blade down his throat.

"I'm afraid, my dear, we may have to give him what he wants," Havarti's tone was that of pure dread.

Ophelia growled, even as the tip of the dagger sliced the man's lower lip open. Her entire hand wrapped around Travus's throat.

"Open wide," Rubenesquire laughed as Travus tilted his head back and pushed the blade down.

The woman's grip around his neck tightened, "Don't do this to me, Travus." she whispered, her voice full of rage and regret, "Don't make your little girl an orphan."

Travus's eye rolled back in his head and he slumped back until he was laying flat on the cold floor. His entire body was limp and his hand fell away from the handle of Havarti's dagger.

Ophelia pulled the blade out of the man's mouth with great care, wiping the blood and saliva on her pant leg before returning it to the bastard sword's proper hilt. When she looked up at the door to the chapel, the svartalfar cleric was already gone. She ran after him anyway.

Entering the chapel, the woman heard struggling at the other end of the wide room. Pulling her bastard sword free of his scabbard, Ophelia looked between each row of benches as she made her way toward the grunting and wrestling noises.

By the main entrance, General Dende had Rubenesquire flat on his back and pinned to the floor with a hand around his obsidian neck. The cleric grunted and gurgled under the man, with one dark hand on the Light Bringer's wrist and the other trying to push the man away where his shoulder and neck met. Without success.

As the former assassin neared, Rassilon looked up at her, "Would you be a dear and collect the two guards I kept outside to arrest this," the Colonel, instinctively looking around, remembered where he was before he called Rubenesquire what he actually wanted to and went with the far more sanitized version, "*suspect* and take him to a cell?"

Ophelia nodded. Making sure her coat was all buckled and buttoned shut, she pushed one of the heavy doors open and called to the guards. They came running.

"Arrest him," the Colonel motioned down to the svartalfar under him, "Take him into a solitary cell. I'll need to question him later."

With three Light Bringers surrounding the unarmed cleric, it was easy to clap irons around his wrists. He didn't even really have to leave the cathedral under his own power. The guards practically carried him with one hand under each arm.

Rassilon waited until he and Ophelia were alone again, "Where's Travus?" he kept the volume of his voice under control but his tone was practically in a panic.

When the woman tried to answer the question, Ophelia found herself unable to come up with the words. She simply motioned for the Colonel to follow her. When Ophelia opened the door to the rectory they were hit with the smell of blood and death almost immediately.

Stepping inside, Travus wasn't lying where she had left him. As far as she could tell, he had crawled over to Urehara and was slouched over the other man's body. He had recovered faster than she thought he would.

"You're not dead," Ophelia said with a thankful sigh, "Havarti wasn't sure he could avoid everything vital in your throat."

In reply, Travus spat a mouthful of blood onto the floor beside him. Red dribbled down his chin and, upon closer inspection, the former assassin could tell that it was taking quite an effort for him to keep breathing.

"I was luckier than them," his voice came out as a heavy croak as he motioned to Tommaso on the floor before the mantle and the Father, whose head rested in his lap.

"What happened, Travus?" the horror in Colonel Dende's face was unable to be hidden as he more stumbled than stepped deeper into the room.

Ophelia explained everything so that the Night Shield wouldn't aggravate his wounded throat. Rubenesquire somehow hypnotizing Travus and Tommaso, forcing them to attack the Father and her. Then she got to the part where Tommaso stuffed his dagger down his own throat.

"Apparently, that's how the cleric likes to end the services of those he's taken control of," Ophelia said, "He ordered Travus to do the same thing after Urehara died. I had to choke him out to make it look like he died and hope that Havarti could keep himself from actually killing him."

"Travus... how could you?" the Colonel fell onto the leather couch, "You killed the leader of Riverbelt's most prominent religious order."

"It wasn't him!" Ophelia stomped in front of the leader of the Light Bringers, "He was under mind control just like I was and I killed an entire outpost of your people!"

"But you weren't in control..." Rassilon's face fell into his hands, "I'm sorry, Travus. I wasn't thinking."

"No, it is my fault," Travus croaked after spitting out another mouthful of blood.

The woman rolled her eyes, "Oh, please! I'm the one Rubenesquire was looking for, remember? But you know what? I refuse to blame myself. The svartalfar could have just spotted me and ran off. Instead he wanted to kill total strangers who didn't believe in what he did."

Ophelia marched over to Travus and knelt down in front of him. She wrested Urehara's head out of the Night Shield's hands, pulling him up so that the other man could get a good, long look into the dead man's face.

"Even he didn't blame you for killing him," she scowled, "I was here. I heard him. I'll even testify to that if you decide to be stupid and try to get yourself convicted in court."

She gently rested the Father's head back in Travus's lap, "Mourn for him. That's fine. He was your friend," Ophelia said as she stood back up, "But don't you even think that you could have broken whatever control Rubenesquire had. I couldn't break the control the Al Razheem had over me. Do you really think you're any stronger than I am?"

She glared down at the wounded man. All he did in response was shake his head.

"Fine," Ophelia turned her attention back to Colonel Dende, "Why are you here, anyway? No one has ever come to one of my rune inspections before and today is suddenly a packed house."

The Light Bringer leader had to take a moment to collect himself before answering, "I, uh, I just received a report that I thought Travus should hear about. Tilly mentioned that he left to come here so..." he shrugged, they both knew the rest of the story.

"What was in the report?" the Night Shield asked.

His first, immediate response to his question was a glare from Ophelia that silently told him to shut up. He got the message and quickly looked away from the woman.

"A patrol found the bodies of Axesam and Fiona in the forests near Nauterhaus to the northwest," the Colonel answered. "I was going to ask if you thought it was an unhappy coincidence or if the Al Razheem had somehow found them and figured out our ruse. I guess we know the answer to that now."

Rassilon looked around the rectory, his entire being slumped over (not just his shoulders). Finally, he lifted himself back to his feet. The shakiness was gone but the man moved as if he weighed far more than his thin frame could carry.

"We need to get Travus to a healer," he said.

Ophelia nodded and they both stepped over to the wounded Night Shield. It took both of them to get Travus to his feet. She slipped her shoulders under one of his arms while Rassilon did the same under the other.

Like the svartalfar cleric, Travus barely needed to move under his own power as the three made their way out to the chapel. As they neared the main doors, though, Ophelia's step became more and more hesitant.

"I have to leave Riverbelt," She said just as the Colonel reached for one of the handles, "Now."

"What? Why?" the Light Bringer asked.

"I still have the tracking rune on," Ophelia answered, "If Efreeti doesn't sense it leaving town soon, he'll know that I stayed."

"Can you at least help me get Travus help first?" Colonel Dende's entire face betrayed his disbelief, his disappointment in the woman, "And how am I supposed to explain what happened in there without you?"

She slipped out from under Travus's arm, "I don't think Urehara told anyone but Tommaso about me. This was the only place that could hide me but that was only because the Juna priests didn't know I was here. There's no way they'll let me stay after..." she motioned back to the rectory.

Rassilon grunted with the effort at the sudden loss of support from the other side of the wounded Night Shield. The Colonel began to protest but was interrupted by Travus.

"She needs to stay," the man spoke softly, with great effort to avoid further injuring his throat, "Can't expose," he coughed, "location to Efreeti before," another cough, this time with bloody spittle, "a plan."

Colonel Dende frowned as he looked back in the direction of the rectory and then to Ophelia, "Go hole up in Urehara's sleeping quarters. I'll tell the priests what happened. They'll take Urehara's body to the infirmary and won't likely even think about going into his room for a couple of days. They'll be too busy with clean up and figuring out the line of succession. We'll come up with a plan in the mean time."

"The sooner the better," Ophelia said, "Kitanah will figure I'm up to something if they don't sense me leaving town fast after what just happened. That will only make them come in force."

"Why do you have such faith that they'll find all this out so fast?" Rassilon frowned back at the woman.

"For the same reason Axesam and Fiona are dead," she answered, "That blonde guard Tristan (thanks Havarti), he was the only one who would have known that they weren't Weston and Union or us," she pointed to Travus and herself, "just by looking. He's on the Al Razheem payroll."

"I'll take care of that," the Light Bringer Colonel nodded, "Oh, Ophelia, make sure you take the book on your way back to Urehara's room. It has all the notes on your tattoos and we'll need those."

The former assassin nodded back, "What really sucks is that I'll never get to have Urehara's souffle' now."

"His souffle'?" Rassilon didn't pretend to not be confused, "Urehara was a terrible cook. They wouldn't even let him cook for the beggars in the soup kitchen."

A light chuckle slipped out of the woman's mouth, "Get Travus some help. He's starting to get pale."

As she turned back into the chapel, the two men stepped out into the morning daylight. When the door closed, she let out a full laugh at echoed against the unfinished temporary rooftop.

"And what, pray tell, is so funny, my dear?" Havarti asked from his resting place on her back.

"I told you that the souffle' was a euphemism!" one last giggle and Ophelia was once again silent.

TWENTY

THE LAST DAY

The next day...

Ophelia looked up from her seat on the leather couch, surprised to see Travus when he stepped into the rectory. She must have figured that he'd be stuck in bed for several days at least. When she told him as much, he responded by holding up a ceramic glass that held oddly colored water and a selection of herbs that still had frost clinging to their leaves.

"I'm not at full mast but I have some billow in my sails," the man said, "This should keep me able to talk and help heal my *hngg* throat."

He took a long, slow sip of the liquid. It had a lousy flavor but it wasn't the worst thing he had ever tasted. Still, the look on his face must have betrayed his opinion of the concoction.

"Whatever that tastes like, booze could only make it better," Ophelia said.

Travus cringed at just the idea, "This is iced and burns my throat. I'd probably be able to breathe fire if I tried to drink alcohol right now."

"Too bad," she shrugged, leaning onto the armrest, "I would have probably stolen a sip anyway."

The rectory had been cleaned up, mostly, after the events of yesterday. The long, thin table was gone, as well as one of the cushioned chairs that rested beside the leather couch.

Travus looked at the remaining chair resting beside the couch, on the side further away from where Ophelia was perched at the moment. He looked from the unoccupied seat to the woman who was watching the fire burn with her legs crossed.

His long red coat, which she had been wearing since arriving in town, hung off the corner of the mantle. Havarti rested inside the compartment that obscured swords from view with only his handle poking out over the left shoulder of the red material. She wore the same green shirt and gray pants that she wore yesterday (had she even taken them off to sleep?) but her boots were nowhere to be seen.

The Night Shield sat down on the couch beside the woman, "Are you still planning on leaving today?"

"Unless you have a better idea," Ophelia answered, "Rubenesquire thinks you are dead, which means that the Al Razheem think you're dead, so you don't have to come. You and Tilly can go back to your normal lives."

Normal lives. Travus scoffed at that. Nothing was going to be normal about his or his daughter's lives again. Inara was dead and Tilly was just starting to enter puberty. How in the world was he supposed to help her through that? What did he know about teenage girls? The enormity of just the idea of guiding his little girl through the years long process of no longer being his little girl automatically ate holes in his stomach.

"I don't suppose I can get you to change your mind," he asked, staring down into the mouth of his tall ceramic glass.

Ophelia shook her head, "Efreeti will need to sense the tracking rune soon. If he doesn't, he'll know I'm still hiding here. He's bound to have received a message from the cleric by now."

"That reminds me," Travus said, "You were right about Tristan. Rassilon caught him trying to break Rubenesquire out of the holding cells."

"At least he won't get out then," Ophelia said back, her pale eyes locked on the crackling fireplace.

"You still think the Al Razheem received a message," it wasn't a question.

She nodded, "Especially if they were already trying to get the cleric free. They had to promise Tristan something good to risk his position in town."

"He couldn't have just taken some initiative to try and get in with the Al Razheem?" the man asked.

"It's risking a lot for a what if," after silence filled the room for a moment, Ophelia turned to look at Travus, "I think I'm going to wait for nightfall before I go."

The Night Shield was silent for a long minute. Even when he started to talk, the words were slow in coming out at the start.

"What if I removed the tracking rune?" he asked, "You still have Urehara's book, right? We can look over his notes, see which one he thought was the tracker, remove it and send it away so that the Al Razheem think you've left Riverbelt."

Ophelia's eyes narrowed and a uncertain scowl pulled at her lips, "You feel up to doing that?"

Travus took another sip from his cup, finding the cooling sensation that washed down his throat and into his chest actually comforting right now. He would have to ask the healers how they got the liquid solution to get so cold.

"I told you, I'm not up to challenging an ogre to a game of arm wrestling but I can hold a scalpel," he answered, "I can cut a straight line and everything."

"I think the allegory you used before was about your mast," Ophelia smirked back.

"So it was," was Travus *blushing*?

"Want me to go get the book?" Ophelia leaned forward on the couch bringing the glowing tattoos on her back into the man's field of vision.

He caught himself staring at the bright symbols for a moment too long. After a quick shake of his head, he changed its direction and nodded.

"Sooner is better than later, right?" he smiled, trying to appear confident, "I'll go get some supplies from the priests and meet you back here."

A SHORT TIME LATER...

Ophelia was on her knees, her shirt again pulled off and just covering her chest. She knelt in front of the large fireplace, its flames washing light over her left arm and side.

The Night Shield stood behind her, half of him illuminated by the flames from the fireplace while the other half was bathed in shadow. Father Urehara's book was in his hands. Errant ink stained the leather cover and blood was spattered over the edges of the pages.

When Travus reached the portion where the religious leader's notes about the woman's tattoos rested, they were stuck together thanks to a small pool of ink that had dried between the pressed together pieces of parchment. He placed the ceramic cup that held the herbal solution (that wasn't as cool as it was only minutes ago) on the mantle to free up his hand.

It only took a finger getting a streak of black on its side to separate the pages. The man looked the sketches over, his brown eyebrows pressing together so tightly they almost became one.

"It looks like he had an idea of how most of your runes work," Travus said, keeping his voice soft (to keep from straining it) while looking over top edge the book at the former assassin.

"You're sure that you wouldn't rather bring a priest in to try and finish what Urehara started?" Ophelia asked.

Travus shook his head, "Time and trust are the issues of the moment. The more priests we tell, the bigger chance word gets back to you know who about what we're trying to do. My only real worry is whether the rune will keep working after I cut it off. Assuming I pick the right one, of course."

"We'll know when it comes off," she answered, "If the rune fades away like the one that symbolized the General's control over me, it doesn't work anymore."

"And they'll come here to find you anyway," Travus scowled.

"I'll have to stay then," the former assassin said, "If they come, my blinking should still work so I'll be able to help fight. If they don't, we'll know that you picked the right rune to cut."

The idea of not having to run with Ophelia both pleased and saddened Travus in ways he didn't expect. Not having to evade and fight assassins every few days was more than appealing. But, as vexing as the former assassin had made it for him the past few months(!), she was one of the main reasons he and Tilly were still alive.

He couldn't even look at her for long the first few days after they left Paimae, knowing that she was the one who killed his wife. Travus had to remind himself, at first, that she was under mind control by the Al Razheem then. As time passed, the fact that his wife was dead still snapped him into random bouts melancholy but he didn't blame Ophelia for being the instrument any longer.

The fact that she was equally clueless as to how to help Tilly should have infuriated him. Especially after the events in Wildesvale. Instead, he found himself comforted by the fact that Ophelia could be there to at least try to help his daughter. It was all he could offer Tilly himself.

"Sooner is better than later," the woman snapped the Night Shield out of his reflections.

"Right. Sooner is better than later," he repeated what seemed to have become their mantra for the day.

Ophelia leaned toward the base of the fireplace to retrieve the scalpel. It was the piece of metal with the fingertip sized blade that Urehara used during his examinations. The small, razor sharp end had been set so that the flames could lap at it, making it as clean as possible under the circumstances.

The woman handed the implement up to Travus, "I'd do it myself but I'm not *that* flexible."

The man cleared his throat and immediately winced as he took the metal tool. He refocused on the pages as he tried to decipher which rune on Ophelia's back was the one that the assassin guild was using to track her.

Keeping the tome open on the pages with Urehara's notes, Travus rested the book on the couch beside them opposite from the fireplace. Beside the book, on the next leather cushion, was a pile of clean cotton rags, bandages and a palm sized tin box that the priests provided. They didn't know why Travus wanted them but they had no reason to question him on something that was such simple little things, really.

He traced a finger over her smooth skin, along a small rune that looked something like a lightning bolt with a little triangle growing out of the side. It rested just to the right of the topmost rune that looked like a crown with an eight-point star in the middle of it.

"According to the notes this one glows the brightest of all of them even when you're just laying down and not doing anything," he told Ophelia, tapping the lightning symbol, "Urehara figured that it was because it was expending the most energy to try and be sensed through the interference of the ley line. Plus, he thought that in some ancient language it means *journey* or *movement*."

She had to concentrate to keep from shivering as the man brushed his fingers her back, "It sounds like the culprit to me."

"He does note that he isn't completely sure on the meaning," Travus warned.

"It's his best guess, right?" Ophelia leaned forward, trying to make her back as easy to see in the firelight as possible, "None of the others are really in contention, are they?"

The man perused over the notes and sketches one last time, "No, although he was able to piece together Kraven's old family seal from where your skin is just a little less sensitive than the rest on your back."

Mention of the General's name made Ophelia tense. But before Travus could say anything she forced her shoulders down and her breaths to be slow and deep. Successful or not, this process was going to be painful for her and knotted muscles were only going to make it worse. They both knew that.

But Travus did say, "Sorry," for mentioning something that he should have realized would upset her. Then he focused all of his attention on the rune that was the cause of all their current troubles.

The blade of the scalpel rested only a hair's breadth from Ophelia's skin, "If you blink, do we try again?" he asked.

She chewed on her lower lip, "I don't think we have a ch-OW!"

Travus pushed the blade into her skin. The distraction worked, she didn't even think to tense up in anticipation of the initial cut. The man wished he could say he was pleased but he so wasn't. Blood rolled out of the wound immediately but the violet glow of the tattoos below shown even through the thick red liquid.

Ophelia's hands curled up into fists, ripping hand sized holes into the thighs of her gray pants. She would have to get a new pair after this. With all the blood staining the garment now, that was going to be an inevitable outcome anyway.

"Remember to... get all... the skin," Ophelia shakily said through grinding teeth, "But don't... cut the muscle!"

They figured that she would be less likely to blink if they didn't slice into muscle. The logic was that, while painful, whatever triggered the defensive measure wouldn't think of the wound caused by the scalpel as life threatening if it stayed superficial. This was all based on the assumption that there wasn't some enchantment to protect the runes from what they were specifically trying now, of course.

Travus felt sweat drip from his eyebrow, just missing his eye as it continued down his cheek like a heat induced tear. He knew it wasn't from the anxiety that suddenly gripped him and his stomach in iron clad clutches. Not even a little. Not at all. (Stop that!)

He kept sawing away at Ophelia's skin as if she was some animal that the Night Shield had taken down in the grasslands and was readying for cooking later. That mental image forced him to stifle a gag thanks to its combination with the smell of the woman's fresh blood.

He'd finally cut the rune halfway off. No sign of any kind of defensive magicks had attacked him yet and Ophelia hadn't blinked. They must have been right. The enchantments didn't think what was happening was life threatening.

He started up the opposite side. It was odd, seeing the muscle in the woman's back shudder as she struggled to stay still. Not like how her entire back shook but the red, bloody tissue that made up the muscle itself. It just felt *wrong* to watch.

"Almost done," Travus struggled to keep the tone of his voice as gentle as he was being forced to not be with the scalpel.

One more slice, about the width of the blade, and the rune should simply fall away from her back and into the hand of the Night Shield. If something was going to go wrong, this was going to be when it was going to happen.

The glowing violet lightning bolt shape pulled away from Ophelia's back and the woman let out a heavy, relieved gasp. She fell forward, ending up on her hands and knees with blood covering the entire bottom half of her back and staining her pants.

"I need to stop the bleeding," Travus said.

Holding the extracted rune in his left hand, he dropped the bloodied scalpel onto the couch and took a rag from the top of the pile with his right. Just as he turned back to face Ophelia she disappeared, along with about a foot of the stone floor under her. Her green shirt dropped into the newly formed hole.

Travus lifted himself to his feet, looking around the room. Ophelia's blinking range was usually only a couple of paces away from where she disappeared but something was different. She didn't leave that violet shape behind this time, although violet wisps floated in front of him like dust in rays of sunlight, and the woman had always reappeared almost instantaneously every other time. But she was nowhere in the room.

Until the next second. Ophelia reappeared behind the couch and about three feet in the air. She landed on the stone floor, the impact knocking out her breath as she ended up face down on the floor.

Where were the stones that disappeared with her? The thought had just occurred to Travus before crumbled stones started raining on him and the couch like an avalanche from some invisible mountain.

He shuffled out of the way as the last of the rubble tore the backrest of the couch to shreds, letting the soft fabric that made up the cushioning spill out. Travus stepped around the couch to check on Ophelia, who lay motionless.

As he bent down to touch the woman's shoulder, she disappeared again. This time, that familiar purple shape was left behind. Along with her blood soaked pants, about a foot of her hair and one of the braids she kept tied beside her face.

Again she reappeared, this time standing right in front of the fireplace. The completely nude Ophelia reached out to grab the mantle before she fell. Her fingers just avoided the cup of iced herbal tea that Travus had been nursing.

The oddest thing was that both braids were still there, hanging on either side of her face. As was all of her hair. Enough of her back was to Travus that he could see that there was no sign of the blood that had coated her only moments before or of any wound where the Night Shield had cut.

He looked down in his left hand. The hunk of flesh that he removed was still there, the rune still glowing bright. Travus looked at Ophelia's back again. The rune wasn't there but her skin had regrown as if nothing had ever been on that part of her back. Not even scar tissue.

"Ophelia?" the Night Shield didn't even try to close the distance between them this time, "Are you alright?"

Ophelia covered her mouth with her free hand. She looked as if she was fighting the urge to retch.

"Just a little motion sick," her voice was barely a whisper, "I think."

She slowly opened one eye and then the other. Lifting her hand away from the mantle of the fireplace, Ophelia tested her equilibrium. Finding it enough to at least stand, she let out a soft sigh and straightened to her full height. She looked around, noticing the shredded couch and the new hole in the floor over which her bare toes draped over the edge.

"If that's what it's like to remove one rune, I'd hate to see what would have happened if we tried to take them all off," she said with a quiet whistle at the end.

The queasiness Ophelia was dealing with passed quickly. Once she was able to really focus on her surroundings, the woman realized the state of undress she was in. Ophelia didn't dive for cover or show any sign of embarrassment.

In fact, her eyes turned toward Travus and a wide smile pulled at her lips. She stepped toward the couch that sat between them. She wagged a finger at the man to have him come closer.

Ophelia leaned over the back of the couch as Travus stepped up, their faces only inches from each other. The only sound in the room was that of their breathing. The man could feel Ophelia's warm breath wash over his mouth as they looked at each other.

"I need you to give it to me," the woman said.

Travus blinked. (Not an Ophelia style blink but an actual one involving his brown eyes.)

Ophelia's hand slid up from the couch, holding the small tin case that had been resting on the cushion. Flicking the top off with her thumb she held the small box on her palm between the two of them.

"Put the rune in this," she said, looking down.

Travus followed her baby blue eyes to his left hand. His fingers were still crimson with her dried blood. The violet rune continued to glow as he dropped the chunk of Ophelia's flesh into the container.

She slapped the top back onto the tin, sealing it shut. Then she again held the palm sized container out to the man.

"Tell me you have an idea on how to get this out of town," Ophelia said.

Taking the tin, Travus nodded a few more times than he really had to but it took that long to get his brain working again, "One that won't even endanger any Light Bringers. I figure strapping this to a calygreyhound will give the Al Razheem a good chase. It'll probably take them weeks to find it out in the wilds, if they can at all. Even with Efreeti's help."

"That sounds good to me," she replied, straightening back up, "I'm going to get into some clothes while you get that thing out of here."

The woman hopped over the hole that her first blink created. She looked back to the Night Shield over her shoulder as she made her way to Urehara's sleeping quarters.

"You can find me in here when you're done," she pointed to the door, "If you want to."

As Travus stepped out of the rectory, he tapped the small tin against the palm of his other hand. It seemed to be a good offer. Should he accept this time?

FOUR WEEKS LATER...

The weeks passed without a hint of Al Razheem activity. Still, Colonel Dende kept Ophelia in hiding, though no longer in the unfinished cathedral. If the assassins came to try to rescue Rubenesquire, as he was from the allied Xaviour Tribe, he didn't want them to be able to stumble upon Ophelia in her last reported location.

To that end, Travus was among the team of Night Shields that figured what questions to ask the svartalfar about everything from the political dynamics underground to how his ability to control the minds of people worked. The cleric had already had three failed escape attempts thanks to his power to hypnotize, resulting in the death of one Light Bringer that removed himself from the cleric's concern, as Rubenesquire described it.

It was returning from his latest session with the svartalfar that Travus stepped into the old, closed bar, "Please tell me that Havarti is still in his scabbard," he said after he pulled the lock on the door shut.

"He's become familiar with your foot falls," Ophelia answered from inside, "he heard you coming from two blocks away."

Ophelia and Tilly were sitting at a table in the middle of the what would have been the area customers drank their various ales and wine. Since the tavern had been closed for nearly a year, it was devoid not only of other people but even whatever decorations adorned the walls when the place was still in business.

The three of them had been here for nearly a week, so it was dusted and cleaned well enough that they could be comfortable. Technically, Ophelia was the only one that had to stay there as Travus and Tilly were no longer being sought out by the Al Razheem. Still, they went with her to all seven closed down or otherwise deserted buildings that she had been housed in. Another countermeasure to foil the assassin guild if, somehow, they were still able to track her after the removal of the rune.

Ophelia slapped the winning card down on the table top with a big grin on her face, "Redemption!" she declared.

Tilly looked up from her two handfuls of cards with a deeply skeptical scowl on her face, "You have to be cheating somehow," she glared.

"I can assure you that she is not," Havarti chimed in from behind the fully grown woman's left shoulder, "She has been quite honest since you caught her those two previous times."

Travus laughing from behind the bar caused the former assassin to do some glaring of her own. He quit laughing and busied himself by pulling two corked bottles of ale from the trapdoor covered pit that the bar, and now the three of them, used to keep various foodstuffs cool.

Sliding over the top of the bar, the man's long red coat (Ophelia returned it to him once he was again on active duty in the city) flopping down behind him after a few steps. Travus handed one of the bottles to Ophelia. Tilly had a nearly full glass of what looked like cloudy apple juice next to her deck of discarded cards.

"Today's the day," he said as he tugged the cork free from his own drink.

"Moving day again already?"

Ophelia had pulled her cork and wrapped her lips around the top of the bottle as white foam gushed out. After wiping at her mouth with the back of her and a quick smack of her tongue against her teeth, the woman leaned back in her wooden chair to look up at Travus.

He nodded as he pulled a chair up so that he could sit on the empty side of the table between the two women in his life, "Rassilon thinks that, since we haven't seen hide nor hair or the Al Razheem in a month, that this should be the last time before we either leave town or, perhaps, find some permanent lodging together?"

Ophelia froze mid-sip. Foam dripped down her chin but she didn't make a move to try and wipe it up. She didn't even seem to notice it.

Tilly's chocolate colored eyes were practically the size of plates as she stared at her father. The thought escaped his mouth before he had a chance to stop it. Now that it was out there, Travus suddenly felt very, very self conscious. Especially with both of them staring.

The not so little girl was the first to actually say anything. "It *would* be easier financially, right? If we all lived in one place instead of two?" she smiled but there was a lot of anxiety hidden behind it.

Ophelia sat her bottle down on the tabletop. Her forehead sank into her palm and she slumped forward.

"Holy Juna!" she gasped as the fact occurred to her, "I'll have to find a job!"

It was the first time she'd used "Juna" as a curse and the fact wasn't lost on Travus and Tilly (it also marked the first time she edited herself in front of the girl). They both laughed. Although, relief from having to answer the idea of actually living together in an actual house may have also been a factor.

After taking a long, deep drag from his bottle of ale, the Night Shield lifted himself to his feet, "Time to gather up our stuff."

"Now wait a minute," Ophelia, her face still resting in her palm, looked up at the man.

Travus felt his stomach tighten. Was she going back to the subject of moving in together?

"You still haven't told me what Rubenesquire told you today," she finished.

The muscles in the man's legs practically collapsed from under him as the tension that gripped him disappeared, "He finally let slip how his hypnotism trick works. It has something to do with pressure points and nerve manipulation."

"How can pushing pressure points make you able to control someone?" Ophelia asked, "And which ones?" she added as an afterthought with a smirk.

Travus excused Tilly from the table so that she could pack up what belongings she had accrued during their month in Riverbelt. The girl relented to her father's wishes, but only after the expected huffing and puffing about fairness.

The Night Shield spoke again once his daughter was in the back room, "Apparently there's a sequence of nerves he hits going from the wrist, elbow, shoulder and up to the neck that makes it so his victim's blood flow is somehow synchronized with the spiritual energy from Lleuad he wields," he pointed in the general areas he indicated on his own arm as he explained. "It makes obeying him as natural to the target as breathing or hearing your own heartbeat."

"Something that powerful can't last long," the woman observed.

"He can control people for an hour at most," Travus agreed, "There are no lingering effects after the control wears off, which is why he makes his victims kill themselves before they get free."

"But he can only execute the control through touch?" Ophelia asked.

"There's still a lot to learn about it," he nodded, "It's a powerful ability but also pretty limited. I'm curious to know if he can only take control of his targets immediately or if he can plant a suggestion like those stage performers to make someone cluck like a cockatrice later."

"Either way he has to touch you, right? So how are the Light Bringers countering that?" Ophelia drained the last of the liquid from her bottle.

"Now only fully armored Light Bringers are watching him while he's in our care," Travus answered.

Ophelia nodded, twirling her empty bottle on the table until his words fully processed, "While he's in your care? Is Rube going somewhere?"

Her eyes narrowed at Travus. He hoped that she wouldn't have noticed that little turn of phrase. He stalled his response by draining the last of his own ale, which was almost half of the bottle, in one extraordinary sip.

"He's technically a diplomat from the subterranean lands," his eyes flicked in the direction of the back room before returning to the woman, "The Valen Court has ordered that he will be transferred back to them where his punishment will be negotiated between an appointed tribunal and a representative of the Xaviour Tribe."

Ophelia groaned, "You have got to be kidding me."

"Relationships with most of the tribes underground are strained at best," Travus recited the reasoning he had been given at his own protest, "The relationship with the Xaviour Tribe is particularly volatile due to a war in the forests up north that have spilled into their tunnels. They've stayed out of the fighting until now. But holding a cleric of their religion could be just the excuse the Xaviour need to spread the violence down south."

"That was a well reasoned and articulate response," the stone faced woman said, "Did you have to rehearse that in front of a mirror a couple of times to keep from laughing at the joke you just told?"

"I would have if I'd thought it was funny," he confessed, "But it's out of our hands now, regardless," he pointed to himself and Ophelia as he finished speaking.

"No wonder the Al Razheem never mounted a rescue after Tristam failed," she scowled as she lifted herself to her feet, "Who needs covert assaults when you can use slimy bureaucratic excretions?"

Travus nodded in agreement but didn't do so vocally. Instead he stood up and started for the back room to gather up his own belongings.

He opened the door so that not only Ophelia but Tilly could (officially) hear what he said next, "Rassilon has the coach waiting around the corner in front of the Hotel Gruber. As soon as we're all packed, he'll take us to our last hiding spot."

Ophelia picked up the polished leather bag that had been resting at her feet. Travus got it for her as a gift a couple of weeks ago. She could also tell that it cost a pretty coin or two so she figured that it was an apology for having to move around so often (which wasn't necessary) as much as it was a gesture of appreciation of their budding *friendship* (which was greatly appreciated). It also happened to have plenty of room for the few things Ophelia owned at the moment.

Judging from the look on Travus's face he hadn't noticed it resting there before then. But he didn't look surprised, either, especially when he saw that Tilly was standing awkwardly beside the door while not only hers but his bags were packed and ready to go in the middle of the room.

Neither woman was stupid. They must have figured the time to move was due and Tilly must have also realized that it was easier to eavesdrop when you didn't have something else to do at the same time.

He sighed, shaking his head at this daughter, but he couldn't hold back at least a hint of an amused grin, "Okay, let's go." he said.

Ophelia wasn't sure where the coach was going. That wasn't saying much, considering that all she had seen of Riverbelt was through the thin space between the red drapes that covered the small windows of the vehicle.

But Travus didn't seem to know where they were going, either. When the view outside changed to headstones and statues, both he and the former assassin looked at each other uneasily.

The carriage came to a stop beside a cliff face that was roughly twenty feet tall. It served in the place of the city's outer wall in this area as the actual granite brick wall started a good distance away where the cliff started to shrink not only into the distance but in height.

The Night Shield pushed the door open and looked up at the driver's bench, "Why did you bring us to a cemetery, Rassilon?" Travus asked.

"There are only so many unoccupied buildings, you know," the Colonel shrugged down at him, "This isn't as bad as you think. It's not far from the town proper. The cathedral is just beyond that clump of trees there."

The dirty blonde haired man pointed to the south, to the left of coach. He shimmied down from the top of the vehicle and hopped down onto the grass just in front of Travus.

"Besides, didn't we agree that you're coming out of hiding after this?" Colonel Dende said.

The other man nodded back and stepped out of the carriage, "Just assure me that we aren't going to be sleeping with a dead body."

"No dead bodies where we're going," the Light Bringer replied, "I'm putting you all up in the living quarters of the priestesses of the goddess Saga Rhiannan. They used to watch over the dead in town ages ago."

"I've never heard of Saga Rhiannan," Travus said as he helped Ophelia and then his daughter out of the coach.

"Their sect died out decades ago," Rassilon explained, "The only reason this place is still around is because of my appreciation of city historical sites."

"Does this appreciation mean that we don't have to clean it up this time?" Ophelia slung her leather bag over her shoulder as she looked around for the building that housed these living quarters.

"Dusting at worst," Colonel Dende said, "The entrance is over here."

The Light Bringer led the trio to the other side of the carriage. In the cliff face was little more to the entrance than a tunnel that both Ophelia and Travus would have to duck to enter.

"It's underground," Tilly pouted.

"Don't be like that," the blonde Light Bringer bumped into the girl's shoulder, "It actually looks like real rooms down there, not some converted cave."

Tilly tried to smile back at the man but it just didn't quite make it. So she busied herself by collecting hers and her father's bags, except for the one that was already slung over his shoulder. That held his sword and various other equipment that came with performing the duties of the Light Bringer.

Like shackles. The corner of Ophelia's mouth twitched with the slightest smirk at some *unofficial* uses for those that she would like to try, preferably on Travus.

Colonel Dende stepped into the tunnel first. He was just short enough that he didn't have to lower his head, although his hair brushed against the support beams that stretched across the top the tunnel every couple of yards as they went deeper inside.

Both Ophelia and Travus had to duck as they walked through, just as the woman thought they would. Tilly brought up the rear, focusing more of her attention of the condition of the bags she was carrying that looking ahead into the darkness.

As the light from the cave mouth started to fade, Ophelia heard Rassilon rustle around in his pockets for something. After a few moments it was revealed to be a little set of flint and steel that he used on a lantern that was hanging on a hook hammered into the support strut holding up the beam stretched across the tunnel, waiting for them.

"From here on out, it will start looking like a real building," he held the now glowing lantern up to his face so that all three of them could see him as he spoke.

He was true to his word. The tunnel opened up into a spacious, square shaped room. The walls were mortared brick, the same kind of granite that was used for the city walls rather than the plain brown rock that the tunnel burrowed through.

It was dusty, also just as Rassilon said. Especially the long table that stretched across the middle of the room. There were doors in each wall, although the one opposite from where the group entered was set deeper into the rock than the others.

"The kitchen is that way and already stocked," the Colonel pointed to the right, "You'll find a good room for Tilly to the left. I think it was originally for body prepa–" he looked back at Tilly, who was still unable to smile at the idea of being down there, "–I'll move your bedroll to a different room."

"And I presume that there are more rooms back there?" Travus pointed at door in the far wall.

"A lot more," the Light Bringer answered, "Rooms that were quarters for the priestesses and then a series of tunnels that led to the Saga chapel, the sacrificial altar and the," again his attention snapped over to the little girl but, this time he couldn't find a way to edit what he was going to say into something more benign sounding, "the crypts."

Tilly turned visibly pale at that. She fought the urge to run back out the way they had come in. That is, until Travus stepped up to her and rested a hand on each of her shoulders.

"You'll never have to go down there," he promised his daughter, "In fact, since we're in the clear we're probably only going to be here for a day or two anyway. I'll start looking for a place to move into tomorrow."

Tilly seemed to settle a bit at that declaration. Then she leaned her head far enough to the side to look toward Ophelia.

"What about her?"

"Well, that's up to her," Travus turned to look at Ophelia himself.

Now it was the woman's turn to look uneasy. Shifting her leather bag from one shoulder to the other, she turned all of her attention to the dusty but otherwise well kept table.

"Are there rags in the kitchen?" she asked as she ran a finger along the wood, leaving a trail that revealed a polished surface beneath.

"We'll talk about it," Travus said to the girl before pulling his hands away and turning to the Colonel, "Will you be staying for dinner, Rassilon?"

The other man shook his head, "Sorry. Not tonight. We'll rain check it until your house warming. In fact, it has to be getting close to sunset. I have a few concerns to alleviate before nightfall."

Though he said that, Colonel Dende lingered for some time afterward. First, he had to move the bedroll he'd provided for Tilly to a room that hadn't been used to prepare corpses for their funerals, as he promised (but he also wanted to make sure it wasn't too close to the room the adults were going to use). Then, discussing the schedule of Travus's duties for the following day since the svartalfar cleric would be leaving town in the morning.

As he emerged from the tunnel the sun was getting intimate with the horizon. To the point that the color had long faded from the landscape.

He slipped into his carriage despite the driver's bench being empty. Rassilon's sword made sitting awkward so he pulled it free of its scabbard.

He was done. All of his responsibilities had been fulfilled. The man had done everything he'd been told. Everything Rubenesquire told him to do.

The Colonel blinked in confusion. When did the cleric tell him to do anything?

Ophelia was now in the place. Rassilon slid his hand from the handle of his longsword down along his blade, careful not to cut his fingers.

The space in the back of the carriage was limited so he had to lean forward as he opened his mouth wide. What was he doing?

The notes of the cleric's interrogation. How he pressed nerves and pressure points in the arm and neck. Rubenesquire hit those parts of his arm when Rassilon pinned him down and arrested him. But that was over a month ago! His control only lasts an hour.

As the tip of the blade slipped between Rassilon's lips, a dreadful realization came to him. He left the outpost almost an hour ago. He heard the cleric say something, telling the Colonel that the time had come.

He thought it was hyperbole, one last snide remark from the svartalfar before he was no longer the Colonel's problem. As Rassilon gagged on the cold steel sliding down his throat he realized that Rubenesquire had triggered something, some latent instructions he'd given the Light Bringer that he didn't remember.

Before the cross guard of Rassilon's sword met his lips, his consciousness was completely gone. After only a few seconds more, death claimed him.

YOU ONLY LIVE TWICE

"OPHELIA," THE WHISPER came into the woman's mind, "Ophelia, wake up!"

She refused to open her eyes or her mouth, "What is it, Havarti?"

"You are in danger, my dear," the sword answered, "The door to the room just opened and closed. I think someone came in."

"You're not sure?" Ophelia thought back, opening one eye cautiously.

"I may not see exactly like you do but I do still need light and it is awfully dark in here."

"You're sure it's not just Tilly?" she thought the question at the sword.

"Positive," Havarti answered, "She has never been this quiet."

The drowsy former assassin scanned around the room. If there was indeed someone in there, she didn't want to alert them that she was awake and searching.

The doorway that led out into the hall was right in the middle of the wall toward Ophelia's feet. She and Travus, on separate bed rolls, were lain out in the corner in the far left corner from the entrance. The brass chamber pot was nestled in the corner opposite them, to the right of the doorway.

Other than that, there wasn't really any furniture or other decoration in the space. The Saga Rhiannan priestesses apparently weren't big on worldly items and whatever was here had either been removed or rotted away years ago.

Beside the woman was Havarti, leaning against the wall. Just beyond her sword was the lantern that they would need to be able to see in the room. Being underground, it didn't matter the time of day.

Ophelia was just about to scold her sword for raising a false alarm when she saw *something*. No more than a flash of movement. The woman couldn't identify what it was although with it being just Travus and her alone in the room, there shouldn't be anything moving.

"I think they're skirting along the far wall," Ophelia thought to her sword.

"I agree," Havarti replied, "They are endeavoring to avoid detection, taking the long away around the room to get to you and Travus."

Ophelia glanced up at her sword leaning against the wall, still firmly in his scabbard. He was too tall for him to just reach for his handle, that would also open her up for any kind of attack from the intruder. The glowing runes on her back would serve as a perfect target for them to aim.

"Oh, no. That is not a wise plan, my dear," Havarti said when the woman's eyebrow quirked up.

"It will keep Travus from being targeted," Ophelia answered and started reaching for her sword with her right hand.

There was a hiss in the dark then another hint of movement. Ophelia's bedroll was skewered but she was already gone, the violet silhouette unable to be seen with normal vision.

It only took the woman a moment to get her bearings. Travus was lying on the floor to her left. That meant that the shadow in front of her...

The former assassin's left hand, her stronger hand, snapped out and wrapped around her barely visible opponent's neck. Just as she started to squeeze, Ophelia felt her wrist and arm suddenly get bombarded with what felt like a barrage of pin pricks.

A surge of vertigo washed through her senses, causing her to stumble back, letting her grip loose and dropping down to one knee. Her left hand and arm started burning and Ophelia was suddenly having trouble breathing.

"You've been poisoned," Havarti said, his voice calm in her mind, "But you've not blinked so it won't kill you. But you must fight! Travus is defenseless!"

Nodding, Ophelia forced herself to her feet and lunged at the attacker. The woman immediately lost balance and tumbled into the would be assassin, wrapping her arms around the person's *very* thin waist and pulling them down to the stone floor with her.

Ophelia tried to speak but she couldn't find the air. It was as if her lungs had been completely closed off. It didn't hurt, really, but the sensation was... it felt unnatural and she wondered why her blinking hadn't kicked in for this.

"Still some fight in you?" a hissing whisper came from the figure lying prone beside Ophelia, "Then we shall end it now!"

"Travus, get up!" Havarti vocally bellowed, "Ophelia is being attacked!"

The trained paranoia of the Night Shield kicked the shirtless man into cognizance. He was immediately sitting up with an unsheathed dagger in his hand. It only took him a moment to see the two figures in shadow beside him and the violet glow coming from one letting him know which was which.

He plunged the blade into the figure of the assassin, right where their heart should have been. Judging from the surprised yelp from his target, he was right on.

The would be assassin's entire body convulsed, knocking Travus into the wall. That shouldn't have been possible from behind the attacker but it did happen. He felt something snap in his shoulder when he hit the cold stone.

The intruder crawled for the door, coming to a nonliving stop in the middle of the room. Cradling his arm, Travus shuffled on his knees next to where Ophelia lay.

"Are you alright?" he asked, his innate sense of caution keeping his voice a whisper.

The woman's hand wrapped around his arm like a vice grip and the Night Shield knew something was wrong. He reached for where the woman had left the lantern when they turned in for the night.

Thanks to a lot of practice, he was able to light it with one hand. The flame light quickly filled the room and Travus could finally see what was happening. Ophelia was lying on her back on the floor immediately in front of him. Her left arm, the hand wrapped around his own, was swollen twice its normal size and it was cherry red. His view moved to her face and, while her mouth was moving, as if she was trying to fit paragraphs of words into a few seconds, no sound was coming out. That was when he noticed what was in her chest.

His kill strike on the assassin was too late. Ophelia had another dagger buried in her chest. Blood was pumping around the gash the blade had made. The attacker must have twisted the weapon when they fell away.

"But, your blinking," he was honestly confused, "You can't die!"

He looked back at the woman's face. Her lips had already turned blue due to lack of oxygen. Tears started welling in her eyes even as her mouth vainly tried to keep speaking.

"No, no, Ophelia," Havarti again spoke vocally, "I will not tell him. You will."

"Tell me what?" Travus asked the sword that rested in Ophelia's limp right hand.

"Her blinking works. She did it when the killer first attacked," the sword said out loud, though it seemed more to himself than the man and not answering what he asked, "For some reason, the runes didn't detect the poisoning or the last strike as lethal blows..."

Travus pulled the blankets from the bedroll behind him and wrapped the cloth around the dagger in Ophelia's chest, trying to slow the bleeding, "What does it matter? She's dying!"

"Slash her throat, Travus," Havarti ordered.

"What?" he shook his head, "You're insane. That will only kill her faster!"

"Ophelia agrees with me!" the sword pleaded, "She will be dead if we don't get her to blink!"

Travus looked back at the Ophelia's face for some kind of confirmation. He didn't get it, her eyes slowly drifted shut.

His entire body tensed. After a moment's hesitation, he threw the blood soaked blanket away and pulled the dagger free from Ophelia's chest.

"Juna forgive me," he muttered as he rested the edge of the ichor covered blade at the base of her neck.

Closing his eyes, he pushed down. His knuckles slammed into the cold stone of the floor.

It took a few seconds for Travus to realize that Ophelia wasn't there anymore. His brown eyes opened. On the floor in front of him was a puddle of blood and a yellowish, clear fluid beside it, just under his knee.

His attention darted up to look around the room. Ophelia was kneeling at the foot end of the bedrolls. Her green shirt, the only thing she wore to sleep, was soaked with her blood. Her forearms stretched out from the rolled up sleeves, both of them looking normal now.

Havarti was still in her hand and her auburn hair was draped in front of her face, obscuring it from Travus's view. He was quiet, waiting to make sure that she was breathing again. It took a little bit but he was finally able to see that her chest was indeed moving up and down with continuous breaths.

"You're alright?" he asked the woman.

Ophelia wiped the long hair from her face. She was pale, shock still washing through her, but her lips were again a healthy shade of pink. The former assassin pulled the front of her shirt down to reveal where the dagger had run through her chest.

The wound was closed, dried blood holding the sides together. The wound was more severe than what one blink could repair but she was alive. Apparently the poison was somehow removed from her body during the blink, as well. That was the puddle of yellow liquid! It literally fell out of Ophelia's body!

"I, I think I'm fine," the woman finally answered, tentatively lifting herself back to her feet.

Travus felt himself relax until a sharp pain shot through his shoulder again. He stifled a yell but not enough for the woman not to notice.

She rushed to the man's side, "What's wrong?"

Her hands hovered over the bare arm that the Night Shield cradled, afraid to touch it. He wrapped the hand of his uninjured arm around Ophelia's and she helped him stand up.

"The assassin knocked me into the wall," he motioned behind him.

Both of them turned to the body of the one that almost killed them, "What in the blue hells?" Ophelia chimed in.

The dead body lay face down on the floor, a pool of dark indigo blood expanding under it. It was a woman but definitely not human. Her scale covered hair looked like snakes, except the heads were eyeless and not well defined. They all had fangs, though.

Ophelia reflexively rubbed her left arm when she noticed the "hair" still writhing around. After a few seconds, though, even that fell still.

She had legs but they didn't look right. They were longer than they should have been by about two feet. They also didn't bend at the knees like Travus and Ophelia's. At the point where her knees should have started, scales instead covered the backs of her curled lower legs from her calves down. They were what whipped the man into the stone wall.

"That's impossible," Havarti broke the silence, "That looks like a gorgon but I thought they were nothing more than myth."

"Fill me in, Havarti," Ophelia ordered her sword.

Again, the room was left to drown in silence. This time, though, Travus knew that he simply wasn't a part of the conversation happening in the woman's head.

"If they can turn people into stone just by looking at them, how come I'm not a statue?" she asked out loud.

"I presume she could not see you in the darkness, either," Havarti answered, "If gorgons share more than just some cosmetic aptitudes of reptiles, she was likely tracking you via smell."

"So you're saying this thing could have been on our trail since Paimae?" the Night Shield asked.

"I doubt it," the bastard sword answered, "It would have had ample opportunity to strike in the last month if that were the case. I would have to hazard a guess that it recently arrived in Riverbelt specifically for this ambush."

"So the Al Razheem never lost track of us but have been simply biding their time," Ophelia said.

"It's possible," Havarti confessed, "It may be that the rune Travus removed wasn't the one tracking you after all."

"Great. So much for being the big hero," the Night Shield scoffed at himself but then a new terror fell over him, "Tilly!"

The man dashed past Ophelia and into the hall. The former assassin raced after him as they ran past door after door, finally stopping at the room that held his daughter.

Then Travus realized, in his panic, that he didn't bring his sword. Looking back at Ophelia, who was just a step behind, he brought his hands together in a twisting motion.

"Dagger?" the shirtless man mouthed.

Ophelia pulled her bastard sword free of the scabbard, dropping the sheath to the floor. She twisted the handle, removing the hidden dagger, and gave it to the man.

She positioned herself on the side of the door nearest the handle. Wrapping her hand around the handle.

"One, two," she quietly counted, "Three!"

Ophelia threw the door open and Travus charged into the dark room. There wasn't any sound of a struggle. She thrust

Havarti into the darkness and he confirmed that the only thing happening in the room was Tilly sitting up on her bedroll and rubbing her eyes.

"Daddy?" the girl yawned, "What are you doing in here?"

As Travus started to explain himself to the girl, the other woman excused herself. Picking up the scabbard and replacing Havarti inside, Ophelia jogged back to the other room. Things were different than when they left.

The gorgon seemed flatter than before. As she neared the body, Ophelia realized that it was a trick of the limited lighting. The gorgon was actually sinking into a newly formed hole in the stone floor.

"Havarti, are you seeing this?" the woman stepped deeper into the room and picked up the dagger that the Night Shield used to make her blink.

"Indeed," the sword replied, "I am relaying this to Travus as well."

Ophelia crouched down at the edge of the hole around the gorgon. She dug the tip of the blade into the pitted stone that surrounded the monster's body.

The metal started to smoke almost immediately. When she lifted the weapon up to get a closer look at the curved steel, the point was completely eaten away.

"This thing's blood is like some kind of acid," Ophelia observed.

Again Havarti agreed, "Apparently so. Who knew mythical beasts were still dangerous after they died?"

The woman straightened herself up, "What do you think the odds are that this is isn't the only assassin coming for us tonight?"

"Tilly wasn't attacked so... only slightly worse than a sure thing?" the bastard sword didn't sound overly excited.

Ophelia dropped the dagger onto the dead monster's back, "Tell Travus that I'm on my way back."

Grabbing her bag as well as the Night Shield's, the woman had a wicked thought. Slipping a satchel over each shoulder freed up her hands. She walked over to the chamber pot, picked it up and, after pulling the top off, dumped the contents onto the corpse along with the pot itself. It was the closest thing to punishing her would-be murderer she had. Then Ophelia picked up the lantern and headed out into the hall.

She made her way back to Tilly's room, stepping through the still open door. Ophelia gently kicked the door shut with her heel before focusing back on Travus and his daughter.

When Tilly saw Ophelia, worry covered her face like a theater mask, "Are you all right?" she asked.

The woman looked down at herself, forgetting that her shirt was mostly dyed the color of her own blood now, "I'm fine, kid. The one who attacked us got a lucky shot in but then I blinked and I'm all better now."

It was mostly true. The wound in her chest ached and itched but it was no longer life threatening.

Travus handed Ophelia back Havarti's dagger and then she set her sword against the wall by the door. Digging into her bag, the woman pulled out her last shirt (the last few weeks had been rough on her wardrobe due to enthusiasm rather than battle) and pair of pants.

It took a little hopping and wiggling to get into the gray pants but they fit well, if snugly, once they were actually on. Then she turned so that her back was to the man and his daughter to protect both of them from blushing, although for different reasons, and also so that the already worried girl didn't see the wound on Ophelia's chest.

She pulled off the bloodstained shirt and tossed it into the corner. It landed with a heavy, wet flop that actually made Tilly stick out her tongue in disgust.

Then Ophelia pulled on her new shirt. It was white but, with what was going on, who knew how long that was going to last. As with her other shirts, the back was cut out and held together with some ribbon so that as little material touched the tattoos on her back as possible. In this case, red ribbon. Once she was buttoned up, she turned back toward Travus and Tilly, although she did almost immediately dig into her bag for her boots.

It had become a habit for all of them to keep their clothes in their traveling bags when they went to sleep, partly due to not having anyplace to really store their clothes in the abandoned places they had been staying.

The former assassin realized that, if they did get out of this, it was a habit that was going to change. Having a place to put her things, even having "things" beyond what she could carry was bordering on a new idea for the woman. It sounded... nice.

As she finished pulling on her knee high black leather boots Travus, who was already again dressed, tossed his long red coat onto Ophelia's lap. She looked up at him questioningly.

"It looks better on you anyway," he grinned, but only for a moment before he returned to being serious, "Besides, we need to hide those glowing tattoos of yours."

Ophelia slipped the coat on, tucking Havarti into the hidden pocket in the back so that only his hilt was visible, "What's the plan?" she asked.

"One of us should recon up to the entrance, see if we're clear to get out of here," he said, stepping toward the door.

"I'll do it," Ophelia stepped in his path on the way to the door.

"No, I can– GAH!"

When Travus started arguing with the woman, she simply lifted a finger and poked his left shoulder. Just that caused him to reel back several steps and cradle his injured arm.

"What happened to Daddy?" Tilly rushed to her father's side.

"The one who attacked us broke his shoulder," Ophelia answered as she reached for the door handle, "See what you can do for him while I check out there."

With that the former assassin stepped out into the hallway. Despite wearing boots with an unusually high heel (she just fell in love with them when she found them back in Wildesvale), she walked without making a sound. Must have been some magical assassin sneaking rune mixed in with all the others on her back.

With the entire place being underground, there wasn't even any ambient light to guide the woman on her way. She had to keep a hand on the wall and hope she didn't walk into the door that led into the greeting room face first.

In fact, her toe hit the door just around the time Ophelia figured she was about there. Thankfully, her boot didn't hit so hard that anyone would notice.

She pressed an ear to the flat wood. If she heard anything, the woman would know that they weren't alone.

They weren't. Ophelia could hear talking but not what they were saying, the words themselves were little louder than whispers.

Now she had to try and figure out what they were up against. That required opening the door.

Ophelia tugged at the door so lightly that it didn't budge. She pulled a little harder. Still it didn't move. Resting a hand half on the door and half on the doorjamb, the woman risked pulling even harder.

The hand on the doorjamb kept it from opening more than a sliver. Ophelia, though, grimaced when the door made a sound like a crack when it moved.

The former assassin was sure that someone or something was going to barge through the door any second. When nothing came to kill her, she slowly leaned in to the thin spacing she'd opened.

At least one lantern was lit in the room but Ophelia couldn't see it, just the light it threw off. Her stomach dropped when she saw not one but two assassins were waiting for them in there. They were both gorgons.

"Ja, Stheno is sure taking her sweet time," one said to the other (with the door open, Ophelia could now just make out the words).

The first was taller than the second. Still, Ophelia figured, based on the size of the dead Stheno in her sleeping chambers, that only brought the larger remaining gorgon up to her shoulders.

Both of them had the same writhing hair. With poisonous fangs. The hair of the shorter one seemed, for lack of a better term, more aggressive than the other even though there wasn't anyone else in the room.

Both of them moved the same way. Their legs looked human but, once you looked below their knees, the lower portion of their limbs curved back like the body of a snake rather than bending at the knee. One leg moved in front of the other, but in more of a slithering motion rather than a step.

Neither wore clothes. Stheno didn't either, thinking about it. But they also had the ability to speak the common upworld tongue. That meant that, rather than being of animal intelligence, clothing wasn't a part of their culture. Even if no one in Ophelia's group had ever heard of them, that didn't mean they didn't have a culture, right?

Not that they had much to hide. Being of reptilian blood, they didn't have breasts like Ophelia. Their chests, though, did bulge beyond their rib cage like there was extra muscle or fatty tissue around where breasts would have been.

They were well armed, though. The larger one carried a crossbow, along with a quiver of bolts on her back. The other had one scimitar in her hand and another still in its sheath on a belt around her waist.

Even if Ophelia didn't eat for a week she couldn't have made herself as thin as these two. Still, one whip of their tail or legs was able to injure Travus. They had to be stronger than they looked.

"Ja, she is simply being cautious, Euryale," the shorter gorgon said to the first, "We were warned not to underestimate her resourcefulness, remember, ne?"

"Ja, still, I could have crawled into that room and swallowed Ophelia whole by now!" the taller gorgon, apparently named Euryale, protested, "What if something *has* happened to her, ne?"

Ophelia couldn't help but wonder if they had forked tongues like snakes or whole like humans. They were too far away for Ophelia to be able to tell.

"Ja, We'll give her a few more minutes. Ophelia isn't alone so whoever she's with may have tried to fight. Ja, that may have slowed Stheno, ne?" the smaller monster folded her arms in front of her chest, "Ja, if she doesn't come back then I supplicate that we take that lantern, hunt the human down and do what our sister wasn't able."

The hairs on the back of Ophelia's neck stood up when the gorgon spoke that last sentence. Not about taking the lantern and hunting her down, although that was worrisome at best. It was the word "supplicate".

Ophelia had only ever heard one other person use that word: Doctor Efreeti. It was true that the thin man didn't own a monopoly on using unusual words but, "supplicate" just happened to be one of his favorites. If this monster that was thought to only be a myth was using the word, it stood to reason that they could be part of the same menagerie that held the crinotaur, another creature of unsure origins.

The two gorgons spoke only to each other, so they appeared to be the only ones in the room. That meant that they were the only ones blocking the way out and into the safety of the city.

She had to get back to Travus and Tilly. They had to figure a plan to get out of here that involved either avoiding these monsters or killing them before they killed Travus, Tilly or herself.

Resetting the door into the doorjamb very, very softly, Ophelia then started back to Tilly's room. She figured the door to the greeting room would block out the sound of her footfalls so she didn't bother to run quietly, only quickly.

"We don't have much time," she told the Night Shield and the girl everything she had heard, as well as her suspicion that the gorgons were from Efreeti's collection.

"If Havarti's right about their sense of smell, hiding isn't going to be an option," Travus scowled.

"I am confident, based on this Stheno's comfort when she was moving around in the dark," the sword answered.

"What are you guys talking about? How do you know how well they can smell?" Tilly looked as happy as her father, meaning not at all, on top of the feeling of missing something.

"I examined the gorgon back in," her eyes darted over to the man for just a split second, "my room. Its blood had eaten a hole in the floor. Havarti was able to tell your father about everything because he was holding the dagger from Havarti's hilt."

"Is that what was happening every time you zoned out and just stared at the wall?" the girl asked.

"I guess so," Travus shrugged his good shoulder, "I didn't realize I was doing that. Sorry."

"So the only option we really have is to fight," Tilly laid out the conclusion that was obvious to all of them but was unspoken.

"These things have blood like acid so Havarti's not touching them," Ophelia declared, "Give me yours, Travus."

"I'm going to need it," Travus frowned at the woman, "You're not going to be fighting alone, you know."

"Your shoulder," Ophelia frowned at the man, "If we had time to set it, maybe you could do something. Besides, Havarti doesn't mind me using your sword, do you, Havarti?"

"I've no desire to be melted by a monster's blood," the bastard sword answered, "Better it than me."

The Night Shield reluctantly tossed the weapon, still in its scabbard, to the woman. Then he started digging into his bag, pulling out a wound up circle of nearly invisible thin line that wrapped around his hand a dozen of times.

"We should be able to make use of Scaram's Thread of Fate, don't you think?"

Ophelia slipped the scabbard into the belt on her hip as she looked over the offered wire, "That could be useful. And that would have a pretty strong whiff of my scent, wouldn't it?" the woman pointed to the bloody shirt crumpled in the corner.

Travus furrowed his brow as Ophelia slipped the Thread of Fate around the hilt of his sword on her hip, "Yeah but– what are you thinking?"

"We can use that to as a scent decoy to draw them past the first few rooms in the hall. I'll wait for them down the hallway and when they pass you and Tilly can run for the exit," the former assassin answered.

"What about their dead sister?" Travus said, "They're bound to smell her corpse, even over the blood in your shirt."

Ophelia rubbed at the back of her neck, chuckling uneasily, "Not necessarily. I, uh, I dumped the chamber pot on Stheno's body."

"You what?" Travus cringed at the idea, "Why?"

"I never said I wasn't vindictive," the woman shrugged, "Even if they do see her first, that will only ensure that they'll come after me more aggressively. Remember that I'm still their primary target. The Al Razheem thinks you're dead," she pointed at the man.

"What about you?" Tilly had practically been the avatar of worrying since Ophelia had come into the room.

"I still have my blinking and I can fight," she stared down Travus before he could speak up again, "Even if I don't kill them, I can still get past them and out right behind you."

"What's to stop them from coming outside after us?" the girl obviously didn't like the plan.

"They've been sneaking around all night," Ophelia knelt down so that she was eye level with the girl, "As much as they want me dead, they want it done quietly. We get out to the streets we're in the clear."

When Travus tried to speak up again, Ophelia quickly straightened up and pressed a finger to his lips, "We don't have time for a debate. They could already be coming and all this could be for nothing anyway."

She turned and picked up her blood soaked shirt, "We'll move you closer to the greeting room door. I'll smear my shirt down the sides of the hall to block your scent and leave a trail for the gorgons to follow. If we're lucky they won't check the rooms as they go."

"And if they do pass us, we run off like spooked deer," Travus finished.

"Like a father keeping his daughter alive to have a family of her own someday," Ophelia corrected him.

The Night Shield sighed, relenting, "Come on, Tilly. Ophelia and I will argue about the wisdom of her plan later. After we're all safe."

The little girl nodded and, after Ophelia checked to make sure that the hallway was still dark, they left the room. Feeling along the wall for guidance, Ophelia found the next door and pulled it open.

After ushering Travus and Tilly into the room, the former assassin smeared her bloody shirt over the handle. Hopefully, it would hide their scents inside and, with blood all over the handle, hopefully discourage the gorgons from even touching it.

Ophelia counted the number of doors until she came back up to the room where Stheno attacked her and Travus. Another heavy smear of blood except, this time, Ophelia started dragging the soggy garment along the wall.

If all went well, Euryale and her sister would think that Ophelia was wounded and follow the trail to finish her off. As Ophelia kept walking down the hall, she heard the door at the far end of the hall open. They were coming.

The wicked part of the woman's brain clicked on again. Tossing the shirt down the hall, toward the crypts, Ophelia started unraveling the Thread of Fate.

She pulled the door open just enough to poke one end of the nearly invisible line past the doorjamb. Remembering that the monsters were shorter than her, she held the thread up at the height of her chest and closed the door.

Then she crossed the hall, stringing the line across the width of the hallway, and did the same thing with the opposite door. The light from what was likely the lantern being held by one of the gorgons started to take away the darkness hiding the human.

Walking faster, but quietly, the woman rushed to put distance between the trap and herself. She finally reached the archway that marked the beginning of the spiral staircase that led down into the crypts. Her bloody shirt was draped over the first step. This was as much space as she could give the father and daughter. This was where Ophelia would make her stand.

The light steadily got brighter and brighter. Ophelia didn't hear doors opening and closing so they must have been following the trail of blood just as the woman hoped.

"Ja, Stheno has obviously wounded Ophelia," the rasping voice of one of the gorgons carried down the curved hall, "Losing that much blood, the human could not have run far, ne?"

If they started talking they would slow down. The former assassin couldn't have that. They could spot Travus and Tilly if they weren't focused elsewhere.

"Actually, it was just a flesh wound!" Ophelia called out to the monsters, "You should see the other lady!"

"Ja, she's alive!" one called.

In your mind, you expect to hear boots falling hard against the floor when someone is charging at you. With the gorgons, it sounded more like a patrol of brooms sweeping against the stone floor violently towards her.

The one with the sword pointed the lantern at Ophelia when they came into view, "Ja, there she is!"

The one with the sword dropped the lantern to the floor to free her other hand to draw the second sword. As she charged toward Ophelia, the taller one, Euryale, took aim with her crossbow.

The human noticed a flicker in the light where the Thread of Fate waited for its quarry. She just hoped that neither of her opponents did, as well.

Euryale loosed a bolt at Ophelia, who threw herself to the side. The arrow buried itself into the angled ceiling just inside the staircase. The woman would have been relieved if the metal arrowhead didn't suddenly suddenly send an arc of lightning back into the feathers of the fletching and explode!

Ophelia hunched over, feeling bits of stone pummel her red leather covered back but, otherwise she was unharmed. Then the charging gorgon screamed.

The woman reached for the sword on her hip but then she realized that the monster had run into the Thread of Fate.

"Ja, my eyes!" she screeched as she reared back and fell to the floor.

Her swords clattered to the stone as the palms of her hands pressed against her eyes. Indigo blood dripped between her fingers and thumbs.

"Sesklo!" the gorgon with the crossbow pressed the butt of the weapon against her hip and pulled back on the string.

This was Ophelia's chance to escape. She started running toward the reloading Euryale, drawing her borrowed sword as she jumped over the now blinded gorgon squirming in pain on the ground.

The Thread of Fate had been eaten in half by Sesklo's blood. Otherwise, Ophelia would have either blinked or decapitated herself because she was running all out.

"Coming through!" Ophelia whipped her blade from side to side as she neared the only gorgon still upright.

Euryale had just started to take aim when the human started swinging. She dove to avoid Ophelia's sweeping attacks, giving the woman the space she was looking for to pass.

Ophelia sprinted for the greeting room door. It hung open and she could see Travus and Tilly running for the tunnel on the far side.

The woman dashed through the doorway, slamming the door shut with a quick spin and grab of the handle. The move barely made her miss a step.

She jumped to hurdle the table that separated the two sides of the room when a heavy crash came from behind. The gorgon smashed through the door with her shoulder as if it had been made of matchsticks.

Her face a mask of rage, she stared down the shaft of the arrow in her crossbow, aiming for the woman's back, "Ja, damn you!" She howled as she loosed the bolt.

Ophelia suddenly ran into the edge of the table, wondering why she was facing the closed door that led into the kitchen. She had blinked. Looking to her right, she saw the arrow hit the support strut in the mouth of the tunnel where the Night Shield and his daughter were waiting for her.

"Travus run!" she called.

The man reflexively turned to cover his daughter just as the arrowhead arced lightning. The tunnel collapsed when the support beam was shattered by the blast.

Ophelia couldn't do anything but look on in horror. Travus... Tilly... They were so close to where the arrow hit.

Fury suddenly filled the woman like air in her lungs and it suddenly felt more vital to her than breathing, "You *BITCH*!" Ophelia hollered, jumping over the table again but this time in the direction of the gorgon murderess.

Her pale eyes locked onto Euryale. The hardest part for the woman was deciding what part to chop off first. No. Nothing fancy for this piece of... decapitation. That was it. She will chop her head off!

"Ophelia, no!" Havarti screamed in her mind, "Don't look at her face, she'll turn you into stone!"

The human averted her gaze just before the gorgon was able to focus on her. She whipped the sword up where Euryale had been. Ophelia felt resistance and then heard the gorgon hiss in pain. She'd hit the monster.

There was no way Ophelia was getting out through the tunnel. It was completely filled with rock. Her only chance now was to hope that the crypts had some old, forgotten entrance. That also meant getting by Euryale.

She chanced looking back in the direction of the gorgon. The monster was huddled against the wall away from Ophelia. Several of the snake-like tendrils that served as her hair wriggled free on the floor, spouting acidic blood onto the stone.

Ophelia turned back and dashed back down the hall. First the light from the lantern came up ahead, then Sesklo came into view. She lay flat on her back, still cradling where the wire had sliced through the bridge of her nose and into her eyes. Her chest was moving. The monster was still alive.

"Hey, Euryale!" Ophelia called down the hall as loud as she could. "Welcome to the club of being an only child!"

Sesklo gasped, suddenly realizing that she wasn't alone and that the one with her had every advantage. Blood coated her entire face, also covering some kind of a green... something in the middle of her forehead. Ophelia didn't bother to take the time to look closely. Before the gorgon even had a chance to raise any kind of defense, the human slammed the heel of her boot flat on her windpipe.

Sesklo's entire body shuddered. Ophelia looked at the blade that Travus had given her. Holes were eaten throughout the length of it thanks to drops of gorgon blood from Euryale's hair tendril things. It wouldn't be of any use in a fight anymore. It could perform one last duty, though.

Putting her whole body weight behind the weapon, Ophelia stabbed the blade through the monster's heart. Sesklo's body fell still.

Then the almost invisible line caught the woman's eye where it laid atop the gorgon's corpse. A quick tug and... it was a tangled mess that found its way into the woman's pocket.

Then Ophelia ran down the stairs into the crypts. She didn't worry about balance as much as speed, especially when she heard the pained wail of the last gorgon mourning over the body of her sister.

Trying to fight Euryale hand to hand would be suicide, even with a few tendrils less than Stheno. The poison slipped past the detection of her blinking before, who's to say that it couldn't again?

The woman's mind raced as she reached the crypts deep inside the hill. They were much like the brick and mortar halls above. The only main difference was that there must have been some kind of water source in the rock above. Stalactites formed in the worn out mortar between bricks hanging from the ceiling about ten feet up but stalagmites lined either side of the pathway ahead, giving Ophelia the impression of a dragon with a gap in its teeth.

Why was her blinking not working like it did before? Urehara seemed confident that the rune Travus ended up removing was the one that was used to track her location. If he was wrong, why did the Al Razheem take so long to mount an assault like this?

The hall almost immediately came to a four way intersection. It suddenly occurred to her that she shouldn't be able to see as much as she could. Looking up again, she realized that the stalactites had some kind of glowing moss on them. While not exactly torchlight, it was enough to navigate by.

Ophelia's mind started to wander again as she moved from hall to hall, taking one turn and then another. There were literally dozens of runes tattooed onto her back. The only one that she actually knew the use of was the one that matched the General's family crest. Although, that was only after the fact, after it disappeared when he died.

That green stalagmite looked familiar. She was snapped back into her current predicament long enough to realize that she was lost. The woman had passed this particular moss covered pile of mineral deposits at least twice. Not only was she no closer to any possible exit, Euryale was likely that much closer to her now.

What if the other runes on her back weren't so singularly focused? The General's was based on his crest but every other one was based on alchemist symbols that had been used in different ways throughout the ages. Who said that Ophelia didn't pay attention when Urehara lectured on and on... and on... and on?

What if every other rune on her back had more than one function? That would explain why her blinking wasn't quite right. It would also explain why they had to get hunters that could track by scent to come and search in her last known location.

Wait a minute. The gorgons hunted by scent!

"My dear, I," Havarti started to say something as Ophelia neared the next intersection.

She was met not by another choice of direction but a scaled fist. She reeled back, lucky that her nose didn't break.

"I was going to say that I thought I noticed some movement ahead," the bastard sword finished, sounding dejected.

"Thanks for the warning," the sarcasm dripped heavy from Ophelia's lips.

Euryale stepped out from around the corner to face the human. The former assassin's eyes were still watering from the punch so she couldn't see the gorgon clearly. Even as her vision cleared, she had enough sense to not look the monster in the face.

"Ja, I saw how you left Sesklo," Euryale growled, "Ja, I saw the disrespect you showed Stheno in death, also."

"You came after me, remember?" Ophelia answered, "I just wanted to be left alone to argue with my man and then have make up sex repeatedly."

"Ja, then I have taken as much from you, too," Euryale lifted two scimitars that glinted in the faint light, "Ja, I used every last shot from my crossbow to bring down the entire hill down on the halls upstairs. There is only you and me now, ne? Ja, no family to join, no Efreeti to command us. Ja, you shall die and I will mourn in solitude for millenia."

"Ooh," the human pursed her pink lips mockingly, "You gorgons are an immortal species, eh? Sucks to be you."

"Ja, I will not kill you quickly," Euryale started slithering toward the human, "I do need something to occupy myself, ne?"

"Nice to know that you think ahead," Ophelia smirked at the gorgon.

"If you have any ideas, Havarti, now would be the time," the woman thought to her sword.

"I'm thinking, my dear. I'm thinking," the bastard sword said, "For the time being? Run!"

"Brilliant strategy," Ophelia muttered, spinning on her heels.

Euryale slashed at the former assassin with her two blades, each missed as the human sprinted in the opposite direction. Ophelia turned at the next corner and kept running.

"Ja, you cannot hide forever!" the gorgon called out, "Ja, yours is the only other living scent down here! Ja, the air does not move! There is no way out, ne?"

"You think she's right?" Ophelia asked the sword.

"We must hope that she isn't," Havarti answered, "The Saga Rhiannan sect had to have another way for mourners to come visit their deceased loved ones without going through the servants' quarters, didn't they?"

"You'd think," she whispered back, "All we can do is keep looking."

Two days passed as Ophelia wandered the halls, avoiding Euryale while simultaneously searching for any sign of an exit, until she found the stairway that brought her and Havarti down here in the first place.

The woman was only able to walk up about thirty steps before she was stopped by an impassable pile of rock and rubble. The gorgon hadn't been lying about what she did to the halls above.

"Okay, at least we know where we are now," Havarti said, "We need to be more systematic in our search for the exit."

The gorgon's hissing call echoed throughout the halls. As if answering, Ophelia's stomach growled loud enough that she actually wondered if Euryale could have heard it.

"I'm having trouble seeing a point here," Ophelia rested her forehead against the cold stone, "All that's waiting for us outside is even more people that want to kill us. Anyone who cared about us is dead."

"We don't know that for sure, my dear," Havarti said, "We didn't see Travus or Tilly get hit by falling rock. They could have escaped."

"After an entire hill falling on them?" the woman scoffed.

"They could have made it out of the tunnel before Euryale had her tantrum," the sword answered, "They could be waiting for you right now."

Ophelia walked back down the stairs. She had to keep moving to make it harder for the gorgon to pick up her trail.

"They're gone, Havarti. I got them killed," she whispered then changed the subject, "We'll keep making left turns at each intersection. Eventually we should hit something new, right?"

"In theory, yes. I'm sure that there are tunnels we haven't been down yet," Havarti replied then changed the subject back, "It is something to hope for, Ophelia. We both need hope to keep going."

"False hope isn't going to put food in my stomach," the woman turned left, hoping the monster wouldn't pick up on the pattern and get ahead of her, "It's coming down to how I choose to die. I can probably last another few days without food. More if I didn't have to keep moving to avoid Euryale. Can you die from lack of sleep?"

The awkward transition was honest. Euryale always caught up with Ophelia and Havarti just when the former assassin thought they'd put enough distance between her and the gorgon to get some real rest. Ophelia even tried slipping into several different sepulchers in the walls, some holding bodies and some not, but the gorgon found the woman each time.

The human was lucky that time and seeping water had made some of the walls between the sepulchers crumble, making them into an interconnected maze of narrow tunnels. That saved her from being cornered. But the gorgon was smaller and had the advantage in those spaces. So Ophelia hadn't slept since being trapped down here.

"I think the process would take more than a couple of days," Havarti said.

Ophelia waved her hand dismissively, "Doesn't matter. If I am going to starve to death, it's going to be over Euryale's corpse. That means I need to take the fight to her soon."

The bastard sword couldn't think of anything to say to that. The two continued on their system of turning left at every intersection. A couple of times they hit a dead end and had to turn back but that just meant that they took the next left.

"I've been debating telling you some things I've learned from Travus," Havarti spoke up after a couple more hours of wandering from hallway to hallway.

"And when would you have done this?" Ophelia didn't bother to pull her mouth away from the dribbling stream of water running off the tip of the stalactite with less moss than the others where they decided to take a break.

"He's wielded me quite a few times since we've met him," the sword responded, "While he hasn't told me much of this information directly, it has come into his mind while I've been in his hand."

The woman giggled even though her companion hadn't said anything funny, "That sounded dirty," she snickered.

Havarti continued, "I was thinking that, perhaps, if you knew what I did, that may keep you on the path of searching for the exit rather than seeking some final, climactic clash with Euryale."

"If it's something I should know, why didn't Travus tell me himself?" Ophelia wiped her chin clean and continued.

"I have to admit that has been one of my concerns," Havarti answered, "I think I can understand some of his reasoning, although another part of it may be that he just never found an opportunity that he felt was appropriate to tell you."

"Let me guess," she said, taking another left, "You still think he's alive and that he was trying to find an opportunity to ask me to marry him. So I have to stay alive for a chance at true love," the woman scoffed.

"How *melodramatic*," Havarti's voice was heavy.

"Fine. Tell me then."

Ophelia had to admit that they had finally come into a hallway that didn't look familiar. The walls were a lighter, drier shade of gray. The plaques that sealed many of the sepulchers didn't have as much rust.

That brought one thought to Ophelia's mind: that she may finally be able to find a salvageable weapon! The woman started tugging at the edges of the plaques. Crumbling the stone behind was the only way to be able to pull the seal open. There weren't any seams where the stone that made the seal *lid*, of which the metal plaque was the middle, met the stone of the wall.

But, unlike the rusted out ones closer to the entrance, these didn't budge. Finally, Ophelia let out a curse of frustration and punched the last plaque on the wall. All that she had gained from this endeavor was two bloody knuckles.

"Well?" she shook her hand, trying to lessen the fresh pain.

"Well what?" Havarti responded.

"What did you learn from Travus that's supposed to make me want to keep trying to escape?" she asked.

"What if I told you that," Havarti was suddenly reluctant to continue but he forced himself, "he knew your family?"

Ophelia's brow furrowed, "What?"

"That was how he came to be in the Oasis. He was there to not only rescue Tilly but you as well," he explained.

"I actually have a family?"

Havarti harrumphed.

She groaned, "Come on! You started this. Tell me!"

"When we get out," the bastard sword said, "I promise."

Ophelia's hands gripped her hips so tightly that it hurt. Her foot tapped so fast that it sounded like a small rabbit dashing for cover. The scowl on her face looked like it threatened to become permanent.

She pulled the sword from her back and stared at him, "You swear that you have real information about my family and that this isn't some trick to get me to keep moving?"

"I do, on penalty of being used to disembowel Euryale," Havarti said.

Ophelia looked up the hall one direction and then the other. Nodding to herself, she slipped her sword back into his scabbard.

"Okay. We're in a new area anyway," she started further down the new hallway, "Maybe we'll find a clue or something in this neck of the woods."

Another left, another left into a dead end, and one more left. After about thirty feet, the hall opened up into a square room much like the greeting room upstairs. Just remembering that felt like it was so long ago to the woman.

There was a long table in the middle of the room, just like above. It was caked with dust, just like when they arrived before. Unlike the other greeting room, though, there was only one other door in the wall opposite where Ophelia entered.

"You don't suppose–" the woman motioned to the door.

"That this could be the way out?" Havarti didn't want to sound overly optimistic but there was a new bounce to his cadence.

Ophelia started walking around the table. She was starting to believe that the ordeal was about to end and she had to control the feeling. If she was wrong, she needed to keep herself together. If she was right, and she was about to get back above ground... the woman felt her dry lips stretch into a smile.

"Ja, so this is where you wandered off to," Euryale slithered into the room from the same hall Ophelia just stepped out from.

The smile snapped out of existence.

"Don't you have a rat to go pounce or something?" the human snapped at the gorgon.

The smile on the monster's face made Ophelia queasy, "I told you that you and I were the only things living down here, ne?"

"I think the moss feels insulted," the woman pointed up to the ceiling.

The stalactites were gone but the glowing moss still coated the upper half of the room. The monster looked up and was unimpressed.

"Ja, I do not count fungus," she answered.

"Whatever," Ophelia sighed, then pointed at the exit, "But I think I can beat you to the door and make you the only living thing down here. Until you starve, anyway."

"Ja, you are a foolish, what do you say, moron, ne?" Euryale smirked.

The human cocked an eyebrow, "What makes you say that?"

The gorgon motioned to the door, "Ja, that is not the way out. Ja, I told you that there is no way out now."

"And I think that you're an ugly... (the sentence devolved into a steady string of cursing and vulgar descriptions that focused primarily on the poor quality of Euryale's lineage) ...so what you do say to that?" Ophelia actually had to take a moment to catch her breath.

"Ja, be my guest," Euryale slithered over the table, disturbing the even layer of dust, and bowed next to the door. "Once you have realized how thoroughly wrong you are, I will kill you and you will sustain me for a century, ne?"

Ophelia was suddenly dreading the possibility that the gorgon was right. She had been able to explore far more of the area than the woman had been able in the days they had been down here. If this was the exit, the monster could have been long since gone and sealed the entrance long before Ophelia got here herself.

But, if Euryale had been in this room before, she would have left tracks like she did over the table and the dust in this place was laid over the surface of everything like fresh snow when the human arrived. And she had vowed to kill Ophelia. That kind of a grudge could keep her down here until the human was dead by her hand and not some innocuous or peaceful cause. Then she could leave and return to Efreeti and the Al Razheem at her leisure.

The woman decided it was worth a shot. She wrapped her hand around Havarti's handle, promising him that if she had to use him to fight, it would only be with his pommel and only until she could run.

Ophelia figured that Euryale would attack her when she reached the doorjamb but the gorgon stayed still. The human took hold of the handle with her free hand and pulled the door open. Still the monster didn't move.

Ophelia stepped through and found herself... in another ante-chamber. It was very similar to the rectory that Father Urehara used as an office back in the cathedral above ground (only without comfortable couches). It even had shelves of books lining the walls, though many of them had rotted to the point that they would fall to pieces at the slightest touch.

There were two tables, both made of stone and built into the floor. There were no other doors but the one she had just stepped through. And it slammed shut behind her.

"Now you understand, ne?" Euryale was practically giddy, "Ja, there are rooms like these throughout the crypt. They were used to hold separate funerals at the same time, a common occurrence during plague ridden times, ne?"

Ophelia refused to collapse into a blubbering mess. Redirect the feeling, she ordered herself. The monster is toying with you, where is your anger?

She found it. That frittering remnant of an ember. It roused quickly until the woman's breathing started to become ragged.

She spun around to face the gorgon with her eyes closed. She bent over and yanked Havarti from his scabbard, burying his blunt pummel just under where both sides of the monster's rib cage met.

"Direct me, Havarti," Ophelia thought as she slipped the sword back into his resting place.

"She's doubled over," he said. "You cut the tendrils off the left side so you should be able to land a punch there without taking a strike from the fangs!"

The woman did as the sword said, snapping her hand back as quickly as she slammed it into the gorgon's head.

"Jump back, she's swinging-"

The woman was already doing what the sword said. She felt the wind whip in front of her face.

"-her swords!" Havarti finished, "Open your eyes, my dear. She is circling around to find an opening, the risk of looking directly into her eyes is minimal."

Ophelia opened her eyes. She hustled over to the nearest table, keeping that between her and the gorgon. Now if she could get a clear run to the door...

Euryale must have realized what she was thinking. The gorgon threw scimitar and it spun through the air, right into Ophelia's path just as she started to sprint for the exit.

When the human stopped, the monster charged, slicing for Ophelia's throat. The former assassin suddenly found herself standing to the now unarmed side of the gorgon. She almost laughed.

But then Euryale looked her way. The gorgon's face, it was... she hesitated to say *human*, which was wholly unexpected from a monster. Except for what looked like a yellow jewel under the

Euryale's right eye. At least, it looked like a jewel until an eyelid closed and opened over it like a third eye.

Ophelia raised an arm to try and shield her eyes, a last reflexive defense. It was too late. Her fist was already frozen shut and turning the same color of marble, like statues in the cemetery.

She was beaten. By this *thing*. She failed Travus and Tilly, allowing them to be buried under tons of rock. The Al Razheem had the means to create an immortal army to take or destroy everything. Worst of all, Kitanah was in control of it all. Ophelia's failure couldn't have been more complete.

The last thing she saw or heard or felt was the monster telling her: "Ja, I live only to mourn my sisters now, at least you did not have to live with your failure for long."

TWENTY-TWO
WHAT DO THEY SAY ABOUT THE THIRD TIME

"...SURE THAT SHE isn't an actual statue?" some unfamiliar voice said, "I mean, even her clothes are stone."

Was Ophelia hearing? She still couldn't see anything but hearing was new.

"While Harby is playing doctor, Lily and I are going to make sure we're not going to wander into an ambush," another voice, a woman, chimed in, "Don't let him linger between her legs for too long, Raiko."

What in the wide expanse of Honua was this "Harby" doing? Whatever it was, it did make Ophelia aware of her surroundings. But why did he have to be between her legs to do it?

Her vision started to return, dimly at first. Everything was gray, and her eyes wouldn't move, but she could make out the room around her.

An elf suddenly stood up in front of her and another new sensation washed through the woman. Was she feeling a, a thumb in her mouth? Rubbing the roof of her mouth?

The elf, presumably this "Harby" was thin and was about a head shorter than the woman. She was estimating, of course. While she was standing stiff, Ophelia wasn't standing up straight.

Harby's hair was black (but that could have been because everything looked to be various shades of gray at the moment) and pulled back into a short ponytail. He had big pointed ears and wore what looked like a knee length white tunic with baggy sleeves and toggles fastening the front together running down the middle of his narrow chest.

"I don't know if this stuff will work. We definitely don't have enough to cover her entire surface but if I apply dabs of it on her key meridian points, it may counter whatever has frozen her in this state and allow her to move again. She at least deserves a chance," the elf said, turning to look back at the other man in the room, who Ophelia figured was this "Raiko".

He was big, even taller than Travus. He had silver hair that stretched down to his waist. Despite his hair color, Raiko didn't look old. He looked to be maybe in his late twenties at the most.

He wore a long brown coat (was she starting to see color?) with a silver brooch that was some kind of seal or family crest on the left side of his broad chest. Raiko also had a pompous look about him that reflexively made her want to punch him right in his pointy nose.

"She doesn't look that bright," he said as he strode up to the still frozen Ophelia, "She has the same look as a cow chewing cud."

He leaned in close to her, until their noses were almost touching. His eyebrows curved up at the outside corners like a little set of silver horns.

And Ophelia could feel his breath on her face. Ugh. This big man's breath smelled bad. Wait, she could smell!

"I'm doing this because its the right thing to do, Raiko," Harby clapped a palm sized circle of tin on top of another one that was filled with some kind of cream, "I'm not doing it to gain any favor or use out of someone else."

Ophelia felt like a voyeur spying on the two men. Not that she could participate in the conversation, at least not yet. As she listened, she found herself rushing from severely annoyed by this Raiko to touched at the sentiments evoked by the elf.

"I do appreciate the cut of this Harby's jib," a familiar voice popped into the woman's head, agreeing with her feelings, "Oh my, Ophelia, you are back with me?"

"Havarti! You're okay?" the woman's relief was obvious to the sword.

"Never mind me," the sword replied, "Whatever that cleric did appears to be working. Juna be praised!"

"Are we religious now?" Ophelia chuckled.

Apparently some of the reaction made it out physically and Raiko's hazel eyes narrowed. His face tilted one way, then the other as if he was inspecting her.

"Only when things go well for us," Havarti let out a soft laugh, "There is something about this Raiko fellow that instantly makes me dislike him. Don't you think?"

The woman suddenly felt pressure on her left breast. This ogre was groping her chest even though she was still stone!

"It boils down to two things for me, Havarti," Ophelia thought, fuming, "First, he has no concept of personal space and second..."

"Raiko, keep your hands to yourself!" Harby looked back and saw what the other man was doing, "She's a real person and I'd hate to have to tell Saya what you're doing to a complete stranger!"

He immediately pulled his hands away from Ophelia and stepped back, "Come on. She can't feel a thing. So who's getting hurt here?"

That put him at the perfect distance. It took some concentration, but the hand that was stuck rising in front of the woman's face whipped out, smacking the big man square in the nose.

"...he called me a cow," Ophelia finished her thought for her sword, "Bastard."

Raiko tumbled back, cradling his face with both hands. The woman's entire body loosened up and she stumbled forward. As she caught herself, Ophelia noticed a metal cuff on Raiko's right arm that wrapped around his wrist all the way up to his elbow.

"Oh, sorry," Ophelia said, obviously not meaning it, "You were saying something?"

Looking down at herself, the flesh on the woman's hands looked healthy and pink. The rest of her body felt normal, too. The last vestiges of the gray in the red trench coat had even faded away.

The tall man let out a loud curse and glared at Ophelia. She simply stared back, unblinking.

"You dezerbed dat, Raiko," the elf said, although his voice sounded muffled, "But you Shouldn'd hab been zo close to her adyway. She wad probubly doing dat before she waz eben petribibed."

"Yeah. Yeah, that was it. That's what I was doing before I was petrified," the woman grinned at the big man before turning her attention back to the shorter elf, "So who do I thank for, um, are you okay?"

She was surprised to see the elf pinching his nose shut with two thin streams of blood running down his chin as if he was the one that Ophelia punched. It was then that she noticed that the smaller man had a cuff that looked identical to the one the worn by the man in the long brown coat, except it was on his left arm. She never would have seen it under his sleeve if he weren't stopping the nose bleed.

The elf nodded, reaching under his long tunic and pulling a rag from one of the many pouches that were hanging from his belt, "I'll be fide but, blease don'd punch 'im agaid."

After some nose blowing and wiping away of blood, Harby folded the rag and tucked it into a different pouch on his back. He pulled another clean rag out and handed it to Raiko, who followed the elf's example and started cleaning himself up.

"My name is Harbenigyr. But most everyone calls me Harby," the man in white spoke up again, his voice was back to normal, "And this is Raiko, for whom I apologize in regards to his behavior."

The big man gave Harby an unamused smile back. He tossed the rag over his broad shoulder, where it landed on the dusty floor next to the gash that was made by Euryale's scimitar when she threw it at Ophelia. The weapon was long gone, as was the gorgon, but the men (as well as others who weren't here at the moment) had wandered around the room and disturbed so much dust that Ophelia couldn't even guess how much time had passed.

"I am a cleric of the Order of Kuan Yin," Harbenigyr continued, "We came down here a few hours ago and in our wanderings we came upon you. I applied an ointment that helped restore you from being petrified," he ran his thumb and forefinger along the edge of one of his long ears, unsure of what to say next.

"Who else constitutes *we*?" the newly reanimated woman asked.

"Don't you think you should introduce yourself before you get all inquisitive?" Raiko crossed his arms over his chest, "We did just save your life, after all."

"No, *he* just saved my life," Ophelia pointed at Harby, "You called me cow and took a grope before I'd even softened up."

"You heard that?" Harby asked, "It took that long for you to be able to move? I am so sorry!"

The cleric's apologetic outburst cut off whatever vindictive reply Raiko had before he could make it. Slipping the half drawn rapier on his hip back into its sheath, the silver haired man huffed and stomped toward the door where a couple of other fresh sets of footprints came in and out of the room.

"You don't have anything to be sorry for," Ophelia said to the cleric although her pale blue eyes stayed locked on the other man, "You brought me back to life for all intents and purposes. He, on the other hand, is asking for something to get chopped off."

"I understand how you feel. Really, I do," Harby said then held up his left arm to display the metal cuff wrapped around it, "Raiko was accused of murder in the village where I found him. He was about to be lynched and I begged for them to keep him alive to stand trial."

"And they listened?" the woman was genuinely shocked, "You must have been pretty convincing."

The cleric shrugged, "People want to be good, for the most part. They made me agree to take him to the Valen Court to face his charges. They put these shackles on us and a constable walked us out of town. When we were out of the city limits he," Harbenigyr let out a regretful sigh, "he killed the constable."

She didn't realize that she could like this Raiko any less than she had before. She was wrong.

"Why are you still traveling with him then?" Ophelia asked.

Again the elf held up the shackle, "We have to stay within a certain distance to each other or we start getting weaker and weaker until we die. These things also make us share, um, damage."

"Hence why you got a bloody nose when I punched him," the woman shook her head, "Sorry about that."

"There's no way you could have known," Harby gave her a kind smile (he seemed more like a kid to Ophelia than even Tilly, despite looking like he was in his early twenties), "Neither Raiko or I knew until after he killed Lot and tried to get away from me."

"Lot was the constable?" Ophelia stepped around the cleric, making her way to the door.

"Yes," the elf answered, "Anyway, you said that you wanted to know who *we* were, right?"

She looked back over her shoulder at the cleric, "Oh yeah, I almost forgot."

"Raiko is out in the hall waiting for Saya and Lily to return. They decided to scout on ahead while we waited to see if the ointment I applied made you flesh again."

"What are you doing down here?" Ophelia asked, "How did you get in, anyway?"

"I, um, I have no problem answering all your questions. I'm sure you have tons of them," Harbenigyr frowned, "But would you mind if I asked *you* your name first?"

"It is only fair. The young cleric has been more than accommodating under the circumstances," Havarti chimed in Ophelia's head.

The woman nodded back, "You're right. Sorry, I do have a lot of questions but I shouldn't get too carried away."

Ophelia introduced herself to the cleric, complete with a handshake. Then she shared a very streamlined version of her history. After not mentioning being an assassin for the Al Razheem, being hunted from town to town or bringing up Travus or Tilly, the story didn't take long.

Raiko had been listening in and wasn't even interested himself until she mentioned the gorgon right toward the end. He stepped back into the room and strode toward Ophelia with the same look Travus had when the Night Shield was going into interrogation.

"You were turned to stone by the gorgon wandering around down here?" he asked, although he kept talking, "Where does she keep her nest? Does she have any weapons? How can we avoid her gaze? Oh, well... I guess you wouldn't know that last one, would you?"

Ophelia's hands balled up into fists again but her bastard sword reminded her that anything she did to Raiko would also happen to Harbenigyr, who did not deserve a disjointed pelvis.

She turned back to face the cleric, "You're down here for Euryale?"

The elf chewed on his lower lip for a moment before reluctantly answering, "Raiko has to pay a debt to a man who beat him in a duel up in Riverbelt. He has to retrieve something called its *divine eye.*"

"Divine eye?" she asked.

"Legend says it's what turns the unworthy into stone," the big man said, bouncing on his heels, "So you must have seen it."

The yellow gem on the gorgon's cheek came to mind.

"I would hate for Harbenigyr to fall into the same fate we did, my dear," Havarti said, "Unfortunately, it seems that preventing that means protecting this pompous lubberwort."

"Lubberwort?" Ophelia quirked an eyebrow, though the two others in the room must have figured the reaction was for what Raiko said.

"Just trust me when I say it was an insult," the sword replied mentally, "I vote that we help but I really do not like this Raiko fellow. Is there anyway we can help without benefiting him?"

"Maybe. I'll see what I can do," she said telepathically to Havarti before speaking up to the big man, "Yes I've seen Euryale's divine eye. Because I have, I even know how to remove it now. But why in the vast greenness of Honua would I want to help you get it? I can just wait for you to become a lawn ornament, take you upside, and watch birds crap on you for fun."

"I see Raiko has been his charming self since I've been gone," a woman with long silver hair not unlike the man with the rapier stepped into the room.

She was dressed in form fitting black leather from her high collar all the way down to her boots. The only parts of her body not covered by black were her pale face and her right arm which just had a glove covering her hand to the wrist.

The woman was indeed pale. Her skin was as white as ivory and just about as flawless. Her eyes were a darker shade of purple than Ophelia's tattoos, which wasn't a color you saw every day. Then the former assassin noticed that she had pointed ears, although quite a bit smaller than Harbenigyr's.

Only the new arrival's pasty left shoulder peeked out from between her skintight top and arm length black glove. In fact her left arm was noticeably longer than her right, by about a half a hand length.

"I am Saya Khushrenada," the pale woman gave Ophelia a formal curtsy, showing her to be a woman likely of noble birth, "Whatever my beau has done to offend you, I feel we should extend an apology for any discourtesy. Don't you agree, beloved?"

She focused her eyes on the big man in the long brown coat. After an awkward silence of his narrow eyes darting around to find some way out of answering, he finally nodded.

"Yes, dearest," he mumbled.

The pasty woman smiled, "Now we can be friends again. Lily, no one is killing each other in here, it's safe to come in," she called back to the doorway.

"Oh, good, the pheromone level in here was up to a worrisome level," a woman who was easily shorter than every other person in the room entered.

Lily had a pleasant smile on her face, the plain brown curls on her head spilling in every direction without any semblance of control. She was plump, not a body type one often came across among mercenaries and treasure hunters, who were often as hungry as they were often sick or injured.

She wore a dress anyone of common birth could buy from any tailor, except for the permanent earth stains around about where her knees were. Her nails told the same story, that she liked to dig around in dirt.

Lily carried with her a staff that was as tall as Ophelia. It looked to be made of interwoven vines that ultimately wrapped around a glowing stone at the apex. The jewel served as their main source of light.

"Now, did I hear that you have intimate knowledge of this divine eye that we've been commissioned to retrieve?" Saya stepped up to Ophelia, returning to business.

The former assassin nodded, "But your boyfriend there wasn't exactly motivating me to be all that helpful."

The pasty woman quirked a silver eyebrow, "Despite reanimating you from stone?"

Ophelia pointed to Harbenigyr, "That was the elf's doing. I could hear him," she nodded at Raiko, "complaining about waiting around every step of the way. Are you saying I owe you just because you're both elves?"

Saya let out an obviously annoyed sigh, "No, no I would never presume such a thing. Harbenigyr is of a truly *selfless* spirit. I must admit that I and my kind are not."

"Her kind?" Havarti queried.

"Your kind?" Ophelia asked out loud.

"I was born under the Griffin Mountains to the north, among the svartalfar Tribe of the Kizoku. All of us are albino," Saya spouted of the explanation so flatly that she was obviously asked about it often.

"I haven't heard of svartalfar having last names that weren't that of their tribe," Ophelia rested her hands on her hips.

Saya turned to face her *beau*, as she called him, looking in his direction even as she addressed the other, taller woman, "My father was not svartalfar."

"Thank you for the genealogy lesson," Ophelia weaved her way around Saya and Lily to the door, "Still not seeing why I should stick around."

Harbenigyr opened his mouth as if he were going to say something. Apparently, he couldn't think of anything so it shut moments later.

Again, Saya let out an annoyed sigh as she turned to face Ophelia, her purple eyes glaring at Raiko for every second she was able before focusing on the woman, "Would gold provide you enough incentive?"

The look on the big man's face was making every moment of this negotiation worth it for Ophelia, "How much were you thinking?"

The going rate for the services of an Al Razheem assassin was one hundred, one ounce size coins of gold per target, assuming no other objective besides the kill, of course. Hearing the number she'd throw out should be interesting.

"Five hundred gold," Saya offered, then added under her breath, "*Raiko had better stop costing me so much blasted money or Folken will cut me off again.*"

And thanks to Havarti's help, Ophelia heard it. Inside, the human woman was nigh unto giddy but, outwardly, she kept her face so still it could have still been stone. It was unfortunate that the pasty woman was going to be collateral damage to hurt Raiko in a way that wouldn't cause pain for the one who actually did help her back into the land of the living.

"Seven," the former assassin countered, "And I get paid if you turn into a statue or not."

Saya's left hand curled into a fist and Ophelia could have sworn that she'd heard it *humming*. Finally, though, the pasty woman nodded.

"Seven hundred gold," she agreed, "Provided that we obtain the divine eye, not just give it a valiant effort. Payment only comes from success."

Ophelia let herself smile wide, "Perfect! I'm pleased to be part of the team."

"My dear," Havarti's tone in her mind sounded more reserved than Ophelia's, "you do realize that we don't actually have any idea how to remove the divine eye from Euryale's face?"

SEVERAL HOURS LATER...

Harbenigyr leaned against his quarterstaff as the group stopped for another break. Lily was talking Ophelia, not giving the other woman a chance to get a word in edgewise. The cleric couldn't help being amused, he had his time as the target of the horticultural wizard's one sided conversation.

"We shoved the book in Raiko's hands, pushed him forward and told him to show the statue the book," Lily hadn't seemed to notice that they'd stopped, at least the news hadn't reached her mouth yet, "And he did. He held the book out right in front of the statue of the lion and do you know what happened next?"

Ophelia didn't even bother to try and answer, She made that mistake three times before she realized that the short woman's questions were rhetorical.

"The lion came to life and pounced him," Lily laughed, "It was the funniest thing I'd ever seen!"

"You do realize that the golem did almost kill us, don't you?" Saya asked Lily.

Saya was only diverting some of her attention to the plump wizard. Most of it was focused on the leather bladder now filling up with water thanks to a stalactite with a steady stream of water dripping from the tip.

"I didn't say that it wasn't terrifying then," Lily protested, "Looking back, though, it was hilarious!"

Raiko grumbled to himself as Saya handed the now full bladder to him. He snatched the water away from her and took a deep draw from the leather.

"Oh, don't take it personally," Ophelia had the most disingenuous air of sympathy as she spoke to the man, "Everyone has that moment where they're pounced by the lion. Figuratively, anyway."

"Like you with the gorgon?" the silver haired man snapped.

Ophelia worked hard to look nonchalant. Inside, though, she ran from enraged, depressed, to vindictive and back. Finally, she shrugged.

"I guess so," she said.

"How long do you figure you were in that state?" Harbenigyr asked as he took a seat where the floor met the wall.

"You would know better than I would," Ophelia said back to the cleric, "How long can someone be stone before they're past where they can be revived?"

The cleric shrugged, shaking his head, "I've never heard of it happening. If I had to guess, I would assume that a petrified person's condition would be like a real statue. Any wear would reflect your condition if you were returned to life."

"And how much *wear* did I show?"

"None. So it's likely that you haven't been down here too long," Harbenigyr answered, "But if I hadn't had this, I wouldn't have been able to even think about trying to bring you back."

He handed the former assassin the round tin that held the cream that he applied onto Ophelia's body when she was still as statue. She opened the tin and leaned in close to give it a sniff. If bland had a scent, this stuff had it. The woman thought that medicine and stuff like this always had to stink.

"What is it?" Ophelia shut the tin and handed it back.

"The man that beat Raiko in their duel gave it to me," Harbenigyr explained, "He said that we would need it to even get into these caverns. And he was right," the elf shivered.

"What can a cream do to open a door to get down here?" the woman looked from one member of the party to the next.

Lily answered, "The application we ended up having to use it for was on a long bricked over entryway beside the cathedral. It transformed each brick from granite into flesh. Without a circulatory system, though, the bricks quickly rotted away to open the path for us."

Ophelia felt her tongue reflexively slip from her mouth, "Gross."

"Yeah," The cleric quietly agreed.

"So you and you," Ophelia pointed at Saya and Lily, "met Raiko and Harby in Nauterhaus. But what why did you go there anyway? There can't be much call to go to a defunct wizarding school these days."

The two other women looked at each other. For the first time, Lily seemed reluctant to speak. The pasty lady was quiet for a long moment before she decided how to answer.

"For the same reason we are all still traveling together," Saya said, "We have similar motivations, if not related goals. Raiko seeks out relics and other treasures to finance his dueling. Despite losing his last *unofficial* match he actually is quite talented with the sword."

"And Harbenigyr doesn't really have a choice but to tag along at the moment," Ophelia added, "But what about you and Lily? What were you looking for in Nauterhaus?"

"Information," Saya answered, then continued, "My people have been attacked by a svartalfar tribe looking to expand its influence. There was word that some of their weapons came from the remains of the school."

"The Xaviour Tribe?" the former assassin guessed.

The noblewoman shook her head, "The Lytyl. The Xaviour Tribe has been keeping to themselves since the clan war treaty was signed. I'm sorry to say that your knowledge of subterranean politics is out of date."

"As it is for everyone above ground, Saya," Raiko chimed in as he stuffed the stopper into the bladder.

The pale woman nodded as she took the bladder back from her lover, "We should get moving. Where do you figure this Euryale is hiding?"

Ophelia looked at Saya quizzically, "Hiding? You haven't noticed that she's been tailing us for at least the last hour?"

The other woman's purple eyes narrowed, "What are you talking about?"

"That's how she caught me off guard last time," the woman in the long red coat explained, "I was so busy trying to find a way out I didn't realize that she was following me the whole time. She's following our scents, especially mine now that I'm moving again."

"And why is that?" Saya didn't like where this was heading.

"Did I forget to mention that I killed Euryale's sisters?" Ophelia said as she wiped stray dirt off her backside.

"No. No you did not mention that," the albino svartalfar spoke with a deliberate, slowly delivered tone, "Why didn't you mention that we were now sitting prey?"

"Oh, I wouldn't go that far," the former assassin started pulling her long coat off her shoulders, "I told you that she's tracking our scents. I doubt that she's close enough to hear us. She'll be cautious. Euryale won't just jump into a fight, especially now that I outnumber her."

"What are you talking about?" Saya asked.

Ophelia tossed her long coat to the pasty woman, "You are going to put that on and meander toward the exit, like you're not sure where it is. She'll be sure to catch up before you get there."

"And meanwhile you will be…?" the noblewoman scowled.

The former assassin had already turned away from Saya and knelt in front of Harbenigyr, "Do you have something really smelly?"

"Smelly?" the cleric's brow furrowed.

"Come on, healer types always have medicine that stinks to high heaven," Ophelia smirked, "I'm not asking for any powerful potion or elixir. Just some run of the mill herb or something that can mask my scent."

Now the rest of the party caught on to her plan. While Euryale followed Saya, Raiko, Lily and Harbenigyr, Ophelia would circle around and take the gorgon by surprise. Or she was going to rush for the way out while the monster hunted them, thinking that the one who killed her sisters was still with the party. That was the very concern that Raiko brought up, although in much less civil terms.

"And miss out on seven hundred gold coin?" Ophelia looked positively shocked at the idea, "What kind of mercenary do you take me for?"

"One that realizes she's out of her depth and trying to cut and run to save her own literally worthless hide," the big man snapped.

"You see that coat? That belonged to a Light Bringer who was very important to me," The human woman pointed at the very garment in Saya's hands, "If you rip it, get it turned to stone again or even stain it with gravy, I will personally chisel it off you whether you're a statue or not."

"Fine, Ophelia," Saya, not looking at all happy, slipped the long coat on, "We'll keep going west for seven more intersections, then we will turn north. We will stop at the last rectory before the exit. I presume that is where Euryale will intercept us?"

"Likely," the other woman agreed, snatching a green vial from the cleric's hand the moment he held it up to her.

Ophelia put a couple of dabs of the liquid on either side of her neck. Then she winced.

"I said smelly, Harby," again, she stuck her tongue out, "Not hair curling."

"It's lubberwort," the elf explained, "It's generally used to treat hyperthermia and heat exhaustion by slowing down the bodies natural processes when it's ingested."

"Why didn't you mention that before I started putting it on like perfume?"

"I said when it's ingested. Drank when it's liquid or eaten when it's still whole." Harbenigyr rose to his feet, "The liquid won't affect you by skin contact. But the smell won't last more than an hour or so."

"Outside of medical uses, it's considered a useless plant," Havarti added in the woman's mind, "Hence why it can be used as an insult."

Ophelia smirked, "Clever boy."

The former assassin walked around the intersection, dripping the contents of the vial at random points, even splashing some on the covers of the various sepulchers. Once the vial was empty, she tossed it back to the cleric, who tucked it back into one of the many pouches on his belt.

Then Ophelia stepped up beside Saya, sliding her hand up along the woman's back, "You better get moving. After."

Saya stopped just short of glaring but definitely stared at the other woman, "After what?"

"I get Havarti back," Ophelia pulled her bastard sword, scabbard and all out of the compartment in the back of the long coat, "You better get moving."

"You named your sword after cheese?" Lily asked, looking as if the idea itself was silly.

The former assassin looked from the wizard to her bastard sword. A tense moment of silence passed and Ophelia finally shook her head.

"It's a sore subject. I'll explain later."

Slipping Havarti into her belt the woman climbed into one of the sepulchers from which the plaque cover had fallen away. After she slipped out of view, Saya and the others started down the hall.

"Why are we counting on this woman again?" Raiko spoke quietly, his eyes darting around to try and spot whatever was stalking them.

"We aren't," Saya answered, equally muted, "We've come up with a plan to anticipate the ambush. If Ophelia shows, it will only make the fight turn in our favor earlier."

The noblewoman shrugged uncomfortably in the long leather coat. It felt... cumbersome around her body. She tucked her left hand into the pocket and was surprised when her fingers found something.

Removing her hand, Saya pulled out a leather string. Hanging from the bottom of it was what looked like a basilisk claw holding a shield.

"Am I wrong, or is this the insignia of the Night Shield?" she presented the thong and pendant to the man beside her.

He nodded, "So she wasn't lying about that, at least."

"Do you think she was a Light Bringer or a Night Shield before she was petrified?" Harbenigyr chimed in to the conversation.

Both Saya and Lily shook their heads.

It was the horticultural wizard who actually answered, "If she was a Light Bringer, she never would have agreed to payment. It is against the organization's code of conduct. If she was a Night Shield, she never would have mentioned the Light Bringers at all. The Night Shield isn't recognized for field work, their responsibilities revolve around criminal defense in the Light Bringer tribunal system."

"How do you know all this?" the cleric asked.

Neither answered that.

Raiko's hand suddenly wrapped around the handle of his sword. He motioned behind the walking group, down the left branch of the last intersection they just passed.

This was early. They needed the space of the rectory to use their number advantage. With no other way out, the gorgon wouldn't have any place to hide. Fighting in the halls, the monster would be able to duck in and out of the intersections and being out-numbered wouldn't matter.

"Ja, you're not her!" a voice echoed from the intersection, "Where is she, ne?"

"Who?" Saya motioned for everyone to continue as she turned back to face the still unseen gorgon.

"Ja, the one whose clothing you are wearing," Euryale slithered out from around the corner, holding scimitars in each hand.

"This thing?" the noblewoman tugged out on the collar of the long coat, giving it a little sniff and cringing, "I admit it's not my color but the previous owner didn't seem too attached to it."

"Where. Is. She, ne?" the gorgon closed the distance between herself and the pale woman.

It wasn't until then that Saya felt so alone. The rest of the party had already turned the corner. That was the plan, of course, that she would stall the monster while they continued on. Still, it didn't make the next part any less unnerving.

"I just realized," the pale woman started tugging at a string tied in the palm of the glove on her left hand, "You've not told me your name. I am Saya Khushrenada of the Romefeller Guilds."

"Ja, you are in my way, spy," Euryale started to pull back her left scimitar to strike the woman down.

"I see you have heard of us," Saya smirked, "Although, I personally prefer *intelligence operator*. Do you know why that term is more agreeable than *spy*?"

"Ja, I do not pretend to care!" the curved blade slashed for the silver haired woman.

Saya lifted her left hand, a small pocket untied and open in her palm, "In my guild, we pride ourselves in considering every contingency."

She pushed a fingertip into the back of her hand and polished, charcoal colored metal emerged from the woman's palm. The sword struck the revealed piece of metal and there was a sudden flash of light, a flare of smoke, and Saya no longer where she had been.

Euryale coughed and spat as she rushed through the rolling cloud of white, her amber eyes watering as she searched for any sign of the woman wearing Ophelia's coat. With the smoke behind her, the gorgon caught the scent again.

Following it, the gorgon realized that the Romefeller spy turned the corner and ducked into the rectory down the hall. The monster felt a smirk stretch her lips as she caught the scents of the others who had been walking with the pale woman. It was a trap and she would not fall for it.

"Ja, I do hope that you enjoy it in there," Euryale called before slithering beside the open door.

Slipping the curved back of one of her swords into the handle of the ajar door, the gorgon pulled it closed. It slammed shut, echoing through the halls of the crypt. With a heavy grunt, the monster stabbed her sword into the doorjamb, effectively using the weapon like a makeshift deadbolt.

"Ja, I will bury this room!" the gorgon pressed her lips to the worn wood as she screamed through it into the rectory, "Ja, no one will even know you were here! You will remember this when you realize that all you had to do was give me Ophelia, ne?"

Inside the room, Raiko slammed his massive shoulder against the door. Wincing, his eyes bore into the unforgiving barrier. He took pleasure in the mental picture of Euryale jumping back in surprise, maybe with a bloody nose, at hitting the door so quickly that it was like he was responding to her message.

"Apparently, Euryale wasn't as blinded by hatred as Ophelia thought," Harbenigyr said.

"Apparently," Saya folded her arms in front of her chest.

Raiko pressed his hands to the sides of the locked entryway, "This would take me some time to get through," he concluded before looking back at the plump wizard, "Can you do something, Lily?"

The short woman with the wild hair looked around the room, her little mouth pursed tightly shut, "The ventilation in here is not very good... any fire would suffocate us before we burned through... ice would only further fortify the door rather than make it brittle... vines could wrench the door from the jamb" her talking was more muttering to herself than answering the duelist's question, "if we could upend a stone to get to soil."

"So no," the big man grumbled.

Raiko reared back and then slammed his foot into the door. The sound of the hit echoed with painful intensity in the room but surely through the halls outside as well. He threw his other foot forward when the gorgon's sword suddenly pierced through, just missing the man's leather boot.

The man fell to the floor. The blade pulled back through the door. No one was positive, or said anything about it, but they all could have sworn they heard the gorgon chortling outside.

"That thing is strong," Raiko panted, "I couldn't even shove a blade through that."

"So she can keep us away from the door," Saya knelt down beside her lover, "But she said that she was going to bury us. How could she accomplish that?" She looked from Raiko, to Lily, and then to Harby.

All looked equally clueless.

"I don't think that we should wait around to find out!" Ophelia's voice floated into the room.

Each member of the party looked in every direction but couldn't see the woman. Yet her voice was as clear as if she was standing right beside them.

"I mean, come on!" The former assassin started talking again, "Even if Raiko does get stabbed, we can just keep throwing his body against the door like a battering ram!"

"That woman is in there, ne?!" The door shuddered as Euryale assaulted it, "Ja, Ophelia, you coward! How did you slink your way in, ne?"

Ophelia laughed, "The same way we're getting out, snake face! Why do you think you couldn't find me? I cleared the way out!"

"Ja, liar!" the gorgon screamed, her voice muffled by the door, "There is no way out!"

Harbenigyr and Saya shrugged at each other. Neither could figure out how the former assassin was doing this. Lily was digging through one of the leather bags that hung off her rope belt. She wasn't sure what was happening but she had an idea of what the next step was going to be.

As did Raiko. He lifted himself back up to his feet, drawing his rapier free of his belt. The big man strode over to the door, leaning against the wall beside it, and waited.

"Say goodbye to the scaly monster, kids!" Ophelia's voice ordered.

Harbenigyr chewed on his lower lip for a long moment before actually speaking, "Goodbye!" He yelled, sounding far more excited than he felt.

The elf bumped Saya on the shoulder. She looked back at the cleric as if he'd violated some unwritten rule but then, after a quiet sigh...

"I would say that we will meet again, Euryale," the Romefeller operative lent a regal air to her words as she spoke, "But you and I both know that is a lie. I'll see you buried in the rubble after we leave."

The gorgon shrieked with rage. The door was jostled with a heavy crack. Then it buckled after another fierce hit.

One more hit and the wood door crumbled into little more than kindling. Euryale charged into the room, wildly swinging her swords as she dove headlong at Harby and Saya, the first two people she saw.

The cleric blocked her first strikes from hitting Saya and him with his quarterstaff. Before another blow landed, the pale woman wrapped her right hand around her left forearm and pulled a curved dagger with a short blade free from under the black leather glove. She slashed up at the gorgon's wrists, drawing blood and making Euryale drop one of her swords.

When Saya withdrew the weapon, the blade was already more holes than steel anymore. Tossing it away, the woman and the cleric scrambled away from the monster.

"Her blood's acid, Raiko!" the woman yelled to the duelist.

That stopped the charging man in his tracks. He suddenly realized that his weapon was gone if he hit a good wound. He glared down at the hilt, cursing himself for his sudden indecisiveness.

Seeing the big man's hesitation, Lily stepped up, throwing a dull brown disk, about the size of the gold coin, at the monster. It landed on the gorgon's back, somehow sticking to one of the faint, pale skin colored scales.

Then the wizard pulled another disk from her bag, licking it and then spinning it between her fingers. A bolt of lightning suddenly leaped from the wizard and struck Euryale in the back. Unlike a natural bolt, though, the crackling light stayed hanging in the air between the monster and Lily. The gorgon was suddenly unable to move of her own volition other that convulse in pain where she stood.

Ophelia dashed through the doorway into the room. As she ran, she interrupted her stride just enough to slow down beside the duelist.

"You wuss," she muttered into Raiko's ear.

She snatched the duelist's sword from his hand and charged at the gorgon. Lily wrapped both of her hands around the dull coin in her hand, cutting off the flow of lightning as Ophelia jumped onto Euryale's back.

"Your hair looks lopsided, darling," the former assassin wrapped her legs around the monster's narrow waist as she raised the rapier, "What you do say we even it out?"

With two slashes, Ophelia severed the tendrils from the gorgon's head that she didn't get to in their first confrontation. Spreading her legs, Ophelia fell from the monsters and rolled away before the acidic blood could dribble onto her skin.

She tossed the hilt of the rapier, the six inches of remaining blade still steaming, back to Raiko. The weapon landed at the big man's feet with a quiet clatter.

Euryale, her face and hands drenched in her own indigo blood, fruitlessly tried to stop the bleeding with her own palms. Every drop that fell from her chin or elbows landed on the stone floor with a burning hiss.

The monster was now unarmed and in so much pain that she was practically defenseless. Except for her blood. No one dared get too close lest they get burned by its acidic properties.

Ophelia rushed over to the cleric. His black eyes were locked on the shuddering monster. He looked as if he was in almost as much pain as Euryale was. It took the woman shaking the elf by his shoulders to get him to acknowledge her.

"Do you have anything that can neutralize the acid, Harby?" she asked.

The cleric went through a mental inventory in his head. Something occurred to him, but he hesitated to say.

"Come on!" Ophelia snapped, "You know she was going to have to die. Did you think she was going to just give you one of her eyes?"

The woman looked over at Euryale as she curled her long legs around herself. She wasn't wailing and thrashing around anymore, in fact, she was weeping and whispering something that Ophelia and the others couldn't understand.

For something that was such an enraged beast only moments before, Euryale's cries reminded Ophelia of Inara Browder's pleas as she carved the life from the woman's body. The former assassin lost her grin and her stomach tightened.

Euryale was a monster, that was true. But Ophelia had been so preoccupied with what she had lost in their battle that she had forgotten that the gorgon had lost her entire family as well. And, like Ophelia, Euryale had been a pawn of Efreeti so it was possible that they had not wanted to come after Ophelia, Travus and Tilly in the first place.

Even if she had been a willing minion of the Doctor, he had left Euryale down here for who knows how long to linger alone in her misery. It was a misery that Ophelia had only made physically manifest thanks to her attack.

"I didn't–" Harby stammered, "I knew it had to happen. I just– didn't expect her to sound so much– like a person."

Ophelia turned back to the cleric, "I know. I'm sorry to ask for your help killing her but at this point, Harby, it would be mercy. Let me end her pain, okay? She'll be with her family again. Euryale's been mourning them as long as we've both been down here."

His hand shaking, Harbenigyr pulled a leather packet out from one of his pouches, "This powder can neutralize several different types of organic acid. It should stop her bleeding and make her safe to... touch." His voice was flat, hopeless.

"Thank you." Ophelia said, her voice gentle.

She stepped away from the cleric but didn't turn immediately toward the gorgon. Instead, she walked toward the corner where a couple of stalagmites had formed, the two tallest coming up to her chest.

"I need you Havarti," she said.

"Of course, my dear," the bastard sword vocally responded.

Ophelia bent down and pulled the sword, scabbard and all, from behind the pointed deposits of minerals. After slipping him into her belt, the woman tugged at something else. Something that no one else could see but it whatever it was seemed to be coming from the thin ventilation hole near the ceiling. Her hands moved as if she was winding up rope.

Then she turned her attention to the gorgon. Stopping just outside of the monster's reach, Ophelia opened the packet and poured the powder. She was careful, just covering the wounds on her head. Just that much seemed to sting as it was.

The bleeding quickly slowed, then stopped. Euryale's amber eyes slowly opened and turned to look up at the human, not understanding what just happened.

Ophelia knew precisely where not to look now, not that the gorgon seemed intent on attacking again. At least not at the moment.

"What are you doing, ne?" Euryale whispered.

"You just reminded me of someone I killed awhile back," the human answered, "It made me remember how much I regretted it, even though I didn't have a choice in the matter."

"Ja, I would have thought killing me would have been a great boon for you," the gorgon said.

"I thought it would be, yeah," Ophelia agreed, "As far as I know, you came willingly to kill me, right? Then you took my family."

"Ja, as you took mine," Euryale hissed.

The human rested her hand on Havarti's hilt, "That's why we're talking now."

"You are not going to kill me then, ne?" the gorgon looked skeptical.

Ophelia shook her head, "Don't misunderstand me, Euryale. I have to kill you. You see them?" She pointed at Harbenigyr, Lily and Saya (Raiko did happen to be in their general vicinity, as well).

Despite being told that she was going to die, the gorgon did not jump to a defensive posture or lash out in a preemptive attack. She simply looked in the direction the human indicated and nodded.

"The big guy has to pay a debt that includes having to retrieve your divine eye," Ophelia explained, "Now, if reneging on this only affected him, I'd say let him rot but that one," she pointed at the cleric in white, "he's the one who brought me back to life. Seeing you in pain horrified him so I know he doesn't have it in him to finish you off but, if you live, he'll suffer the same fate as Raiko."

"So knowing that another's life is a bartering key is supposed to make me willing to sacrifice myself, ne?"

Ophelia shook her head, "What I wanted you to know, to hopefully understand, was that I wanted to kill you out of anger before. Now, it's to protect them."

"Ja, I have become... tired after all this time," Euryale said, "Ja, I have been alone as I never have before. Ja, I used to think my sisters constant nattering was dreadful but I have found myself longing to hear it again."

Ophelia quirked an eyebrow, "Are you saying that you're going to let me kill you?"

The gorgon shook her head. The motion caused a wave of nausea to shoot through her as twinges of pain made her face twitch. After a few seconds, she had recollected herself.

"Ja, now you must understand me," Euryale spoke softly, "Ja, I will not resign myself to death. Ja, I will fight fang and scale to send you to meet it rather than I. Ja, it is our way and my sisters would be ashamed if I simply laid down for you. Ja, if I were to die in battle, I know that my sisters would welcome me."

The human was quiet for a long moment, "What were you whispering?" she finally asked, "Before I put the powder on your wounds, you were whispering something to yourself."

"Ja, it is what we gorgons call the Death Note," Euryale answered, "Ja, if we've breath when we are defeated, we are to chant it so that our loved ones beyond can find us faster."

"So you considered yourself defeated?"

The gorgon reluctantly nodded, "Ja, I was in so much pain I could not see. Ja, could not hear or taste the air. Ja, however I can now. Shall we finish this, ne?"

Ophelia look a deep breath, held it for a long moment, then finally let it go, "You're ready then?"

Slowly, with deliberately careful movements, Euryale stood back up. Ophelia followed suit and the two warriors stood facing each other.

The gorgon motioned to the rest of the human's party, "They will not interfere?"

Ophelia pulled Havarti and his scabbard free of her belt. She tossed the bastard sword to Harbenigyr, who caught him awkwardly. He even had to press his knees together to keep the sword from sliding out from between his arms and clatter onto the ground.

"Hold onto him for a minute, will you?" she requested of the cleric.

The elf nodded. None of the party even pretended to understand what was happening but none of them stepped forward to intervene. Raiko was even less inclined to do so than the others as he bitterly clung to the remains of his bejeweled rapier's hilt.

Euryale slashed her sharpened claws at the human, who ducked under the strike and countered with a punch of her own that was as easily avoided. The two women circled each other as they sized each other up, looking for an opening.

Finally, the gorgon dove for Ophelia's legs, trying to pull them out from under her. The woman hopped back, driving Euryale's face into the stone floor. The former assassin jumped on top of the monster and the two grappled, trying to pin the other to the ground.

Euryale didn't appear to have a solid bone in her body as she bent and twisted all around Ophelia. The gorgon wrapped a leg around the woman's neck and started to squeeze.

The world started to fade away and Ophelia could only move one part of her body. She opened her mouth wide and sank her teeth into the flesh of the inside of Euryale's thigh.

The gorgon's leg involuntarily loosed its grip. It wasn't much but Ophelia was able to pull herself up from between Euryale's legs.

Again the women struggled for dominance. This time, the human pinned the gorgon down, wrapping a hand around the monster's throat.

She didn't just squeeze, Ophelia pushed the gorgon back until her head struck the stone floor with a dull thud. Euryale couldn't wrench the human's hand free so she did the only thing she could... she stabbed her sharp claws into Ophelia's throat.

Ophelia blinked, disappeared and reappeared three feet above the gorgon in a violet fog. Falling on top of the monster, the woman focused the weight of her whole body down on the few inches of Euryale's neck.

The former assassin felt the gorgon's windpipe snap under her forearm. Euryale's entire body tensed as air gurgled from her mouth, not able to figure out which way it was supposed to go.

Finally, the gorgon fell limp. But Ophelia didn't feel like much of a victor. She took her sword back from the cleric and returned to the body of her fallen opponent.

"We should be able to use what's left of the Thread of Fate to take her head off," she pulled the nearly invisible wire from around the crossbar of her sword and starting to do just as she described, "The powder will keep her blood from eating everything and then you can give it to your better, Raiko. He can remove the divine eye himself."

Lily produced a bag for Ophelia to put the gorgon's head. After sprinkling the last of the powder all over Euryale's now severed head, it was put in.

Ophelia then tossed it to Raiko, who didn't look at all thankful. The former assassin stepped up to Saya, who was missing the middle of her left hand, and was inspecting the missing part of her palm.

"Can we get out of here now?" Ophelia said to the pale woman, "I don't want to be down here anymore."

TWENTY-THREE

THE BEGINNING IS THE END IS THE BEGINNING

At sunrise...

Back in her long red leather coat, complete with Havarti back in his proper place on Ophelia's back, the party emerged from the side of the grass covered hill. This part of the cemetery was far more decrepit than the part where Ophelia, Travus and Tilly had initially entered.

Looking at the various headstones, they were too worn to be able to read. The statues were barely shaped like angels or people or whatever beasts they were carved to be originally.

For some reason, Ophelia was reluctant to look up. When she did, though, a gasp that took her entire breath escaped her mouth.

"What is that?" she could barely whisper.

Harbenigyr looked confused by the question, "That is the Juna Cathedral," he answered simply.

It was huge! The last time Ophelia saw it was only one floor tall. Now there were at least three spires on each corner of the building.

The cresting morning light reflected from the many stained glass windows that lined the side of the cathedral's silhouette.

Urehara said that it was going to be at least ten years before it was finished. Ten years.

"How long has the cathedral been *finished*?" she asked.

Harbenigyr shrugged, "I haven't been on the continent long and Juna isn't the goddess of my Order. So I have to admit that I have no idea."

She turned toward Saya.

"It's been complete as long as I remember," the pale woman answered.

"Is the Hotel Gruber still around?" Ophelia scanned the rest of the skyline of the city even though there was no way she could see the place she mentioned at any time.

The Romefeller operative nodded, "That is where we are all staying at the moment."

"I'll be there by sundown," Ophelia said starting to march toward the city, "Have my money then."

She didn't even linger long enough for Saya or anyone else to answer. The former assassin walked up to the main doors of the cathedral. They looked exactly like they did the last time Ophelia stepped through them, although the long shadow the building cast beyond the stairs and onto the road beyond was new.

The woman thought about going in, seeing what else had changed but she didn't. But she wasn't quite ready to move on yet. Looking around, the street was deserted except for her. The town had not awoken yet. Since there was no one to overhear...

"So what were you going to tell me?" Ophelia asked.

"Pardon me?" Havarti replied.

"You were going to tell me something before I became a lawn ornament," the woman said, "About my family."

"Oh," the sword answered, "I don't know if it would be *appropriate* now."

"Appropriate?"

"You forget, my dear," Havarti said gently, "I know where you want to go. What I was going to tell you was from him, remember?"

Ophelia nodded. The sword was subtly hinting that there was no more putting it off. It was time to move on to the Light Bringer outpost, assuming it was still there. She knew how to get there from the cathedral.

The trip was a lot longer on foot than it was in a coach. By the time she reached the familiar looking building, the sun had climbed a good distance into the blue sky. The sign in front was different, made from a different wood and painted in different colors than the previous but it said the same thing:

LIGHT BRINGERS
RIVERBELT OUTPOST
#1701

"Go on," Havarti urged.

Ophelia stepped down the walkway to the door. Then stopped. She took another step forward but her other foot wouldn't rise from the street.

"My dear," the sword spoke gently, "you want to know what happened to them. Staying out here will not give you that."

"Yeah but what if I'm right and they did get crushed?" the woman stuffed her hands into the pockets of her coat.

"You aren't sure," Havarti answered, "Neither am I. But whatever their fates were, we will be better off for knowing, rather than have the uncertainty gnaw at both of us."

"Alright. Okay," Ophelia took a deep breath and started forward again.

Her knuckles cracked when her fingers wrapped around the handle of the door. It took everything Ophelia had to pull the door open, then she had to find more to actually step inside.

"Welcome back, Light Bringer," the man sitting behind the window in the wall said as she stepped inside, "What was your duty assignment?"

It took Ophelia a moment to realize that he was talking to her. She stepped up to the window which was set high in the wall, just like before. It was then that she had no idea what to say.

"Um, er," her mouth opened, closed and even made sounds but nothing that made any sense that came out until, "ah, I don't suppose that Colonel Dende is still in command here?"

The man looked up from whatever paperwork he was looking over. His skin was dark brown, the same shade as melted fudge. His dirty blonde hair reminded the woman of the very Colonel to whom she was referring, although it was a bit longer. It just threatened to go down past his eyebrows.

He smiled politely, the little tuft of gold hair on his chin barely budging, as he looked her over. Tucking the stack of parchments off to the side, he focused all of his attention of the woman as he answered.

"I'm afraid I don't know that name. Our current commanding officer is General Pierce."

"Oh," Ophelia was again at a loss.

"You're not a Light Bringer, are you?" the man tapped the symbol of the shining sword on the front of his tunic.

The woman shook her head, "No, a Night Shield gave me this coat a, a long time ago."

"What brings you here then?" the Light Bringer asked, giving her a look that Ophelia didn't know how to interpret (beyond maybe indigestion?).

"I was hoping I could find out what happened to the one who gave me this," Ophelia tugged on her coat, "And his daughter."

The man in the window grunted (an argument for the indigestion theory?), "Maybe you should speak with Colonel Mitchell. I'll send a runner."

"Thanks, Captain...?" the woman trailed off.

"My name is Cameron," he gave her an almost formal bow as he stood up.

The Light Bringer disappeared from the window but reappeared only seconds later when he opened the door to give her access to the rooms beyond. The man guided her to an office that was only a couple of doors down the hall.

He asked her to wait there for Colonel Mitchell. Ophelia agreed, although she didn't sit in the lone chair that wasn't behind the desk.

The wall behind the polished desk, cherry wood if she had to guess, had two separate book cases resting in front of it. One had tomes on the various laws of different lands and instructions on procedures that Light Bringers and Night Shields utilized in different circumstances.

The other had a clepsydrae that told anyone in the room the time of day and books of a more whimsical nature. Everything from *Maiden Peridot and the Revenant* to some books that had titles that sounded downright scandalous.

Before Ophelia could explore any further, the door to the office opened and a woman in a red cape stepped inside. Under the cape she wore leather armor that had bronze and silver swirled together to shape into the symbol of the Light Bringers.

The woman that Ophelia presumed to be Colonel Mitchell had auburn colored hair, cut to the length of her shoulders. She wiped a few stray strands out of her eyes and behind her ear, exposing hidden streaks of gray.

Her eyes were chocolate colored with thin lines that fanned out from the outer corners. When she saw Ophelia standing in the middle of the room, Colonel Mitchell didn't look as if she was expecting her. Had the runner missed her and she found her way to her office regardless?

"Are you the one who was asking about a Night Shield?" the armor wearing woman asked.

So she did know that Ophelia was in here, "Yes. My name is Ophelia."

"Ophelia what?" the other woman asked as she stepped around the former assassin, heading for her well cushioned chair.

"Just Ophelia." she shrugged.

The woman nodded, as if expecting that answer, but Colonel Mitchell didn't look as if she believed her, "What Night Shield are you asking after, just Ophelia?"

"Travus Browder," she answered.

"That's a name I haven't heard in a long time. A long time," the Light Bringer leaned back in her seat.

"You know him?" Ophelia's stomach bounced.

"Knew him," the woman nodded, "He was my first trainer when I joined the Libs."

"The Libs?"

"Our pet name for the Light Bringers," the Colonel explained.

Despite what the other woman said, Ophelia felt her stomach sink when she realized, "You said that you knew him. In the past tense."

The Light Bringer let out a breathy sigh, "He died about five years ago."

"Five years," Despite the news of the man's passing, Ophelia couldn't help but smile, "Then he did survive the tunnel collapse."

"Tunnel collapse?" Colonel Mitchell wrapped her hand around her chin, "He was almost killed by a cave in on the graveyard grounds thirty years ago."

"That long?" the former assassin had to grab the edge of the Light Bringer's desk to keep standing, "What about Tilly?"

"What about her?"

"She was in the tunnel when it collapsed, too," Ophelia said, "Did she survive, too?"

The Colonel's eyebrows pressed together. "Yes."

The other woman waited for the Light Bringer to clarify further. When she didn't Ophelia spoke up again.

"Is she still alive now?" she asked.

Colonel Mitchell chewed on her lower lip, her brown eyes slowly drawing across the other woman, "She is."

With that, Ophelia found her way into the only other chair in the room. She looked relaxed to the point of melting, at least figuratively, as she leaned back in the leather wrapped chair.

After a peaceful, if unsure silence, Ophelia finally looked up at the Light Bringer, "She's alright, isn't she? She has a family of her own, or a successful career or something of the like?" she asked.

"I think it's safe to say yes to that," Colonel Mitchell leaned forward and rested her elbows on her desk, "She traveled around for a few years but she finally came back here to settle in Riverbelt around the time of her father's passing..."

She trailed off when Ophelia started staring at her, her pale blue eyes narrowing at the Light Bringer before she had even finished speaking. The Colonel straightened up in the chair, interlacing her fingers on her lap before actually speaking. It had been a long time since anyone's gaze was able to make her uncomfortable.

"Tilly?" Ophelia's pale blue eyes dropped down to look at the cherry wood desk rather than the other woman as she finally spoke up, "You're Tilly aren't you? You have the same little mole in your left eyebrow."

"How in the world can you see that from there?" the other woman asked, raising a hand to her temple.

It was the Colonel's turn to wait for Ophelia to explain further. Like Ophelia before, though, the Light Bringer didn't receive any further information.

"I go by Tillyria now," the middle aged woman said, "or Colonel Mitchell or Ma'am to my subordinates."

Ophelia lifted herself from the chair, again shaking her head, "I couldn't see your mole, Tilly, er, Tillyria. It just occurred to me that no one as high ranking as you would see someone off the street asking about a," she gulped, "long dead Night Shield."

"You never were stupid," the older looking woman sighed, "You're right, of course. I wanted to make sure that you were, well, really you before I told you. I would think seeing me now compared to when I was twelve would be a bit of a shock."

"You are right about that," Ophelia nodded, "But Mitchell now? That means you're married?"

"I am. In fact, you met my husband up front. He recognized who you were from the stories I've told him," Colonel Mitchell rose to her feet herself and stepped around her desk toward the other woman, "Where have you been all this time?"

"I was… trapped in the crypts with Euryale," Ophelia answered, "I only got out just around dawn thanks to a party of, well, a mish mash of a group anyway, that found their way in."

"I am so sorry I didn't come back for you," the Light Bringer closed her eyes tight as she leaned back against the front of her desk, "I mean, I've tried to find ways down off and on over the years but, apparently, not hard enough. Can you forgive me?"

"Forgive you?" the former assassin's thick eyebrows pressed together as she looked up at the other woman, "For what? I'm the one who turned your life upside down and made you a target of the Al Razheem in the first place!"

"The Al Razheem?" Tillyria's still closed eyes flicked one way and then another, as if she was searching through some kind of mental filing cabinet, "They're stuck underground playing some part in the unrest between the Lytyl and Xaviour Tribes. I haven't even heard the name in years."

"To me, it has only been a couple of days since I last saw you, Tilly," Ophelia sighed, "I wanted to ask you to forgive me every time we had to run to a new town."

"You had that when you convinced my father to let me surf on top of the carriage that took us out of Wildesvale. Remember? He never would have let me do that without you there," The Colonel chuckled, "Looking back at our time together, you, Dad, and me, he and I both agreed that it was one of the most *exciting* times of our lives. When we weren't about to get stabbed, anyway."

Ophelia wanted to ask, but she wasn't sure if what she wanted to know was appropriate, "Your father, Tilly, did he ever remarry? Did you ever get a new mother?" the questions came out anyway.

The Light Bringer looked taken aback at the suddenness of the questions. The shock only lasted for a moment, though.

She shook her head, "No, he never remarried. He couldn't find anyone that could match up to Mom. Or you."

"Or me?" Ophelia let a wry, soft laugh slip from her lips, "He could have just strolled up to any trollop at any bar to find someone like me."

The Light Bringer had to bite her lip to keep the rush of anger from slipping out in words she'd likely regret. She was Ophelia, all right. She was the only one that could make her this angry that quickly.

"I need to show you something," Colonel Mitchell said, her voice slowly calming as she circled back behind her desk and pulled a drawer open, "Daddy always had a feeling that you would come back. Before he passed on, he wrote a note for me to give you."

Tillyria pulled a folded piece of parchment out of the drawer and held it out to the younger looking woman. It was sealed with stamped wax that had the basilisk claw and shield symbol of the Night Shield on it. Ophelia stood and took it, looking down at the document unsurely.

"Have you read it?" she asked.

"He dictated it to me," the Light Bringer answered, "I wrote down every word he said. Being his daughter, some of it was *awkward*," she blushed.

Ophelia did little more than breathe for a long, long moment. Finally, though, she nodded.

"Thank you."

The other woman smiled back, "Would you like to be alone to read it?"

The woman in the long red coat shifted her weight from one foot to the other, trying to decide. Her pale eyes shifted to look at the brass hilt of her sword just over her shoulder.

"Yes, yes she would," Havarti answered for her, "Thank you, Tillyria."

The woman's eyes lit up at recognition of the disembodied voice. The dripping of the clepsydrae was the only sound in the room as she walked around the desk.

"I'm glad you're still with her, Havarti. She'd be a real mess without you," the Light Bringer's smile only got wider as she gave the sword a playful flick on the hilt before stepping to the door, "I'll be just outside. Let me know when you're done."

Ophelia nodded but otherwise stayed motionless as the door closed. This was more than she could have hoped for. She'd come back to life certain that Travus and Tilly were dead. Now known by her full name, Tillyria, she had followed her father's footsteps and become a Light Bringer. And she was married to boot!

Travus had lived for decades after they were separated. While she and he wouldn't have some kind of tearful reunion (or a night to get reacquainted), Travus had left her a message.

"Perhaps you should sit down before you read it," Havarti suggested.

"Hmm?" Ophelia shook her head to pull herself out of her stupor, "Oh, yeah. Good idea."

She did just that. Dropping back into the chair she'd just vacated. Her hand shook as she slipped a finger under the wax seal and broke it. She unfolded the parchment and started to read.

Dearest Ophelia,

Yes, I know you never would have expected me to address you in such a manner but, as time has passed, I have come to think of you that way. Perhaps you expected me to start with something more melancholy like the death of my wife.

It's true, Ophelia, that you were the instrument that killed her. Remember, though, that you weren't in control of your actions at the time. It took that bastard Rubenesquire to make me understand just how powerless that can make someone feel.

It was not your fault! Inara would agree with me, too. Even Tilly thinks so. (She goes by Tillyria to try and seem more grown up. She's glaring at me now because she promised to write down every word I said and she didn't want you to know that.)

But now we come to the reason that I decided to write this letter. My health is failing but there are some things that were taken from you that I think you deserve to have back. I know you will return someday and I won't let that (a colorful word for minotaur excrement. I couldn't bring myself to write that, sorry. -Tilly) Efreeti win.

Your parents, Ophelia. You deserve to know about your parents. You were taken from them a few months before Efreeti put those runes on your back and took your memories.

I only knew them for a short time but they told me so much about you as a child. Their love for you was so obvious.

They came after you, Ophelia. You parents fought so hard to try and get you back. I know you didn't realize it at the time, but you actually saw them.

It was shortly after we first met and–

Ophelia's vision became so blurry that she couldn't read anymore. She blinked and blinked but tears kept streaming down her cheeks.

The woman wasn't sure she wanted to read anymore. It was that one word that Travus used: "try". That means that they failed and that Ophelia could have been the one to kill them. Especially if it was the night that Travus stormed the Oasis with his band of mercenaries.

She had killed over half of them herself. What if she *had* been the one to run them through? Did they die cursing their own daughter?

"Ophelia," Havarti's voice was gentle, "Ophelia, you need to keep reading. It isn't what you think."

How couldn't it be? She wondered, aware that her sword could sense the question as well. Ophelia steeled herself to continue, wishing that she had something to fight to the death with at the moment. Surely, that would be easier.

It was shortly after we first met and you were escorting me up to see the General. Remember the animal pens? The woman who sacrificed herself to kill the hell hound. I think you realized that there was something familiar about her.

That was your mother Ophelia. Her name was Perse. She was a brilliant chemist. She was the one who made the explosives that were strong enough to breach the walls. No, that's not the important part that you should know about her.

You look so much like Perse. She said that you both even had the same jade green eye color, although you definitely inherited your father's nose. Perse was the one who taught you to braid your hair the way you do. Apparently, it's a family tradition. You still do it the exact same way she did, Ophelia. Efreeti couldn't take that from you.

Your father was the mountain of a man you saw in the General's office. Even as he was dying, he told you that he loved you.

He was the one who brewed that honeybark ale that you liked so much. He would let you sneak sips of it when you were growing up, much to your mother's chagrin.

Even though you can't get that honeybark ale brewed by him personally anymore, I made sure his recipe was distributed to every tavern owner I knew. Have a drink in your parent's honor, Ophelia.

Remember that they loved you and fought for you. They may not have lived to see you regain your freedom but you have it now.

I'm sure Tilly has told you that I never remarried. That is because I could never bring myself to love someone as much as I loved Inara.

I know that is an odd thing to write in a letter to you, Ophelia, but it is true. I loved my wife and still hold our vows sacred. I still feel that way. But I do love you, too. We never had the chance to go through with taking vows, although I am not sure if you were ready for that step by the time we parted. I am thankful for the time we had.

I was lucky enough in this life to fall in love with two women. One was the mother of my beloved daughter, the other showed us how to carry on regardless of the challenges and dangers put before us. In case that was unclear, that was you, Ophelia. You taught both me and Tilly to carry on.

That and that thing with the candle wax. It was the only time we had a proper bed but... Tilly is practically glowing, she's blushing so bright! So, for her sake I won't go into more detail. Besides, I'm sure that you remember that little escapade...

Ophelia found herself devouring every word Travus had written after that. He told her all about her family. She saw so much of herself in every story he related about them. Her parents really were still part of her somehow. Efreeti wasn't able to take everything from her after all.

Finally, though, the letter came to a close. After tucking the letter into the inner pocket of the coat Travus had given her so long ago, Ophelia struggled to dry off her face and make herself presentable for the upcoming return of Tillyria. It was her office, after all.

IN THE HALLWAY JUST OUTSIDE...

After a few minutes alone and leaning against the wall, Cameron walked up to the Colonel who was also known as his wife. He wrapped his hands around hers before she rested her head on his shoulder.

"Was it her?" he asked.

Colonel Mitchell nodded against his tunic, "She hasn't aged a day since I saw her last. But she still recognized me."

The woman's vision blurred as tears overflowed and spilled. She softly sniffled as the man pulled her close, resting her head on his shoulder as he wrapped his arms around her.

"How could that be possible?" he whispered, planting a soft kiss on her temple, "Her not aging, I mean. Not whether or not she recognized you. You are quite sexy as an adult, you know."

"I don't know. Staying out of the sunlight, I guess?" she chuckled, her voice was only slightly muffled by the man's tunic, "Her only worries were about us. Me and my Dad. She thought we'd died in the cave in when I was a kid. You should have seen the relief on her face when I told her we survived."

"So you *did* tell her who you were?" Cameron said.

Tillyria shook her head, "She figured it out on her own."

"Still, she had no reason to worry," the man smirked as he rested his cheek on the crown on her head, "A Colonel in the Light

Bringers who commanded an entire division in the Clan Wars? Not someone that can be taken down easily."

"She doesn't know all that," Tillyria shrugged, "It seemed a lot to get into at the time."

"So what are you going to do then?" Cameron wrapped his hands around her waist.

"Up to the day he died, Dad didn't understand why the Al Razheem hadn't made a move. I wonder if word of Ophelia being back will change that," the Colonel mused, "Regardless, I think I'll ask if she's willing to join the Light Bringers. I'd like her close, maybe get a chance to get reacquainted."

"Sounds awfully generous to me," he nodded, "After being gone for thirty years, she's bound to need a place to stay."

Tillyria sighed, "I swear, honey, if I'd known half of what happened to her and her parents back then, well, I guess I still would have given her as much trouble as I did but I would have felt worse about it!"

"You were a kid," Cameron quirked an eyebrow, "And she was the reason you had to go on the run at such a tender age. A little embitterment would only be natural."

"When my Dad and she were considering having her runes removed, Ophelia thought that she might regain her memory about her family, maybe even be able go to find them again," the woman wrapped her arms around her husband's shoulders, "She didn't know that she'd already seen them die. Ophelia gave all that hope up just so she could protect me and Dad. And now I'm taking that all away from her by showing her that blasted note."

"You and I both know that it's better that she know the truth," Cameron kissed her forehead, "False hope only brings very real disappointment."

The door opened to reveal Ophelia, who invited the Light Bringer Colonel back in. She looked quizzically at the dark skinned man that had guided Ophelia back into the office initially.

Separating himself from his wife, Cameron introduced himself. His eyes bulged in surprise when Ophelia hugged him tightly...

and then proceeded to let him know what horrors would be visited upon him if he ever did anything to hurt Tillyria.

"Juna forbid," he smirked back at her as Ophelia let him go, although something must have told him that the woman was serious because it was followed by an awkward chuckle.

Tillyria hadn't expected the introduction to happen so suddenly. She hadn't even realized that she had been holding her breath before her chest started burning to remind her of the fact. Freeing the air, she stepped back into the office and sat back on her desk.

Moving to stand beside the Colonel, Cameron spoke up, "Forgive me if this sounds rude but Tilly says that you haven't aged a day since she saw you last. How is that possible?"

Tillyria looked up at her husband in a mix of shock and horror. The man was direct, as always, but she thought that he might have tempered it for someone he'd not met. Especially someone that was obviously so important to her.

"I wish I could say clean living," Ophelia grinned as she sat back down.

She related the story of everything that happened to her after she was separated from Travus and Tilly. Ophelia told them almost everything, including killing Euryale, but neglected mentioning that they took her head as a trophy.

"And you came straight here?" the man asked, shifting behind his wife and resting his hands on her shoulders.

"Pretty much," Ophelia nodded, "The last I saw of Travus and Tillyria, they were getting buried under tons of stone. I had to find out if they survived. Although, I didn't realize so much time had passed."

"Which leads us on where to go from here," the Colonel waved her hand as if she were erasing their previous topic of discussion to make way for the new, "Did you need a place to stay, Ophelia? Cameron and I have a house here in the city. It's small but we can make room."

The other woman shook her head, "Thank you, Tilly. I appreciate it but, but I already have a job."

"A job?" the Light Bringer cocked her head to the side, "Already?

"Remember that cleric I mentioned?" Ophelia explained, "He's the victim of some kind of enchanted artifact that has bonded him to this idiot with raging hormones and an attitude problem. If the pile of roc droppings gets hurt, so does the cleric. I'm going to protect them both until we can break that bond somehow."

Tilly had taken years to discipline herself to not outwardly show her emotions. It worked on most everyone with the exceptions being her father, her husband and, apparently, Ophelia. She felt herself pouting in a way that made her feel like back when she was that twelve year old girl and the younger looking but actually older woman's reaction showed that she recognized it, too.

"I'm sorry but he saved my life," Ophelia pressed her palms together as if she were pleading, "I owe him."

"I understand," the middle aged woman frowned, "But I was hoping I could talk you into joining us."

"Me? You would want me as a Light Bringer?" Ophelia pointed at herself in disbelief, "A former assassin? I'm surprised I was let into the building as it is."

The Colonel smirked, "I can pretty much guarantee a good recommendation from a senior officer."

Ophelia glanced back at the hilt of Havarti and stayed quiet for a long moment. Finally, she shook her head as she lifted herself back up to her feet.

"I appreciate it, Tilly. Really. But there's no way that I could hold up the standards that you represent. In fact, I shouldn't even be wearing this," Ophelia tugged at the long leather coat and shrugged it off her shoulders, "It was your father's, so it's only right that you–"

Again the Light Bringer Colonel held up her hand and the other woman stopped talking mid-sentence. Tillyria had to stop herself from smirking. She thought it only worked on Light Bringers she outranked.

"It's yours, Ophelia. Dad gave it to you and I'd like you to keep it to remember him by," The Colonel said, "Besides, Night Shields wear blue capes now so there's no chance that you'll be mistaken for one of them anymore."

"He mistook me for a Light Bringer when I came in," Ophelia nodded at Cameron.

"Only because he gets too absorbed in his paperwork and barely glanced up when you first came in," Tillyria replied as if it had happened more than once before, "All Light Bringers wear capes to avoid just that confusion now. You don't have to worry about representing the Light Bringers badly."

The former assassin pulled the long coat back around her body. The other woman rose to her feet, stepping up to Ophelia. Ophelia was about a half a head taller than Tilly, but she was used to staring down soldiers that towered over her. The woman in the red coat was more curious than intimidated.

It wasn't really in either woman to back down. Not that there was any kind of contest of wills going on at the moment.

"Could I ask one thing of you, though?" what Tillyria said didn't sound like a question.

"Of course," Ophelia replied.

"You aren't beholden to my rank or anything but, if I send for you, will you come back here?" the discipline Tilly tried to project cracked with the little, sheepish smile that crossed her face.

Ophelia reached out and hugged the other woman tightly. It was mostly to hide the tears that started welling out again from Tilly, but Cameron saw them and would tell his wife about them later. He told his wife everything.

"As fast as I can," Ophelia nodded, "I'll blink all the way back here if I have to."

Both women held each other for a long, long time before Ophelia reluctantly pulled away. Looking at the clepsydrae, she saw that it was after midday. As much as she didn't want to leave, Ophelia did have a job to do.

"I'm sorry, but I have to get back to the cleric and his party," she said to Tillyria, "That, and I need to collect my first payment."

THE HOTEL GRUBER, WHILE OPHELIA WAS AT THE OUTPOST

The door men pulled the double doors to the tavern open for Raiko, Saya, Lily and Harbenigyr. The leather sack holding the gorgon's head bounced on the duelist's hip as his narrow eyes scanned for the person he sought.

The tall top hat stood above the rest of the gathering breakfast eating crowd like a signal buoy. The party weaved their way between the round tables until they stood before the man who was so thin that he looked practically emaciated.

How that was possible was hard to fathom. Especially considering the fist sized cauldron of boiling chocolate sauce, complete with a little tuft of flame under it to keep the heat up in the metal serving dish, and the various fruits and breads that lined the clothed surface of the table.

The duelist motioned for the rest of the group to linger behind as he closed the remaining dozen steps between him and his target. The man had just pulled back the sleeve of his tweed cloak so that he could dip a piece of bread that had several types of nuts baked through it into the sauce when Raiko sat down at the table across from him.

"Less than two days," the thin man's mouth spread wide into a painful looking smile, "Either I am about to be jubilant or a very, very discontented at what I am about to hear."

The big man set the leather bag on the table, not bothering to avoid the plate of peeled apples on the table between them. As the sack settled and the now mashed fruit spread out under it, the thin man idly tossed the piece of bread covered in steaming chocolate onto the plate from which it originated.

"Your behavior still poorly reflects your noble lineage, as it did before," he said, pushing the two round pieces of glass higher on his face, "Passive aggressive behaviors like this only demonstrate how easy it was to best you at your own favorite sport to begin with."

A flicker of red came to life behind the eyes of Raiko but only for a brief moment before he took a deep, steadying breath. Then he tapped the top of the bag.

"I've brought what you asked for," the big man said, "Now give me back my collateral."

"I do miss the days when one would announce their presence, await permission for an audience, and show appropriate respect to one who was of higher breeding and physically capable of killing them," the thin man in the top hat replied, "These days even when one is thoroughly defeated, they feel they are owed by their betters."

"I'm not kidding, Eligos!" Raiko snapped back, "I've paid my part of the damned bet. Now give it back!"

The man with the long silver hair suddenly found an equally silver fork pressed against his skin where his jaw met this throat. Still warm chocolate sauce smeared over his pale skin while the sharp tines of the utensil pressed through the chunk of bread and scratched against the soft tissue.

The thin man's arm stretched much further than it should have been able to in order to reach Raiko. But reach it did.

It pressed so firmly against the duelist that even Harbenigyr felt scratching on his neck. Lily took his reaction as a request for a glass of water that she took from a pitcher resting on the empty table beside them.

"Remember, plebeian, that I was and still am the victor of our previous altercation," the man calling himself Eligos hissed between his closed set of white teeth, the smile never leaving his face, "You know that it was not mere fortuitousness that caused this turn of circumstance but skill. Do not test my patience further by trying to evoke your impotent will over mine."

Raiko didn't dare utter a sound in agreement or defiance as the other man held the makeshift weapon firm. His eyes darted from side to side and, while there was noticeable reaction to what was happening at this table, various members of the inn's staff quickly rushed to assure the concerned customers that all was under control.

That meant that this Eligos was indeed powerful not only financially but politically in this region. Chances were that he could kill Raiko and no one would even think that he should be taken into custody by the Light Bringers. All because the duelist didn't have that kind of leverage.

But Saya did. Motioning as her lover did for the wizard and cleric to stay behind, the albino svartalfar strode up beside the table occupied by Raiko and the one they knew as Eligos.

"I humbly apologize for Raiko's immature behavior," she said, giving the thin man a formal curtsy, "Raiko is simply eager to continue on so that he may, someday, better himself enough to perhaps provide you a more formidable opponent next time we meet."

The fork pulled away from the big man's neck, coming to rest again on the plate of bread. The man in tweed leaned forward in his seat resting his chin on his palm.

"You are most fortunate to have one of such a fine pedigree advocating for you," his smile widened, "Before I return your space rock, Raiko, I–"

"Meteorend," the duelist corrected him.

Saya's purple eyes snapped to glare at him in that instant. Thankfully, Eligos didn't seem to notice Raiko's outburst.

"–would like to know how you were able to procure my new divine eye so efficiently."

The thin man motioned to Lily and Harbenigyr to come join the others at the table. After Saya nodded back at the wild haired wizard, they both did so.

The elf pulled a chair out for Lily, who took the provided seat. Eligos nodded his approval while Harby awkwardly stood between Raiko and Lily, as the table was out of chairs.

The thin man didn't appear to notice or care as he turned his attention to the cleric. "Harbenigyr, wasn't it? Did that compound I provided you prove as useful as I'd hoped?"

"Yes, sir. It opened up the sealed entryway just as you said it would," the elf nodded, though he turned pale as the memory returned to his head.

"Excellent, excellent," Eligos's attention shifted to the plump wizard, "Were you the one who figured out how to retrieve the divine eye without suffering from the rumored ill effects?"

Lily shook her head, "No, I can't claim credit for that, unfortunately. My services came down to my knowledge of the various languages of the region and of the local flora," her hazel eyes flicked back to Harby for a brief moment before returning to the thin man, "Of which no part of your compound is made."

"Very astute, young lady," Eligos nodded, his hand reflexively reaching up to steady his tall hat before turning to Saya, "Knowing what I do of Raiko's tactical abilities, you have to have been the one to figure a safe methodology to recover the divine eye."

The big man frowned at the not so subtle affront but, this time at least, didn't say anything in protest. The pale woman tapped her cheek with her still partially deconstructed left hand thoughtfully for a brief moment before speaking.

"Each of us had a role to fulfill in this success."

Eligos let out a slow, quiet grunt, "Your hesitation tells me that there is an element to this that you have not revealed yet. What, pray tell, could it be?"

Each of the four members of the party looked at each other uneasily as the entire tavern seemed to sink into silence despite being full of people eating their first meals of the day. Finally, it was Harbenigyr who spoke up.

"We had help from a woman that your ointment was able to return to the living after being petrified."

The thin man suddenly looked very interested, "It was able to bring a victim of the gorgon back to life? That was far more ambitious a use for it than simply opening a blocked door!"

"To be honest, it seems rather convenient to me," Lily spoke up.

The wild haired young human regretted it almost immediately after the look Saya gave her. Eligos, though, seemed only pleased at her statement.

"I can understand that," he agreed, "But you do remember that I was the very one that sent you down there after the gorgon? Of course I would be aware of its more dangerous properties but it had not seen the light of day in years. There was no way that I could know that there were any victims still down there, let alone ones that could be recovered from such a simple concoction."

"A very lucky coincidence," Saya said to the thin man although her eyes were locked on Lily.

"So why did you not bring this woman with you?" Eligos asked, "Surely, if the cream brought her back from stone it would have kept her from returning upon the next encounter with the gorgon."

Raiko scowled, "She ran off the moment we were above ground."

"Ah," the man in tweed nodded, "Surely, she would want to reacquaint herself with things familiar. I do hope not too much time had passed between when she was turned into a statue and when you saved her. Such a disparity in time would be... vexing to the mortal mind."

"When she was petrified, she didn't show any degradation from the elements down there," Harbenigyr answered, "Ophelia said that she would meet us back here later today."

"And that explains Raiko's eagerness to leave," Eligos pointed a curved claw at the big man, "He feels as if she's wronged him and doesn't want her to receive whatever was agreed upon to gain her services."

"She melted the blade of my rapier in the gorgon's blood," the duelist growled.

The thin man laughed, the sound something like poorly tuned lute mixed with the whistling sound one gets when they blow into an empty bottle. He practically fell back into his seat, making the back creak.

"It will be a shame that I'll not be able to meet her," Eligos finally said when he was able to get enough control over himself, "Alas, I am already overdue for my next destination. I trust that you will be more discerning when selecting opponents with which to duel from now on?"

The thin man held a black stone that was a big as Raiko's fist out to the duelist. It had barely had enough time to reflect a glint of sunlight before the big man snatched it and stuffed it back into his coat. Oddly, despite its size, it did not leave any sign of where it rested within his brown leather coat.

He didn't bother to answer Eligos and Eligos didn't seem to really care. The thin man simply rose from his seat and gave the group a deep, formal bow.

"Please, feel free to finish my breakfast for me or, if you prefer, order a separate one for yourselves," he said, "It will be my treat."

He turned away from the table and started away. Then he jumped and quickly dashed back to grab the apple smeared leather sack.

"Wouldn't want to forget our reason for coming today, would we?" he giggled before finally leaving for good.

NEARING SUNSET...

Ophelia stepped through the doors into the Hotel Gruber just as the sun was starting to kiss the tops of the many new buildings and few recognizable to the woman. She strode up to the wide desk that rested beside the doors where a svartalfar woman with soft green hair pulled back in a ponytail stood and waited for such an eventuality.

"How may I help you today?" she asked.

"I'm looking for Saya Khushrenada," Ophelia answered, "Could you call her down please?"

The gray skinned woman flipped through the pages of the thick book that listed every guest in the hotel and in what room they were staying. After finding the specified entry, she motioned for a bell hop and instructed him to retrieve Miss Khushrenada.

By the time Saya came down to the first floor, Ophelia was already at a table sipping on a massive mug of honeybark ale. Somehow, the woman in the red trench coat had convinced the barkeep to give her a mug that was usually only reserved for half-ogres or dwarves, pretty much any species with a heftier constitution (not to mention bladders) than humans or elves.

The pale woman stepped up to the table and sat down. A waiter appeared, took the new arrival's order and disappeared just as quickly. Ophelia didn't say anything, she simply leaned back in her wooden chair, lifted her mug, and drank deeply.

Finally, Saya decided the silence had gone on long enough, "You look troubled," she stated the obvious.

"I found out how long I was down in that crypt," the other woman answered, wiping foam from her upper lip.

"And I would hazard that it was much longer than you had thought or hoped," again, the silver haired woman stated the likeliest conclusion.

The waiter returned, placing a flute of bubbling, golden wine in front of Saya. The woman picked up the glass by the stem, giving the liquid a quick smell before starting to take a sip.

Ophelia nodded, "Thirty years."

Saya froze mid-sip. That wasn't as long for svartalfar or elves, to be sure, but that was still an entire phase of life for one of her kind. She forced the drink she had swallowed down her throat and placed the flute back on the table.

"I'm sorry," Saya said, although the words sounded hollow, even to her.

"It wasn't like I had family waiting for me or anything," Ophelia shrugged the platitude off then took a heavy drag from her mug, "And it's not like I've aged while I was down there, so it really shouldn't bother me, I guess."

"Regardless, it is an adjustment," Saya idly tapped on the cloth covered surface of the table, "Do you have a place to go? Is your former employer still in business and able to take you in?"

Ophelia shook her head, "I wasn't a local here when I went into the crypts. I had just, er, left my previous job and came out west. So that gold you owe me would go a long way in getting myself reestablished."

"Seven hundred," the pasty woman nodded, "Would you be willing to listen to another offer?"

The former assassin sighed, "Don't tell me you don't have the gold."

"Not at all," Saya said, "Money is not the issue. I was wondering if you would mind joining our little band. At least until we return to Emerald City."

"Emerald City?" Could it be more obvious that Ophelia had never heard of it?

"That is where my people are headquartered," she explained.

"To be honest, Saya, I think I've had my fill of underground for awhile," Ophelia said.

"Emerald City isn't underground," Saya replied.

The other woman frowned, "But you said that it was where the Kizoku Tribe was headquartered."

"The Kizoku are not my people," Saya corrected, "At least not primarily. My father is the chairperson of the Romefeller Guilds. We're a network of mercenaries, intelligence operatives and various other services available to nobles and governments. You were instrumental in getting Raiko out of his self imposed troubles. I think you could do well with us."

"Have I mentioned that I really don't like that guy?" Ophelia's voice echoed slightly as she spoke into her mug just before taking another drink.

"Despite his skill in bed, he has been *falling* out of my favor of late, as well," Saya finally admitted, to herself as well as Ophelia, before taking a long sip of her sparkling wine, "But he is bonded to Harbenigyr, who has proven himself quite useful over the past weeks."

"So if we can figure out a way to break the bond from those shackles, we can kick Raiko to the curb?"

Ophelia felt her lips spread into a wide grin at the idea of being able to stab the duelist without any collateral damage to the cleric. Havarti didn't even seem to mind the idea himself.

"If he continues to act like a petulant child," Saya said before draining the rest of the golden liquid from her flute, "I would, of course, compensate you for your time. Although seven hundred gold per diem would be a steep fee if our trek takes us as long as I figure."

"Oh, that. I only made you agree to that because I knew it would make you annoyed with Raiko," Ophelia chuckled, "But you do still owe me that, you know."

"Of course," the pale woman agreed, "Khushrenadas are a family that prides themselves on our honor. Besides, you do need to obtain proper equipment if you do agree to come with us. In particular, a horse."

Ophelia smirked, "You're so sure that I'm going to come with you, aren't you?"

Saya didn't react one way or another as she looked back at the other woman. A couple of familiar voices suddenly spoke up from beside the table.

"We didn't mean to intrude," Lily spoke up, her cheeks flushed pink, "but we overheard you talking and thought that, maybe, you would want to have dinner all together?"

"If it isn't too much trouble, that is," Harbenigyr added, "We can always get another table if you two still have, um, business to discuss."

"Oh, not at all, Harby," Ophelia waved welcoming hands at the two unoccupied wooden chairs around the table. "Since I'm a part of this merry band now, it would behoove us to get to know each other better. Wouldn't it, Saya?"

"Absolutely," the pale woman nodded in agreement, "Shall I call for Raiko to join us?"

Ophelia shook her head to very much the same rhythm that Havarti shook to express his displeasure at the idea, "I was thinking we would want to enjoy our dinner tonight."

"Very well," Saya agreed, and honestly didn't look overly heartbroken, "Harbenigyr doesn't eat red meat and Lily is a vegetarian. Do you have any dietary restrictions of which we should be aware, Ophelia?"

"Dietary? No," the former assassin and now newly hired adventurer said, "Although I think I would like to take a little nibble out of those ears later."

She playfully pinched the point of one of Harbenigyr's long ears and the young elf turned from tanned to bright red in a matter of seconds. Lily giggled and even Saya couldn't hold back a snicker.

She was going to come along to look after the cleric who saved her life anyway. But now Ophelia was going to get paid for it. And the Al Razheem surely thought that she was long dead, so she was free of their schemes. This really was a fresh start.

"I do suppose that this is as pleasant a beginning to a new life as we could have asked for. Isn't it, Ophelia?" Havarti seemed pleased with the turn of events before the two of them.

Ophelia silently agreed with Havarti's words. Then she drained the rest of her mug, that was still over half full beforehand, and called for a refill.

BACK IN BLACK

A DOOR OPENED in the darkness, allowing Doctor Efreeti to step inside. Tossing the stained sack onto the familiar marble table, the not-quite-a-man pulled his hat off and rested it on top of the leather containing Euryale's head.

"Ophelia," he smiled so wide that every tooth in his head was fully exposed, "Darling, I'm so glad to have you back."

After only a matter of moments, a knock came from the only actual, physical door in Efreeti's lair. He already knew who it was.

"Please come in, Madam General," he said.

Kitanah pushed the door open. Stepping inside, she practically glowed green from the various runes and symbols tattooed all over her skin. They covered her from her neck, down her arm and wrapped around her torso, some peeking out from under the blood red corset she wore.

Her brass sleeve undulated with every step she made toward the man in the tweed cloak, a faint hint of green light glowing from inside the hooked ring. Thanks to the chartreuse light, she looked younger than even the day she joined the Al Razheem and Efreeti had noticed an increase in her already *formidable* appetites as she has only become stronger over the years.

"Did you find it?" she asked the eerily thin man.

"Indeed," Efreeti nodded, "I have acquired a divine eye. I should warn you, though, that I do come bearing some unexpected tidings with my prize."

"Unexpected tidings?" she cradled the metal sleeve in her free hand.

"The party I conscripted into the retrieval of the divine eye," the thin man explained, "One was a cleric from the Silver Herald Isles. He brought with him some kind of *compound* that can turn stone into flesh, including petrified flesh back to its normal state."

"What are you saying, Doctor?" the assassin's emerald eyes narrowed.

"What I am ever so delicately trying to inform you of, Madam General, is that this party followed the stories of a gorgon haunting the crypts under Riverbelt. During their hunt, they stumbled upon the petrified body of your nemesis, Ophelia, and *restored* her to life."

"No. No! NO!" Kitanah screeched, "You assured me that she was dead!"

"She was," Efreeti fought hard to keep from smirking, "Any other cleric, even if they had the compound this one did, could have bathed the statue in it and Ophelia would have never recovered. The clerics from Silver Herald, however, have special knowledge of how energy ebbs and flows through the body. He knew precisely how to apply it to bring her back. The chances of that happening are exactly the same as you, even with your immense influence, praying to your deity and requesting a corpse be returned to full life."

"Is she still in Riverbelt?" the woman hissed, "I will see her dead AGAIN!"

"Alas, Madam General," the thin man shook his head, "Ophelia is surely long removed from the city of her former grave now. And you have a procedure that must happen now in order to see it be successful," he pulled the leather bag out from under his hat and held it up, "Any delay will jeopardize the viability of the tissue you wish transplanted into you."

Kitanah let out a breathy curse before stomping toward the marble table, "How much recovery time am I looking at after this?" she asked.

"This one is difficult to determine, Kitanah," his voice was meant to come out sounding comforting, the success of it was debatable, "There has not been much call for inter-species organ transplants in this plane of existence. We will have to keep you under close observation for months to ensure the viability of the tissue but you could return to action in a matter of weeks."

The assassin jumped up onto the table in a huff, "Fine. See to it that searchers are sent out to find Ophelia and keep her under observation. The second you feel I'm physically able to kill her myself, I'm going out and going to enjoy every second of watching her suffer."

"By your command, Madam General," Efreeti grinned as he popped his top hat back onto his balding head, "I would hate to be the one to keep your plans from coming to full fruition!"

TO BE CONTINUED...

ABOUT THE AUTHOR

Spencer Stoner was born in the state of Nevada, where he still lives today. His day to day life includes weekly meetings with the patrol for whom he serves as an Assistant Scoutmaster. He is also a black belt in American Kenpo Karate who is always willing to teach a willing student.

As for hobbies, he loves comics and hopes to eventually spread his storytelling to that format. He draws portraits of his characters to make sure their descriptions stay consistent through all his stories because of the art form's influence.

To waste time, he plays video games... a lot. In particular, he enjoys role playing and fighting games. Spencer also has almost every older video game system from the original 8-bit NES up to the Wii and PS4.

Even though he's not currently married, Spencer's family (including his mother and three sisters) comes first to him. Did he forget to mention his brother-from-another-mother Jim? After thirty years, you would think his memory would be better.